Plain Jane re...
seduction...
the b...

HIS
Cinderella
HOUSEKEEPER

Three of your favourite authors deliver
three glamorous fairy-tale romances!

THIS Cinderella HOUSEKEEPER

SHARON KENDRICK
ANN MAJOR
LUCY MONROE

DID YOU PURCHASE THIS BOOK WITHOUT A COVER?

If you did, you should be aware it is **stolen property** as it was reported *unsold and destroyed* by a retailer. Neither the author nor the publisher has received any payment for this book.

All the characters in this book have no existence outside the imagination of the author, and have no relation whatsoever to anyone bearing the same name or names. They are not even distantly inspired by any individual known or unknown to the author, and all the incidents are pure invention.

All Rights Reserved including the right of reproduction in whole or in part in any form. This edition is published by arrangement with Harlequin Enterprises II B.V./S.à.r.l. The text of this publication or any part thereof may not be reproduced or transmitted in any form or by any means, electronic or mechanical, including photocopying, recording, storage in an information retrieval system, or otherwise, without the written permission of the publisher.

This book is sold subject to the condition that it shall not, by way of trade or otherwise, be lent, resold, hired out or otherwise circulated without the prior consent of the publisher in any form of binding or cover other than that in which it is published and without a similar condition including this condition being imposed on the subsequent purchaser.

M&B™ and M&B™ with the Rose Device
are trademarks of the publisher.
Harlequin Mills & Boon Limited, Eton House,
18-24 Paradise Road, Richmond, Surrey TW9 1SR

HIS CINDERELLA HOUSEKEEPER
© Harlequin Books S.A. 2010

Italian Boss, Housekeeper Bride © Sharon Kendrick 2007
Shameless © Silhouette Books SA 2003
What the Rancher Wants… © Lucy Monroe 2007

Special thanks and acknowledgement are given to Ann Major for her contribution to THE COUNTRY CLUB series.

ISBN: 978 0 263 87397 9

026-0710

Harlequin Mills & Boon policy is to use papers that are natural, renewable and recyclable products and made from wood grown in sustainable forests. The logging and manufacturing processes conform to the legal environmental regulations of the country of origin.

Printed and bound in Spain
by Litografia Rosés S.A., Barcelona

Italian Boss, Housekeeper Bride

SHARON KENDRICK

Sharon Kendrick started story-telling at the age of eleven and has never really stopped. She likes to write fast-paced, feel-good romances with heroes who are so sexy they'll make your toes curl!

Born in west London, she now lives in the beautiful city of Winchester – where she can see the cathedral from her window (but only if she stands on tiptoe). She has two children, Celia and Patrick, and her passions include music, books, cooking and eating – and drifting off into wonderful daydreams while she works out new plots!

To Bryony Green, the best editor in the world

CHAPTER ONE

NATASHA didn't have to see his face to know something was wrong.

She could tell from the slamming of the door and the heavy footfalls in the hall. From the momentary hesitation which was not like Raffaele at all. The barely muffled curse; some Italian expletive, she thought. She listened while he hung his suit jacket up in the hall and heard him go into his study. Then silence—and something very much like fear stirred within her and she didn't understand why.

He had been away to America—where he owned real-estate on both the east and west coast—and whenever he returned from a trip he always came to find her. To ask her how she'd been. How Sam was.

Sometimes, if he was flying by commercial rather than private jet, he would even remember to bring the child some soft toy or game that he'd bought at the airport. Once she had seen him remove a shiny gold box of perfume from his briefcase, and her heart had begun to thud with a ridiculous excitement. But she had never seen it again.

The scent had not been destined for Natasha. Presumably it had gone to the leggy supermodel he had been seeing at the time—the one who'd always used to leave a stocking or a scarf behind in the bathroom, like some territorial trophy, marking out her pitch.

The study was still ominously silent, and Natasha began making a pot of mega-strong coffee—just as Raffaele had taught her to when she'd first gone to work for him. Wasn't it crazy how memories could stay stuck fast in your head, even though they meant nothing? Natasha could still remember the shiver she'd felt as he'd bent close to her, too close for her comfort—though, not, it had seemed, for his. He had been too intent on showing her what to do to notice the mousy-looking woman at his side.

His voice had dipped, like soft velvet underpinned with steel. 'In Italy we say that the coffee should look like ink and taste like heaven. Very strong and very dark—like the best kind of man. You understand? *Capisci?*' And the black eyes had glittered at her in mocking question, as if it amused him that a woman should need to be taught how to make coffee.

But she had. Oh, she had. Back then she had needed teaching about pretty much everything that someone like Raffaele took for granted. While he was used to only the very best, she'd always been the kind of person who usually spooned instant out of a jar—until the time had come when she'd had barely enough money to buy any. Just thinking about the mess she had found herself in still had the power to make her tremble with apprehension. She never wanted to go back there—to those days of hunger and uncertainty and real fear—to before Raffaele had stepped in to save her.

Was that why she'd put him on a pedestal ever since?

Natasha placed the coffee and cup on the tray, along with two of the small almond biscuits which were Raffaele's favourites. She had learnt how to make those, too, from the Italian cookbook he had bought her one Christmas.

Then she checked her appearance in the kitchen mirror, just as any employee would do before going in to see their boss—even if they didn't happen to live in the same house, as Natasha did.

She would do. Her pale brown hair was neat, her dress carefully ironed and her features unadorned by make-up. She looked efficient and unthreatening. The way she liked it.

Going bare-faced was a habit she'd gotten into when Sam was a baby, when she'd been terrified of being judged by other people more than she already had been. She had wanted to send out the message that being a struggling single mother didn't mean she was sexually available.

Besides, Natasha had learnt that it was easier if you kept things simple. There were advantages to almost everything in life—it all boiled down to your attitude. No make-up meant more time in the morning—just as tying her hair back did. She looked just what she hoped she was—a respected and respectable member of Raffaele's staff.

'Natasha!'

She heard his peremptory summons couched in the distinctively accented voice as it carried down to the basement. Hastily, she picked up the tray and carried it upstairs to his study, but in the doorway she paused, her attention caught and arrested by the sight of him. Natasha frowned. Her instinct had been right—there *was* something wrong.

Raffaele de Feretti. Billionaire. Bachelor. Boss. And the man she had quietly loved from almost since the first time she'd set eyes on him. But who wouldn't love him? *Not* loving him would have presented a greater challenge—despite his arrogance and that disdainful air he had sometimes, when he wasn't really listening to what you said.

He hadn't heard her now and was standing with his back to her, gazing out onto the drenched garden at the centre of the London square, where raindrops dripped down the trees like a woman's tears.

Today the garden was deserted, but on fine days you could see nannies with their boisterous young charges running around the paths to the tiny playground section at the far end. Or mothers with prams, before they went back to work—as many of the mothers around this affluent part of the city seemed to do whether it was because they needed the variety or because they wanted the independence. Natasha could never quite work it out. She used to think that it would be bliss not to *have* to work, but that was probably because the option had never been open to her.

Natasha used to take Sam to the garden when he was younger—feeling very privileged to be able to do so, but slightly nervous, too, as if someone was about to move her on, to tell her she had no right to be there. Her son, of course, had been unaware of the exclusive location of his playground, but every time her beloved little boy had patted his bucket and squealed with delight as sand flew out, Natasha had thanked a be-nevolent fate for bringing Raffaele de Feretti into her life.

'Raffaele?' she said quietly.

But Raffaele didn't look round. Not even when she

put the tray down on his desk with a little clatter. His tall, lean body just remained there—as unmoving as a statue and as silent as a rock—and there was something so *perturbing* and so *alien* about his stance that Natasha cleared her throat.

'Raffaele?' she prompted again.

Her soft English accent filtered into his fractured thoughts and slowly Raffaele turned round, his eyes taking in her familiar face and the gentle concern in her eyes. He sighed. Natasha. As ever-present and un-threatening as the air he breathed. He frowned, brought back to the present with a jolt. He had been miles away. 'What is it?'

'I've brought you your coffee,'

Coffee? Had he asked for any? Probably not—but he could certainly do with some. How like her to guess. He nodded, gesturing for her to pour some and then he sat down in the leather chair at his desk, run-ning his fingertips along the dark rasp of his jaw, the way he always did when something was on his mind. It was usually a high-profile takeover of some big company, but today it happened to be something much bigger. His mouth hardened—because unlike corporate affairs, which he could practically deal with in his sleep, this particular problem was something he usually steered clear of. The personal.

'Has anyone called this morning?' he demanded.

'Not a soul.'

'No press?'

'No.' The tabloids had upped the ante ever since a reality-TV star had claimed that Raffaele had bedded her in a *'Five Times a Night!'* romp, when he had barely met the woman. The matter was currently in the hands of his lawyers, and just the thought of it made

Natasha feel quite sick, even though she knew it wasn't true. She tried a joke, to try to help ease that terrible tension which was tightening the face she knew so well. 'Well, no *visible* press—I guess, there could always be a couple of reporters hiding in the bushes. It's happened before!'

But he didn't laugh. 'You've been in the whole time?'

Natasha nodded. 'Except when I dropped Sam off at school, of course—but I was back by nine-thirty.' Her mouth softened with concern. This close, she could see he looked somehow *different*. His brilliant black eyes were shadowed and the tiny lines which fanned outwards from them seemed somehow more pronounced. As if he had gone without sleep while he'd been away. 'Why? Were you expecting someone?'

Not exactly *expecting*—because that might imply that he had invited someone, and there had categorically been no invitation issued. Raffaele gave a small shake of his head. He was a man who did not give his trust easily—his suspicions had been fuelled by a lifetime of mixing with people who wanted something from him. Sex or money or power—the magical trinity which he had in spades. With Natasha he had come pretty close to implicit trust—but he was still aware of the dangers of confiding in others except when absolutely necessary.

The more people you told, the weaker you became. Because knowledge was power—and, surely, this quiet Englishwoman already knew far too much about how he lived his life. For now, he had her loyalty, because she owed him a great debt—but what if greed reared its ugly head and persuaded her to sell out, as he had seen happen so many times in the past? What if she discovered that she could make enough to keep her in comfort for many years if she sold her story to the papers, who were always hungry to find out more about him?

'No, Natasha—I wasn't expecting anyone,' he said, with blunt honesty.

'You're back from America early.'

'I haven't been in America. I flew to Italy, instead.'

'Oh? Any special reason?' She pushed the sugar towards him, knowing that she was being unusually persistent—but she had never seen him look quite so troubled before.

'It doesn't matter.'

But, because she loved him, Natasha chose to ignore the sudden dark, repressive tone of his voice. 'Something's wrong—isn't it, Raffaele?'

Inexplicably, he felt the flicker of temptation for one brief moment, before his mouth curved with an aristocratic disdain he rarely used on her. 'It is not your place to ask me such a question,' he answered coolly. 'You know that.'

Yes, she knew that—and mainly she accepted it. Just as she accepted so many other things about his life. Like the women who sometimes shared his bed, who would wander down to breakfast in the morning, all tousle-haired and pink-cheeked, long after he had left for the City. They would giggle as they demanded she make them French toast and orange juice and Natasha's jealous heart would break into a thousand pieces.

It was true that there hadn't been any of those *inter-lopers* for some time—in fact, he was probably gearing up for another any day now. Maybe *that* was what was bugging him? Was some woman giving *him* the run-around, for once—instead of the other way round? In which case, why didn't he damned well tell her? At least, that way she would be able to steel her heart against the pain to come. Against the projected and mostly hidden fear that, this time, his affair might be serious.

But then Natasha felt ashamed at her self-seeking—for wasn't there another part of Raffaele's life which threatened to mar its near perfection? His beautiful half sister, who was nearly a whole generation younger than him. Could that be the reason behind his unscheduled trip to Italy?

She cleared her throat. 'Elisabetta's okay, isn't she?'

Raffaele stilled, the coffee cup almost to his lips. He put it down with a clatter, untasted. 'What makes you ask about my sister?' he questioned, in a voice of dangerous stealth.

She could hardly say *Because, in your charm-filled life, she seems to be the one area which causes you concern.* That really *would* be stepping over the boundaries of acceptable behaviour. Natasha shrugged, remembering the anxious phone call he had taken from Elisabetta's psychiatrist a couple of weeks ago, which had resulted in him sitting in his study until darkness had fallen. It had been left to Natasha to wander in unnoticed and gently wonder if he wanted to put the light on, to remind him that he had a dinner engagement that evening.

'Just a hunch that all wasn't well.'

'Well, don't *have* hunches!' he flared. 'I don't pay you to have hunches!'

She stared at him, and his words felt as if they had

lanced through her heart. 'No, of course you don't. I shouldn't have said anything. I'm sorry.'

But Raffaele saw the faint tremble of her lips, which she'd tried and failed to hide, and relented with a sigh. 'No, I am the one who should be sorry, *cara*. I should not have spoken to you that way.'

But he had—and maybe he would continue to do so—and could she bear that? Natasha pinned her shoulders back as once more she felt the distant beat of apprehension—and this time it wasn't about Raffaele, but about her.

Didn't they say that familiarity bred contempt— was that why he thought he could talk to her any old way and she would just take it? Oh, yes, sometimes he called her *cara*—but that was more a term of endearment. He certainly didn't mean it in the romantic 'darling' sense.

Was she blinding herself to the fact that her position here was slowly being eroded? Was she going to wait until it became untenable before she had the courage to walk away from him?

She was beginning to recognise that as Sam grew older he would begin to notice the things which made him different from his schoolfriends. That the sumptuous home in which he lived was not really *his* home, but belonged to his mother's billionaire employer. How long before that started to matter and his friends started making fun of him for being different?

'I'd better go and get on,' she said stiffly. 'I want to make a cake—Sam's bringing a friend home for tea.' And she turned away before he could see the stupid tears which were threatening to prick at the corners of her eyes.

But Raffaele saw the rigid set of her shoulders and,

for once, he realised he had hurt her. He knew that whatever else happened, Natasha didn't deserve that. Maybe it was time that he told someone other than his attorney. Troy saw things only in black-and-white, in the way that lawyers did. That was what they were paid to do—to deal with practicalities, not emotion.

But, even for a man who had spent his life running from emotion and all its messy consequences, sometimes, like now, facing it seemed unavoidable. And Natasha was a woman—they seemed to do emotion better than men. Certainly, better than this man. Wouldn't a feminine perspective from an impartial party be useful? What possible harm could there be to run it past her?

Maybe it was true what they said—that if you spoke the words out loud it made you see them differently.

Raffaele had spent most of his thirty-four years pressing all the right buttons and had achieved huge international success, but what he liked best was the control that success gave him and the power which came with it. But these past weeks he had felt it slipping away from him—and the sensation made him uneasy.

'Natasha ?'

'What?' she answered, but she didn't turn back; she was too busy blinking away the last of her tears.

Natasha would tell him the truth, even if he didn't want to hear it. 'Elisabetta's in a clinic,' he said bluntly. 'She has been secretly flown to England, and I'm terrified the press are going to find her.'

CHAPTER TWO

NATASHA froze, her own fears crumbling to unimportant dust as she tried to take in what Raffaele had just told her—a lightning bolt from the blue. *'What?'*

'My sister has been admitted to a private clinic in the south of England, with an acute anxiety attack,' Raffaele said, as if he were reading from a charge sheet.

Natasha blinked away her thoughtlessly self-indulgent tears and turned round to face him, her hands automatically reaching out towards him in an instinctive gesture of comfort. But she saw him flinch and stare at them as if they were something untoward—which she guessed they were—and they dropped to her sides like stones.

'We've been trying to keep it out of the papers,' he said, still in that same, flat voice.

'We?'

'Me. Troy. The doctors in charge. They're worried that it will add to her stress. If the papers get hold of it, then she'll be harassed when they discharge her—and it'll drag her right back down. The security at the clinic is tight, but there are always photographers loitering around in the hope of sniffing out a new story. And you know how everyone loves this particular modern fairytale—"the girl who has everything suddenly fighting for her sanity".'

'Oh, Raffaele,' she breathed, her blue eyes growing worried as she heard the cynicism which made his voice sound so harsh. 'Poor Elisabetta! What's happened?'

He tried to make sense of it. He wanted to tell Natasha not to look at him like that, or to say his name in that sweet, soft way, that her sympathy was making him feel all kinds of stuff that he didn't need to feel right now. Like he wanted to go straight into her arms and put his head against her pure pale skin and just *hold* her. But he shook the thought away with a corresponding shake of his head.

He was supposed to be taking control—not sleepwalking into disaster by looking vulnerable in front of his damned housekeeper! He forced his mind back to the unpalatable facts.

'You know that she never had a particularly stable upbringing,' he said, swallowing down the bitter taste in his mouth. 'She was born when my mother was trying desperately hard to please her new husband. She knew that he wanted a child—and even though she was in her early forties by then she moved heaven and earth to get pregnant.' Raffaele had been a teenager at the time, and he remembered feeling pushed aside by his mother's new obsession. But he had been protective of the baby girl when she'd arrived—though, shortly after that, he had been relieved to leave for university.

His eyes narrowed as he remembered. 'Elisabetta once told me that they were disappointed she wasn't a boy. Her father wanted someone to take over the business, and this artistic, fey girl was the antithesis of what he'd needed. Maybe that attitude sowed the seeds for her anxiety—or maybe it would have happened anyway.' He shrugged, and his face darkened—for analysis was not in his nature unless it concerned a column full of figures. 'Who knows what caused it? All I know is that it exists.'

'But has something happened?' Natasha questioned quietly. 'To bring matters to a head?'

Raffaele's black eyes pierced through her like dark lasers. 'How did you guess?'

Because that was the way of the world, thought Natasha. 'Was it a man?'

'How perceptive of you, Tasha,' he said softly, and then his mouth hardened. That wasn't the word *she* would use to describe him. 'A relationship,' he corrected acidly. 'Someone Elisabetta thought had fallen in love with her—but, of course, it was her enormous wealth which had seduced him. *Damn* the money!' he exclaimed bitterly. '*Damn* it!'

Natasha bit her lip. Sometimes working for a man as powerful as Raffaele meant telling him things that they didn't really want to hear—because no one else dared to. Except maybe for Troy, Raffaele's lawyer. He never shied away from the facts.

'That isn't really fair, is it, Raffaele? I mean, you're enormously wealthy and it doesn't impact negatively on your life, does it? You *enjoy* your money,' she pointed out, softening the home-truth with a smile. 'So you can't always say that money is the root of all evil.'

Raffaele's mouth tightened. So this was what happened when you took someone like her into your confidence! His simmering rage was directed at Natasha now, his eyes sparking ebony fire. 'You think to criticise *me?*' he demanded. 'You dare to do that?'

'No,' she replied patiently, 'I'm just trying to help you see it more clearly, that's all.'

'She should not have been mixing with such low-life!' he stormed.

'She is a young woman, Raffaele. You haven't always—'

'Haven't always, what?' he prompted dangerously.

'You haven't always displayed the greatest judgement with some of your choices of women, have you?'

'What?'

She met the look of smouldering disbelief in his eyes without blinking, but somehow the thought of his doe-eyed half sister breaking her heart over some gold-digger gave Natasha the courage to stand up to him. 'I draw your attention to the woman you're currently suing.'

'Madonna mia!' he exclaimed. 'I met her twice—and there was no intimacy. Am I to be held responsible for some lying actress who wants to use my money and my reputation to boost her career? And Elisabetta is my *sister*,' he continued stubbornly. 'It is different.'

Natasha sighed. It was that age-old double standard again, which some men—particularly the old-fashioned macho breed, like Raffaele—applied to all women. That there were two types. Madonna and whore. She bit her lip. Which category would *she* fall into?

Her behaviour since she'd first entered the de Feretti household had been beyond reproach—but she was still a single mother, wasn't she? And, surely, that would score negatively when measured by Raffaele's exacting standards?

'Why don't you tell me what's happened?' she said softly.

He shrugged his shoulders restlessly. Her voice was cajoling—it was like the warmth of the sun on a summer's day—but, instinctively, he fought against its comfort. 'What's to tell? This *scum* bled her bank account until her attention was drawn to it—and then he ran.' His face darkened. 'But not before he had convinced her that she loved him and that she could love no other as much as him. She stopped eating. She stopped sleeping. Her skin is like paper and her arms—they are like *this*…' He joined his forefinger and thumb together in a circle to illustrate Elisabetta's emaciated limb, and another wave of pain etched its way across his features. 'She's sick, Tasha.'

His eyes narrowed as he saw the look of concern on her face. Thank God, this was only Natasha he was talking to, came one sane, fleeting thought. Nobody had ever seen Raffaele de Feretti even close to vulnerable before—and, surely, this came close. At least, Tasha didn't count.

'Are you all right?' asked Natasha anxiously.

The image of Elisabetta came floating into his mind—with her huge eyes and the waterfall of black hair which fell in a heavy curtain to her waist. Clenching his fists together, he thought how much he would like to be able to protect his vulnerable half sister from the knocks that life had waiting in store. 'I should have been able to protect her!'

Natasha opened her mouth to say that modern women were strong enough not to need protectors—but that wasn't really true, was it? Hadn't Raffaele done just that with her? Brought her in from the cold. And hadn't he treated her son as…well, if not as his own, then certainly as some distant and fondly regarded relative?

Had she forgotten how despairing she had been when she had thrown herself onto him for mercy?

She had rung his bell one night in answer to an advertisement in the newspaper for a housekeeper, and he had opened the door himself. Some time in the hours between Natasha deciding that there was no way she could carry on living in a damp house and working like a slave, the heavens had opened and she had been soaked to the skin.

'Yes?' Raffaele had demanded, 'What is it?'

Natasha had barely noticed the autocratic and irritated note in his voice—or that his black eyes had narrowed to something approaching astonishment as he took in the sodden mess she must have made.

'I've come about the job,' she'd said.

'You're too late.'

Her face'd crumpled. 'You mean, it's taken?'

He'd shaken his head impatiently. 'I mean, that you're too late. Literally. I'm not interviewing any more today. See the agency and I'll try to fit you in tomorrow.'

But Natasha was desperate—and desperation could make you do funny things. It could fire you up with a determination you didn't know you had until your back was against the wall. Particularly, if you were looking out for someone else.

'No,' she said firmly, and rushed on as she saw his expression of incredulity—because it was now or never.

'No?' he demanded. She dared to say no? To *him*?

She took a deep breath. 'If I go away now, then you might appoint someone else before me, and no one will do the job as well as me. I can promise you that, Mr de Feretti.'

'*Signor* de Feretti,' he'd corrected flintily, but his

interest had been awakened by her passion and determination and by the cold light of fear which lay at the
back of her eyes.

He'd opened the door a fraction wider, so that a
shaft of light had illuminated her, and Raffaele'd found
himself thinking that she certainly wouldn't provide
much in the way of temptation—and maybe that was
a good thing. Some of the younger applicants he'd
seen that day had been pretty *conturbante*—sexy—and
had made it clear that working for a single and very
eligible bachelor was at the top of their wish-list for
very obvious reasons. And the ones who'd been older
had seemed itching to mother him. 'So what makes
you think you'd do the job better than anyone else?'
he'd demanded.

There was no possible answer to give other than the
unvarnished truth, and Natasha had heard her voice
wobble as she told him.

'Because no one wants the job as much as I do. No
one *needs* it as much as I do, either.'

He had seen she'd been shivering. Her teeth had
been chattering and her eyes had a kind of wildness
about them. He thought at the time that he might be
offering house-room to someone who was very slightly
unhinged, but sometimes Raffaele allowed himself to
be swept along by a gut feeling that was stronger than
logic or reason, and that had been one of those times.

'You'd better come in,' he'd said.

'No! Wait!'

He frowned, scarcely able to believe his ears.
'Wait?'

'Can you give me a few minutes and I'll be back?'
As Raffaele'd nodded his terse agreement he'd told

himself he was being a fool—and he didn't even have the fool's usual excuse of having been blinded by a beautiful face and body. She was probably the head of some urban gang—the innocent-looking stool-pigeon who had arrived ahead of her accomplices who were even now bearing down on him.

But Raffaele was strong and fit and, deep down, he didn't really think the woman was any such thing. Why, she was little more than a girl and her desperation sounded real enough, rather than the rehearsed emotion of some scam.

He'd tossed another log on the fire, which was blazing in his study, and poured himself a glass of rich, red wine. He'd almost given up on her coming back and thought that it was probably all for the best—though, his curiosity had somehow been whetted.

And then came the ringing on the door—only, this time it was even more insistent. His temper had threatened to fray as he'd wrenched it open.

'You are not showing a very good example in interview technique!' he'd grated, and then had seen that the woman was carrying a bundle—evident, even to his untutored eyes, as being a sleeping child—and there'd been a buggy on his front step. 'What the *hell* is this?'

Without thinking, he'd pulled her inside out of the howling storm, swearing softly in Italian as he'd directed her in towards the fire, where she sank to her knees in front of the leaping flames, the child still in her arms, and let out a low, crooning sound of relief.

'My friend's been looking after my b-baby in the bus shelter while I came to see you.'

For a moment, he'd felt fury and pity in equal

measures—but something else, too. He would help her, yes—but only if she proved she was worth helping. And, unless this mystery woman dried her eyes and pulled herself together, he would kick her back out on the street, where she belonged.

'Hysterics won't work in this case,' he'd said coldly. 'Not with me.'

Just in time, Natasha had recognised that he'd meant it and, sucking in a shuddering breath, she'd looked down at Sam. How did he manage to still be asleep? she'd asked herself with something close to wonder.

'How old is he?' Raffaele'd asked.

She'd lifted her face to his. It glowed in the firelight and had been wet with rain and tears, and he'd suddenly found himself thinking that her eyes were exceptionally fine—pale, like a summer sky.

'How on earth d-did you know he was a boy?' she'd questioned shakily.

He'd heard the strong and fierce note of maternal pride and, unexpectedly, he'd smiled. 'He's dressed entirely in blue,' he'd said, almost gently.

Natasha had looked down and, sure enough, the hooded all-in-one and baby mitts had all been in variations on that shade. 'Oh, yes!' And, for the first time in a long, long time, she'd quivered him a smile. 'He's nearly eighteen months,' she'd added.

Raffaele had hid the sinking feeling in his heart. *Porca miseria!* What he knew about children and babies could be written on his fingernail, but even he knew that children around that age were nothing but trouble.

'But he's really good,' Natasha'd said.

It was perhaps unfortunate that Sam had chosen that precise moment to wake up. He'd taken one look at Raffaele and burst into an ear-splitting howl of rage.

There'd been a pause.

'So I see,' Raffaele'd said wryly.

'Oh, he's just tired,' Natasha'd babbled, clamping him tightly to her chest and rocking him like a little boat. 'And hungry. He'll be fine tomorrow.'

He'd noticed her assumption that they would still be around the next day, but didn't remark on it. 'Why are you in this situation? Where have you been living?'

'I've been working in a house—only, they keep asking me to do more and more, so that I hardly get a minute with Sam. And the house is damp, too—he's only just finished a cold, and I'm terrified he's going to get another. It's not somewhere I want to bring a child up.'

His eyes had narrowed. 'And what about his father? Is he going to turn up and want to stay the night with you here?'

'We don't see him,' Natasha'd said, with an air of finality.

'There isn't going to be a scene? Angry doorstep rows at midnight?'

She shook her head. 'No way.'

Raffaele'd looked curiously at the boy, who had been attempting to burrow into her shoulder, his thumb wobbling towards his mouth. He'd frowned. 'Where's he going to sleep?'

And with those words she'd known that she was in with a chance. That she'd had one foot in Mr—or rather—*Signor* de Feretti's expensive door and she had to prove to this rugged, but rather cold-eyed, foreigner that she deserved to stay. *They* deserved to stay.

The child had spent his first night under the Italian's roof in the same bed as his mother and when, the next morning, Raffaele'd caught Natasha trawling through the second-hand column of the local paper he'd overrode all her objections—which admittedly weren't very strong when it came to her beloved boy—to order a top-of-the-range bed which was fashioned out of wood to look like a pirate ship.

And there mother and son had been ever since.

It suited all parties very well. Raffaele knew that it was far better his big house be lived in—especially as he was away a lot, not just in the States, but Europe, too, for the de Feretti empire spread far and wide. Once, Natasha had plucked up the courage to ask him why he bothered keeping on a house in England when presumably a hotel might have been more convenient.

But he had shaken his jet-dark head. 'Because I hate them,' he'd told her, with a surprising vehemence. Hadn't he been in enough of them as a boy, following the death of his father, when he had been trailed from pillar to post by a mother determined to find herself a new rich husband? 'Hotels have no soul. All the furniture is used by faceless hundreds. The pillows slept on by others and the mattresses made love on by countless couples. Yet, when you buy stuff of your own and put it down somewhere at least you can make any house a home.'

If she hadn't been so busy trying not to bite her lip with embarrassment when he'd said that bit about making love then she might have disagreed with him—telling him that a home consisted of more than just furniture and belongings. It had to do with making it the place you most wanted to be at the end of the day. And, anyway, who was Natasha to disagree with him, when he had provided the only real home she and Sam had ever known?

When Sam had been old enough Raffaele had insisted on enrolling him to attend the nursery section of the highly acclaimed international school which was situated nearby.

'Why not?' he had queried, rather arrogantly, when she'd shaken her head.

'It's much too expensive,' Natasha'd said defensively. 'I can't afford it.'

His voice had gentled in a the way it rarely did, but which was impossible to resist when he turned it on. 'I know that. I wasn't expecting you to pay. I will.'

'I couldn't possibly accept that,' Natasha'd said, feeling as if she ought to refuse his generous offer even though her maternal heart leapt at the thought of Sam being given such a head start in life.

'You can, and you will. It makes perfect sense,' he'd drawled. 'All the other schools are far enough away to eat into your time when you take him there, and ultimately *my* time. Listen, Natasha, why don't you look at it as one of the perks of the job—rather than me giving you the use of a car, which so far you have refused to drive in London?'

Put like that, she'd found she could accept his offer gratefully, and she would never forget her joy, when Sam spoke his first few words in French and then Italian. After that Raffaele had taken to always speaking to the boy in his native tongue, and while Natasha had revelled with dazed pleasure at this evidence of her son the linguist, there had been a tiny part of her which had felt shut out. It had been enough to make her start taking Italian lessons, herself, though she kept quiet about it—in case it looked as if she was *expecting* something.

It hadn't all been plain sailing, of course. There had been the time when Sam had fallen over the step into the back garden and sustained a nasty bump to his forehead. Natasha had rushed him to the emergency room and though Raffaele had been out of the country at the time, he had listened grimly on the other end of the line as she recounted how a social worker had been round the next day to check everything out.

'Well, you should have damned well been watching him!' he had flared.

It had been unjust and unfair, but Natasha had been too eaten up with guilt to tell him that her back had been turned for just a few seconds.

And the time when Sam had found a handbag belonging to one of Raffaele's girlfriends and had decided to reinvent himself as his favourite character, Corky the Clown.

'But that's my best lipstick!' the girlfriend had screeched, as she'd dodged Sam's pink-glossed and podgy hand as he attempted to hand the decimated piece of make-up back to her.

Raffaele had laughed. 'I'll buy you another.'

The woman had pouted. 'You can't buy them over here—they're exclusive to America!' she spat. 'What a horrible little *brat!*'

And Raffaele had looked at her and known that no amount of fantastic sex was worth having to look at a nasty, spiteful face which could make a little boy cry. 'Tell you what,' he said coldly, 'I'll buy you a one-way air-ticket and you can go and get yourself a replacement.'

The girlfriend had flounced out, and Raffaele had told Natasha to make sure she kept her offspring under control next time. But that weekend he had purchased a huge, floppy clown for Sam as a kind of silent thank-you for doing him a favour he hadn't realised he was in need of.

Of course, he never enquired about Sam's father— it was none of his business, and he didn't want to get involved in the bitter stuff which came after a couple split up.

Besides, he never really thought of Natasha in those terms. She was Sam's mother and his housekeeper, and it seemed to suit them all….

'*Dio!*' he swore. What the hell was he doing, thinking about the past, when he had the biggest problem of his life on his hands right *now*—in the present? 'What on earth am I going to do about Elisabetta, Natasha?' he demanded.

'You're doing everything you can,' she soothed. 'Presumably, she's in the best clinic that money can buy. You can support her by visiting her—'

'She isn't allowed visitors for the first four weeks,' he said flatly. 'It's one of the rules.'

Natasha nodded. How would he find that? she wondered. He, who had made up his own rules in life as he went along. 'Well, the other stuff, then. You know. Like keeping her safe.' Her eyes shone. 'You're good at that.'

But he barely heard a word she was saying, because the sudden shrill ring of the doorbell pealed out with its own particular sense of urgency.

He strode off to answer it, checking first in the peephole that it wasn't the dreaded press-pack. But it was Troy standing on the doorstep, and when Raffaele opened the door and the other man stepped inside the lawyer's grim face confirmed his worst fears.

'What is it?' he demanded. 'What's happened?'

There was a pause. 'The press have got hold of the story,' Troy said. 'They've found out where Elisabetta is.'

CHAPTER THREE

'ARE you certain—absolutely certain?' demanded Raffaele, feeling an overwhelming sense of rage run through him at the thought of his vulnerable little sister being at the mercy of the unscrupulous press hounds. Had Elisabetta really had her cover blown? His black eyes bore into his lawyer. 'They've found out where she is?'

Troy nodded. 'I'm afraid so. I've just had a telephone call from one of our people. They're outside the clinic now,' he said.

Raffaele swore very softly and very quietly in the Sicilian dialect he had picked up one long, hot summer on the island, when he'd still been railing against the intrusion of his new stepfather. Few people could understand the language, but it had remained with him in times of anger ever since. But he recognised now that his fury was a nothing but redundant luxury and would not help solve the problem. Every problem had a solution—he knew that. Hadn't he demonstrated it over the years, time and time again?

He thought quickly. 'Come through to my study,' he said, and then glanced at Natasha, who was standing there, looking as if she wanted to say something. He waved his hand at her impatiently. 'Can you bring some coffee for Troy, Natasha? Have you eaten? I'm sure Natasha can make you something if you want.'

Troy shook his head. 'No. Coffee will be fine. And maybe one of those biscuit things, if you have them?'

'Yes, of course,' said Natasha, nodding with a brisk smile and turning away, telling herself that *of course* Raffaele was going to dismiss her like that—because what was happening with Elisabetta was *nothing what-soever to do with her.*

She was an employee, for heaven's sake, not Raffaele's confidante—no matter how much she longed to be. And that was one of the drawbacks to the strange position she had in his life—she was part of it and, yet, nothing to do with it. Always hovering on the outskirts of it, like a tiny satellite star which relied on the mighty light of a huge planet, so that sometimes she felt she was consumed by him. But at times like this he would send her away to provide refreshments, just like the servant she really was.

After she'd gone, the two men walked through the long, arched hallway which led to his study, where they sat on either side of the desk.

'Can we kill the story?' Raffaele asked.

'Only temporarily. The *London News* is threatening to run a piece in its gossip column tonight.'

'Then slam out an injunction!'

'I already have done,' said Troy. 'But the trouble is that they aren't actually breaking any privacy code. It's just a general piece, with a few old photos, about concerns for "party-loving heiress, Elisabetta de Feretti".'

'But this is intolerable!' gritted Raffaele from between clenched teeth. 'Doesn't anyone give a damn about her well-being?'

'Not if it sells more newspapers.'

Raffaele shook his dark head, his frustration accentuated by real concern. Had he failed his sister? Been too enmeshed in the world of business to notice that her life was disintegrating around her? 'How the hell did they find out about it? Didn't the clinic give me a thousand assurances that Elisabetta's anonymity would be protected? Do we know the source of the story?'

'We do now. It's a member of staff, I'm afraid,' said Troy slowly, sitting back in his chair as if putting distance between himself and the outburst about to follow.

For a moment Raffaele's long olive fingers curved, so that they resembled the deadly talons of some bird of prey. *'Madonna mia!'* he said, with soft venom resonating like liquid poison from his voice. 'Do you know what we shall do, Troy? We shall hunt down and find the cheating Judas who betrayed my sister. And, much as I should like to inflict a Sicilian form of punishment that they will never forget, we will discipline them formally.' He punched his fist over his heart. 'And make sure that he or she never works in a position of trust or authority again!'

There was a pause. 'You *can* do that,' said Troy, with the smooth diplomacy of his profession. 'But it will be a waste of your time and ultimately of your resources—and at a time when you can least afford to squander them.'

'You are saying that this kind of behaviour should go unpunished?' Raffaele demanded icily. 'Is that the course of action you are recommending to me?'

Troy held his hands up in a don't-shoot-the-messenger pose. 'Of course I can see that to carry out such a threat would give you satisfaction—but it would be a short-lived achievement and it would detract from your real aim of making sure that Elisabetta gets the treatment she needs without anything making it more difficult for her. And, unfortunately, all the railing and lawsuits in the world won't change human nature or the lure of big money—haven't you said that yourself, Raffaele, more times than you can count?'

Raffaele was silent for a moment while he digested the other man's words. He had known and admired Troy since both men had met at the Sorbonne in the concluding year of their international law degrees—and he had discovered Troy was that rare thing, an Englishman who spoke several languages. They had been educated as equals, had good-naturedly fought over women, and Troy had never been cowed by the black-eyed Italian who was held in so much awe wherever he went because of his presence and his unforgettable good-looks.

The fact that the Englishman had also been considered to be a bit of a sex god by the women of Paris had meant that there was no rivalry between the two men.

As well as Troy's fluency in both Italian and French, he possessed the valuable impartiality which was so much a characteristic of his nationality, and all these factors had made him the perfect choice to be personal advocate for the powerful Raffaele de Feretti. There were not many men to whom Raffaele listened, but this was one of them—and he was listening now.

'*Si,* Troy, *mio amico*—you are right, of course,' Raffaele said heavily, still feeling that he had somehow failed his sister—even though logic told him otherwise. 'So, what do we do?'

Troy placed the tips of his fingers together in an almost prayerlike gesture of careful thought. 'We run a spoiler. We take attention *away* from Elisabetta by giving them a bigger story.'

Raffaele gave a sceptical laugh. 'And how do you propose doing that?'

Troy leaned forward. 'Elisabetta is newsworthy because, yes, she's young, and beautiful, very rich and occasionally flawed—but ultimately she's famous for being your sister.'

'I think that you overestimate my interest value,' demurred Raffaele—because he had sought no publicity for himself.

Troy gave a short laugh. 'It's true that in terms of your power and your money everything that can possibly have been written on the subject already has been. But don't forget, Raffaele, that there is one area of your life which has held a particular fascination for the press ever since you passed puberty.'

Raffaele stared at him, his black eyes narrowing. 'Be a little more *specific,* Troy,' he instructed softly.

'They've been trying to marry you off for years!'

'So?'

'So the only story which could draw interest away from Elisabetta would be if you finally did it.'

'Did *what,* precisely?'

'Got yourself a wife,' said Troy, just as there was a rap on the door and it began to open. 'Maybe it's time you married, Raffaele!'

Natasha entered the room just in time to hear Troy's enthusiastic statement and, for a moment, she honestly thought that she might drop her tray. She felt the blood drain from her face and her knees grow weak and some terrible roaring sound deafened her ears—like the sound of an express train racing through her head.

'Natasha?' Raffaele was frowning at her. 'Are you sick?'

'I…'

'Put the damned tray down,' he instructed tersely, but he had risen from his chair and was taking it from her himself. He put it down on the desk and caught her by the arm. 'What the hell is the matter with you?'

But with a few deep breaths Natasha had quickly recovered her equilibrium and she shook him off, telling herself that it was very important she didn't make a fool of herself.

Raffaele had been nothing but decent and fair to her over the years, and he had done more for Sam than could reasonably be expected of a boss. So she was not going to blow the whole thing by showing her distress at what was, after all, a long overdue piece of news. Or had she really expected a man like Raffaele to remain single for the rest of his life, just so that she could maintain her little fantasies about him?

'You're getting married?' she exclaimed brightly, and then forced the next word out, even though it felt like a fishbone stuck in her throat. 'Congratulations!'

Raffaele was staring at her as if she had taken leave of her senses. 'So this is how gossip begins!' he objected moodily. 'Something half overheard and then, before you know it, you are dealing with "fact"—only, it isn't fact at all. Just some crazy conjecture!'

'You mean, you're *not* getting married?' questioned Natasha cautiously, unable to prevent the wild leap of her heart, and thankful that he wouldn't be able to detect it.

'Of course I'm not getting married!' he retorted.

'I'm trying to persuade him to get married,' said Troy.

'Oh.' Natasha forced a smile as she looked at Troy, hating—just *hating*—Raffaele's smart-aleck lawyer at that moment. She cleared her throat as she began to pour their coffee. 'Isn't marriage an honourable institution that isn't supposed to be entered into lightly?' she asked, as casually as if she was enquiring whether they wanted milk or sugar. 'Who's the lucky woman?'

'I'm not talking about a *real* marriage,' said Troy. 'I'm talking about a pretend one.'

'A pretend one?' said Raffaele and Natasha at exactly the same moment, and Natasha began to fiddle around unnecessarily with the sugar bowl.

Troy nodded. 'You don't have to actually go through with it—just make the gestures. You know— you buy a whopping engagement ring and then you pose with your fiancée for the papers and she gives them a few interviews telling them where the wedding will be, where she's going to buy her dress. They love all that kind of stuff.'

'You seem remarkably well informed on the subject,' remarked Raffaele, with a sardonic elevation of his black brows.

'I try,' said Troy modestly.

'And even if I *were* to entertain such a bizarre remedy, aren't you forgetting one thing?'

'Like what?'

Raffaele's black eyes were like hard, cold jet. 'That there isn't a candidate.'

Did he hear Natasha's pent-up sigh of relief? Was that why he turned his head and fixed her with an impenetrable stare. 'Didn't you say you had a cake to make?'

Natasha blinked. Of all the times to prove that he had actually been listening to something she had to say he had to choose *this* one! 'Er…yes.'

'Well, then, run along, *cara,*' he said softly.

'Right.' Reluctantly, Natasha headed for the door, while they just carried on with their conversation as if she was invisible. Which I might as well be, she thought furiously.

'You just need someone who is prepared to go along with it,' Troy was saying.

'Like who? Oh, I can see your reasoning. It's a good idea, Troy—but there's just one problem, and it's the nightmare scenario.' Raffaele's eyes narrowed thoughtfully. 'Most women I know would be only to happy to go through with it—the difficulty would be getting them off my back afterwards.'

Troy laughed. 'Which is why we choose someone who wouldn't dare try to hang around.'

'Again, I say—*who?*'

Fascinating as she found the subject, Natasha knew that she really couldn't justify hanging around any longer, and she was almost out of the door when her eagle eye spotted a rogue little yellow plastic brick lying underneath one of the two wing chairs by the bookcase.

Now, how the hell had that gotten in here—especially when Sam wasn't even supposed to go into Raffaele's study? She was so fastidious about keeping all signs of young children carefully hidden away. Raffaele might be tolerant, and kinder to her son than his position warranted, but he certainly didn't want to be tripping up over model soldiers every time he came home.

She made a little exclamation of annoyance as she leaned over to retrieve the brick, and as the sound diverted his attention Raffaele found his eyes drawn to her bent figure.

Nobody could accuse Natasha of vanity—indeed, the garments she wore for work wouldn't have been out of place in a boot-camp and they'd never have been Raffaele's choice for a woman—never in a million years. He'd often used to think that here was a woman who would never distract him as she went about her work.

Maybe it was something to do with the fact that his nerves were on edge, or that it had been a long time since he'd had someone in his bed. Or maybe it was just something as simple as the fact that the moment had caught her with the material of her dress stretched tight across her derrière. Raffaele swallowed. And a very attractive derrière it was, too.

He narrowed his eyes and became aware of Troy's gaze following exactly the same path as his.

'Oh, yes,' said Troy softly. '*Yes.* That is *perfect.*'

Why was it that Raffaele found himself looking at his lawyer with cold distaste, wanting to tell him not to *dare* look at Natasha in that way—that she deserved his respect, not his predatory gaze? He shook himself. Predatory? Over *Natasha?*

She was straightening up now, with a piece of yellow plastic held between her fingers, and the fabric fell loose away from where it had been moulded to the tight, high curve of her buttocks. And all Raffaele could think was *why the hell had he never noticed that before?*

'You wouldn't have wanted to have stepped on *that* with bare feet!' she said triumphantly, and put it in her pocket as she marched out without a backwards glance.

Raffaele watched as she shut the door behind her, and suddenly there was Troy, sitting with some dumb, expectant grin on his face, looking at him as if he had found the key to the universe.

'Well? What do you think, Raffaele? Isn't this the answer to our predicament? Wouldn't *Natasha* do?'

CHAPTER FOUR

'No!' RAFFAELE snapped back, in an icy voice. 'Natasha would *not* do! She's my housekeeper, for *Dio's* sake!'

Outside the study door, the sound of her name halted Natasha right in her tracks and presented her with an age-old moral dilemma. Should she stay or should she go? Should she listen or not? But, surely, if they were talking about *her* didn't she have every *right* to listen?

Heart thumping, and with misgivings which were making her forehead ice into a cold sweat, she put her head close to the door. Their voices were muffled, but she could make out certain words like *unsuitable, inappropriate*. And then something else, which ended with Raffaele saying, quite loudly and quite forcefully, 'No one would ever believe it!'

And Troy's response. 'Why not ask her?'

She heard the sound of a chair being scraped back, and instinct made her move quickly away from her giveaway position. She hurried down to the kitchen, realising that time was tight if she wanted to have the cake made before she went out to collect Sam.

The radio was blaring as she changed her mind

about lemon drizzle and instead made cupcakes, which she iced in lurid shades of green and blue, especially designed to appeal to small boys—and to hell with the additives!

Despite the apron she'd put on, she'd still managed to get splodges of cake mixture over her dress—and she was going to have to leave in a minute. She ran upstairs and changed into something warmer—because the autumn afternoons were beginning to bite.

She put on a pale blue sweater, which brought out the colour in her eyes, and a pair of old jeans Then she brushed her hair and wove it into its habitual French plait. Her fingers hesitated over the little tub of lipgloss which had been on special offer at the chemist back in the summer, and which some impulse had made her buy. She'd only used it a couple of times, and it didn't really seem to be *her,* so she'd put the top back on and had never used it again.

So what was it that made her pick it up today? Did it have something to do with the way the two men had looked at her in the study—or rather the way they'd *not* looked at her? As if she was some old piece of furniture—reliably comfortable, but not something you'd want to show off to a guest.

Defiantly, she opened it and stroked on some of the strawberry-scented gloss. Perhaps some of her reluctance to dress up had come from knowing that she could never compete with the other mothers, who arrived at the school looking as if they'd stepped out of the pages of a glossy magazine. Maybe that was why she was always being mistaken for one of the nannies—though she had to admit that most of *them* made more of an effort than she did.

Outside, the late-afternoon sky was a clear blue and

the trees were etched against it in startling relief. All the leaves were turning rich shades of bronze and toffee and gold and, in the distance, she thought she could smell the faint drift of smoke, which was unusual in London, though this area was exclusive enough to have gardens big enough to cope with bonfires.

Natasha was suddenly overcome with the sense of nostalgia which autumn always provoked. The end of the summer and the start of winter and soon Sam beginning full-time school. During no other season was she quite so aware of the passing of time as this, when the leaves began their dizzy spiralling dance to the ground below.

There were luxury cars in abundance parked in the streets near the school—most people had to travel from all over the capital to get there—and Natasha never forgot to count her blessings that she lived close enough to walk there.

She watched as the children began to file out in their rather old-fashioned uniform of knee-length shorts for the little boys and kilts for the girls, along with thick sweaters which looked like home-knits, and sturdy shoes and dark socks. Sam was excitedly anticipating the time when he would graduate to long trousers—like the 'big' boys at the middle school—and Natasha began to wonder how long she could let things continue like this. With Sam getting more and more used to the luxurious lifestyle which Raffaele could afford to give him. Was it time for her to start getting real? To live within *her* means?

'*Maman!*' Sam called as he came running over, his little friend in tow. 'You're wearing lipstick!'

'Hello, darling—was it a French day today?'

'You're wearing lipstick!' accused her son again.

'Yes, I am—do you like it?' She smiled down at Sam's best friend. 'Hello, Serge. How are you?'

'*Très bien, merci!*' replied Serge, with the solemn confidence learnt from his French diplomat father.

'Well, that's good,' she replied, as the three of them began to walk the route home, which took them past the area's best conker tree. 'I've made monster cakes!'

'Monster cakes?' Serge frowned as Sam began to scoop up the shiny brown nuts. 'But what are monster cakes?'

'It means you turn into a monster if you eat them!' chanted Sam. 'Will Raffaele be there?'

'He's probably busy, darling—we'll see.'

'*Oh!*'

The boys played with their conkers in the garden and then came inside for supper. Because it was Friday, there was no homework, so she left them playing a complicated game with battleships. She was just wondering whether Raffaele wanted her to make him supper when she almost collided with him.

'Just the person I wanted to see,' he said grimly.

It didn't sound that way. And why was he looking at her like that, with an expression on his face she had never seen before? The black eyes were brilliant and piercing and they narrowed as they swept over her, as if they were assessing her for something—but what?

Some kind of sixth sense set off a distant clamour which seemed to make Natasha acutely aware of the pulsing of her blood—as if something had just sprung to life within her. Alarmingly, she felt the tips of her breasts begin to rub against the rough lace of her bra and the corresponding flood of colour to her cheeks.

'Well, here I am,' she said.

But Raffaele wasn't listening. He was struck by the

way her cheeks were looking uncharacteristically pink—like the wild roses of summer. And by the way…the way… *Madre di Dio,* but this could not be happening!

Irresistibly, he found his gaze locked onto the luscious curve of her breasts, and he started wondering whether this was because of what had happened earlier—an awakening which had been triggered by something as simple as a woman bending down to pick up a toy. The sudden realisation that behind the guise of her unerring efficiency Natasha *was* a woman. A real flesh-and-blood one at that. He found that he wanted to cup his palms over those buttocks and bring her right up close against him.

'Any more news about Elisabetta?'

Her question was like an icy bath on his senses, and he discovered that he had been guilty of some very impure thoughts, indeed—and *that* wasn't on his agenda at all. He hardened his voice. Elisabetta was the reason he was about to do all this—and the *only* reason, he reminded himself.

'No,' he said, staring at her mouth and thinking that there was something different about *that,* too. Was it all shiny and pink? Or was that just his imagination? He frowned. Was he out of his mind to go through with this crazy scheme? And yet hadn't he been racking his brains all day and coming up with remarkably few solutions to this particular dilemma? For all his wealth and power and connections there were some things he *couldn't* control, and the press was one of them. 'Is Sam here?'

'He's downstairs with Serge. He's got a new conker he wants to show you.'

For a moment the tension on his face eased, the

faint smile nudging at the corners of his mouth completely transforming his rugged features.

'I'll go down and take a look.' He raised his brows. 'And later—will he be here then?'

She shook her head and frowned. 'No, he's going to stay over at Serge's—it's his turn this week. Is there a problem?'

'Not really,' he said smoothly. 'I suggest that you and I eat together.'

Natasha shrugged. It wasn't as if their eating together was unknown. She didn't go out that often—and certainly not when Raffaele was around. She felt that being there was part of the fabulous deal he had made with her—she made the house warm and comfortable when he was home.

She wanted to ask him what was on his mind and, yet, there was something very censorious in his eyes which dared her to even try—a dark, warning light that made her very aware of his position over her. Because—despite all their familiarity and the usual ease with which they lived their lives—sometimes Raffaele unmistakably pulled rank, and he was doing it now. This wasn't a casual suggestion that they might eat supper together, it was an order, and Natasha's pulse began to race. 'Sure. Would you like me to cook something special?'

'No. That won't be necessary. I'll cook.'

Raffaele? *Cook?* 'R-right.'

Her anxiety grew as she saw the boys off when Serge's impossibly glamorous nanny came to collect them. Natasha could tell that she was dawdling unnecessarily in the hall.

'Signor de Feretti—he is at home?' the girl asked guilelessly, her enormous dark eyes like velvet saucers, searching the tempting spaces behind Natasha's shoulders.

'He is—somewhere. Quite busy, I expect—unless it was something specific?'

'I want to go to Italy to be a nanny next year—I thought maybe he could tell me some things.'

'Signor de Feretti is very busy,' said Natasha, a little more crisply than she had intended. 'Perhaps you should try one of the agencies? I'm sure they can tell you everything you need to know.'

After they'd gone, the house seemed more echoing than usual, and Natasha could hear the sounds of Raffaele clanking stuff around in the basement kitchen in between the phone ringing and ringing. He shouted up to tell her to leave it on the answer-machine, but then his mobile started, and he must have picked it up because she could hear the low, urgent sound of his voice.

She felt odd—as if she wasn't quite sure of her place anymore, as if something had changed but no one had bothered to tell her about it.

Slowly, she went downstairs, where Raffaele was stirring something in a pot. He wore jeans—old, faded and blue—hugging his lean hips and skating down the muscular shaft of his long legs. With the jeans he wore a shirt made of thick white cambric, through which she could just make out the hard outline of his torso.

He heard her come in and turned round and, inconsequentially, she noticed that there were two buttons of his shirt undone and that dark hair curled there—a shadowy dark triangle, contrasted against the snowy material. His black hair was still damp, as if he had recently showered and his feet were bare. Natasha was suddenly filled with an overwhelming wave of longing and weakness.

'Hungry?' he questioned.

She shook her head, wanting to ask him what was going on—why he was talking to her and treating her in a way which made him seem like a stranger to her.

'Not yet. I'd like a drink, please.'

He frowned. 'You mean, a *drink* drink?'

She glanced over at the already open bottle of red. 'If that's all right.'

'Sure. It's just that you don't usually—'

'Drink? No, I don't.' But Natasha had had enough of this walking-on-eggshells feeling. If he was about to tell her he wanted to sack her, then why the hell didn't he just come out with it—instead of all this awkwardness which left her feeling lost and helpless? 'And *you* don't usually behave like this.'

'Like what?' he demanded.

'Oh, Raffaele—I don't *know!*'

He stared at her and, for a moment, he almost made a joke about the glaring lack of feminine logic, the way he might usually have done, but he poured her a glass of wine, instead, and turned the heat off from underneath the pan. Then he drank a large mouthful of his own drink and sat down on the edge of the large kitchen table, his black eyes fixed unwaveringly on her face. 'You know what Troy and I were discussing earlier?'

'You discussed rather a lot. And then I left,' she said pointedly.

He realised that there was no *correct* way of going about what he was going to propose. That maybe being businesslike was the only way in which either of them might find it acceptable.

'I have a favour to ask you, Natasha,' he said quietly.

'Go on.'

'You've heard the phone ringing? *Si?* It was the editors of two national dailies, asking about Elisabetta—wanting to know more details. For now, a blank refusal to tell them anything seems to have worked, but they won't let up—I've seen it happen before. I've spent the afternoon going over and over what might be the best course of action. I thought of taking her to the States, or back to Italy—but the former is a long way for her to travel at the moment, and, as you know, the worst place in the world for her at the moment is Italy—and that man.'

There was a pause while he looked at her—at the mediocre jeans she wore, with a very ordinary sweater. At the cheap canvas shoes on her feet—footwear which no woman of his acquaintance would ever be seen wearing. He thought about all the things Troy had said and found himself agreeing with some of them. What alternative did he have? No woman knew him the way she did—and no other woman would be prepared to take him only on *his* terms.

Would she do it? he wondered, and—more importantly—would anyone really believe that he, Raffaele de Feretti, would enter into a relationship with someone like Natasha Phillips? But his mind was made up. In a day of ever-decreasing possibilities, this remained the only one which made any sense to him.

'I want you to become engaged to me, Natasha,' he said slowly.

For a moment her mind played tricks on her as a thousand latent fantasies sprang into glorious Technicolor life. Dreams that she'd tried desperately hard not to nurture were suddenly given life—dreams about a man who had seemed way beyond the grasp of someone like her.

Yet sometimes, when the dark cloak of night banished all reasonable objections, her hopes would flare as she allowed herself to think about his glowing olive skin, with his black eyes set in it like dark jewels. Or the autocratic and proud features and the body which was all hard muscle and sinew. She would allow herself a heavenly glimpse of what it would be like to be held in his arms, to be kissed by such a mouth as Raffaele's. And then be left aching and empty when the morning light mocked her for her foolish longings.

But Raffaele was asking her…to *marry* him? If Natasha hadn't been so befuddled by events she might have made the connection with what she'd overheard earlier—as it was, she just stared at him, her lips parted.

'You want to marry me?' she questioned breathlessly.

'No. I want us to become engaged.'

The first cold drip of reality pinged into her brain. 'Why?' she asked numbly.

Why the hell did she think? 'Because it will kill the Elisabetta story stone-dead.'

Somehow Natasha kept the hurt from her face—the stupid hurt which might let him catch a glimpse of the crazy fantasies she had been nurturing. Instead, she used her matter-of-face voice—the one she sometimes used if she thought he looked tired and said so. 'You don't think that it might look like a set-up? That any editor worth their salt will realise that?'

'What they think and what they print are two different matters—and no editor will be foolish or cynical enough to come out and say that the engagement is just a—'

'Publicity stunt?' she put in shakily.

'A damage limitation exercise,' he corrected.

There was a long pause while Natasha tried to work though what the repercussions might be, but her head was whirling with it. 'And just when are you proposing that we get 'engaged'?' she asked quietly.

Raffaele relaxed by a fraction. 'We can go and buy a ring as soon as you like.' His eyes narrowed as he saw her bite her lip and, for the first time, he began to consider how such an action might sit awkwardly with such a quiet and plain woman. 'I can understand your reservations—'

'Can you?' She gave a short laugh.

'Of course I can. It seems a little *theatrical,* but we really ought to make it look as real as possible.'

As real as possible. Natasha kept her face in check. Not a hint of disappointment would he read there. 'But it isn't real, is it?' she questioned, almost brightly. 'None of it.'

Raffaele laughed, some of the tension beginning to leave him as he realised that she was joking. This was going to be ridiculously easy! 'No, of course it isn't! Don't worry, Natasha—it can be the shortest engagement on record, if you like. Just long enough to take some of the heat off Elisabetta. You can even keep the ring afterwards, if you want—or sell it, of course.'

There was a dreadful kind of silence. 'That won't be necessary,' she said, in a choked kind of voice. 'I'm not asking for any kind of payment.'

He realised that he had said the wrong thing. 'I didn't mean it like that. Really, I didn't.' He stared at her, waiting for some light-hearted response and, when none came, he softened his voice in the way he only dared risk doing with her—because Natasha was sensible enough not to see anything in it other than friendly concern. 'You're the only woman I know who won't read anything else into it. It makes perfect sense, when you think about it—since we know each other so well.'

Natasha looked at him. He just didn't get it, did he? They *didn't* know each other at all. If he had known even a *fraction* about the way her mind operated, then he would know that he'd really insulted her with his crass suggestion that she keep the ring or sell it. As if such a ring wouldn't be anything other than a mocking reminder of what could have been but which never would.

His words had opened up the great, gaping chasm which lay between pointless dreams and harsh reality. She was useful to Raffaele, nothing more than that—and never more so than now.

Raffaele's eyes narrowed as another far more unsettling objection occurred to him. 'Unless you have some man-friend of your own?' he suggested silkily. 'Someone who might object on the grounds of your relationship with him?'

Had Natasha stupidly thought that her pain threshold had been reached? Because as she shook her head in answer to his question she was discovering a capacity for more. And, oddly enough, this suggestion hurt more than anything preceding it—that he could think she might be seeing someone. *And that he shouldn't even care!* But Natasha forced herself to embrace the pain which washed over her.

Maybe this was the wake-up call she needed. The one which would banish all her wistful longings once and for all and allow her to move on with her life. To maybe start looking out for herself—even to think that one day she might meet a man she cared about enough to consider spending her life with. It was true he wouldn't be Raffaele de Feretti—but if she chose to compare other men with *him,* then she was going to end up a very bitter and lonely woman.

'What *exactly* will this so-called engagement entail?' she asked.

'We'll announce it, obviously—and then just a few high-profile occasions when we'll need to be seen at together. Nothing too onerous,' he added, with the glitter of a smile.

How *privileged* he was, she thought suddenly—and not simply in the material sense. Here was a man who could snap his fingers and get exactly what he wanted.

'And what about Sam?' she asked, her heart undergoing a swift somersault of misgiving.

'What about him?'

'It's going to confuse him,' she said quietly.

There was silence for a moment.

'Will a five-year-old boy even notice?' he questioned. 'This isn't something that's going to make any difference at home. Nothing is going to change for Sam, is it? We can explain about Elisabetta being sick, if you want, and that us being a couple is simply to help her— as long as he doesn't tell anyone else. Or we can just answer his questions if and when they come up. All Sam needs to know is that we're still going to be friends afterwards.'

She stared into his uncomprehending eyes. Friends? Not really. *And he doesn't even realise that, either, does he? Nor does he have any inkling of how much my little boy worships him and would love more than anything for the engagement to be real. I have to leave*

this house and this man, Natasha thought suddenly—
and I have to do it soon. Perhaps this whole peculiar
scheme would make it that bit easier....

'You want some time to think about it?' asked
Raffaele, frowning.

'No. I've made my mind up. I'll do it.' After everything he'd done for her, it was the least she could do.

He slanted her a smile and held his glass up to chink
hers in a toast. *'Stupendo!'* he said softly. He saw her
lips tremble and idly wondered what it would be like
to kiss them, to seal their 'engagement' in the more traditional way. He was surprised by the stir of interest
he felt. But this was a game. A pretence. Nothing more.
And the rather more worrying question of authenticity
began to rear its head.

'You're going to have to do something about your
wardrobe, of course,' he said abruptly.

Natasha nearly choked on her wine. 'What's that
supposed to mean?'

The good thing about knowing someone as well as
he did Natasha, was that Raffaele could tell it like it
really was—and the truth was a luxury you didn't get
to use with most people.

'Well, obviously, the press are going to love the
rich man-poor girl aspect of the affair—the fact that
you work for me—but if you look too…well, too…'

'Too, what, Raffaele?' she questioned, in a high,
clear voice.

'My taste in women is well known,' he said bluntly,
wondering why she hid her bottom when it happened
to be such a shapely one. 'And, at the moment, you do
not fulfill any of the criteria.'

There was a pause, as if he was letting the full, hurtful implication sink in.

'You will need to dress in beautiful things,' he continued. 'Tomorrow you will go and buy yourself an entire new wardrobe and charge it to my account. Buy what you like,' he added. But even thinking about her shapely curves was making made him grow hard—something which was *not* part of the deal. 'And perhaps you should do something with your hair while you're at it,' he finished.

There was a space of about ten seconds when Natasha was seriously tempted to tell him exactly what he could do with his bogus engagement and then tell him how incredibly *insulting* he had managed to be before storming off. But the possibility dissolved away—because there was no way she could follow through. How could she fail to do anything other than help Raffaele when he needed her help just as he had helped her that wet, dark night when she'd turned up on his doorstep? Doing this would make them even. Quits. And then she could leave him.

Because after this there would be nowhere to go with this relationship—and she had no right to get angry simply because Raffaele looked on her as nothing more than someone who worked for him. She did! If she had invested too much emotional energy and hopes in her boss, then she had only herself to blame.

'I haven't done anything with my hair for years.' Natasha touched her fingers to the thick French plait which hung all the way down her back. Wasn't Raffaele giving her the opportunity to do what all those TV makeover programmes aimed for—make her into the woman she'd always wanted to be?

And what kind of woman is that?

The sobering truth was that she didn't know.

CHAPTER FIVE

THE NEXT day, Natasha went to the most famous department store she could think of and booked an appointment with a personal shopper.

'Call me Kirsty,' said the grinning redhead. 'And then tell me what it is you're looking for.'

Natasha drew a deep breath. She knew what Raffaele wanted—someone who looked as little like a housekeeper as possible—so why not give it to him?

'I want a complete change of image,' she said.

She noticed that Kirsty didn't contradict her. 'We can do that. And what's your budget?'

This part took a little getting used to. 'I don't actually have a budget,' admitted Natasha.

Kirsty's eyebrows underwent a rapid elevation. 'You mean, money's no object?'

'Kind of,' Natasha agreed, but some stubborn frugal ethic forced her to add, 'Of course, I don't actually want to *waste* any money.'

'There's no such thing as waste—not where clothes and beauty products are concerned,' said Kirsty smoothly. 'We women owe it to ourselves to look as good as possible. Remember that, Natasha.'

'I'll try,' said Natasha faintly.

It was not something she had ever done—blazed her way through a shop and kitted herself out from head to toe. When she'd been growing up, money had been tight, then she'd been a student and then Sam had come along. The array of goods on sale was dazzling, and Natasha was glad to have Kirsty to run an experienced eye over colour and design.

As Kirsty told her, most women didn't get to the age of twenty-five without some of idea of what colours suited them—but what most of them failed to do was to try some unusual and different shades which would not have been their first and obvious choice. She put Natasha into deep leaf-green and terracotta, deep blues and purples, as well as her more usual pastels. There were silk-satins for evening, deliciously filmy underwear and clothes that were described as 'leisure-wear'.

'Now the good bit—shoes. Here, try these!' suggested Kirsty.

Natasha tottered around in front of the mirrors on a pair of impossibly high heels—which she resolutely rejected.

'But they make your legs look like stilts,' objected Kirsty.

'I'm not sure I *want* legs like stilts—and, anyway, I can't actually walk in them!'

In the end she compromised with something lower—but Kirsty insisted that if she didn't buy the sinful-looking shoes in scarlet patent she would regret it for the rest of her life. And Natasha supposed that she must have been on some kind of a high, because she found herself agreeing.

She shopped until she almost dropped, but her fatigue was quickly put to flight by a pedicure—

possibly the most heavenly and restful experience of her entire life. Her feet were pummelled and scrubbed and soaked in sweet-smelling warm water, her toenails buffed and polished, so that, in the end, they didn't look or feel like Natasha's feet at all. She felt so comfortable that she allowed herself to be shown how to make her face up, and she bought the foundation, mascara, eyeshadows, blusher and lipsticks which a fancy-looking chart said were suitable for her particular colouring. Then the beautician suggested a leg and bikini wax.

'Oh, I'm not sure,' she said doubtfully, wondering when it would ever end.

'Is it a gentleman paying for all this?' asked Kirsty delicately. 'Yes? Well, then, let me assure you that a leg wax *will* be required.'

Natasha could hardly object to the insinuation—just as she could hardly tell Kirsty that sex wasn't part of the deal. Hadn't she told herself that if she was going to enter into this elaborate subterfuge then she would do it with good grace? More importantly, that she would actually try to *enjoy* herself.

'Now, you're ditching those jeans,' said Kirsty determinedly, 'and you're going to wear some of your brand-new wardrobe. The old Natasha is dead—long live the new one!'

The new Natasha was then taken to a fancy hairdresser close to South Molton Street where, magically, their most talented stylist managed to find a slot free at the end of a busy afternoon. That was money talking again, Natasha guessed.

'So, what are we looking at, dear?' he questioned, lifting long strands of hair one by one and then letting them drop down again—so that in the mirror Natasha thought she looked like a kind of octopus. 'One inch? Two?'

'Make it look fabulous,' said Natasha recklessly, because she'd bought Kirsty a champagne cocktail for helping her and had had one, herself, and had rather glowingly decided that it would be ridiculously easy to get used to having a lot of money.

'Fabulous it is!' trilled the stylist with camp excitement.

Natasha had missed out on the frivolous side of growing up. The aunt who had brought her up had been kind, but distant—and terribly old-fashioned. She had thought it demeaning for women to rely on their looks to help them get on in life. 'A woman should use her brains, not her body,' she used to tell Natasha as she pored over her schoolbooks.

Little wonder that Natasha had been ill equipped to deal with all the pitfalls of a modern world from which she had been rigorously shielded. Her arrival at university after her all-girls' school had been like being hurled down a wind tunnel—it had left her gasping and reeling. Her prim innocence had attracted a certain type of man—the kind who saw the taking of virginity as his due, but who ran a million miles when he discovered she was pregnant.

As the colourist pulled various strands of hair through an alien-looking, silver cap and the cutter snipped away, Natasha wondered whether she had just stayed stuck in a rut. She had been safely cocooned at home with her aunt, and now she was safely cocooned at Raffaele's. Her one foray into the outside world had left her feeling scorched and so she had retreated from it. Well, not so safe anymore, she thought, as the dryer whooshed the shorter, brighter strands of hair around her head.

'There!' said the stylist, beaming.

Natasha blinked, hardly recognising the face which gazed back at her from the mirror. The dress and the make-up were amazing, yes—and the lingerie she was wearing underneath made her feel completely different from the usual drab mum she considered herself to be. But it was the hair which effected the most dramatic transformation of all. No wonder thieves wore wigs to disguise themselves, she thought.

The stylist had lopped several inches off and cut into the ends of it, so that it hung in a thick, scented curtain to her shoulders. With the colourist's help it was now a mass of subtle variations, a warmer and lighter version of her original shade, so she would have described it as golden or honey instead of the ubiquitous pale mousy-brown.

'What do you think?' the stylist asked excitedly. 'There's still enough length to wear it up, if you want to.'

'It…well, it doesn't look like me,' she breathed.

'That was the idea, dear!' he commented wryly.

It had been easy during her makeover to forget just why she was doing it. But as the taxi neared the house, laden down with enough shopping bags to sink a battleship, Natasha began to feel nervous.

Would Raffaele think she'd lost it and had gone completely over the top? More importantly, could she actually go through with this whole crazy scheme?

But something had happened as she had stared at herself in the mirror in the hairdresser's. Something which she couldn't really put into words, but it had a lot to do with giving her a certain *sense* of herself—as if when she'd gazed back at that calm, perfectly made-up face she had seen someone different from the person she considered herself to be.

Not Natasha the mum.

Nor Natasha the housekeeper.

Or Natasha who knew nothing about men.

She had blinked at the very real discovery that she could be whoever she wanted to be—she just hadn't found out who that was. Not yet.

The taxi drew up outside the imposing townhouse and the driver tooted his horn. 'Anyone inside? You'll need a crane to help you get those in,' he joked.

Raffaele appeared at the door. And stood for one long, silent moment staring down at her, black eyes narrowed and impenetrable, before he ran down the steps.

He paid the taxi and took the shopping bags from her, and Natasha was suddenly and acutely aware of his proximity, of the raw masculine heat radiating from his body and the sensual trace of lemon and sandalwood aftershave which was so particular to him. Her newfound confidence began to seep away, drained by the ebony blaze of his gaze as it raked over her. *Say something,* she pleaded silently.

The taxi roared away and they stood on the pavement—facing each other like two people who'd just met.

His eyes travelled from the tip of her expensively shorn head down to the dress of fine cashmere which moulded itself to her body in a way he'd never seen a dress do to her before. A leather belt was slung low on her hips and leather boots slouched midway down her slender legs. Raffaele was unprepared for the savage kick of lust.

'Where's S-Sam?' she questioned unsteadily.

Reluctantly, he tore his gaze away from her legs to

her face—to eyes that were newly huge and the soft glimmer of rose-petal lips. 'Inside. We were watching a DVD but he's just fallen asleep—worn out from playing football. He's had a busy day.' There was a pause, and when he spoke again, it was with a soft and almost dangerous stealth. 'And so have you, *cara mia,* to judge by your appearance.'

Her heart missed a beat—for that was surely disapproval which glimmered from those coal-black eyes, a note of condemnation which had deepened his voice? 'You don't like it?'

'I didn't say that.'

'You didn't say the opposite, though, did you—that you liked it?'

His mouth pursed into the mockery of a kiss. *'Madre di Dio,'* he mused. 'Is this what a little finery does to a woman? It changes her from demure to demanding?'

'That's not fair, Raffaele!'

'Isn't it? And is it fair to dress like a siren—to say to a man you may look but not touch?'

'I didn't say that!'

'Oh, you *didn't?'* His eyes widened, like a cat's. 'That is exactly what I wanted to hear, *bella mia,'* he murmured. He dropped the bags to the pavement, pulled her into his arms, and Natasha found herself being almost lifted against the hard, muscular length of his body. With a low laugh of what sounded like triumph he raised his hand to catch hold of her beautifully cut hair, winding his fingers through its silken depths and bringing it towards him so that her gasping face was lifted to his.

'Raffaele!'

'What is it, *mia bella?'* he taunted. 'You want me to kiss you? Is that it?'

She opened her mouth to say no, but the word never came—and, if it had, it would have been a lie. Maybe he knew that—just as he seemed to know the precise moment to crush his lips down against hers in a powerful kiss that was about possession as much as passion, like a man staking his claim.

Was it because she had not been kissed by a man for so long that Natasha reacted so completely and instinctively to Raffaele's kiss—or was it simply Raffaele effect?

Whatever lay behind it, all Natasha knew was that she seemed powerless to do anything other than close her eyes and open her lips and submit to the sweet, heady pressure. Her hands flew up to grip at his shoulders as she felt the soft graze of his teeth, the tantalising flick of his tongue against the roof of her mouth. Did he sense how helpless she felt. Or was her little cry of disbelieving pleasure a giveaway in itself?

Because hadn't Raffaele's kiss been her greatest and most forbidden wish of all—the one which had used to eat away at her when she least expected it? When he curved her that hard smile before he left in the mornings. Or when he returned from abroad and she had missed him more than he would ever know. Or occasionally—and much too dangerously—when he had just taken a shower and his black hair still glistened, and she'd imagine the hard, olive-skinned body standing beneath steaming jets of water.

Well, this kiss was real enough and, for once, reality far exceeded the kiss of her imagination. She moaned as she felt her knees weaken and her grip on his shoulders tightened.

He felt her unspoken surrender, and it blasted into his senses simply because it was so unexpected. He felt confused—because this was *Natasha* he was kissing. Natasha whose sleek curves he could feel beneath his seeking fingers. Natasha who was inciting him to the kind of kiss which only led to one place, and that place was bed. And Raffaele knew that if he didn't stop doing what he was doing then she was going to get a whole lot more than she had bargained for.

He tore his mouth away from hers, the thunder of his heart seeming to drown the sound of traffic which hummed in the nearby street. Her lips were still parted, wet from where he had licked them, and the pale blue of her eyes was almost completely obscured by the blackness of desire. He felt some strange feeling over-power him—more anger than frustration—as if he had been just playing with her and she had damned well played him back at his own game. So, was she sexually more experienced than she let on? Her quiet evenings nothing more than a bluff for when he happened to be in residence?

Natasha stared up at him, her kiss-crushed mouth trembling, trying and failing to read that dangerously wild, dark glint in his eyes. 'Why did…why did you do that?' she whispered.

Why, indeed? To punish her for the crime of mak-ing him want her when she was out of bounds? Or for having worked too effective a transformation from housekeeper to wife-in-waiting? Or maybe because he couldn't ever remember wanting to kiss a woman that badly in a long time?

But all this was a pretence, he told himself furi-ously, and maybe they both needed to be reminded of that fact.

His autocratic mouth curved into a close approxi-mation of a smile, but it stayed light-years away from his eyes. 'Didn't you know that there's a journalist hiding nearby, sniffing around for a story? And I think we may have provided him with one,' he whispered, steeling his heart to the dawning hurt in her eyes. 'What a pity there wasn't a camera to hand!'

For a moment, she thought he was joking, but one look at his mocking face made her realise he was deadly serious and she began to try to wriggle out of his arms. But Raffaele's grip was too firm for her to be able to move away effectively. In fact, all it was doing was... Her eyes widened.

'*Si,*' he said grimly. 'You feel it? You feel me? What you do to me? How much you make me want you?'

'Let...me...*go!*' she breathed.

'But you should not kiss a man like that if you are not prepared to take the consequences!'

'You...you *bastard!*'

But now the spark of fire in her eyes was doing the impossible, turning him on even more, and he wondered why the hell that should be—until he realised that her usual role in his life was docility. Suddenly, she had stepped out from behind that role and he found himself wondering what else he might find beneath.

'Shh, *cara,*' he said softly. 'We don't want that nice journalist to think we are rowing, do we? Not when we are about to tell the world we're engaged.'

'Will you let me go?'

'In a minute.' But still he held her, unable to relinquish the softness of her body as he willed the exquisite pain of desire to subside. He felt her relax against him, heard her soft sigh of submission and saw her eyes briefly close in surrender. '*Si,*' he whispered. 'This is the way of it. You see how helpless we all can be, Natasha—held in thrall to our most primitive longings?

You and I, we choose to play a game—to concoct an elaborate masquerade—but underneath it all we are just a man and a woman, programmed by nature to join together in the most fundamental way possible.'

But, oh, how that hurt. That almost *anatomical* dissection of their kiss, which was poles apart from her crazy longings. If anything could have painted a picture of just how heartless Raffaele de Feretti really was, then his words had done it with perfect clarity.

'Will you let me go?' she whispered.

'I will.' He snaked his tongue out over his dry lips and his eyes sparked with provocation, but the ache in his body was real enough—as was his fleeting sense of regret that this *was* a game. That he couldn't just haul her upstairs and let this mad desire burn itself out in a few hours of delicious sex. 'Unless you want one last kiss before I do?' he murmured.

The awful thing was that she *did*—even though he had done it just to give the reporter an eyeful! But it was—as he had gone to great pains to remind her— nothing but a physical hunger. It wasn't something rooted in the emotions—well, certainly not in his— and she mustn't forget that. *I don't want to end up being badly hurt,* she thought fiercely, and this time she *did* pull away.

'No, thank you,' she said. 'I'd like to see Sam—and then to hang all these beautiful clothes up before they get too creased.'

Anger carried her along to flounce past him, enjoying his faintly bemused expression as she left him to carry in all her bags. Let him wait on *her* for a change, she thought!

But inside, her negative feelings dissolved into love as she found Sam fast asleep in the garden room, as

Raffaele had said. In front of him ran a film showing *The World's Greatest Ever Goals*—her little boy was football-mad, and didn't Raffaele occasionally take him to see a match on one of those rare Saturdays when he was free?

She stood and watched his snuggled little form, feeling a huge lump constricting her throat, knowing that one day soon she was going to have to take her child away from a man he had grown to love—almost like a father. But Raffaele *wasn't* his father, and what choice did she have but to leave? To grow old before her time in this house, not living at all except in his formidable shadow—what example would *that* be to set for her young son?

She touched her fingers to his soft cheek. 'Wake up,' she said softly. 'Wake up, darling.'

Sleepily, Sam blinked up to her. 'You look different, Mama.'

'Mama's had her hair cut, that's why.' And Mama's wearing fine clothes and underwear. All paid for with Raffaele's money. She felt the stain of guilt flare into her cheeks. 'Are you hungry?'

'No,' he said absently, and then murmured something in Italian, as he often did if he'd spent a protracted period of time with Raffaele. Usually, she delighted in how he could practise his language skills, but today all it served to do was to emphasise the advantages that this life gave him—advantages which would swiftly disappear, like a bubble popping, once she left the Italian's employment.

Raffaele walked in the room and saw her lean over to tenderly brush a lock of hair away from the boy's head—but it was as if he was looking at someone he'd never met before. Yes, she was an exemplary mother and a reliable worker—yet, today, it was as if someone had waved a magic wand and made her into someone else. Where was the Natasha he knew?

He had brusquely told her that his taste in women was exacting—but he had not in his wildest dreams believed that she could have so magnificently become the very embodiment of his ideal woman. Was this going to complicate matters? Mercilessly, he quelled the raw rush of desire, knowing that he couldn't afford to let it.

But then his phone rang, and Raffaele went out of the room to answer it. It was Troy, and he sounded both bemused and pleased.

'I've just had the *Daily View* on the line, saying that you've been spotted kissing a glamorous blonde outside the house and they want a comment,' he said. 'What's going on, Raffaele? This is pretty confusing. I thought that it was Natasha who was going to be the decoy—though you know I always had my reservations about her ability to carry it off. So who is it? Who's the mystery woman?

'There is no mystery,' said Raffaele, with a beat of satisfaction whose source he did not recognise. 'The woman was Natasha.'

There was a stunned silence. *'Natasha?'*

'Yes, Natasha,' Raffaele answered coolly. 'As for a comment—there is none. But you might like to mention that I shall be taking the glamorous blonde in question to a charity dinner on Monday night.' His voice dipped. 'And she will be wearing my engagement ring.'

CHAPTER SIX

'NATASHA!'

She could hear the note of impatience in his voice.

'Natasha!' he called again.

'I'll be two seconds, Raffaele!' she called down, and turned back to her son.

Sam was sitting before an open drawing book at the little desk in his room, silvering the stars which were sprinkled through a unicorn's mane. 'Good night, darling,' she said—feeling as if she were proposing to leave him for a month, instead of just one evening.

''Night, Mama,' he murmured, and smiled. 'You look nice.'

She didn't feel *nice*. She felt like a fraud—or whatever the feminine equivalent of a wolf all done up in sheep's clothing was. Natasha shivered. And she was *cold*—unused to having such large areas of flesh on show, even though she knew that other women would wear dresses such as these to the charity ball she and Raffaele were due to attend that night.

'You're sure you don't mind being left with the babysitter?' she asked anxiously, as she had asked him several times since supper. It occurred to Natasha that if Sam had been a more manipulative child then he might have said that, yes, he did mind, that he wasn't used to his mother leaving him with other people—and demand that she stay behind. And wasn't there a part of her that would have been hugely relieved to have done just that? Surely, just *being* Raffaele's fiancée would be enough to fool people—without them having to turn up and appear at parties like a pair of performing seals?

Sam shook his head. 'No, I like Anna. She's fun. She sings songs into a hairbrush!'

Natasha forced a smile. 'Does she?' The drama student daughter of some people down the road was certainly lively—and she adored Sam—but it was the first time Natasha had ever used her. Would she be able to detect a fire if one started in the basement? Or would she use this opportunity to import a load of unsuitable friends, leaving Sam forgotten while she partied?

Telling herself that her own nervousness was being transmitted into worrying about her son, Natasha set off downstairs, where Anna was waiting in the hall, talking to Raffaele. They both looked up as Natasha carefully began to descend the wide and sweeping staircase—still finding the scarlet patent shoes a little high and her dress a little long—the red silk gown making soft whispering sounds as it slithered down to the ground around her.

It seemed to take for ever to get to the bottom, especially with Raffaele's eyes fixed on her like that—an ebony spotlight which spilled over her with dark light. 'Here I am,' she said brightly.

There was a heartbeat of a pause. 'So I see.' Raffaele's gaze was steady as he watched her unaccustomed movements. He was used to seeing Natasha in jeans and trainers, striding around the place at a fast pace, but this Natasha moved differently—probably because of those killer heels she was wearing. If he stopped to listen carefully enough, would he hear the silken sound of her thighs brushing together? And was she wearing stockings underneath that bright waterfall of a dress? He felt a pulse spring to life deep in his groin.

'Wow—you look *amazing,* Natasha!' said Anna. 'I can't believe it's you!'

'I know the feeling,' said Natasha wryly, relieved to have reached the bottom of the stairs without tumbling over.

'Come here, over to the light, and let me look at you properly,' murmured Raffaele.

He stepped back to survey her, one hand cupping his elbow, a forefinger pressed to his lips—in exactly the way people did when they were studying a painting in an art gallery. *As if I'm on show,* thought Natasha indignantly, *as if I'm a possession*—until she reminded herself that there was no point in being indignant. She had known exactly what she was getting into. This was exactly what it was supposed to be. A game.

So play it. She tipped her head slightly, feeling the heavy mass of her hair, which was piled high in an elaborate confection courtesy of a hairdresser who had arrived earlier this evening for just that purpose. The circle of platinum around her finger felt heavy, too—as if her slender hands were too fragile to cope with the weight of such a colossal gem, and the imbalance was threatening to make her topple and fall.

Deciding that to go and shop for a ring like normal mortals would be too crass in light of the exceptional circumstances, Raffaele had sent out for the jewels in the way that other people might send out for a takeaway!

A tray of engagement rings had been brought to the house in a window-darkened car which had housed two hefty bodyguards as well as the jeweller and gem expert. Before he had ordered a selection Raffaele had demanded to know which stones she would like to look at.

'I don't really know,' she'd blustered.

Raffaele had frowned. 'You must have *some* idea?'

'Why should I? It's not something I've ever given a lot of thought to.'

'No?' His voice had been frankly disbelieving. 'I thought that all women dreamed of engagement rings?'

For once, Natasha's gaze was genuinely cold. Of all the arrogant assertions he could have made—that was possibly the most offensive! 'Maybe in your circles they do!' she retorted.

'Oh, they do.' He gave a cynical laugh. 'Most certainly they do.'

Oddly enough, that made Natasha think. Of course he was eligible—she didn't have to see the articles in all the glossies to know *that*—but she had always thought that he would be liked...loved...for sheer charisma alone. But Raffaele had power and prestige, as well as a hard body and the face of a fallen angel—wouldn't that make *any* woman want him? Enough to plot to get him? she wondered. She felt her heart softening, wanting to defend him against such scheming women—until she reminded herself that Raffaele was well able to look after himself.

'No, you choose,' she said evasively, because there was part of her that wanted nothing to do with the ring. It was a prop, she reminded herself— nothing more. If she started telling him that she liked one gem more than another, if she started investing it with her likes and dislikes, then it would assume an importance which would be unnecessary. More as a defence mechanism than anything—Natasha didn't want to become in any way attached to a meaningless bauble—she bit back the information that she had always rather liked aquamarines and insisted that he decide.

Yet wasn't it a very feminine reaction to be disappointed when he opted for a diamond? For its cold, precious fire seemed so totally lacking in feeling. It was a huge, pear-shaped stone of a seriously significant carat-size—according to the jeweller.

'It's a good investment, *Signor* de Feretti.'

Raffaele had turned to her. 'Do you like it, *cara?*'

Did he see her wince at the jeweller's crass observation? And was she supposed to go through the pantomime of dazed fiancée as he slipped it on to her finger? Apparently, she was.

'It's magnificent,' she said truthfully.

And now, tonight's charity ball was the ring's first outing—and *their* first outing as a couple.

Raffaele slipped the velvet evening wrap around her shivering shoulders, his fingertips brushing against her pale smooth flesh, and he noticed how dark his skin looked against hers. Unbidden and unwanted, came another image—the one which couldn't seem to stop burning itself with searing clarity into the fevered recesses of his mind. Of his hard dark body pinning down her submissive milky whiteness. Of running his hands and his tongue over every curve she possessed.

Beneath the exquisitely cut evening trousers Raffaele felt the ache of sexual hunger—surprising in its intensity. Was that because he knew he couldn't have her? Because she was not his equal and to take her to his bed would be to take advantage of her—was that her sudden inexplicable lure for him? Surely, to a man who had everything, the forbidden would have a powerful lure all of its own.

'The car is here,' he said huskily.

Outside the night was clear, the indigo sky star-sprinkled, and Raffaele could see the faint cloud of his warm breath against the cold air as he watched her get into the back of the limousine.

'So, do you like going to these kind of dos?' asked Natasha, as he slid onto the backseat beside her.

'They serve a purpose.'

'You mean, they raise money for charity?'

In the darkness he gave a brief half-smile. How genuinely innocent she was in the ways of the world he inhabited. 'Something like that.'

'What else?' she persisted—because they had to talk about *something* if they were going to get through this evening.

He turned to her. The shadows and the flickered illumination from the passing streetlamps were playing interesting combinations of light and shade on her face. Her lips glistened with unaccustomed lipstick and her eyes looked huge, almost startled. This new Natasha was taking some getting used to.

'You don't want to know,' he murmured. 'Keep your sweet, idealistic view, Natasha—believe me, it's a rare quality.'

Idealism was all very well—but not if it meant you were always on the outside, looking in. 'I want to learn,' she said stubbornly. 'I might as well get something out of the experience.'

Surprisingly, her comment wounded him—though whether it was just his pride which was hurt, he wasn't quite sure. Raffaele gave a short laugh. Maybe it served him right. What did he expect? Fluttering gratitude at all times of the day? 'Okay, then, I'll teach you all about the big, bad world. Yes, of course these events raise money for worthy causes—but, for a lot of people, it's important to be *seen* to be giving.'

'But not to you?'

His eyes narrowed. 'Was that a question or a statement? Should I be flattered or offended?'

Natasha might have been worried about the evening ahead and feeling out of her depth, but she always tried to be scrupulously fair and she shook her head. 'I don't think you need your ego bolstered by other people's opinions of you.'

'Why, thank you, Natasha,' he murmured.

The look which washed over her filled her with ridiculous pleasure and, quickly, she turned to look out of the window, afraid that he might see. It was important that he didn't. He must not see how vulnerable she was to his praise. She had already let herself down by responding to his kiss like that—much more and he might begin to guess at her feelings for him. And then what?

Wouldn't he be appalled? Embarrassed? Even outraged that she had dared to presume to nurture longings for a man like him?

'Here we are,' he murmured, his voice butting into her thoughts. 'Now, take a deep breath before you prepare to enter into the fray, *cara.*'

Natasha peered out of the window at the dazzling sight which awaited them. The venue was one of London's most glitzy hotels, its exterior bright with lights so that it looked as if there was a whole galaxy of stars burning at the front of its upmarket site opposite Hyde Park.

A roped-off red carpet made a startling red river and, on either side, were banks of photographers with huge and rather intimidating lenses which looked like alien eyes. Natasha sucked in a breath. Could she really go through with this?

Raffaele saw the way she had stiffened, and he tilted his dark head. 'Are you sure you're ready for this, Natasha?'

She was tempted to say that she wasn't. That she was hopelessly miscast for this role and no one would ever believe that a man like Raffaele de Feretti would have proposed marriage to someone like her.

But if she backed out now, then wouldn't she always be left feeling some kind of wimpish failure, as well as letting Raffaele down horribly at the very last moment? Shouldn't she just seize on this as a glamorous adventure—a taste of real luxury which she could store in her memory bank?

Turning a little, she shook her head and smiled. 'I'm as ready as a woman could possibly be!' she said.

He thought that if it had been any other woman looking like that in the backseat of the car then by now he would have kissed her and touched her—why, they might even have…

'Raffaele!'

'Mmm?' His erotic daydream shattered.

'The chauffeur is holding the door open,' she scolded.

Adjusting his jacket and trying to quell the dull ache of frustration, Raffaele got out of the car first and then held his hand out for hers. Her left hand. The one with the ring on it.

Natasha trembled as the massive diamond caught the light, It seemed to flash and sparkle with the significance of a beacon shining on top of an isolated lighthouse. But the wearing of this ring was simply to send out a message—it was not a symbol of how two people felt about each other.

The press went wild.

'Natasha! Hey, Natasha! Look this way!'

'Over here, Natasha!'

Countless flashbulbs exploded—bleaching the night with blinding white light so that Natasha blinked and swayed a little. Raffaele's hand tightened on her elbow.

'You okay?' he murmured, his head distractingly close to hers.

More flashbulbs exploded.

'I'm…fine. Just a little dazzled.' She wobbled back a smile. 'Literally!'

It occurred to him that Natasha could be witty and clever even during a stressful occasion like this—or was that the most insufferably patronising thing to think? Had he forgotten that she'd been midway through a degree when she'd become pregnant with Sam? He frowned. And that women's lives were changed by having babies in a way that men's never were.

'Come on,' he said, his voice suddenly raw and he wondered why the hell he was concentrating on inconsequential things like *that* when he had a whole evening of subterfuge to get through. He slipped his hand around the silken span of her waist in an unashamedly proprietorial gesture, spanning his fingers out to increase the area of her body he was touching, and realised that he was enjoying it. He was enjoying it very much.

'Raffaele!' someone shrieked. 'What made you want to marry your housekeeper?'

'Natasha!' shrieked another, as if they had known her all their lives. 'What's it like being engaged to a billionaire?'

'Just keep smiling,' he murmured. 'Don't say a thing.'

'I wasn't intending to.'

Once inside the foyer, which was filled with blooms so scented that momentarily Natasha felt quite faint, different members of staff converged on them like well-oiled parts of a huge machine.

'Can I take your wrap, madam?'

She slipped it from her shoulders and handed it over to the female member of staff, unused to the deference she was being shown. And, suddenly, she identified far more with the girl in uniform than with the glamorous creatures who were milling around, laughing as if they had all been let in on some secret and fabulously funny joke. *I'm just like you!* she found herself wanting to say to the smiling girl.

Without the silk-velvet cloak Natasha felt bare and exposed—and as Raffaele led her into the chandelier-bright ballroom she realised that she was. Exposed to the lenses of the cameras outside, and now exposed to the penetrating gazes of the women within the spectacular interior of the room.

Were her nerves so on edge that she imagined the faint murmur of comment? No. And neither was there anything the matter with her vision. She saw the heads turn and gazes look her over—from head to toe.

'Okay?' questioned Raffaele, for he'd felt her tense beneath his hand.

She wasn't—not really. But neither was she going to give up at the first hurdle. 'Suddenly, I can identify with exhibits at the zoo!'

'It's that bad?' There was a sudden gleam of understanding in the jet-dark eyes. 'You need a drink.'

Did she? Maybe she did. 'Thanks.'

Taking two flutes of champagne from a passing
waitress, he handed her one, and, as Natasha raised it
to her lips, the bubbles fizzed up her nose. She wrinkled it.

'You are not used to champagne,' he commented.

'Don't patronise me, Raffaele,' she remonstrated
softly as she drank some and thought how dry it tasted.

'I'm not. It was an observation, not a criticism.'

'Of course I'm not used to it. I don't come from a
champagne-drinking background—more the glass-of-
wine-at-Christmas type. I drank some for the first time
at university—but it certainly wasn't anything like this
stuff.' She shrugged, wondering why the hell she had
taken the conversation down to this particular dead-
end. 'The bubbly I drank wasn't real champagne.'

'Was that with Sam's father?' he demanded, seeing
the way her features had become shuttered and finding
himself suddenly—inexplicably—wanting to know.

He had never asked her anything like that before,
and it occurred to her that now was not the right time.

'Yes, it was,' she said, her cheeks flaring with the
memory. But she was saved from saying any more by
a couple bearing down on them. Nervously, she drank
a little more champagne, fleetingly thinking that
maybe she *could* see what the fuss was all about. It
really was *very* moreish!

'Raffaele! So this is why you have such a fearsome
reputation as a poker player! You have a beautiful
woman like this tucked away at home—and nobody's
ever seen her!'

The immaculately groomed man who spoke looked

as if he was in his fifties, but the woman with him was about half that age—more like Natasha's. She, too, had an expensive-looking head of blonde hair and a silken dress which clung to her firm, lush young body. Had she always looked like that? Natasha wondered. Or had she, too, been subjected to the perfect makeover courtesy of someone else's money?

Natasha suddenly had a horrible feeling of predictability—as if she had just been plucked off a production line of eager wannabes. Was that what other people thought of *her*—that she had bargained away her youth and her rather lowly position to be at the beck and call of a wealthy man?

Except that Raffaele is only in his thirties, she reminded herself. And it wasn't his *money* she was interested in. Biting her lip, she swallowed some more champagne. It wasn't her place to be interested in him at all!

'Yes, this is Natasha,' Raffaele was saying. 'Natasha, meet John Huntingdon—he and I have done a little business together.'

'A little business?' laughed John, as he shook her hand. 'He bought my office block in Canary Wharf!'

Raffaele was now narrowing his eyes at the blonde. 'I'm sorry—I don't think we've met?'

The blonde gave Raffaele a fluttery smile which matched her fluttery voice. 'No, we haven't—I'd certainly have remembered *you!* Hi, I'm Susi.'

'Hello, Susi,' said Raffaele gravely.

'Congratulations!' Susi had now turned her attention to Natasha, picking up her hand and looking at the ring with barely disguised greed. 'You must tell me how you did it—I've been trying to get John to buy me a sparkler for—'

'Oh, all of three months,' put in John smoothly. 'In fact, almost from the moment we met! Anyway, we're all on the same table—so we'll see you in a little while.' He placed his hand in the small of Susi's back and propelled her forward, like a horse who was refusing to jump. 'Come along, darling—there's a good girl.'

Natasha felt slightly humiliated on the other woman's behalf—but hadn't she rather set it up for herself, by playing the part of gold-digger whilst flirting with Raffaele? And now more people were coming over, flocking round them like ants to a dollop of spilled jam, and she suddenly experienced a frightening feeling of vulnerability as they were surrounded by curious eyes.

Natasha was glad to sit down for dinner—though she had little appetite for the seemingly endless array of tiny but luxurious dishes which kept appearing in front of her. Quite honestly, the dress was cut so close to her figure that anything more than a morsel would have made it uncomfortable to sit in. No wonder these women managed to stay so thin!

Candles flickered and perfect white flowers cast their heady scent over the select gathering. John Huntingdon sat on one side of her and a corporate lawyer named Charles on the other. All the men at the table seemed to be headhunters, or something to do with finance—not really Natasha's area of expertise at all.

Everyone seemed to belong—as if they were all members of the same exclusive club who all went to the same events on the city's star-studded social calendar.

'How come I haven't seen you before? You weren't at Wimbledon?' one of the women asked Natasha.

She admitted she hadn't been.

'Oh! What about Cheltenham?'

'That's a horse race, *cara mia,*' Raffaele enlightened her in a wry voice as he saw her frown.

Fleetingly, she thought how ironic it was that this Italian should know more about England than she did. Because it's not your world, she reminded herself. It never has been, and that simple fact is not about to change.

As Raffaele watched her he thought how *sweet* she looked. And how simple—for all her expensive clothes and the ludicrously large ring which completely dwarfed her slender hand. Whereas the other women had the definition of gym-worked muscle, which rippled rather unattractively against the silks and chiffons, Natasha's physique came from running round after Sam, or going from the top to the bottom of the house with a vacuum cleaner in hand.

Even after her glossy transformation she still had some quality about her which marked her out. Some stillness—almost a purity. She looked, he thought, like a flower which had been picked from somebody's garden—all soft and natural and a complete contrast to the scentless perfection of the hothouse blooms which surrounded them.

His mouth hardened. What was this cynic thinking? Was he projecting some kind of wishful fairytale onto this particular woman because they inhabited different worlds? It was easy to fantasise about someone when you knew that reality would never be allowed to intrude to shatter it.

Yet you wanted her when you kissed her, didn't you? *And—more than that——you wanted to pin her down somewhere and to thrust into her until you had lost yourself.*

He barely tasted the fine wines and the food was un-remarkable—despite the cost and the lavish attention paid to its preparation. But Raffaele wasn't hungry.

He glanced across the table at Natasha again—it seemed that she had overcome her initial shyness and was now nodding intently at something the man opposite her was saying. She said something to John Huntingdon, who was sitting beside her, and Raffaele was surprised and not pleased to see both men laughing.

He felt the unfamiliar thump of jealousy—bizarre and inexplicable—and instead of inwardly groaning at the sound of the orchestra, which was just starting up, he found himself rising to his feet to walk round table and hold out his hand proprietorially.

'Dance with me.'

As so often with Raffaele, it was an order and not a request, but that didn't stop Natasha excusing herself to the people she'd been talking to. Because, even if Raffaele hadn't been her boss and even if they hadn't been masquerading to the world as a newly engaged couple, she just wanted to dance with him.

She had been trying her best not to feast her eyes on him during the meal, but she hadn't made very much headway, blown away by the knee-weakening vision he made in formal evening wear. Black suited him. Well, everything seemed to suit him—but black especially so. It accentuated the charcoal depths of his hair and his eyes and contrasted with the golden-olive glow of his skin. There were many men there tonight—all of them rich and well-connected—but there was not another in the entire ballroom who could have held a candle to her Raffaele.

'I'd love to,' she responded softly, 'seeing as you asked so nicely!'

Raffaele's eyes narrowed as he led her onto the floor—the only time he could remember ever being first up to dance. Was she…*teasing* him? Was she perhaps taking this whole subterfuge a little far—responding to him as his *equal?*

But all thoughts evaporated into insignificance when he pulled her against him. She felt…well, *sconosciuta*…strange—and not just because it was a brand-new woman in his arms. They began to move in time with the music.

With Natasha he felt acutely aware of her body. Of the undulation of her waist as he wound his fingers around it, sinuously as a snake. Of the light brush of her breasts against his chest, the knowledge that her amazing bottom was so tantalisingly close. That he could reach out his hands and cup it with possessive anticipation, then grind her hips towards his, so that she could feel for herself the hard ache of desire which was threatening to—

He groaned, experiencing a confusing mixture of wanting the forbidden and yet being confronted with the sweetly familiar. Had he thought this was going to be easy? Of course he had.

'It's…it's a fantastic band,' said Natasha, sensing his tension and feeling more than a little tense herself. He felt so good. He smelt so good. She found that she wanted to reach up on tiptoe and whisper her lips over the dark curve of his jaw. Beneath the thin silk of her evening gown she could feel the wild, uncontrollable flutter of her heart. Unseen, with her cheek close to the dark shoulder of his dinner jacket, she whispered. 'Isn't it?'

What the hell was she talking about? Ah, yes—the music. He wished it wasn't there—for he would have preferred to have listened to the soft sigh of her breath and the heavy beat of her heart. The music of her body as it began to play out the familiar melody of desire.

He found that he wanted to press his body against hers, to slide his hard thigh between the giving softness of hers. And, yet, while such a display of intimacy might almost be expected of a couple who had just announced their betrothal, he knew that he could not do it. If it was anyone other than Natasha then, yes—he could pretend. But the game might get out of hand and, if it did, then wouldn't he be tempted to do it properly, to make love to her? And that really *would* be taking advantage of her subservient position in the most despicable way possible.

'I'm bored with dancing,' he said curtly. 'Let's break, shall we? Do you mind?

Natasha shook her head as he led her off the dance-floor. *Or does he really mean that he's bored with me?* she wondered, somehow managing to stop her smile from slipping. But this isn't about *you,* she reminded herself. Ultimately, it's about Elisabetta.

He caught her by the arm, his fingers gripping into her soft flesh. He saw the way her eyes widened as they searched his face anxiously——and something about her concern put him on the defensive. Why the hell were they still here? Hadn't they done enough for their diversionary plan to succeed? 'I can't face any more sitting around that table and making small talk.'

'I thought you were discussing deals—*I* was the one making small talk!'

'So I saw. You seemed to have all the men round the table eating out of your hand.' His mouth hardened into a determined line. 'So why don't we just leave quietly, before anyone actually notices we're gone?'

As if no one would notice that Raffaele de Feretti was no longer in their presence! 'Won't they think it rude?' Natasha asked, turning her face up to his.

'They'll think it perfectly understandable for us to want a little time on our own,' he clipped out, because when her lips parted with innocent question he wanted to crush them beneath his.

'Okay, then—but I really think we ought to say goodbye first,' said Natasha stubbornly.

He opened his mouth to tell her that what *she* wanted was irrelevant, but to his astonishment she was already walking away from him, the taut curves of her bottom drawing his eye irresistibly as she made her way back to the table.

CHAPTER SEVEN

OUTSIDE, the press had multiplied like bacteria, and two heavy-looking security men had to clear them a path to the waiting car.

'Blame yourself!' Raffaele snapped, as he pushed Natasha into the back of the limousine and then jumped in behind her, slamming the door on the jostling pack as it moved away.

'Wh-why?' Natasha didn't like to ask him to move his thigh from where it was pressing against hers—not when his eyes were spitting irritated black fire at her.

'You went around saying goodbye to everyone like they were long-lost friends, meaning that someone got word out to the press that we were leaving!'

'It was just good manners,' said Natasha, her determination to remain cheerful at all costs evaporating under the onslaught of his quite unreasonable display of temper. And there was still that leg, of course.

He could hardly believe what she had said. 'You think that I...*I* need a lesson in manners?'

She stared right back. He thought he was immune to criticism, did he? 'Right now, yes. Yes, I do!'

'From you?'

'Why not from me?' she retorted furiously. 'If I'm

good enough to be engaged to you and brought here on your arm, then I'm reckon I'm good enough for just about anything else!'

'Oh, you do?'

'Yes, I do!'

There was a heartbeat of a pause.

'Good enough to kiss, perhaps?' he questioned deliberately.

The confined atmosphere of the car closed in on them. The hungry flash of warning in his eyes. The gleam of his lips. And still the warm, hard pressure of his thigh. She should have seen it coming. She wanted to say *Raffaele, please don't do this!*

And she wanted to beg him to just do it—*and do it now.*

'Raffaele,' she breathed, her voice low and husky and complicit.

'*"Raffaele!"*' he mimicked, almost harshly—for she had him in her power, something he had not anticipated nor prepared for, and she would now taste the consequence of that for herself. He was going to kiss her, and it was wrong, more than wrong—she knew that and he knew that. But—*Madonna mia*—he was going to do it all the same!

With a throaty sound halfway between a groan and a tiny roar, he pulled her unprotesting body into his arms, his hands digging into her sweet, yielding flesh and drove his mouth down on hers in a kiss that was filled with anger as much as lust.

With an answering cry of need Natasha fell back against the skin-soft leather seat of the car. His hands were on the bare flesh of her back, his lips coaxing hers open—while that rogue thigh was pushing its way insistently between hers. She shivered with violent need. She knew she should stop him and, yet, nothing could have made her call a halt to the debilitating sweetness of that kiss.

Trying to ignore the doubts which were flaring in her mind, Natasha took his hard and proud face in her hands, cupping its sculpted shield shape as if to reassure herself it was real. That he was real. That this was really happening.

Oh, but it was.

With a gasp, her hands fell away at the precise moment that his fingers grazed over her nipple—so hard it was almost painful, pushing against the silk-satin of her evening dress as if it wanted to be free of the constricting gown. And as if he had read her thoughts, he slipped the delicate strap of her gown down over her shoulder, so that her breast was bare. She felt first warm air against the naked skin, and then—shockingly—the flick of his mouth on it.

Shuddering, she looked down—and there was Raffaele's dark head, suckling her. And that shockingly intimate touch jarred the growing voice of her conscience even as her body silently screamed out its answering desire. *This isn't right,* she told herself frantically. *You know it isn't. Especially in the back of a car!*

She tasted sweet. She tasted salty. She tasted of woman and of need. Raffaele was nearly exploding as his tongue played with the puckering bud, and he felt her squirm beneath his hands, heard her tiny gasps of pleasure. It was so unexpected. So *bizarre.* In a few short days the woman who brought him tea in the afternoons had been transformed into this passionate creature who was writhing around in his arms!

He felt the hard need of his desire pressing against him. If it had been anyone else but Natasha he would have guided her hand there. She would have unzipped him. Taken him into her mouth…

What the hell was he thinking of?

He didn't care. It didn't matter. Nothing mattered except—

'Raffaele!' Sanity prevailed for the single instant it took Natasha to push at his chest, the word indistinct because it took every bit of determination for her to say it.

But the muffled protest was like being showered with icy water. With a groan, Raffaele tore his mouth away from her, letting go of her as if she had suddenly become contaminated. He slid over to the opposite side of the seat, steadying his ragged breathing, his pounding heart.

She waited until she had pulled her dress back up before she risked a glance at him, and she bit her lip, sensing his anger. Yet she'd *had* to stop what was happening. Surely, he realised that. 'Raffaele?'

He turned his head then, and Natasha almost recoiled at the icy look of detachment in his eyes. 'What?'

What had Kirsty told her to acquire along with her brand-new wardrobe? Attitude—that was it.

'That…well, that shouldn't have happened,' she said coolly.

He looked at her almost with admiration. How effortlessly she had slipped into the role of fiancée! 'You think I don't know that?' he growled softly, and yet he was aware that something remarkable had happened. A woman had stopped Raffaele de Feretti from making love to her. When had *that* ever happened before? His mouth became a grim line of realisation. *In nessun momento*—never!

And while his pride and his ego made him want to

capture her in his arms and kiss her again, in a way that would leave her gasping and reeling and *begging* him to do it to her, infuriatingly, he could see that she had made the right decision. 'You think I want to complicate further this damned ridiculous situation?' he snapped. 'By adolescent fumbling in the back of a car? That certainly wasn't included in the deal!'

She was about to say that she didn't think any particular *deal* had been hammered out—but perhaps he was referring to his offer that she could keep the costly ring? More hurtful was to hear that mind-blowing kiss dismissed in such a careless way.

'Do you always kiss women like that?' she demanded.

He gave an arrogant smile. 'What do you think?' he challenged softly. Was her *ego* growing at the same pace as her ease with her new role? 'Do you think I turn on simply for *you?*'

His mocking tone tore into her. But she was damned if she was going to show him that he'd hurt her—because he might just start to question why.

'Obviously not,' she said smoothly. 'You don't get a reputation as a superstud unless it's well founded.'

He stared at her, outraged, scarcely able to believe what he'd heard. *'Superstud?'* he repeated dangerously.

How formidable the feeling of getting your own back could be—and what a marvellous way of distracting her aching body from the sweet pleasures she had denied it. He had wounded her and now he was having a taste of his own medicine.

'Oh, come on, Raffaele,' she protested. 'You are listed and photographed in the international gossip columns with a series of glamorous women on your arm—some of whom have actually gone on record to boast about your sexual prowess. If that isn't being a superstud, then I don't know what is!'

There was complete silence apart from the quiet thrum of the car's powerful engine, and Raffaele was so livid at her assessment that, for once in his life, he couldn't think of a thing to say. But that didn't last long, and he turned to her, his eyes spitting dark fire.

'You think that I am defined by my ability to plea-sure women—like some kind of *gigolo?*'

She had never seen him look quite so indignant and, in spite of everything, Natasha burst out laughing.

'What's so funny?' he demanded furiously.

'You are! Of course I'm not calling you a gigolo— I don't expect you've ever had to pay for sex in your life—'

'Natasha!' he put in warningly.

But she blazed on. 'People say things when they're…' *When they're* what, *Natasha?* When they're head-over-heels in love with a man who sees them just as an object in their lives? So quit while you're ahead. Show him that it's no big deal. But was she re-ally that good an actress? 'There's no need to over-react, Raffaele,' she finished softly.

Oh, wasn't there? Did she have any idea of how much he was aching for her right now? How if he wasn't such a gentleman he would be sliding that dress up her thighs right now and letting his fingers entice her. He swallowed, made a barely perceptible curse. The irony did not escape him—even at such a moment of high desire—that no one had ever accused Raffaele de Feretti of being a gentleman before, least of all himself!

Yet, infuriatingly, she was right. There were two ways this could go—and the most obvious one would certainly be the easiest and most pleasurable to carry through. He could carry on kissing her, and she could carry on responding, and things would inevitably progress to the next stage of having sex with her. Maybe not in the back of the car—but certainly when they got back to the house.

But think of all the complications that would throw up along the way. How would they both feel about it in the morning, when the heat of passion had been vanquished and sated? When she had to go and get Sam his cereal and take him to school as if nothing had happened? Then what? He wanted them to play-act at being engaged—but that would be taking method-acting one stage too far!

No, the most rational thing to do, under these circumstances, was to put it down to a cocktail of proximity and the raging hormones of two people in their sexual prime.

Raffaele scowled. When was he going to stop thinking in this crazy way? This was *Natasha,* and he needed to remember that. Maybe he should tell her to get changed into her ordinary clothes as soon as they were home—to make him a pot of decaffeinated coffee, the way she always did when he arrived home late.

It had been she who had insisted on the decaf, he remembered rather inconsequentially—after she'd once commented that he'd looked tired and he had confessed to lack of sleep. It had been during the Palladio takeover, he remembered, and frowned.

Crossing one long leg over the other, relieved to see the end of his street, he decided that maybe such a request wouldn't be the wisest course of action. There was no way of second-guessing how she might react. The old Natasha seemed to have disappeared—lost in her brand-new hairstyle and her brand-new and overly provocative wardrobe. Would he ever get her back? he wondered.

Once again, he scowled. 'We're here,' he said flatly, as the car drew to a halt.

She got out of the car before the driver had time to open the door for her. *I'm off-duty now,* she thought defiantly as she walked up to the front door and let herself in.

Anna was curled up in the television room, reading a weighty looking book on mime and dance, and she looked up when Natasha walked in, and smiled.

'Oh, you're back earlier than I thought. Did you have a good evening?'

'It was fantastic,' said Natasha, with the kind of enthusiasm she thought would be expected of her.

Anna frowned. 'You look a bit pale,' she commented.

'I'm just tired,' said Natasha lamely.

'Mmm. Me, too,' came a voice as smooth as honey-eyed cream, and Raffaele walked straight over to her and slid his hand possessively around her.

Half in alarm, Natasha looked up to see a sensual glint in the ebony eyes, and her heart began to pound in spite of everything.

'I guess it's an early night for us, *mia bella,*' he murmured, and began to teasingly caress the indentation at her waist.

'Oh, I *quite* understand!' said Anna, jumping to her feet and grinning.

With a tight smile, Natasha shook herself free of his

embrace and walked over to Anna. 'Sam's okay?' she questioned.

'Sam's fine. I read him two stories and then he fell asleep. I haven't heard a peep out of him once!'

'I'll walk you home,' said Raffaele.

'No, please. It's just down the road!' protested Anna. 'Honestly, I'm a big girl now—you should see where I live during term-time.'

'I'll walk you,' he repeated obdurately.

After they'd gone, Natasha automatically began to tidy up—but as she straightened from stacking some magazines neatly in the rack she caught sight of herself in the mirror, and was momentarily transfixed by the image which gazed back at her. Anna was right. Her face was pale and her eyes were like huge, dark saucers—dominating her face with a look of restless uncertainty.

The front door slammed, and Natasha hastily turned away from the mirror as Raffaele walked slowly back into the room, loosening his tie, an inexplicable look in his eyes. She was reminded, all too vividly, of the sweet sensation of his kiss, the sensational feel of his hands on her breasts.

'What's the matter, Natasha?' he mocked. 'You don't look very happy.'

'Was that display really necessary?' she questioned.

'And what display would that be?' he questioned, flinging his tie onto the table.

'All that touchy-feely stuff in front of Anna,' she retorted, resisting the urge to pick up the tie and fold it for him, picking up the babysitter's used coffee mug instead.

He shrugged, his eyes dancing as he recognised the tell-tale signs of sexual frustration in her expression, the angry little way she was wriggling her hips. 'But we're engaged to be married, *cara*,' he protested innocently, and drifted his eyes over the pinpoint thrust of her nipples against the slippery scarlet satin of her gown. 'Or had you forgotten? Bedtime, I think—don't you? Oh, and don't forget to turn the lights out, will you?' he added deliberately, and then he was gone.

Natasha was left staring at the empty space in the door, feeling as though some psychological battle had just been fought.

And Raffaele had won.

CHAPTER EIGHT

NATASHA didn't see the newspapers until after she took Sam to school next morning. She had overslept, and only just remembered to put on her engagement ring after throwing on yet more new clothes.

She woke her son and went downstairs to make coffee and toast, with the massive diamond winking and flashing on her finger like a star. Would anyone at the school notice? she wondered, but doubted it. Early on at the school she had been assessed by the super-rich mums and accorded her own particular status—which was why she mainly mixed with the au pairs.

She did her best not to react when Raffaele walked into the kitchen, waving his one free hand around in the air as he spoke in animated and exasperated French into a mobile phone. But it wasn't easy. She wondered if that little scene in the back of the car had given him the same concern which had left her staring at the bedroom ceiling for most of the night.

'He's talking to a bank in Paris,' translated Sam as he carefully poured honey over his porridge. 'An' he's *very* cross.'

Natasha thought that you wouldn't need Sam's superiority with languages to be able to work *that* out!

Though, to be honest, Raffaele might as well have been singing in Swahili for all the notice she would have taken of what he was saying. She was too busy trying not to ogle him.

He was wearing a city suit, but even the formal design of the outfit was unable to detract from his raw sexuality and masculinity. His black hair was faintly ruffled and he looked the picture of glowing vitality.

Natasha held up the *cafetière,* the way she always did, and Raffaele nodded his head vigorously—just the way *he* always did. Or did she imagine a faint quirk of his lips and that slight narrowing of his eyes? Even if it *was* simply her imagination her memory came thudding in to add to her discomfiture. Natasha was very aware that her hand was shaking, and she slopped some coffee into the saucer.

Raffaele raised his brows fractionally, his eyes dancing dark mischief as he clicked off his phone and shook his head when she offered him toast.

'*No, grazie,*' he murmured. 'Strangely enough, I have little appetite for food this morning. Why, Natasha—you've spilt the coffee! You seem a little on edge—is something troubling you?'

Yes, she wanted to shout. *You* are! But, of course, she couldn't do that because Sam was sitting in the room—and there would be no explanation in the world you could give to a five-year-old to explain why you had started shouting at your boss and behaving so uncharacteristically.

And then—to Natasha's fury—the two of them began to chat to each other in Italian—making her feel completely redundant. She really was going to have to work a bit harder at the language—she hadn't really progressed much beyond the days of the week and being able to ask for directions to the railway station.

'Have you nearly finished, Sam?' she asked pointedly as the minutes ticked by. 'Yes? Then run up and brush your teeth and we'll go.'

'Yes, Mama.'

Sam jumped up, grinned at Raffaele, and ran out of the room. Natasha grabbed an apple from out of the fruit bowl and made to follow him.

'Oh, Natasha?'

Keep it neutral, she told herself. 'Yes?'

'You're in the papers. Or should I say *we're* in the papers.'

Heart pounding, she stared at him. 'Have you seen them?'

He gave a short laugh. 'You know I don't bother reading the tabloids.'

'How do you know, then?'

'Troy rang me first thing. He seems pleased with the results.' The expression on his face told her nothing about his own feelings on the matter. 'You can buy them on your way back from school, if you're interested.'

'Of course I'm interested!' She turned her head and noticed for the first time the faint blue shadows underneath his eyes. 'Aren't you even a little bit curious about what they say?'

'What they *say* is largely irrelevant—getting the item in the papers was the main purpose of this exercise, remember?' he questioned coolly.

Was that designed to put her in her place? To remind her that they might have shared kisses and intimate embraces but that she remained the woman who served him his coffee and offered him his toast.

'Of course I remember,' she said lightly. They stared at one another across the of the wide expanse of the basement kitchen, with its huge range and its copper pots and the exquisite antique tiles which had been imported at great expense from Italy. A bowl of fruit lay in the centre of a scrubbed wooden table which stood on the beautiful worn stone floor tiles.

It looked like one of those illustrations from a magazine—everyone's dream kitchen. Natasha had heard some of his friends expressing surprise when they saw it for the first time, especially the girlfriends. Perhaps they expected something streamlined and slickly modern, instead of the traditional. But Natasha had recognised early on that there was a side of Raffaele which was fiercely traditional.

It was why she had dared to make the odd little addition to the room—the slim coloured glass bottles lined up on the windowsill which she'd discovered as a bargain in a junk shop, the small jug of flowers on the dresser.

But this morning the familiar terrain of the kitchen seemed different—or maybe it *felt* different, just as Natasha did. It seemed that it was impossible for a man to awaken your senses and for you to carry on treating that man exactly the same as you'd done before.

She kept wavering between wanting to put as much space between them as possible and wanting to run into his arms, to have him hold her tightly and to kiss her again in that almost unbearably sweet way. He had made her feel like a woman—a real flesh-and-blood creature—with desires she had hidden away for so long she'd almost forgotten they existed.

She turned away before he could see her sudden rise in colour and guess its cause.

'Oh—and just one more thing, Natasha.'

She swallowed down the erotic memory. 'Yes?'

'I've been invited to a cocktail party at the Italian Embassy on Wednesday. You will, of course, accompany me.'

'Of course.'

'And next weekend I have a business meeting which will spill over into the social.' His voice dipped. 'Is your passport up to date?'

Her embarrassment forgotten, she turned back to face him. 'Why?'

'Because, *mia cara,* the meeting will most probably be abroad.'

She shook her head. 'Well, I can't do that.'

'Oh?' Raffaele's eyes narrowed. 'Why not?'

Was he being completely dense? 'Because of Sam, of course.'

'Because of *what* about Sam, *mia bella?*'

'I can't leave him for a whole weekend to go *abroad!* Why, I've only ever even left him for a single night before. You know that.'

'*Si,* I know that,' he said, and his black gaze locked on hers with piercing thoughtfulness. 'And maybe it is something you ought to think about.'

She certainly wasn't imagining the reproachful note in his voice, or that faint flicker of censure in his eyes. 'You make that sound like a criticism,' she said shakily, knowing that she could stand almost anything but that. Because in a way her whole life was centred around Sam's needs—and any disapproval of that would surely throw into question her whole existence.

'It was not intended to be quite that.' He paused, spread his hands in that typically continental gesture he sometimes used. 'But it might do you both good to have a break from each other.'

'You're saying we have a claustrophobic relationship?' she demanded.

'I can see I've touched a raw nerve,' he said acidly.

'Maybe you just can't stand the fact that someone else's needs might come before *your* wishes.'

She was clearly spoiling for a fight, and Raffaele almost gave a low, cynical laugh. Almost. But he recognised that this wasn't getting them anywhere. There was a reason why they were both so tetchy—and it was the same reason why sleep had refused to come last night. It was the needs of their hungry bodies, demanding to be fed—and so they would be.

'It is pointless arguing about it, since I will need you with me,' he stated tersely. 'Arrange for Sam to go to a friend's—it will be fun for him, and good for you to have a break. What about Serge—they get on well, don't they?'

Natasha nodded. She hadn't been aware that he'd noticed—but, as usual, he had a point. And Sam *did* love Serge. Natasha was sure the French boy's parents would be only too pleased to have her son for a few nights.

But a weekend away in the company of others with the man she was pretending to be marrying threw up a whole new set of problems. She put the apple in her handbag. 'Won't we be expected to share a room?' she said slowly.

He studied her. 'Oh, Natasha—come on!' he remonstrated softly. 'What do you think? Unless they're having a Return to Chastity Weekend most modern engaged couples *do* have sex and *do* share rooms.' His eyes fired her a challenge, but deep down he felt the aching insistence of desire. 'And do not look so shocked, *cara*. Not to put too fine a point on it—you and I were well on the way to having sex in the back of the car last night!'

She stared at him, her heart thundering in her chest. 'How *dare* you say something like that?' she hissed.

He raised his eyebrows in mock-surprise but, oh, he was enjoying this. Whoever would have thought that Natasha kept such fire hidden beneath her mousy little exterior? 'Keep your voice down—or don't you mind Sam hearing you chastising me?'

She shook her head distractedly. What was he *doing?* He seemed to have her tied up in twists and knots and circles, and she should be hating him, resenting him—when all the time, she…she…

'No,' he murmured, as he watched her, 'it would be the best solution, I agree, but, unfortunately, I can't come over there and kiss you, Natasha—no matter how much you want me to.'

He met her indignant gaze and let his own travel with arrogant amusement over her flushed cheeks, and down farther still—to where her breasts peaked against the soft cashmere of her sweater. 'Go on,' he taunted. 'I dare you to deny it with any conviction! You can't, can you?'

'I'm going to take Sam to school!' she declared, and grabbed her bag.

'Running away?' he mocked.

'Running to sanity!' she retorted.

'Well, make sure you're free that weekend,' he said softly.

It sounded more like an ultimatum than a request, and the accompanying look which he sent lancing towards her made little goosebumps ice their way all over her skin.

Natasha tried to concentrate on Sam's chatter as they searched the pavement for conkers, the way they always did, but all she could think about was Raffaele. Matters weren't helped when she approached the wrought iron gates of the school and sensed, rather than saw, people turning to stare at her.

Usually she felt pretty much invisible—but there was no doubt that her makeover had turned her into a much more acceptable version of a woman. Blondes fared better than mouse—Marilyn Monroe had discovered that decades ago.

This morning she had dressed down, and wasn't looking radically different from usual, even though the jacket she wore was softly luxurious—but people were definitely noticing the ring. That's why Raffaele bought it, she reminded herself, with a stab of something which felt unreasonably like disappointment.

She kissed Sam goodbye and watched him running across the playground. Then she saw one of the other mothers approaching, with an expression of grim determination on her face. This was a woman who had barely deigned to glance at her before today—a woman who was clearly very good friends with her plastic surgeon.

'Hello—*Natasha,* isn't it?'

Natasha nodded, and pulled her new jacket closer. 'Hello. Yes, that's right. I'm afraid I don't know your—'

But the woman was in no mood for introductions. 'Someone said that you and Raffaele de Feretti were…' Her disbelieving tone faded away the moment her sharp eyes alighted on Natasha's hand, and she snatched it up as if she had every right to. 'So it's *true!*'

Her hostile and disbelieving tone made the lie

easier—you're doing this for Elisabetta, Natasha reminded herself. 'Yes, it's true,' she agreed pleasantly. 'It's all been a bit of a whirlwind!'

'But…'

Natasha raised her eyebrows in question. 'Yes?'

'Aren't you his *housekeeper?*'

Natasha's heart was thudding like a piston, but somehow she kept her face calm. 'Actually, I prefer to describe myself as his *fiancée,*' she said, with a glow which felt dangerously like triumph.

But that was the wrong emotion to be feeling, she told herself as she hurried away in a sudden bluster of dark falling leaves. She had nothing to be triumphant about because none of this was real. She was simply playing a game, and even if her motives for doing it were sound she had to remember not to get sucked into the fairytale. Particularly when the fiction of being betrothed to a man you'd always secretly desired was so overwhelming. Yes, she wanted him—but what woman wouldn't?

Raffaele wanted her, too—he had made that very plain. He had wanted her in the highly charged atmosphere of the car last night, but she had seen the gleam of desire in the seemingly innocent surroundings of the kitchen this morning, as well. And, in a way, that had been infinitely more dangerous. It was easy to yearn for someone when you'd been drinking champagne all evening and were all dressed up—but to feel the same way in the cold, clear light of day… Well, that could easily send out the wrong message to someone like her.

Because lust meant nothing—it was just a part of Raffaele's restless and seeking nature. His power and his alpha-maleness would put sex high on his list of priorities—for him, it would come as naturally as breathing. And Natasha would get hurt if she wasn't careful. Not just because she was a woman and she placed different values on sex, but because of the way she felt about him.

The little newsagents was tucked away just off the busy main road—it was such an old-fashioned shop that Natasha used to wonder how long it would be able to survive in the face of the supermarket giants who were sweeping small businesses away.

On tall shelves were jars of brightly coloured sweets, and from the ceiling bobbed a few bats, while chocolates, foil-wrapped to look like pumpkins, lay on the counter—for Halloween was fast approaching.

'Getting blustery out there,' said the owner, an old man who wore fingerless gloves and still liked to add up in his head. 'It'll be winter soon.'

'Oh, don't say that!' Natasha protested.

She bought stamps and two tabloids, but she didn't open them until she was almost home. *But it's not really your home,* mocked a voice in her head as she let herself into the garden square. *It's Raffaele's home, not yours.* As the wind flapped the pages of the news-papers, she wondered if it was the 'engagement' which had suddenly made her start thinking like this, and a shiver ran over her skin as she realised that what she had agreed to had changed everything.

That nothing was ever going to be the same again.

She leafed through the first paper and there it was— the shot taken when they'd arrived at the charity ball and first stepped onto the red carpet to face a battery of cameras.

Raffaele had cupped her elbow and bent his head close to hers, asking her if she was okay—his look one of solicitude rather than passion. In a society of easy sex and quick kicks it was the image of caring which had convinced the hacks that Raffaele de Feretti's heart had finally melted.

They said that the camera never lied, but it wasn't quite as simple as that. It picked up on what it saw—and then interpreted it to fit its own agenda. The image selected showed the one true emotion expressed in a whole evening of pretending. Raffaele's concern for her had been genuine, the emotion had been genuine—and that was what had convinced the gossip columnists that this was, indeed, *the real thing!*

Natasha's fingers were trembling as she read it.

After dating some of the wealthiest and most beautiful heiresses in Europe, Italian billionaire playboy Raffaele de Feretti has astonished everyone by becoming engaged to his housekeeper, Natasha Phillips. Ms Phillips, 25, who is a single parent, was photographed showing off her ring—a giant two-carat solitaire—at a charity ball last night. If diamonds are a girl's best friend, then lucky Natasha has one hell of a buddy!

How peculiar it was to read about yourself in the third person like this, she thought—and even more peculiar was the sight of *her* photo featured in a national newspaper. It didn't look like her at all—with her coiled and elaborate hair and her shimmery silk-satin evening gown. She looked like an expensive stranger.

Yet if she examined it more closely she could see her expression as she reassured Raffaele that she was okay. Would anyone else notice the soft look of adoration which was sparking from her eyes as she looked at him? If he gave the picture more than a cursory glance would he guess at her secret, or just think that she was a fine actress?

She walked home slowly, thinking of what Raffaele had said about her rarely being parted from her son. His words had implied that this was a failing rather than a strength, and for the first time Natasha began to wonder if perhaps she used Sam as an excuse not to go out there and live life properly. Did she? Was he one of those children doomed to be tied to his mother's apron strings? And was she in danger of becoming the kind of woman who resented her child growing up and growing away?

Galvanised into action, she telephoned Serge's parents and asked if Sam could go and stay the following weekend. They were delighted to oblige.

'*Mais, oui—bien sûr!*' Serge's mother laughed. 'You wish to have some time alone with your husband-to-be, *oui?*'

That rubbed at Natasha's conscience—but Elisabetta's pinched and wan face swam into her memory. 'If that's okay?' she said.

'It is more than okay. Go and have a wonderful time,' whispered Madame Bertrand.

Natasha didn't even want to think about it and, instead, began to sort out the walk-in larder. It was deeply satisfying to create order out of chaos, and it also served as a kind of distraction therapy.

The ring felt odd and scratchy as she dipped it in and out of a bucket of hot and soapy water, so she slid on a pair of rubber gloves and smiled. If only the *Daily View* could see her now—how different she looked to the image of herself which was plastered over page five of the paper! But she needed to do this. *Because* this *is my reality,* she reminded herself. *After all this is over I'll have to go back to a normal existence—where I won't be whisked in chauffeur-driven cars to charity balls. Or kissed by black-eyed Italians who can make you feel as if you've found heaven in their arms.*

The telephone rang, and she peeled the gloves off and went to answer it.

'Natasha?'

The rich, accented voice spilled over her senses like honey. 'Yes, Raffaele?'

There was a pause. 'On your recent shopping trip, did you by any chance buy some swimwear?'

'Sw-swimwear?' Had he meant the word to sound X-rated, or was it simply what it implied—heat and sun and partially clothed bodies? Natasha closed her eyes as she recalled the teeny bikini which the personal shopper had told her would be a sin not to buy. And the halter-neck one-piece in acid-green which made her body look as curvy as a coiled snake.

'It's a simple question,' he said impatiently. 'And I'm about to go into a meeting! Yes or no?'

'I did.' She swallowed. 'Why?'

From the penthouse suite which housed his office, Raffaele looked out over the skyscrapers of the city and gave a grim smile of satisfaction.

'Then you'd better pack it. You remember I told you to keep next weekend free?' There was a pause. 'We are going to Marrakech, *cara.*'

CHAPTER NINE

'You do realise——' Raffaele paused deliberately as he watched her reach up, the silk of her robe brushing against her waist as she did so, and he found himself marvelling at how such a simple movement could be so damned provocative. He flicked his tongue over lips which were suddenly bone-dry. 'That I need to know a few details about your life.'

Natasha turned round. She had been hanging up clothes in the sumptuous bedroom and trying not to act too dazed by the level of luxury she had been subjected to ever since their private jet had landed in Morocco. But it hadn't been easy. This was opulence on a scale she hadn't realised existed.

A car had been waiting to whisk them to the ancient city of Marrakech, surrounded by the famous rose-pink walls, its streets lined with fragrant orange trees, with old-fashioned pony and traps trotting along amid the spluttering cars.

It was hard for Natasha to believe that a place could be so gloriously hot in October and the sky such a clear, bright blue, and she breathed in the scented air with a kind of startled delight after the misty cool of autumnal England. She had never been abroad anywhere before—something which Raffaele had found hard to believe—and this would have been a wonderful place to start if it hadn't been for her worries about sharing a suite with him.

The opulent *riad* in which they were to stay was situated right in the very heart of Marrakech. It was an oasis of comfort and luxury, with a massage room and sauna as well as large, opulent suites—pure, decadent comfort, and situated only minutes from the bustling Medina, with its narrow alleyways and exotic goods and general air of mystery.

It was also, as Raffaele had pointed out, accessible by car—both a luxury and a rarity in the region. Revelation seemed to follow on from revelation and he had saved the most astonishing fact until last—much to Natasha's amazement—they were to be the guests of a sheikh.

'A *real* sheikh?' she breathed.

'I think that Zahid would be outraged to be described as a fake,' came his laconic reply.

'Would you mind telling me why we're spending the weekend with a sheikh—how you even *know* one?'

Raffaele smiled. 'He's someone I do business with. Someone I happen to like. And he will expect me to bring a woman with me.'

Who would Raffaele have brought if he weren't pretending to be in a relationship with me? wondered Natasha, unprepared for the swift, sharp tang of jealousy—but somehow she kept it from showing on her face. She was getting rather good at concealing her emotions.

'Doesn't he have a palace?' she queried instead.

'Of course he does. He has several, *cara mia.* But he, too, will be accompanied by a woman. Like you, she is a Westerner—and that is frowned upon by his people. So he takes his consorts elsewhere.'

Natasha found herself wondering what this 'consort' thought of being hidden away like a guilty secret. But that was none of her business.

'And, anyway,' Raffaele murmured, 'that is enough about Zahid. I told you—I want to learn about *you, mia bella.*'

Natasha shook her head in disbelief. 'But I've been living in your house for over three years,' she objected. 'Surely, you know *something* about me?'

He could see the faint puzzlement and hurt which had momentarily crumpled her rose-petal lips, and he hardened his heart against it. It wasn't her place to be offended—to look at him with those big blue eyes. Did she imagine that it was some kind of interest in her as a person which made him ask, instead of plain necessity?

The sight of the enormous bed seemed to tantalise him with its allure, and to make him examine his own motives—it had since they'd arrived. Was he going to seduce her? And if so—when? Perhaps that was the real reason behind his question—a kind of distraction while he made his mind up? To see whether she would be suitable to seduce—or whether she would be foolish enough to read more into it than was there.

'On the contrary,' he demurred. 'I need a little of the kind of detail which a man in love would be expected to know.'

A man in love. It didn't mean anything, but that didn't stop her stupid heart reacting, even while she realised that this was simply Raffaele through and through. He excelled at everything he did—and he wanted to excel at being a fiancé! It would be intol-

erable for him to be found out—for other people to discover that the whole situation was a sham—and that
was what had prompted him into asking her. Or did she
imagine that a little heavy petting in the back of a limousine would be enough to win the affection of a sophisticated man-of-the-world like him?

'What exactly do you want to know?' she asked.

'Your childhood. Schooling. That kind of thing. A
whole life to get through.' Shrugging his broad shoulders, he wandered over to one of the cushioned divans
which overlooked the central courtyard and slid down
on it, black eyes like chips of jet. 'Why, if you manage
to keep it brief, we might even be able to cover your
likes and dislikes before we get called for dinner!'

Natasha glared at him. Had the put-down been de-
liberate? Did he just want to get it over with as quickly
as possible because she was boring? Well, *damn* him!

'I was brought up by a maiden aunt—'

'Your parents?' he intercepted swiftly.

For a moment, she was tempted to tell him that if
he kept interrupting they would never be able to 'keep
it brief,' but some instinct of self-preservation told her
not to bring discord into the bedroom.

'My parents both died within a couple of years of
one another. My aunt was older.'

'And strict?'

She sighed. 'Raffaele, is all this necessary? I
thought we had a whole life to get through.'

Something in her gentle admonishment made him
wince, and yet something else disturbed him far more.
The fact that he *wanted to know!* And why was that?
Because for the first time in his life he had met a woman who wasn't gushing to tell him everything bar her
inside leg measurement?

'I want to know,' he said stubbornly.

And, of course, what Raffaele wanted he always got—didn't he? 'Yes, she was strict,' said Natasha, and then to stop him from reaching the obvious conclusion for himself, and thinking that he was some kind of psychological genius, she elaborated. 'In fact, she was so strict that I'd barely been allowed any kind of social life before I went to university.' She met the look in his eyes and nodded. 'That was where it all went wrong. Freedom came as a bit of a double-edged sword, really—I wanted it, but I was scared of it, too. And, of course. I didn't have any real experiences of going out, drinking, dancing. The sort of things that most people my age had grown up with.'

He suddenly caught a glimpse of the girl she must have been then—with the unworldly air which had remained pretty much intact until her recent makeover. 'And what about Sam's father?'

Well, she might be able to see the purpose of allowing him a recap of her past life, but he certainly didn't need to know the fine details of *that*. Sam's father had just been looking for thrills—not a lifelong commitment. And in a way Natasha hadn't been able to blame him—because she hadn't been looking to have a baby, either. But accidents happened—and just because Sam hadn't been planned it didn't mean that he didn't have every right to be loved and nurtured and cherished.

'Sam's father has many attributes,' she said carefully.

'Why doesn't he see his boy?'

Natasha frowned. 'Does it matter?'

'I want to know.' He met the challenge in her eyes. 'For research purposes, you understand,' he elaborated coolly.

'He wanted nothing to do with the pregnancy,' she said flatly. 'He has never even seen his child, and nor has he wanted to.'

He saw the fierce expression of pride masking the hurt on her face and something turned over inside him. 'Natasha—'

She shook her head, shaking away his meaningless expression of sympathy. She didn't *need* that. 'But *I* wanted the baby—no matter how he was created. And, in many ways, it's easier this way. At least I've been spared the emotional warfare which comes when two parents are separated. Sam has never known anything but love and I've never regretted my decision—not for a single second!'

In a way he applauded her fiery spirit, yet also he cursed her—because nothing drew a man to a woman more than a flame. Didn't she realise that he wanted her in his arms, that he desired her intensely and that something seemed to be blocking his desire every step of the way?

First, he had hesitated because of the inequality of their social standing. Yet now her feisty defiance in the face of what must have been a difficult time seemed to be blocking him, yet again. So what was stopping him?

Was it his *conscience?*

Raffaele frowned. He must stop being sentimental—because nobody could accuse *her* of that. She had coolly stated that it suited her for Sam's father not to be around, just as she had coolly agreed to masquerade as *his* fiancé. She was a pragmatic woman who had demonstrated that she had a woman's needs—needs which she'd admirably suppressed during Sam's early years.

But Sam wasn't around now. For once, she was free of responsibility. They were both adults who wanted one another—didn't they deserve a little light relief in the form of a mutually explosive passion?

He studied her. Her hair was a silken tumble around her shoulders and the long gauzy dress she had sensibly worn in such a strict country hinted distractingly at the lush firm body which lay beneath. Her painted toenails peeped out from the front of woven leather sandals, quietly informing him that her long legs were bare, and suddenly he ached to have them wrapped around his naked back. But she was surveying him as warily as a cornered animal, and Raffaele—who was a master of timing—recognised that the time was not right.

He rose from the divan with all the languid grace of some jungle cat and picked up an air-light linen jacket.

'I'm going to have my meeting with Zahid before dinner—you might wish to freshen up,' he drawled, and his eyes met hers as he wished that he could stay and watch her.

Natasha found her cheeks colouring as she watched him go, wondering if there was some kind of acceptable behaviour for sharing a suite with a man. Rules which most normal people were aware of but which had passed her by. Was there some kind of code you used when you needed to go to the bathroom?

She waited until she was sure he had gone, and then gathered together all her fresh clothes and lingerie—terrified of having to emerge from her shower looking in any way vulnerable in case Raffaele should suddenly appear. Because, in a way, all this watchful waiting was playing havoc with her senses.

She knew he wanted her—despite her laughable

lack of experience with the opposite sex. Even if it wasn't for the telltale glint she sometimes saw in the depths of those ebony eyes, a man like Raffaele could not disguise the sexuality which seemed to exude from every pore of his remarkable body.

The trouble was that she wanted him, too.

So where did that leave her? Wondering and worrying about whether to go through with her heart's greatest wish—or protecting that self-same heart by denying it?

The bathroom increased her trepidation even while it appealed to her senses—it was all marble and mosaic and mirrors. Costly essences lined a spa bath so wide and deep that you could almost imagine floating in it, and someone had placed bowls of fresh crimson rose petals on the pristine white surfaces.

But Natasha had spent too much of her adult life catering to other people's needs not to allow herself to enjoy this. Freedom and luxury—what a pleasure. Closing her eyes, she slicked on the creamy soap, creating layers of foamy suds over her breasts...breasts which were growing unusually heavy...

The minutes melted by as the memory of Raffaele's kiss swam into her head with erotic clarity. Her body stirred restlessly beneath the scented water, and in the end Natasha got out. Heading for the shower, she turned the temperature right down until she was so cold that she was shivering as she wrapped herself in an oversized white towelling robe to dry.

She slithered into the brand-new lingerie and a long, silky robe, and when she'd dried her hair and put on a little make-up she stepped back to inspect herself in the full-length mirror.

The woman who stared back at her might have

blended in perfectly with the luxurious surroundings, but it certainly didn't look like the Natasha *she* knew. It didn't *feel* like Natasha, either. The new bra and panties fitted as comfortably as a second skin, but they were making her uncomfortably aware of her body. Of the strange new dull ache which seemed to tingle at her skin just lately. But she would be a hypocrite if she pretended to try and pinpoint when that longing had begun, because it was engraved on her memory as well as her heart.

Ever since the afternoon when Raffaele had kissed her!

Drawing a deep breath for courage, and telling herself that to embroil herself any deeper than she already was would be sheer madness, Natasha pushed the door open and walked into the suite.

He was waiting for her. Reclining on a heap of lavish velvet and brocade cushions, looking such a mass of contradictions. Sexy and passionate—yet cool and calculating. His olive skin glowed softly, like deep golden silk. And those legs. Natasha swallowed. So impossibly long. His whole pose was both languid and watchful, and she found herself wondering how he managed to be all those things at once.

'I note that you have learnt to make a man wait, *mia cara,*' he murmured approvingly.

She swallowed, wishing that the huge room didn't suddenly feel as though it had telescoped into matchbox proportions. 'I'm not playing games with you, Raffaele.'

'Well, you should,' he reprimanded softly. 'Games are good, because men like to believe they are being played with.'

'D-did you have your meeting with the Sheikh?'

'I did.'

Edgily, her fingers pleated at the soft silk which covered her thigh. 'What was it about?'

'You want to hear the details about the new conference centre which is being built in Zahid's country?'

'No. Not really.' Natasha turned away from the mocking distraction of his ebony eyes. 'What time's dinner?' she asked, a note of slight desperation in her voice.

'Not until seven.'

'Oh!' Another hour to kill. Sixty long minutes in such gloriously tempting confinement with him. How the hell was she going to get through it?

'Natasha?'

His deep voice broke into her thoughts.

'Natasha, look at me.'

Reluctantly, she turned back and did as he asked, afraid of what she would read in his face—what kind of new temptation she would find there. 'What?' she whispered.

'You look very beautiful tonight, in your robe of silk and with your hair like coils of satin. Do you know that?'

She wanted to tell *him* not to play games. Not to seduce her with his honeyed words and that look of approbation which seemed to wash sweetly over her skin. Not to tell her she was beautiful when she knew deep down that she was plain and ordinary Natasha Phillips, who just happened to have had a lot of money and care thrown her way.

But the oddest thing of all was that he made her *feel* beautiful. As if it wasn't a game at all. As if the words he spoke were true. As if he were saying them to someone for the very first time.

And how crazy was that?

With his long list of lovers, Raffaele must have told a woman she was beautiful almost as often as he'd made yet another major takeover!

Snapping herself out of the spell he seemed to have woven around her, Natasha forced a smile. 'Do you happen to know your way around this vast place?' she asked.

'No.' A spark of interest flared from the black eyes. 'But I have a pretty good sense of direction.'

'Shall we have a guided tour of the *riad* before dinner, then?' she questioned guilelessly.

Reluctantly, he applauded her manipulation, acknowledging that the air had been becoming fraught with tension and knowing that it might have built up to such an extent that there would have been no alternative but to kiss her.

But you are planning to kiss her, anyway.

'What a wonderful idea,' he said softly, his eyes a dark gleam. 'Let's go.'

She followed him downstairs to the cool, central courtyard she'd seen briefly when they'd arrived and which dominated the ground floor. It was almost as if they were walking on a cool carpet of different kinds of marble—in colours ranging from palest cream to a rich sand and every shade in between.

Tall candles were being blown gently by the lightest of breezes, and by now a soft dusk had begun to fall. The warm air was scented with some heady fragrance which Natasha didn't recognise, and her senses felt as if they were slowly coming to life.

The courtyard led onto a large swimming pool, its turquoise waters illuminated from within, and Natasha gasped.

'Oh, but that's beautiful!' she exclaimed.

'You can swim?' Raffaele asked.

'Of course.'

'We could steal down here later, when the house is asleep,' he suggested, and saw the way she bit her lip. 'You could show me what a nymph you are in the water.'

Abruptly, Natasha turned and began walking away, her heart thundering, wanting to tell him not to make suggestions like that, but afraid that he would hear the longing in her voice if she attempted to carry through such a blatant lie.

His footfall was soft, but he was following her, and she barely knew where she was going other than around a maze of corridors—some light, some dark— as if she was taking part in some bizarre game of hide and seek. Or as if he was the hunter and she the quarry. A quarry that had no desire to escape.

Raffaele knew what she was doing. The language of her body was calling out to him like a siren, but he recognised that she did not want to be seen to be complicit in her own desires. She wanted him to take her, as women had longed to be taken since the beginning of time.

He felt his mouth dry as he quickened his pace and watched hers slow. So easy to reach her. So ridiculously easy. He reached for her, capturing her waist with his hands, and turned her around, seeing the way her eyes darkened and her lips parted as she gazed up at him.

'Natasha,' he ground out, in a voice which was harsh with desire.

Thoughts flew into her mind. That she could stop him. That she *should* stop him. That this was leading absolutely nowhere other than to certain heartbreak.

But wasn't this a dream which Natasha had cherished and nurtured, despite trying not to? Like a tiny seed which someone had planted in a dark cupboard she hadn't been able to help herself from feeding it, occasionally allowing light in on it, so that it had just grown and grown.

'Raffaele,' she said unsteadily, and just the saying of his name was like granting herself a forbidden luxury. Like the turning of a key in a door which had always been locked.

And suddenly his lips were on hers, and Natasha was letting him kiss her, not fighting him—not in any way. She had wanted this for much too long to deny it any longer. Moaning at the first sweet taste of his mouth, she felt the hot chase of her breathing and the eager surrender of her body as he pulled her into a darkened alcove.

CHAPTER TEN

His lips were hot and hungry, his body hard.

'Raffaele!' Natasha moaned against his mouth, gripping at his broad shoulders for fear that she should sway and fall.

'You want this,' he said unsteadily, not asking but stating.

Some last vestige of sanity swam into her mind. 'The servants—'

'There are no servants, *cara*,' he ground out. 'In a place like this they are taught to look the other way.'

Natasha stiffened. Was that how he saw *her*, back in London? Cooking breakfast for the women who had shared his bed and then slipping into the shadows when her presence was no longer required?

The sentiment unsettled her—but not enough to stop her. Not enough to make her hold back from reaching up to grip those muscular broad shoulders, or from sighing out her pleasure as he pulled her closer.

It was as if she had been made to be held by him. To be wrapped in his arms with his heart beating against her breast. She closed her eyes as he slid his palms proprietorially over each of her silk-covered buttocks, letting her feel the hard cradle of his desire.

'Raffaele,' she breathed shakily.

'Our bodies match, *si?*' he murmured. 'They fit together perfectly.'

'Like a jigsaw,' she whispered, barely realising that she had said it aloud until she heard his low laugh of pleasure.

'But a jigsaw with one vital piece missing, I think.'

His voice sounded suddenly different. Deepened with desire and a sense of purpose. But Natasha had no time to be nervous, because now one hard, muscular thigh was parting hers—though it only seemed to increase the terrible growing ache within her rather than relieving it.

'You like that?' he questioned, as his mouth whispered over the base of her throat.

She swallowed. *'Yes!'*

Raffaele reached round to take one soft breast in his hand, his thumb beginning to tease the hard thrust of her nipple as it peaked through the light material of the dress, and he felt the shudder of pleasure which rippled through her body. 'This, too?'

She closed her eyes. *'Yes!'* She knew where this was heading, where she wanted it to go. Something in Raffaele's touch incited her as well as excited her—and she was suddenly filled with the urgent desire to touch him back. To dare to feel him as he was feeling her. She drifted her hands down, over his chest, over the taut board of his torso. He groaned his approval.

'Ancora di piu. More!' he translated huskily, and then groaned again as he felt her fingers tiptoe farther down, seeming to hesitate before cupping him, as if testing the weight there, as if she were intimately assessing his body. And it was a situation so bizarre that Natasha should be doing this—should be touching him

in such a way which was making him harder than he could ever remember being before—that he very nearly exploded there and then, in that dark and scented alcove.

He bent his mouth to her ear, to the perfumed bright hair. Where had his little mouse gone now? 'Take off your panties,' he murmured.

Distractedly, she shook her head.

'No?'

'It's…'

'It's, what?' he prompted on a throaty murmur.

'It's *wrong*… We…we…*shouldn't.*'

'Shouldn't we?'

'N-no!'

But her actions were belying her words and, unseen, he smiled as he reached down to ruck up the filmy fabric of her gown, sliding his hand up the cool silk of her inner thigh with delicate yet ruthless efficiency. Like a dance he had engaged in so many times before, the moves were as natural to him as breathing. And so was her reaction. The shudder. The little cry as his fingertip alighted on that most vulnerable and feminine part of her. But the sense of wonder which made her voice shiver into that incredulous little gasp—surely that was Natasha's and Natasha's alone?

'Are you quite sure we shouldn't?' he urged, as he moved his provocative finger away and heard her muffled and slurred little sound of objection.

'No… I mean, yes… I mean…'

But Raffaele knew exactly what she meant, and he began to tug at the moist little scrap of material with a low growl, his own erection so hard that it was actually painful.

At that moment a low bell began to ring.

They both froze, and Natasha was the first one to act—trying to pull away from him. But he held her firm.

'Let me *go!*'

He could smell the heady incense of her desire and grazed his lips to her earlobe. 'Let me take you first.'

Wasn't it appalling that part of her should thrill to that outrageous demand—or was it only natural when he murmured in that silken, accented voice? And maybe she should be grateful that he'd said it—because although Natasha was terribly aroused, aching for him, the sexist and matter-of-fact way he had stated his intention brought her to her senses.

Or rather, *away* from her senses.

This time, fired by indignation and given strength by just how dreadful it would look should someone stumble upon them, she managed to extricate herself from the enticement of his embrace.

'Raffaele! We must stop it,' she urged furiously, and she began to tug her clothing straight and lift her fingertips to her hot and flushed cheeks in a vain effort to cool them.

Through the dim light he raised his eyebrows imperiously. 'Why?'

'Why do you think? Because our host happens to be summoning us to dinner and is waiting for us!'

He shrugged. 'Zahid will understand.'

For some reason his careless excuse offended her even more. 'Well, maybe he will,' she stormed softly. 'But it would be an unforgivable breach of good manners, and one that *I* certainly wouldn't tolerate.'

He stared at her, seeing the situation through her eyes for the first time and suddenly he understood. She wasn't just thinking of her own reputation—and he had to admit he hadn't really been thinking about it either, had he? She was concerned about all the people who would be waiting to serve them with what would undoubtedly be a lavish dinner.

Raffaele was used to people waiting for *him,* but for Natasha it was the exact opposite. She was always at his beck and call, wasn't she? Waiting on his wishes and his commands. But this weekend was different. He had asked her to masquerade as someone else, and she was obeying him to the letter!

Somewhere along the way she seemed to have acquired all the haughty attributes which actually made her believable as his fiancée. She was telling him what to do—and he could tell by the expression on his face that he would not be able to change her mind. At least, not now.

He nodded curtly as they stepped out into the courtyard once more, but frustration continued to linger in his blood—and something about the way she had admonished him perturbed him.

Because he had thought of them as not being equals—yet hadn't Natasha just demonstrated the exact opposite by her actions? When had a woman last told Raffaele what to do? Never in his adult life, that was for sure. And when had a woman last stopped him from making love to her?

Never.

The bell rang again, and they turned in its direction. But just before they set off he caught her by the arm—and heard her sharp intake of breath, saw the way her eyes darkened at just that light touch.

'Very well,' he whispered, recognising the power he had over her with silent satisfaction. 'We will go in to dinner and we will play the attentive guests—but never doubt for one moment what I intend for us to do later, once we can excuse ourselves. I shall spend the evening feasting on the sight of your kiss-bruised lips, *mia bella.* I shall be imagining the feel of your naked skin next to mine—and I shall be cursing that infernal bell for not ringing a few minutes later, when I should have been safely inside you and when no power on earth could have separated us!'

The sexual boast should have horrified her, but it did no such thing. It started her pulse racing and that melting feeling came to the pit of her stomach again. But Natasha hid it with a look of outrage. Because anger was a lot safer than showing how vulnerable you felt inside.

'Will you take me in to dinner?' she said quietly.

Or *what?* he wondered. For a moment he was tempted to test her. But something in her eyes stopped him. A look which lit the light blue with a fierce kind of fire. He had seen that look before—it had been burning there on the night she'd walked into his life: a mixture of defiance and pride.

'Yes, I'll take you in to dinner,' he answered. 'But I cannot wait for it to be over!' His voice dropped to a husky promise. 'Because once it is over we both know what will happen.'

If it hasn't been for the brittle tension which seemed to radiate from his powerful frame she might have challenged him on that—but she didn't dare. Not least because she was afraid that he was right and that she wasn't going to be able to resist him.

And since when had she treated her impending introduction to a Middle-Eastern potentate so casually? Had she completely lost her senses as well as her heart? 'What am I supposed to call the Sheikh?' she questioned anxiously, smoothing at her hair and wondering if it looked a complete mess.

'You can address him by his first name—once he gives you permission to do so.' He paused. 'And your hair looks wonderful.'

She pushed the remark aside as a servant suddenly materialised from one of the side-rooms, bowed and gestured that they should follow him. Natasha found herself wondering how much he had overheard as they climbed a staircase to the very top of the building. But all her doubts were dissolved when they walked onto the rooftop terrace and a scene awaited her which looked like something out of the *Arabian Nights*.

Polished lamps were burning and softly buffed bronze tables stood before low divans scattered with cushions in gold and burgundy and rich saffron. Beneath them the city lay spread out—the lighted bustle of the main square contrasting with the soaring floodlit monuments and the dark, twisting streets of the Souk. Above them was an indigo ceiling of star-studded sky, with a crescent moon shining like white-gold, and Natasha's impression was of so many different shades of light that she was dazzled by it all.

And then she heard the whisper of someone approaching and became aware of the focussed activity of yet more servants, trailing in the wake of the imperious character who now swept onto the terrace. He was clothed in shimmering robes and a headdress covered his autocratic head. The dark searchlight of his eyes swept over her, burning with curiosity.

Instinct told her to bow and then she raised her eyes and waited for the Sheikh to address her.

'And who is this?' Waving an imperious hand to dismiss the servants, he spoke to Raffaele, as if she had no voice of her own.

'This is Natasha.'

'Ah.' The Sheikh's eyes were like pieces of jet. 'Your fiancée?'

'Yes.'

The Sheikh surveyed her thoughtfully—as if, Natasha thought with slight indignation, she were some object for sale in the marketplace! But maybe that was how he'd been brought up to think, she reasoned.

'You realise how many women would long to be in your shoes?' he questioned softly.

'I count my blessings daily,' said Natasha demurely, and to her surprise, the Sheikh gave a shout of laughter, though Raffaele's eyes narrowed thoughtfully.

'And what of your sister?' questioned the Sheikh, his voice suddenly and unexpectedly soft. 'I understand from my aides that she is unwell?'

Raffaele nodded, acknowledging that this powerful ruler had some of the most thorough information-gatherers in the world. 'She is having the best treatment available—and now her doctors inform me that she is making good progress. I spoke to her this morning, and I haven't heard her sound so upbeat for a long time.'

The Sheikh nodded. 'That is excellent. Natasha—you must call me Zahid, not Highness. And now—let us be seated.' He flicked a look of barely veiled annoyance at a surprisingly modern watch, which seemed a little out of place when contrasted with his very regal and traditional robes. 'We cannot begin dinner until our final guest arrives, but we shall have something to drink in the meantime. You will take champagne, perhaps?'

Natasha shook her head, tempted, but knowing that she mustn't. She would need all wits about her if she was planning to resist Raffaele—and it was imperative for her sanity that she did. Her sensibilities must not be changed or softened by the introduction of alcohol.

'I would prefer something soft, if you have it... Zahid,' she said shyly.

Raffaele watched while Zahid beamed his approval and clapped his hands together in his most sheikish manner. Was Natasha just being extremely disingenuous—or was she aware that Zahid's upbringing meant that he rarely if ever took alcohol?

Or was she simply afraid of the effect that alcohol might have on *her* and her decision-making? Raffaele felt a beat of heat and of satisfaction. No. Not a drop of any intoxication had passed her lips when he had so very nearly made love to her in that darkened alcove before dinner.

A tray of heavy red goblets was carried in, and another containing small dishes of different nuts, and Raffaele watched with a mixture of bemusement and aching frustration as Natasha began to open up under Zahid's unusually gentle questioning.

He had never really seen her in this light before—but then, why would he have? Until recently he had never really looked at her at all—and, yet, now that fact seemed inconceivable. In her long gown she managed to look both modest and extremely sexy—but that shouldn't really surprise him, either. She was a woman in her twenties, with clear skin and sparkling eyes, her figure firm and fertile.

The ache inside him intensified, and suddenly it became about more than just fulfilling his sexual hunger. Raffaele found himself watching with something almost like *jealousy* as he saw Natasha smiling at a remark the Sheikh had made. Was the desert Prince flirting with her?

But, at that moment, the fourth guest arrived, and Raffaele rose to his feet, noticing that Zahid did not—that, in fact, he barely flicked the new arrival a glance.

The woman who entered noiselessly on sandalled feet was not the blonde goddess-type usually favoured by the Sheikh. Her hair was deep brown and her face pale.

Zahid looked up. 'You are late.'

The brunette shot him a reproving glance. 'Forgive me,' she said lightly. 'Zahid—aren't you going to introduce us?'

He frowned. 'This is Raffaele de Feretti, a business colleague, and his fiancée, Natasha—'

'Phillips,' butted in Natasha hastily realising that Raffaele probably didn't know.

Zahid nodded. 'This is Francesca.'

'Hello,' said Francesca, and smiled.

There was, Natasha realised, no explanation as to who Francesca was, or her relationship to Zahid. He hadn't even given Francesca's surname! But why would a sheikh need to explain himself if he didn't want to?

All Natasha knew was that Francesca appeared to be completely oblivious to Zahid's quietly simmering anger. Was he mad because she had been late, perhaps? Even Natasha knew that you were never supposed to arrive after a royal personage.

But Natasha's awareness of Zahid's displeasure was quickly displaced by her own growing feelings of confusion. On the one hand she was finding it ridiculously easy to converse with the eastern ruler and the enigmatic Francesca—but on the other she was becoming acutely aware of Raffaele watching her. And—try as she might—she couldn't seem to stop her body from responding to that very calculated scrutiny.

Did he realise that he was making her skin tingle and her breasts feel heavy and aching? As if they wanted nothing more than to be touched and kissed by him. Did he know that he was awakening memories of the way he had made her feel when his lips and his hands had been familiarising themselves with her body? But even if he knew all *that* he would certainly not be aware of how he had captured her heart without even trying to.

She felt its beat quicken with the awareness that her love for him burned as strong as ever—but along with the raw sting of unwanted emotion came the equally insistent demands of her body, which were making her feel weak with unwelcome longing. She felt debilitated by it, as if she wanted to squirm and wriggle and have everyone in the room just disappear as if by magic and for Raffaele to stride over to her and pin her to the ground and…and…

Natasha hastily crossed one leg over the other—which wasn't terribly easy when you were sitting on a floor-cushion wearing a long dress.

But Raffaele knew of her agitation. She was certain of that, from the way those black eyes were silently sending her sizzling messages of sexual intent. The way that his teeth bit slowly down on the full cushion of his bottom lip. Did he realise that she was imagining him biting down onto *her* mouth in just the same way as that?

'Natasha? You will eat some of this mango sorbet?' asked Francesca. 'You've barely touched your supper.'

'Natasha has little appetite,' observed Raffaele softly, his black eyes alight with mischief. 'I wonder why.'

Aware that everyone was looking at her, Natasha took the dish that was being offered to her. At least the sorbet was deliciously icy—cooling down the heated clamour of her senses. She was acutely conscious of the fact that time was ticking away inexorably and that soon there would be no reason not to go back to the huge suite she was sharing with Raffaele. And then what?

Somehow she managed to get through the rest of the meal—nibbling at all the sweet delicacies which were brought in on beautiful dishes garnished with exotic flowers.

The Sheikh briefly shut his eyes, and Natasha thought how tired he looked. As if echoing her thoughts, Zahid rose to his feet. 'You will forgive me if I retire.' His black eyes were like chips of stone in the hawklike face as he glanced down at Francesca.

'Come,' he clipped out.

There was a momentary hesitation before Francesca stood up gracefully and gave Raffaele and Natasha a quick, forced smile.

'Excuse me,' she murmured, and then she too was gone, in a drift of filmy rose-pink fabric.

The silence seemed immense.

Natasha didn't know where to look, what to do, how to behave—but it seemed that Raffaele had no such reservations, for his movements were decisive.

Walking over to her, he bent to catch her hand in his, drawing it up to his mouth and touching his lips to her trembling fingers, his eyes never leaving her face.

'Bed, Tasha?' he questioned silkily.

Her heart thundered as he pulled her to her feet. Because, unless she decided to sleep *here,* it seemed she didn't really have any alternative. Were she and Francesca really the same woman—just a warm body suitable for the needs of a highly sexed and powerful man?

'Okay,' she said, trying to express a reluctance she couldn't seem to feel.

You don't have to do anything—not a single thing, she told herself fiercely, as she followed him down the seemingly endless staircase and back to their suite.

And the door closed softly behind them.

CHAPTER ELEVEN

His black eyes narrowing, Raffaele observed the look on Natasha's face as she stared at him across the bedroom. No one would have believed that this was the same woman who had been gasping for pleasure in his arms earlier. Now she was watchful. Cautious. Her body language shrieking *Stay away!*

He gave a half-smile. 'Well, I don't know about you—but I'm exhausted.' Kicking off his shoes, he yawned and then headed towards his bathroom—but not before he had seen her fleeting expression of astonishment. The half-smile became even more wry. Did she really imagine that he was some kind of crass individual who would leap on her when she was very definitely sending out messages that she wanted no such thing?

But he was aching as he showered and he was hard. He pulled on a pair of silk boxers and went back into the bedroom.

As he had suspected she would be, Natasha was already tucked up on one side of the huge bed, the linen sheet held up chastely to her chin, her eyes closed as she feigned sleep. He stood watching her for a moment.

'I know you're awake, *cara*,' he said softly. 'You want me to sleep on the divan?'

Natasha's eyes snapped open, and then she wished they hadn't—because the sight of Raffaele's honed olive body wearing nothing but a pair of shiny dark pants was playing havoc with her equilibrium. She'd never realised quite what a magnificently athletic physique he had—but why would she have? She'd never seen him practically naked before.

Yet, though she'd always been taught it was rude to stare, she couldn't seem to help herself, and it was impossible to tear her eyes away from the shafts of his powerful thighs, the broad shoulders and the perfectly defined chest.

His lips curved into a smile which was almost cruel, but the ache within in him was an exquisite agony. 'I asked you a question, *bella*.'

Natasha blinked, dazed by his proximity and the hammering of her heart. 'You...you did?'

'I asked whether you wanted me to sleep over there.' He glanced rather contemptuously at the velvet-covered divan.

Beneath the sheet, she shrugged her shoulders restlessly. 'It doesn't really seem fair, does it? I mean, it looks very uncomfortable.' She met the unhelpful look in his black eyes. 'Perhaps...'

'Perhaps, what? You're going to offer to sleep there instead? Is that it, *bella?*'

She eyed the vast space beside her nervously. 'Well, it's a big bed. Maybe...'

His black eyes narrowed. Was she really that naïve? 'You think so? No bed is big enough for a man and a woman if they are trying to deny themselves something they both want.'

'What are you saying, Raffaele?'

His mouth hardened. 'I'm saying that I won't touch you. At least not intentionally—not if that is what you have decided you now want. But if you press yourself close to me in the middle of the night and then claim you were 'asleep'—or if you clutch at me and afterwards assert that you were having some kind of bad dream—well, I cannot guarantee that I will respond in the way that a *gentleman* might.'

Beneath the Egyptian cotton her body shivered at the vivid images his silken words created. 'Wh-what are you saying, Raffaele?' she repeated shakily.

His black eyes were suddenly as hard and as obdurate as his body, and he wondered whether she was staring at him closely enough to see his arousal.

'I'm saying that I'm going to make love to you,' he said harshly. 'Unless you tell me emphatically that you don't want me to.'

There was a silence broken only by the faint cacophony of the distant sounds of the city.

Their eyes met. He didn't love her. He would never love her. A servant girl, the mother of an illegitimate child. Theirs was a relationship—if you could call it that—forged out of necessity. Only now it was threatening to spill over into desire...

Heartbreak, she kept telling herself over and over again—repeating it like a magic spell, like a mantra. Heartbreak.

Yet his dark eyes and hard body held a far greater lure than any spell, no matter how powerful it was— and all Natasha could think about was that she would never get another opportunity like this. That he would not ask her again. And could she honestly live the rest of her life knowing that she had been so close to the realisation of years of wistful daydreams and then turned her back on it?

'So, tell me you don't want me and let that be an end to it,' he asserted starkly.

There was silence for a moment.

'I can't do that.' Her voice was soft.

But he needed to be sure. He did not want her railing against him tomorrow morning simply because her conscience had got the better of her.

'Say it,' he commanded throatily.

Was this his victory, then, to make her beg? She swallowed. 'I want you.'

The ache within him intensified, but it was the honesty in her voice which moved him—so that the walk over to the bed where she lay felt somehow *significant*.

He shook his dark head very slightly, like a man emerging from the water and trying to rid himself of the last few drops. He really *had* been without a woman too long if that was the kind of bizarre interpretation he was putting on something so simple as having sex.

Yet it *had* been a long time; he could not deny that. Why?

Because he had been working hard?

Well, yes—but that was nothing new.

Because there had been no one suitable?

Hardly. At any given moment of any given day Raffaele could have snapped his fingers and any number of beautiful women would have come running to him.

Maybe that was why. Because it all came a little too easily to him and he was bored, his appetite jaded by the inevitability of it all.

Yet Natasha hadn't exactly been unforthcoming, had she? As soon as he'd waved a credit card in her direction she had dazzled him with the green light. No one in their right mind could really accuse her of playing hard-to-get. So what was it?

He stared down at her, at where the shiny fall of her hair lay like a layer of honey-blonde satin over the crisp white pillow. Her eyes were the clear blue of an Italian spring morning and her skin like freshly poured cream.

Reaching down, he pulled the sheet away from her. She lay trembling in a satin nightgown as pale as her face, and he touched a little shoestring strap.

'Shall we take this off?'

Was this how clinical it was going to be? she wondered wildly. He'd strip her off and then presumably himself? So…so *mechanical?* She shook her head and saw him frown. 'No.'

'No?'

Would she sound ridiculously needy if she said it? But suddenly Natasha didn't care what she *sounded* like. This wasn't about her *image,* for heaven's sake, but the craving of her heart. And if this was to be the night she had long dreamed about then she wasn't going to be shy about conveying what her needs were.

'Kiss me first,' she whispered. 'Please. Just kiss me.'

'Kiss you?' Unexpectedly, he smiled then. 'Is that all?'

He bent down towards her, almost as if he was moving in slow motion, so that it seemed like an eternity before their lips connected. And when they did—well, for Natasha it was as all the books said it should be. A soft explosion, the awakening of a desire

so immediate and so intense that she gave a cry of surrender and looped her arms around his neck, pulling
him down to her, his hard chest crushing against the
soft cushion of her breasts.

And Raffaele was startled by her sudden fervour,
excited by the contradiction she presented—reserved
and then passionate—and he found himself kissing
her back with a fervour which matched hers, pulling
her into his arms and tangling their limbs together.
Only the slippery satin of his boxers and her nightgown
lay between their nakedness and, yet, for once, he
revelled in these sensual barriers.

Luxuriously, he ran his hands experimentally down
over the silk-covered lines of her body, heard her gasp
her pleasure.

And Natasha touched him back in a way she had
never touched a man before—with a kind of delicious
freedom and inhibition—and she rejoiced in the feel
of his skin, the decadent sensation of hard muscle
beneath honed flesh. Tracing the line of his arms and
his thighs, she stroked the flat planes of his belly and
the hard curves of his ribs.

Raffaele shuddered—because this felt almost *too*
intimate. This was *Natasha,* for *Dio's* sake. Sweet,
reliable little Natasha—who, it seemed, had become a
sensual dynamo in his bed!

He groaned as he peeled the nightgown from her,
tossing it aside as his gaze raked over her naked body
and, as the night air washed over her skin, he saw her
purely instinctive gesture of trying to cross her arms
over her breasts. He stopped her.

'No, *mia bella,*' he husked softly. 'Do not be shy—
for shyness has no place between a man and a woman.
Let me look at you. *Si.* Let me look at you. You are

beautiful, do you know that?' he breathed. 'Very, very beautiful.'

Her skin was pale—so pale—and her breasts large, rose-tipped and, oh, so inviting. He gave an odd little cry as he bent his head to one and teased the tip with the soft graze of his teeth, and he heard *her* cry, felt her buck with pleasure beneath him as she clutched him even closer.

And then it was like performing an old, familiar dance but in a completely different way—as if someone had just shown him some brand-new moves. Was it because he knew her that it seemed so *strange*…so *distinctive?* Or because she knew *him?* For once, he could not hide behind the image he wanted to present to the particular woman who lay beneath him— because Natasha knew him through and through. She had seen him angry and sad—even vulnerable. She had seen him all ways.

He felt a stab of something—was it ire?—because in a way she was now seeing him stripped bare in every sense of the word. She would watch him lose control at the moment of orgasm—that one time when a man was as weak as he would ever be other than at the moment of death.

And Raffaele revelled in that sudden anger, because it meant that he could do what he was best at—giving a woman pleasure. He knew so well how to entice and to tantalise, when to advance and when to retreat. He knew all the places where she would be most sensitive.

He pleasured her with his hands and then with his mouth—a virtuoso at what he was doing—and it was with a kind of grim satisfaction that he heard the first of her cries as it ripped through the night air before he had even entered her.

But still he held back on his own satisfaction.

In the aftermath of orgasm Natasha lay reeling, her senses exploding—but she sensed tension in Raffaele, and she didn't know why. From being the man who had clearly wanted her—still wanted her—so badly, he had suddenly become shuttered, almost restrained.

Raising her dazed eyes to his, she brushed his mouth with her fingers and then she followed with her lips, coercing him into a deep and drugging kiss, willing him to let go, to relax. She felt the sigh and the breath and the tension leaving his tightly coiled body— heard the exclamation he made, something in Italian, and not something she recognised from years of hearing fragments of the language at odd moments.

Moving on top of her, he lifted his head and stared down at her for one long moment and then he held her face in his hands, as if he were framing a picture.

'Tasha,' he said simply, and entered her.

It was like nothing she had ever experienced. Ever.

It felt...*right.* Complete. As if the vital part of a jig-saw had just been found. Hadn't Raffaele said that himself earlier? But, of course, he had meant it purely in a physical sense, while, for Natasha, this was emo-tional. More than emotional. She opened her eyes to look into his before great waves of pleasure began to engulf her.

'Raffaele!' she sobbed, and then she felt him tense and begin to shudder within her.

His orgasm seemed to go on and on—tearing him apart with sheer delight—and afterwards he found himself gathering her into his arms and kissing the top of her head almost indulgently—as if *she* had done something special.

It was only when something unknown woke him in

the night that Raffaele was able to come to his senses. Silently, he slipped away from her, carefully disentangling the leg which was snuggled between his and then held his breath to see if she would waken. But she didn't. He pulled on a pair of jeans and a T-shirt and slipped out of the suite, noiselessly climbing the marble stairs to the terrace where they had eaten dinner the evening before.

It was one of those unforgettable panoramas which made you want to just rejoice in the very fact of being alive to see it—no matter how preoccupied you were. The stars were being swallowed up by the rose mist of the dawn sky, and he could see the dark blots of some unknown birds as they circled around a city which was still sleeping.

Raffaele stared out at the startlingly exotic skyline, where the tall, slender towers of the minarets rose up to gleam in stately splendour against the growing gold of the sunrise.

Well. He had done it. He had slept with Natasha and had probably had the most *fantastico* sex of his thirty-four years. He had gotten what he wanted—as he always did.

And now?

He leaned against the balustrade, barely noticing the faint chill of the early morning air, or the coldness of the unforgiving marble against his bare feet.

Now—for the first time in his life—he wasn't sure. Had he been wrong to pursue something which he knew they had both been longing for? Should he have used his wider experience to call a halt to it before it had reached this stage? How was Natasha going to cope with what had happened?

Natasha.

Who would ever have imagined that she could be…

Shaking his head in slightly dazed disbelief, Raffaele gave a ragged sigh. Was it not just one of the exquisite ironies of life that a woman with the potential to be the perfect lover should be the one woman with whom it would be impossible to pursue a relationship?

But just thinking about her soft, scented body was enough to make him start hungering for her once more. He felt…*insatiable* around her. Or was that simply because he recognised that this particular affair had an exceptionally short shelf life?

Snaking his tongue around his bone-dry lips, he moved towards the stairs.

Decisions would wait. Everything would wait. And in the meantime he would wake her—in the most satisfying way possible.

CHAPTER TWELVE

NATASHA stretched lazily, dreamily, indulgently—allowing herself a warm nestle into the mattress and an even warmer recollection of the night before. A warm, Moroccan night....

She blinked open her eyes and looked around, but there was no sign of Raffaele so, yawning, she sat up in bed and picked up her watch. Ten o'clock! Could she really have slept for that long?

Of course she could've. There had been very little in the way of sleep during the night itself. In fact, the whole weekend seemed to have gone by in a blur of slow, sensual nights and lazy, erotic mornings. And after breakfasting late they would set out to explore the city with Zahid and Francesca, and Natasha had wondered if there would be a tremendous fuss attached to being out and about with a royal personage. To her surprise there was not. But that was mainly on Zahid's insistence.

True, there were always a couple of bodyguards hovering discreetly nearby—and they never had to queue!—but Zahid's flowing robes allowed him to blend easily into the background of the exotic city. Natasha wondered what the average tourist would say if they realised that a real-live sheikh was walking among them!

Drums and snake-charmers had provided background music as she had marvelled at the Badi Palace and the Saadian Tombs—at the souks and the astonishingly lush gardens which were unexpectedly dotted around the city. It was a place of smells and sounds and colours where Africa met an Arabian culture, all set against the backdrop of the snow-capped Atlas mountains.

After lunch they would return to the *riad,* where she and Raffaele would retire for their siesta—there seemed to be something so decadent and so wonderful about going to bed together during the afternoon so freely. And not just bed, either. The cushions which lay heaped in velvet and satin piles on the low divans provided soft havens for the slow thrust of their bodies, just as the cool marble of the floor contrasted so erotically with the heated softness of aroused flesh.

Why, once she had been leaning over to peer into the mirror and she had heard Raffaele move behind her. Jerking her head up, she had caught his look of sensual intent, had felt him exploring her, freeing her flesh. And, just like her, he had watched her reflection in the mirror, seen her pupils dilate in delighted pleasure as he had entered her.

Under his masterful tutelage Natasha had become bold, too—flowering beneath the exquisite fingers of her lover, feeling free and uninhibited enough to touch him as she had longed to for almost as long as she had known him.

What delight it brought her to see that hard and autocratic face soften beneath her lips. And to see him momentarily lose himself in that one sweet moment of release was quite something. *I could get quite used to this,* she thought.

A clatter shattered her indulgent reverie, and she looked up to see Raffaele walking into the room, carrying a tray with juice and coffee. He was already dressed and shaved, she noticed, his black hair still damp from the shower and a cream silk shirt clinging to the hard torso beneath. Natasha's heart turned over with love and longing.

Had this weekend changed anything? Did he feel what she felt—that they had forged something between them, something real and unconnected to the reason which had initially brought them together? Was he ready to acknowledge it?

'Good morning,' she said shyly.

There was a pause. 'Hi.' He recognised the tone without surprise as he put the tray down just as he recognised the look on her face and, inwardly, he felt his heart sink. This was what women did. They were like fierce and demanding tigers in your bed, and then they turned coy. They wanted reassurance that you liked them just as much in the morning. That you wanted to take things to a different level.

But he knew from experience that he must be very careful. Too much reassurance always gave them the wrong idea—and he couldn't afford to do that. Not with Natasha—for hadn't he already broken every single rule in the book with her in these few days?

He put the tray down. 'Like some coffee?'

'I'd rather you came back to bed,' she said softly.

He gave a brittle smile, forcing himself to stay right where he was, even though his body was yearning for a little more of her sweetness. 'Well, I'm afraid you're going to be unlucky—I have a few phone calls to make before we leave for the airport,' he said obliquely.

It was as if reality had made an unexpected appearance ahead of schedule—the glass carriage becoming a pumpkin again before midnight had even struck.

'Phone calls?'

His eyes narrowed as he heard the note of objection in her voice, and he wondered if spending the weekend with a sheikh had somehow turned her head. What the hell did she think this was—some kind of honeymoon? Had she forgotten that this was all an elaborate ruse which just happened to have run away with itself because of a little sexual chemistry which he had foolishly encouraged?

His voice became stern. 'Actually, I *do* have to work, Natasha.'

'Of course you do,' she said quickly, and could feel herself slipping straight back into her old role. Obedient Natasha. Compliant Natasha.

Yet some cool new distance in his black eyes made her heart lurch with a nameless kind of dread. This wasn't how it was supposed to be. Not after what had happened between them. Because, surely, even Raffaele wouldn't deny that they had been amazing together? That what had started out as play-acting had become something quite different. Why, last night, in bed he had made her feel as if she was the only woman in the universe

But it was dark in the night, mocked a voice in her head, and you couldn't see his eyes then, could you? All you could feel was his body, and all you could hear were the things he was murmuring to you as he thrust into you—things he probably says every time he goes to bed with a new woman. What makes you think you're so different, Natasha? So special?

Taking the cup he brought over to her, she put it down quickly on the inlaid table beside the bed before he could notice that her hand had started trembling.

'I'll leave you to get dressed,' he said.

'Yes.'

He moved away from the bed and the distracting sight of her softly pink face, still flushed from sleep. 'We'll have breakfast on the terrace with Zahid and Francesca. I'll meet you up there. You can find it on your own by now, can't you?'

He just couldn't wait to get away, could he? 'I think I can just about manage without a map,' she said pleasantly—because she was damned if she was going to let him see her hurt and her anger. But it was mainly anger with herself that she felt—for allowing herself to *feel* hurt. Raffaele hadn't promised her anything, had he? Other than a great weekend and great sex? And he had certainly delivered *that*.

She forced a smile, noticing that he hadn't touched her. Not a kiss. A glance. A murmured comment. Not a single touch which might have made her feel she mattered.

She waited until he had gone before she drank her coffee and thought about how best to handle this. Now that they were preparing to return to England, Raffaele was clearly working hard to reestablish the boundaries and he had obviously decided that the whole bed thing had been a mistake. So she had some choices open to her.

She could seduce him—or beg him to make love to her.

Or she could keep her pride and her dignity and

shrug her shoulders as if it didn't matter—even if her heart felt as if it was breaking into a thousand pieces.

There was no contest, really, was there?

She showered and dressed with particular care, recognising that make-up had another role to play other than that of accentuating a woman's good points. It became a mask you could hide behind—and she was in desperate need of some kind of camouflage this morning.

She chose a plain white silk shift which brushed the floor—the golden-ringed belt worn low on her hips its only adornment. Her hair she caught up into a twist on top of her head—simple and uncomplicated and the opposite to the writhing nest of emotion she was feeling inside.

But she wouldn't have been human if she hadn't felt nervous as she made her way up to the terrace, wondering what the day ahead would bring.

The two men were alone, standing overlooking the city, deep in conversation. When they looked up Natasha wondered if that was an odd kind of *guilt* she read in their faces—or was she now just getting paranoid?

But Zahid could pull charm out of the bag when he wanted to. Almost seeming to compensate for Raffaele's unmistakably cool body language, he bowed to her as if *she* were the royal—and clapped his hands so that servant after servant brought out different dishes of fruits and tiny little sweet pastries and strong, thick coffee in a beautiful silver pot.

With a start, Natasha realised how easily she had slipped into the role of mixing in such exalted circles.

'Where's Francesca?' she asked.

'She is in her room and, unfortunately, she will not be joining us,' said Zahid smoothly.

'Oh?' Natasha looked across at Raffaele, but his black eyes were as expressionless as those of a statue. 'That's a shame.'

'Indeed, it is,' said Zahid coolly. 'But she sends you her good wishes and says farewell. And I have told Raffaele that he must bring you to my country one day, whenever you wish it.'

'I think that Natasha is done with travelling for a while—aren't you, *cara?*'

Natasha nearly choked on a macadamia nut, but at least chewing it gave her something to focus on— something to stop her rage from bubbling to the surface. How dare he? How *dare* he treat her like some commodity he could just pick up and then put down again at will? Did he think she had no feelings? Or was he just afraid that she was about to start booking a two-week trip to Badr al Din, or wherever it was?

But pride was a funny thing—as soon as it was injured it began healing itself in order to protect. Thus it was pride which enabled her to smile widely at Zahid and to tell him how much she appreciated his kind offer. And pride which allowed her to tell him truthfully that she intended to come back to Morocco one day with her son.

'You have a son?' Zahid queried in amazement.

Which answered her unasked question of how much Raffaele had told the Sheikh about her. Nothing, it would seem.

'Yes, he's five.' She could see Zahid doing mental calculations in his head, so she cleared up any embarrassing confusion with the truth. 'I split up with his father when I was still pregnant.' Which would also, she guessed, make her a thoroughly unsuitable consort for the Sheikh's friend.

'Five?' breathed Zahid diplomatically. 'You must have been little more than a child yourself!'

Somehow she got through the rest of the meal—though that nut was destined to be the last morsel which passed her lips. She bade farewell to Zahid and, once he had swept from the terrace followed by a retinue of servants, she rose to her feet.

'What's the hurry?' questioned Raffaele, with a perfect view of her long legs from where he lay back against one of the stacked cushions.

'To pack, of course!'

Maybe it was because *he* liked to be in the driving seat that he now perversely found himself wanting to stay a little longer. Or maybe it had something to do with the morning sun illuminating her so that she looked like some glorious white and golden goddess. But she had turned her back on him almost deliberately and was walking away from him.

His mouth hardening with anticipation, he stood up and followed her all the way down the stairs until they were back in their suite, and then he caught hold of her and turned her round, a question in his dark eyes. 'Maybe we should delay our flight for a while,' he said huskily.

Heart pounding, Natasha stared up at him. 'Really? Why? What else did you have in mind?'

'That is a very loaded question, *cara.*' Snaking his hand around her waist, Raffaele smiled as he pulled her close into his body, his voice deepening as he lowered his lips to her neck, his eyes closing as he inhaled the delicate scent that was Natasha's alone—and so familiar to him. 'I can think of plenty of things I would like to do right now.'

And so could she. Things not entirely unrelated to

his warm touch and the fact that she could feel the hardness of his arousal pressing against her, as well as sense the desire which thrummed in the air about them.

'Can you?' she questioned.

'Mmm.' He nuzzled at her ear. 'Can't you?'

'Raffaele, please—'

'Please, what, *cara?*'

She wanted to say *Please will you stop touching my breasts like that?* But it seemed that her body had other ideas—for it was revelling in the glory of his touch. Was it possible for a woman to know that something was wrong and yet to respond with a kind of unstoppable *greed?*

'Oh!' Her head fell back, her mouth opening in a gasp as he rucked the silk of her gown up around her thighs. He wasn't wasting any time with tenderness, she thought desperately. The golden belt had clunked its way to the ground, and now he was tugging at her panties, tearing at the delicate fabric impatiently. She gasped again—was it to protest at such arrogant disdain for the costly little piece of underwear? She would never know, because now he was touching her where she most liked to be touched, and he was doing it like a man on a sensual mission. And suddenly it was too late to do anything other than breathe his name out loud. 'Raffaele!'

'*Si,*' he said, frantically unzipping himself, levering her up against the wall. He stared down at her parted lips and huge dark eyes for one split second, before thrusting into her so long and deep that his sigh of satisfaction became a ragged and almost helpless groan.

There was no time to think, to speak, to object or even to kiss—because her orgasm happened so quickly and unexpectedly that Natasha felt almost cheated. As if he had robbed her of something and she couldn't quite work out what it was. And Raffaele shuddered within her almost immediately, his big body convulsing as he tightened his arms around her, saying something in Italian which sounded more like a curse than anything else.

She waited until he had stilled and then weakly pushed at his chest, appalled by the sheer *physicality* of the act. Her tongue snaked round her lips, her heart sinking with despair. He had *used* her—used her as a body, simply to satisfy his needs. *And you have used him,* taunted a voice in her head, and she flinched as she heard it.

'Tasha?' His breathing was steadier now, but his eyes were wary—because something about the intensity of what had just happened had taken him by surprise. 'Are you okay?'

She was far from okay. She was hurting like hell. But *signor* would never know that. 'Yes, I'm absolutely fine. Why wouldn't I be?' She opened her eyes very wide. 'And now I'd like to go to the airport and take a plane. Or is it *catch* a plane? I'm not sure. I'd never travelled by air before this—particularly not by private jet—but you're the expert, aren't you, Raffaele? You're the expert on pretty much everything. *You* tell me.'

He frowned and yawned, thinking that bed just might be the best option all round. 'I thought we were going to delay our flight?'

'But we don't need to anymore. Not now.' She moved away from him.

'What are you talking about?'

Say it, she told herself. Confront your worst fears and then they can have no power over you. 'Well, we've just had sex, haven't we? So we can leave right away. Unless you were planning to fit in another couple of bouts before we go back?'

'*Bouts?* This is not a boxing match we are talking about!' he flared. 'And there is no need to put it quite so...*clinically.*'

She stared at him in disbelief. 'Oh, please, Raffaele—let's not dress up the facts just to make them palatable! That's what this whole weekend was about, wasn't it? Sex—pure and simple—a basic human urge that we both satisfied. If that wasn't *clinical,* then I don't know what it was!'

'Why are you suddenly talking like this?' he demanded furiously.

Because she had suddenly come to her senses. 'Because it's the truth! You know it is!' And she turned away from him and ran into her dressing room before he could touch her again, recognising that this was not going to be easy.

Over the years she had learnt to love him—it had crept up on her almost without her noticing—and now she was going to have to *un*learn it. Because to Raffaele she was nothing other than a person who could be useful to him. She could perform a million roles—from making him soup and throwing the press off the trail of his sister to taking him in her mouth under the intimate cloak of the night and hearing him moan his fulfilment.

Biting her lip, she racked her brain as she raced through the possibilities open to her. Perhaps the only way she was going to come out of this with any degree of sanity was to revert back to what she really was.

What she always had been. His employee—nothing more and nothing less.

She was hurriedly piling her delicate lingerie into a suitcase when Raffaele entered the suite. His attention was caught by the lacy thong which she clutched between her fingers and his mouth hardened.

'We need to discuss what we are going to do when we return to England,' he said curtly. 'Are you prepared to continue with this arrangement?'

Taking his statement at face value, she chose her words carefully, damned if she would give him the satisfaction of knowing just how vulnerable she felt inside.

She held up the heavy, cold weight of the diamond ring so that rainbow rays streamed from its faceted surface. 'For as long as we need to we will continue with this engagement,' she said. 'And, seeing as the press don't actually have access to the bedroom, they won't know that it isn't a proper relationship, will they? When Elisabetta is well and you decide that the charade is no longer necessary, then we'll just let it fizzle out all by itself. There'll be a new story by then and my debt to you will have been repaid.'

He stared at her, at an expression he had never seen in her eyes before, and he couldn't quite work out what it was. A new coldness. All the habitual adoration flown. 'Is that how you see it? Is that how you regard all that has happened between us?' he demanded. 'As the repaying of a debt?'

Oh, how *arrogant,* she thought bitterly. And wouldn't he just love it if she told him that, no, he'd captured her heart into the bargain?

'Let's leave our egos out of it and just stick to facts, shall we, Raffaele?' she questioned coolly.

It was at moments like this that she took him completely off guard. For a moment, he thought—with something approaching admiration—she sounded exactly like his lawyer.

CHAPTER THIRTEEN

HAD Raffaele thought that Natasha might relent on the journey back to London? That a hand splayed carelessly over the silken temptation of her thigh might have her breathlessly revealing that she couldn't wait to get home and into his bed?

In truth, yes, he had. But the reality was quite different.

She was cool, polite, distant. At first Raffaele let her get away with it—the flight was turbulent and there were too many stewardesses bobbing around and offering them unwanted glasses of champagne to challenge her resolution with seduction. But when they arrived back to an empty house and she jerked her head away from his slightly impatient kiss his eyes narrowed—at first with suspicion and then with barely suppressed anger.

'Are we going to stop this charade now? I think you have made your point, don't you, *cara?*'

'What point is it I'm supposed to be making, Raffaele?'

His eyes narrowed. How feminine introspection angered him! 'I don't know, *cara,*' he said silkily. 'And to be honest, I don't care—there is only one thing I care about right now, and we both know what that is.'

She stared at him, shivering at the cold detachment in his black eyes. How easy it would be to let him carry on kissing her—his sensual mouth and his practised hands stroking away any doubts she had. But how foolish, too. Every time he entered her body he was chaining himself a little more tightly to her heart. Every kiss was like a brand that nobody else could see but that was going to scar her for ever.

'I told you in Morocco that I will continue with our supposed engagement, but the sex stops. It…it has to,' she finished shakily.

'Do you want to tell me why?' he drawled, ignoring the sudden look of appeal in her eyes. 'Is it because Sam is due back?'

Natasha winced. He was concerned about practicalities, nothing more. 'In England we have an expression,' she said slowly, 'about not playing with fire because you only get your fingers burnt.'

His mouth curved into a cruel smile. As he bent his dark head closer he could see the instinctive tremble of her body, and temptation briefly flared. How easy it would be to make her take her words back—to have her pleading with him to make love to her. But Raffaele never begged. And neither would he waste his time with someone intent on games.

'Then, stay away from the fire,' he said mockingly. 'Let your body grow cold, instead, Tasha.'

Desire left his dark, rugged features as abruptly as if a switch had been turned off, and Natasha watched him walk away from her with a terrible feeling of foreboding. Wanting to call or to run after him, but knowing that if she did so she would be lost for ever.

'I'm flying to Paris,' he snarled.

'When?'
'Tonight.'
Tonight?

Sam arrived back from Serge's house full of energy and enthusiasm, and even *he* looked different—as if he had been parted from her for months rather than a few days. But being apart made you reevaluate things and look at them differently, Natasha realised. Yes, he had missed her—but only in the way a five-year-old boy *should* miss his mother.

I must make sure I never try to live my life through my son, she told herself fiercely. He mustn't become one of those only children of a single parent who feels responsible for the happiness of that parent. She needed to increase his freedom. She had to learn to let go. Of him and of so much more.

If anything had come out of this wild, tumultuous episode it was that lesson.

Once Raffaele rang from France. Natasha tried to convince herself that his clipped tone was due to the crackly international line, but deep in her heart she knew the real reason. Now that their brief sexual fling was over, he had distanced himself from her, and that, too, was inevitable. Yet, for the first time, Natasha recognised that by changing their relationship she had managed to destroy it. That there was no going back to where it had been.

Had she really thought that she could carry on like before after eveything they had shared together? With her serving him coffee and trying to forget all the achingly sensual intimacies they had shared?

At least, the news from the clinic was good. Elisabetta had put on weight and was benefiting hugely from the therapy. She was moving to a sister clinic in the United States, which would give her vast land-scapes in an inaccessible place where no one would bother her. The world had moved on—a high-profile Hollywood divorce wiping away any interest in the half-sister of an Italian billionaire.

The 'engagement' was yesterday's news—even the huge diamond had taken to slipping round her finger so that it wasn't visible. The last two mornings she hadn't actually worn it, and nobody had noticed.

Usually, when Raffaele was away it just felt like a change of routine. This time it felt different. As if there was a huge hole in her life. Natasha couldn't settle to anything. She felt as if she no longer belonged—even the Italian she had been studying now seemed like a faintly ridiculous thing to be doing.

And what the hell was going to happen when Raffaele returned?

Something was going to have to give—and maybe this was the kick-start she needed. She thought about something Sam's headmaster had said to her when the exam results had come in, and made an appointment to see him before school ended.

The door slammed one evening the following week, and Natasha looked up, unprepared for the sight of Raffaele walking in, all windswept and sprinkled with droplets of rain, wearing a dark cashmere coat. That old rush of love came back—only, now it was sharper, stronger, honed by absence and the knowledge of his lips and his body and by a brief taste of what life would be like as Raffaele's woman. Her legs felt shaky as she watched him put down his briefcase, not daring to move or to speak for fear that she would do something humiliating—like beg him to kiss her, to take her upstairs to his bed.

Slowly, he took off his coat, thinking how pale she looked—all her old warmth and approachability gone. He stared at her. At the little pulse which was beating frantically at the base of her neck. He remembered kissing her there.

'How are you, Tasha?

How formal he sounded. 'I'm fine. You? Good trip?'

'Productive,' he answered tersely, and turned away from the soft gleam of her lips.

He made a couple of calls and then went downstairs to the basement kitchen, where the old-fashioned range radiated warmth and a pot of something that smelt like stew was bubbling on top. Natasha looked up with the startled expression of a young animal which had just heard a threatening noise in the undergrowth.

'Would you like…coffee?'

She never usually asked. He shook his head. 'Actually, I need a drink.'

A drink? He never drank before dinner as a rule. 'You didn't tell me you were coming home.'

'You mean, warn you?' His smile was mirthless as he opened a bottle of wine and held it up to her in question. She shook her head. 'I thought I'd surprise you.'

Oh, but this was awful. Horrible. Like walking on something hopelessly fragile that you were afraid was going to be shattered beyond recognition if you took a wrong turn. She needed to act before that happened. 'Look, Raffaele, I need to talk to you.'

'What is it, Tasha?' he questioned, as he poured the wine and drank some, the rich vintage easing just a little of the tension which felt like a tight iron band clamped around his forehead.

'I've got some news.'

His fingers tightened around the glass and he put it down. 'You're not pregnant?'

She heard the horror which had frozen his voice, and its icy tone confirmed all her worst fears—made her realise that the decision she had reached was the best one for all of them.

'No, I'm not.' She blushed, furious with him for bringing the subject up when that was the last thing she wanted to talk about. She was trying to forget it. She *needed* to forget it. 'I'm on the pill.'

'Oh, come on—no contraceptive is foolproof, *cara*. You, of all people, know that.' He saw the stricken look on her face. 'That was the wrong thing to say. I'm sorry.'

'No—please. Don't be. It's true, after all.' She had told herself that she wasn't going to run away from the truth anymore. So she wouldn't. She drew a deep breath. 'Look, I had a chat with Sam's headmaster the other day.'

'Really?' he queried politely, wondering if this was actually relevant. 'He's not in any kind of trouble, I hope?'

Natasha bristled. 'On the contrary. He's doing exceptionally well. So well, in fact, that he's been offered a scholarship at a bigger school.' She paused. 'In Sussex.'

'Sussex?' he said blankly, ignoring her expression of maternal pride. His eyes narrowed. 'But that's miles away.'

'Yes, it is,' she agreed, her voice so bright that she felt it might crack under the strain. 'And it's beautiful. You should see the school. Right out in the country—they've got huge playing fields.'

'But you live *here,*' he objected. 'How the hell will he get to school? Or are you planning to board him?'

Over her dead body! 'No. He'll… Well, we'll…live in Sussex.'

There was a pause. *'We'll?'* he echoed softly. 'You're planning to buy somewhere down there, are you? Or to rent?'

Was he deliberately driving home her economic insecurity in order to make a point? To make her realise how dependent she was upon him? Well, she *wasn't!* Natasha drew her shoulders back, her earlier reservations melting away beneath the determined look she directed at him.

'Actually, neither. The school has offered me a job as Assistant Matron—and there's a little cottage in the grounds which goes with the post. We can move in whenever we want before Christmas.' She took a deep breath to give her words real conviction. 'It'll be a fantastic place to spend Christmas.'

He was staring at her. 'You? Assistant *Matron?*' Raffaele's eyes narrowed. '*Madonna mia,* Tasha— that's a job for an old woman!'

'Actually, it's the perfect job for someone like me!' she retorted.

He wanted to grab hold of her, to haul her into his arms and demand that she stay. But maybe that was her objective. He stilled. Was it? Was this just another attempt at manipulation in his lifetime of women trying to get him to do what they wanted him to?

'Perhaps you are attempting to call my bluff,' he observed softly.

She stared at him and frowned. 'I'm not sure I understand…'

'Aren't you?' His mouth curved into a cruel smile

as he observed how wonderful she looked—how glossy her carefully styled hair, how expensively creased the linen shirt she wore so easily with her skinny jeans. 'I suspect that you enjoyed all the luxuries that our phoney relationship brought with it, didn't you? Perhaps more than you could have ever anticipated? Maybe that's one of the real reasons you agreed so readily to have sex with me—why you slipped so easily and so comfortably into the role of fiancée.' His face darkened. 'But perhaps the outcome of our little *liaison* wasn't quite to your liking, *mia bella*—perhaps you wanted to go one stage further?'

'I don't know what you're talking about!'

'Don't you?' He gave a short laugh. 'I'm talking about marriage! Wouldn't it suit you better to give your role here some official status—as my wife? Hmm?' Arrogantly, he raised his dark brows, seeing the stain of colour which washed over her cheekbones. Was that guilt? 'And what better way of achieving that aim than by threatening to suddenly leave—with all the disruption that would bring.'

For a moment, she thought she might have misheard him. But the dark look of some unknown emotion on his cold face told her otherwise. She shook her head, her heart beating so fast that she seriously thought she might faint.

'How can you think that of me?' she breathed. 'How *can* you, Raffaele? To imagine me capable of such devious behaviour? I went to bed with you because I wanted to—because I couldn't stop myself.' *Because I felt I would die if I didn't.* 'There was no ulterior motive.'

But he had been fighting himself and fighting the aspirations of women for too long to believe her. Had she imagined that he would beg her to stay? Would disclose that he needed her—he, who needed no one?

'Well, then, go, Tasha. Go and sublimate your own life and bury yourself away in some godforsaken school somewhere.'

'As opposed to burying myself away here?' she questioned quietly.

He heard the accusation and deflected it back. 'That was your choice,' he said, his voice equally quiet.

Yes. He was right. Her life there had become what she had made it. She had settled herself into a predictable groove, perhaps hoping secretly that something would rocket her out of that comfortable existence. And something had.

Perhaps Raffaele's accusation was underpinned with more truth than she had at first cared to admit—for hadn't there been a bit of her that had hoped for a storybook ending to the fairytale happiness she'd experienced in his arms?

Was this what was known as getting above your station? Had her head been turned by a hedonistic series of outings with a royal sheikh and his retinue? By her surprise ability to charm strangers at charity dinners?

She swallowed. 'How much…how much notice do you want?' she questioned.

'Go as soon as you want,' he snapped. 'I can phone an agency and have you replaced in an instant.'

Which showed her exactly how important she was to him. It was a sobering reminder, but perhaps a very necessary one. At least, she would be left with no illusions about Raffaele wanting her. 'Very well. I'll arrange it as quickly as possible.' She crossed the room to the door and when she reached it she hesitated, turning round to find him watching her, his face a mask of cold indifference. 'There's just one thing, Raffaele.'

'Yes? You'll need a reference, I imagine?'

Natasha felt dizzy, wondering if he was aware of the hurt he could wield. Was this how it all ended—nearly four years of closeness—with him offering to commit a few words about her to the page? But it hadn't been a *real* closeness they had shared, had it? More like her imagining of what closeness was. Because she didn't have any experience of it. Because she had wanted to feel close to him. But things in life didn't just happen because you wanted them to. Especially not love.

She nodded. 'Yes, obviously I'd like a reference— but I was actually thinking about Sam.'

Sam. For the first time the mask slipped—and Raffaele felt the harsh grit of regret stinging at his heart, because he had grown fond of the boy. 'What about him?' he questioned gruffly.

She opened her mouth to tell him that Sam was going to miss him, but changed her mind at the last minute. If she made too big a deal out of it wouldn't that be another accusation he might fling at her? That she was looking for a rich stepfather for her son? 'He's been very happy here,' she said. 'Thank you.'

The quiet dignity on her face made something twist inside him. '*Prego,*' he said harshly, and then turned his back on her and poured himself another drink.

CHAPTER FOURTEEN

THE house seemed empty.

The house *was* empty.

Raffaele slammed the front door behind him and listened to the silence which seemed to settle down on him like a heavy blanket. Suddenly the silence was broken by the sound of carol singers outside. He flung the door open to see a *variopinto* bunch of boys standing on his doorstep, giving it everything they had—even though their voices were lusty rather than melodic. What was it, he wondered, that made Christmas songs so unbearably poignant when sung like this rather than in the perfect massed chorus of a formal choir?

Was it because they made him think of Sam?

And Tasha?

Tasha.

He narrowed his eyes as one of the boys held up a tin and rattled it. What on earth were they doing out at this time of night?

'Do your mothers know you're here?' he demanded.

'Yes, they do!' called a voice from the end of the path, and a young girl, scarcely out of her teens, came forward. 'I asked permission for them all, and it's fine. I'm the au pair,' she added helpfully.

She looked little more than a teenager herself, he thought, and he found himself staring at her. Natasha wouldn't have been very much older than this when she'd turned up that night. But that had been a long time ago now. She had been a big part of his life in that time—more than he'd realised—was it any wonder he missed her?

'What are you collecting money for?' he demanded.

'For orphans everywhere, sir!'

He withdrew a note from his pocket and stuffed it into the tin.

'Oh, *thank* you, sir!'

'Sing "Silent Night" will you?' he said quietly, and shut the door, wondering what kind of masochistic urge had made him ask for that—because it was so unbearably heartrending that he found he couldn't listen to it all the way through.

That evening he played opera while he was getting ready to go out—the most passionate and angry he could find—and found it as satisfying as it was possible to be satisfied by anything in his current state. He was due to attend a fund-raising dinner that he simply didn't feel he could get out of, though he had told the organiser to give his second ticket to someone else.

'You won't be bringing a guest, *Signor* de Feretti?' she had asked in surprise.

'No, I won't.'

He would leave as soon as it was reasonable to do so. Going was the last thing he wanted, or needed, but his company was making a sizeable donation and he knew that his presence was important to the charity.

There was the usual rag-bag of press hanging around the red carpet, and a couple of questions were flung his way about what had happened to his

fiancée—but he gave a dismissive shake of his head
and continued up the carpet.

Inside, he saw a few people he knew and many he'd
done business with—including John Huntingdon, who
had been there the night he'd taken Tasha to a dinner.
He had a stunning and much younger woman on his
arm, as usual.

Raffaele narrowed his eyes. Was it the same one as
last time? It was hard to tell. They all looked the same.
'I think we've met before?'

She shook her spun-sugar blonde hair and not a
strand of it moved. 'Oh, no—I don't think so! I'd certainly have remembered *you*!' she trilled. 'Johnny
and I have only been dating for two and a half
weeks—haven't we, darling? Will you excuse me—
I must just toddle off to the little girls' room and
powder my nose!'

The two men watched her go.

'Your women get younger every day,' observed
Raffaele.

'Oh, they're all interchangeable!' said John cheer-
fully. 'When you've been married as many times as I
have it's as well not to foster dependence—far too expensive!' He frowned. 'But I liked that woman you
brought with you last time, though. She was *different*.'

'Tasha?' Raffaele nodded, looking at the sea of
glamour, the waves of silk and taffeta, hearing the trills
of high, rather forced laughter. 'Yes,' he said slowly.
'She was certainly different.'

He thought about her all evening—and all night,
too.

She had sent him her new address and telephone
number, accompanied by a rather sweet little note from
Sam, telling him that he was enjoying the country.

And playing football. And somehow that had hurt as much as anything else.

Raffaele stared down at the winter-bare trees in the garden. Shouldn't he drive down there—take the boy a present for the holiday period? See what Tasha was up to? Would he ever be able to rid himself of this nagging disquiet if he didn't at least *try?*

The winter day was crisp and clear, with frost icing the hedgerows and fields and bright red berries daubing the holly trees and hawthorn bushes so that the land-scape looked like a Christmas card. He drove past thatched cottages where trees twinkled in latticed bay windows and wreaths made out of ivy leaves lay hanging on glossy front doors.

The school had obviously been a stately home in a former life, because the approach to it was along a wide and winding gravel drive, through formal parkland. There was even a small lake around which padded a clutch of cold-looking ducks.

He hadn't told her he was coming. Maybe she wouldn't even be there. Why, there might even be some new man on the scene. Raffaele's mouth twisted and his leather-gloved fingers bit into the steering wheel of the powerful car. But why shouldn't she have a new man? She was in no way committed to *him.* Hadn't he made it starkly clear that he didn't want her?

An offshoot of the main drive curved away to the left, on it a sign saying Spring Cottage. As he approached he could see a figure in the garden, bending over and digging furiously and, even though the figure wore a woollen hat and unisex clothes, he knew immediately that it was Tasha.

She must have heard the sound of his car, for he saw

her stop digging and straighten up, then stab the fork into the ground and lean on it as if for support.

Natasha stared. She didn't recognise the car—was it a new one?—but she didn't need to. Nor did she need to see the shadowed face of the man who drove it. She would have recognised Raffaele anywhere—sensed him at a hundred paces on a dark night, so attuned did she always seem to be to his presence. But that's because you're a well-trained worker, she told herself forcefully. Because that's what you spent all those years doing.

She watched as he climbed out of the car and began to walk towards her. His black hair gleamed in the crisp, clear light of the winter sun and his dark cashmere coat was softly familiar. But she didn't move forward to meet him. She couldn't. Her legs felt as if they had been planted into the hard and unforgiving soil which she had been trying to break up all morning.

As he approached she could feel the increased thundering of her heart. She tried to read the expression on his dark and autocratic features, but she couldn't. She wanted to drink in his beloved face, and yet she wanted to turn away from it—as if that might protect herself from the way he was making her feel.

She tried to smile, but the icy air seemed to freeze it onto her face and, inside, she felt the cold plunge in her heart as she realised how much she had missed him.

'Hello, Raffaele.'

'Hello, Tasha.'

They stood looking at one another.

'This is a…surprise.'

He nodded. 'Yes.'

'Would you…would you like to come inside?'

As opposed to standing here freezing? he wondered. He glanced at the ground, which was lying in great, dark chunks of earth—like giant pieces of the ginger-bread she sometimes used to make.

'You're making plans for your garden?' he observed. And didn't that tell him something about her life here? She was settled. You didn't plant things unless you were planning to stick around long enough to watch them grow.

She wasn't going to tell him that gardening had become a kind of acceptable exercise and distraction therapy. That it helped break the constant thoughts of regret and the reflections which sometimes circled round and round in her head like killer-sharks who had scented fresh blood.

'I'm a bit of a novice,' she admitted. But then she remembered that last terrible conversation they'd had—which had started out with similar polite niceties and ended up with him accusing her of wanting to marry him because she had grown used to the luxury he could provide! You don't work for him anymore, she reminded herself. You don't have to be in thrall to him any longer. You're free. Even if you don't want to be. 'Raffaele, why are you here?'

The question—such an obvious one, too—completely threw him. He realised that he hadn't planned what he was going to say and that, for once in his life, his fluent and often acerbic tongue was not providing him with the perfect answer. Was that because there wasn't one?

'Weren't we going to go inside?'

Natasha shrugged. 'Okay.'

She pulled off her gloves and stuffed them in the pockets of her jacket, and he followed her inside, having to stoop his head to accommodate the low doorframe.

Once inside, she took her hat off, too—and he could see that the expensive blonde highlights had partially grown out. It should have looked ridiculous, but somehow it did not—because her hair had the natural gleam of good health, youth and vigour.

Raffaele looked around. Within the small cottage she had created the kind of homely nest which always seemed to spring up around her. There was soup cooking on the stove and drawings of Sam's pinned onto the front of the fridge. A simple little jug of twigs with some kind of furry tips had been stuck in the centre of a scrubbed wooden table, and next to the jug was an open textbook on French Grammar.

He looked at it, then at her. 'Given up on Italian, have you, Tasha?'

She was terribly afraid that she would do something stupid. Like cry. Like tell him how grey her life was now that he was no longer in it. Blinking furiously, she glared at him. Hadn't he got what he wanted—his pound of flesh and a couple of extra slices into the bargain?

'Why are you here?' she demanded.

'I've brought a Christmas present for Sam.'

'Oh.' Funny thing, human nature. You could tell yourself that you didn't want something—like Raffaele bringing up the thorny subject of their ill-fated liaison—and then find yourself bitterly disappointed when you got the very thing you'd wished for. 'That's nice.'

'He's not here?'

'No. He's out with a friend.'

'I see.' That was good. He wanted to see Sam. But

not now. Definitely not now. And then he saw the expression in her eyes—that wary look, like a cornered animal—and Raffaele knew that he couldn't continue to keep playing it safe. He was known in the business world for being a risk-taker *par excellence*—since when had he ever played safe? But this felt different—and he couldn't, for the life of him, work out why. Because he had never had to take an emotional risk before? Or because he was seriously afraid that she might send him away? He drew a deep breath. 'I miss you, Tasha,' he said simply.

Her stupid, needy heart leapt as if someone had just made a loud noise behind her, but Natasha kept her face neutral with the determination of self-protection. Did he think that she was some kind of toy? To be picked up and played with and then thrown away when he'd finished with her?

'Well, that's nice, too,' she said blandly. 'But I'm sure you must have found yourself a decent substitute by now. As I recall, you told me that all you had to do was just pick up the telephone and you'd have me replaced in an instant.'

He winced. Had he really said that? Yes, of course he had. And more. He'd been scared and he'd been angry—running from something that he'd spent his whole life running from. Imagining that all women were like the ones he'd been mixing with since he'd made his first million at an obscenely young age—grasping, greedy sexual predators. Unwilling and unable to believe that he might have discovered one who was unlike all the rest. Refusing to believe the evidence of his own eyes and his own heart.

He had convinced himself that her lowly position made her unsuitable to be his partner, but that too had been a convenient excuse to hide behind—because since when was Raffaele de Feretti ever constrained by convention?

He drew a deep breath. 'Tasha, listen to me. I miss you and I want you back,' he said.

Once she would have leapt like a starving sparrow on those few words, but Natasha had learnt a lot lately. Out of the bitter, broken nights of her heartbreak, and the tears stifled to spare her sleeping son, she had discovered a resilience and a strength which she would not let go of easily—for her sanity's sake, she couldn't afford to.

She smiled. 'There are other housekeepers, Raffaele.'

'I'm not looking for a housekeeper.'

'Really?' she said politely.

He looked at her with admiration. At the composure she wore like a mantle around her shoulders. Oh, but she was magnificent—how could he have spent so many years never realising that? Why, no other woman had ever faced him down like this—whoever would have predicted that Natasha Phillips should be the one who did? 'I am looking for a lover, *cara mia.*'

'Well, we both know there certainly isn't any shortage of candidates for that particular post!'

'But there's only one person who can properly fill it. You know there is,' he said softly. 'And that person is you.'

Of course her heart leapt again. And of course she wanted to squeal with delight and run into his arms, and kiss him, and…and…

Natasha swallowed. This wasn't some game of emotional tennis with all the unspoken power which came from being seen to win. At the moment she held the upper hand. Raffaele probably only wanted her because she had taken the initiative and left before he'd had time to grow tired of her. He was looking for a lover, and she wasn't. Well, certainly not another lover like him—who could hurt her with the kind of pain she hadn't even realised existed.

'I can't operate in your world, Raffaele,' she told him truthfully. 'I can't do stuff like you. For you, I'm just another woman. But for me—' She stopped, aware that she was saying far too much—giving herself away when to do so would be to place herself in terrible danger.

He shook his dark head, the mask gone completely now, raw passion and truth burning unashamedly from the black eyes. 'But you're not just another woman, Tasha! You're the woman I want. The house isn't the same since you've gone—'

'Then, employ someone else! Someone else who will keep it cosy and warm and have pots bubbling on the stove, so you can fool yourself into thinking it's a real home!'

'That's not what I'm talking about and you know it!' he exploded, and he glared at her, raking his hand frustratedly back through his black hair. 'My life isn't the same without you, either.'

'But you're always going abroad!' she objected. 'I was hardly a day-to-day fixture. Your life can't have changed *that* much.'

'And I always used to come back to *you*,' he said stubbornly. 'Now I don't. You can argue with me all you like, Natasha—don't you think I've done the same, myself, over and over, to try to make some sense of all this?' he demanded. 'But the fact remains that I can't. I miss you. I want you.' There was a pause. 'I love you.'

And that stopped Natasha right in her tracks—because she knew enough about Raffaele to realise that he would never say something like that unless he meant it. He might be cold and cruel sometimes, and he had a reputation for ruthlessness in the business world—but he would run a mile from emotional blackmail and from using words that weren't true.

But he had said some awful things to her. Did he think he had the right to do that? That she would just let him? Wasn't it important to show him that if he really had changed, then so had she?

'You think that you can accuse me of trying to get you to the altar,' she said quietly, 'and then just pretend it never happened? As if it's okay to hurt someone?'

He held her gaze, wanting to hold *her,* praying that in a moment she would let him and yet recognising that if they were to have any kind of future as equals in an equal partnership he must let her wield her own power. 'I wish I could take the words back, *mia bella,* but I can't. I was scared of the way you were making me feel and that made me lash out. But I'm even more scared at the thought that I might have lost you. Me, who always thought of myself as fearless!'

He could see her lips soften, and the look in her eyes was telling him that the ice she had fashioned around her heart was slowly melting away. How easy it would be to take her in his arms now, he thought, and to coax her answer from her with his lips.

But this was too important to be dictated by desire.

He played his trump card. 'The question is whether or not you can look into my eyes and tell me that you don't love me. Can you do that, Tasha? Can you honestly do that?'

She looked at him then, and the last of the fight went out of her. 'You know I can't,' she whispered. 'You've known that all along.'

Briefly, he closed his eyes and, when he opened them again, he held out his arms to her. 'Come here. Come to me, Tasha.'

She hesitated for one last, unwanted second before she went into them—like someone who had been standing frozen outside for too long. She had to bite her lip to stop the tears. 'Oh, Raffaele!'

She was shaking, and Raffaele tenderly kissed away the tears which had begun to slide down her face despite all her best intentions. He pulled her closer and held her tightly, and they stayed just like that for a long time, before he bent his mouth to her ear, his breath warm against her silken hair.

'Now, take me bed,' he whispered. 'For I will not wait a moment longer.'

'Oh, won't you?' she teased. But Natasha felt newly powerful as she led him into her tiny room, even when he took one look at her narrow bed and started laughing.

'Dios!' he exclaimed in a low voice. 'I do not think that I have slept on such a bed since I was ten!'

'I didn't think you were planning on doing much sleeping,' she said, both confident and yet strangely shy in light of the look he was now slanting over her.

'Ah, Tasha,' he whispered tenderly, and touched her cheek, brushing away a smudge of mud with the pad of his thumb. 'Look at you. *Bella. Mia bella—sempre.*' And then his voice suddenly became urgent, sharpened by the thought of what he had so nearly lost. 'Kiss me,' he demanded. 'Kiss me now.'

Rising up on tiptoe, she wound her arms around his neck and put her lips to his. He made a little groan of delight, and she found herself smiling through the passion—because she could make this incredible man moan with just a kiss.

It was too cold in the small cottage for a leisurely undressing, and their clothes ended up in a heap on the bedroom floor—Natasha's gardening trousers strewn over Raffaele's cashmere sweater. In the confined space they lay close together under the duvet, exploring each other with eyes and lips and hands as if it was the first time.

And in a way it was—certainly for Raffaele. The first time he'd ever had sex and allowed—no, *wanted*—emotion to enter into the equation. So that afterwards he was dazed, shaken, pulling her into his hard body, his embrace fierce, possessive, protective as their heartbeats stilled.

And later they lit a fire and sat on the floor in front of it while they roasted the chestnuts she'd bought yesterday at the market—and that was where Sam found them.

He took one look at them and a smile like the sun broke out on his face—then he gave a little squeal and hurled himself into Raffaele's arms.

EPILOGUE

IT HAD been—as Natasha said—the worst possible time for a man to turn up on her doorstep and tell her that he wanted to spend the rest of his life with her. She had, after all, just taken on a new job and Sam was due to start at the school after the Christmas holidays.

Raffaele had bitten back his instinctive demand that she go with him instantly, recognising that Tasha's dislike of letting anybody down was one of the things he loved about her. He gave a slow smile of contentment. There were so many!

So they had sat Sam down and asked him what *he* wanted to do—but his answer hadn't really helped, since he'd told them that he didn't care where they lived just as long as the three of them were together.

And, in that moment, Natasha had recognised that Raffaele was a hugely influential force in her son's life— that he was a father to Sam in almost every sense of the word. Sam had been missing him, too, she realised.

In the end they had gone to see the headteacher and explained their predicament.

She had looked at Natasha with a stern expression. 'I can't say I'm not disappointed,' she'd said. 'Because I am.'

Then she'd looked at Raffaele. 'And I can't say I'm surprised, either,' she'd added softly, her face softening.

Raffaele had smiled. 'Thank you. But we've decided that we'd like Sam to come to school here, anyway. We're going to buy a house nearby.'

'Oh, you *are?* Oh, that's wonderful!'

The head had beamed and sent for tea, and afterwards Raffaele told Tasha that he had felt about ten years old, sitting in that study! Once, he would have gone to hell and back rather than make such an admission. But that was one of the greatest things about love—it liberated you in so many ways.

And with the whole world to choose from the two of them had fallen in love with this corner of the English countryside. It was close enough to a major airport for Raffaele to take trips abroad—even though the lure of travel was palling and, for the first time in his life, he could see the attraction of being successful enough to delegate and stay home more. It was also close enough for him to travel into London as often as he wanted—he could do what many other businessmen did these days, which was to fly in by helicopter.

They had found a big old house in a decent-sized plot—with a garden big enough for Sam to have an entire junior football match on if he wanted to. There were stables for the horses that Natasha had always had a yearning to ride, and a flint-walled kitchen garden which got just enough summer sun to provide the white peaches which Raffaele had adored when he was a little boy. They might not grow as big nor quite as sweet as those remembered fruits—but growing them would be a symbol of something he had found with Tasha. Roots.

It was the kind of house that neither of them had ever had but both had longed for. It was a home, in fact. Their first real home.

'Home is where the heart is,' said Natasha, as he touched his lips to hers before carrying her over the threshold and continuing straight upstairs towards their bedroom. 'Corny, but true.'

He could feel his own heart's thundering beat and his body's urgent need to join with hers. 'Then my home is with you, *mia bella,*' he said softly. '*Per sempre.*'

Natasha's Italian had come on well enough for her to know that this meant *always*—but even if she hadn't spoken a word of the language she would have understood what he meant.

She could read it in his eyes.

Shameless

ANN MAJOR

Ann Major lives in Texas, USA, with her husband of many years, and is the mother of three grown-up children. She has a master's degree and is a former English teacher.

Ann loves to write; she considers her ability to do so a gift. Her hobbies include hiking in the mountains, sailing, ocean-kayaking and playing the piano. But most of all she enjoys her family.

This book is dedicated to Ella Mae Lescuer
for all her hard work.

Prologue

Mezcaya, Central America
El Jefe terrorist compound

Lt. Col. Phillip Westin, burly ex-Marine, wasn't dead.

Hell. He almost wished he was. Solitary confinement—it made you crazy.

Groggily, he chafed at the ropes binding his wrists and ankles. Beneath the restraints his skin burned from too much rubbing.

He tried to roll over but he was so weak he could only lie facedown in the dark, gasping. The windowless walls seemed to close in upon him. He wanted to scream…or worse…to weep. One minute he was burning up, the next he was shivering and whimpering on his cot like a baby. The cramps in his legs and arms knifed through him constantly.

Where the hell was he? *Remember! Try to remember.* His thoughts were slow and tortured. It took him a while to realize that he was lying on a dirty canvas cot deep in The Cave that served as the dungeon underneath *Fortaleza de la Fortuna.* The *fortaleza* was a terrorist compound in Mezcaya run by a particularly dangerous group of thugs who went by the name El Jefe.

Westin had been captured a few weeks ago shortly after he'd run Jose Mendoza, one of the terrorist ringleaders, off a mountain road and killed him. Too bad Mendoza's illegitimate son, Xavier Gonzalez, didn't have a forgiving nature.

Westin blinked but couldn't see a thing. The damned dungeon was blacker than the inside of an ape's behind.

His head throbbed where Xavier had smacked him with a rifle butt yesterday. His throat was dry. He was thirsty as hell. Dehydrated probably.

Xavier and his unkempt dirty bunch of thugs had captured him and beaten him senseless and then gleefully trussed him like a pig for slaughter.

He was going to die. At dawn. A single bullet to the head, the final coup de grace. An hour ago Xavier and a couple of short, teenage captors reeking of body odor had strutted inside The Cave like a bunch of bantam cocks in a barnyard and kicked him with their black, muddy combat boots.

"Gringo. ¿Cómo estás?" They'd prodded him with their assault rifles and made cruel jokes in Spanish rather than in their Mezcayan dialect. They'd flipped coins to see who'd get lucky enough to pull the trigger. Xavier, the youngest and the most lethally handsome, had slid a .45 out of a black holster and dried it off on his sleeve.

"You kill my father, so you die, *gringo.* You have no right to be in my country."

"Your drug and gun money was making inroads in *my* town, *bastardo*. *My* town."

The kid was dark with a permanent Mezcayan tan. With one brown hand he'd lifted a cigarette to his pretty mouth; with the other he'd carefully centered the cold barrel on Phillip's forehead.

"*Your* town?"

Xavier's eyes were scarily irrational in his pretty-boy face. His finger had pulled back the trigger ever so slightly. "Bang. Bang, *gringo*. *Your* town is going to be my town."

Before Phillip could argue, the thick, acrid cigarette smoke from the kid's cigarette had made him wretch. Hell, maybe puking up his guts had saved him. Instead of firing his gun, Xavier had burst out into hysterical laughter and shrieked, "*Cobarde*. Coward."

Then the *bastardo* had danced a little jig.

"*Tengo sed*. I'm thirsty," Phillip had said.

Xavier had smiled that pretty smile. "So—drink this!" He'd pitched the cigarette into the vomit in front of Phillip's face.

Bastardos. His death was a game to them. Phillip Westin, ex-Marine, had been handpicked for the Alpha Force. His usual style was spit-and-polish perfect.

He wouldn't be a pretty corpse. He wouldn't even rate a body bag in this hellhole compound that was hidden deep in Mezcayan mountains and rain forest.

There'd be no military honors at his funeral. No funeral, period. No beautiful woman to weep over his grave back home in south Texas.

Suddenly a blond goddess, no a witch, seemed to float above him in the misty black.

Oh, God…. Just when he was weak, wet, shaking and puking with fear, he had to think of *her*—the icy, trampy

witch, who'd walked out on him. Usually, the witch was
satisfied to haunt his dreams. When he was awake, he
was disciplined enough to keep his demons and witches
at bay.

But he was weak and cold...so cold and feverish a
spasm shook him...and so scared about dying he could
think only of her.

Anger slammed him when her sulky, smoky voice began to sing the love song she'd written about their
doomed relationship.

He jerked at his ropes, and to his surprise they loosened just a bit. "Go away! Leave me alone!" he yelled
into the steamy darkness.

The perverse phantom draped her curvy body against
the black wall and sang louder.

Nobody but you/Only you.

"Shut up," he growled even as every cell in his body
began to quiver as he fisted and unfisted his fingers in
an attempt to free his hands.

*I had to say goodbye...but everywhere I go...there's
nobody in my heart...only you....*

Her husky voice had his head pounding. He dug his
fingernails into his palms. Suddenly to his surprise, he
jerked his right hand free of the ropes. "Damn you, shut
the hell up!"

And yet I had to say goodbye, the witch crooned.

"Tramp! You're just a one-hit wonder. You know
that, don't you?"

That shut her up, but she didn't go away. Instead, that
sad, vulnerable expression that could tie him in knots came
into her eyes, which shone brilliantly in the dark. Her
golden hair fell in silken coils around her slim shoulders.

Hell. She looked like a little lost sex kitten in need of
a home and a warm bed. His home. His bed.

Oh, God, all she ever had to do was look at him like that and all he wanted to do was to hold her and to protect her and to make love to her. What would he give to have her one more time before he died?

Everything—

His gut cramped as he clawed his cot with his free hands. He remembered exactly how her hair smelled, how her skin smelled, how her blue eyes flashed with tears if he got too domineering. She'd had a fearsome talent for gentling him.

Escape. He had to escape.

His hands shook. He closed his eyes and tried not to remember how small she was or how perfectly she'd fit him.

Think of something else! Like getting out of here!

But when he swallowed, he tasted her. One taste, and he was as hard as a brick.

Somehow he got the ropes around his ankles loose, but when he tried to stand, the black walls spun and he fell back onto the cot. Weak as he was, his groin pulsed with desire. Hell. The proximity of death was the best aphrodisiac.

Damn Celeste Cavanaugh. He'd asked her to be his wife, to marry him. What a damn fool he'd been to do that. Hell, he'd picked her up in a bar. No. Damn it. He'd rescued her from a bar brawl. She'd been a nobody from the gutter, the prettiest, sexiest little nobody in the whole world with a voice like an angel.

He'd lifted her out of that life, given her everything, and treated her like a lady. She'd moved in with him and they'd played at love and marriage. Why the hell hadn't she bothered to tell him about her ridiculous ambition to be a country-western star? Why hadn't she at least given him a chance to understand it?

As soon as she'd gotten on her feet, she'd run to Vegas with another man. Phillip had come home from a dangerous mission in the Middle East where he'd gone to rescue his buddies. His homecoming had been delayed because he'd been captured and had had a narrow escape. But once home again, he'd thrown his seabag down at the door, stalked through the ranch house, calling her name. God, all those days and nights when he'd been a hostage trapped in that cell in the Middle East, he'd been burning up for her. Just like now.

She'd left him a letter on his pillow.

"I met a man, who's going to get me an audition with a world-famous producer, Larry Martin. I'll call you from Vegas." She'd said her stage name was Stella Lamour.

There had been more letters in the mailbox from Stella. After he'd read and reread those letters, every word carving his heart out, something had died inside him. Maybe his feelings.

Forget her.

But he couldn't. Seven years later, she still starred in all his dreams.

When he died down here, she wouldn't even know. The *bastardos* would sling his bloody corpse into the jungle, and he'd rot. In this rain and heat and mud, he'd be fertilizer in less than a month.

You're an ex-Marine. Forget her.

When he tried to stand again, he passed out and dreamed he was back home in Texas dancing with her at the Lone Star Country Club while his Marine buddies cheered and clapped.

He regained consciousness to heat that was as thick and dark as a sauna, to no-see-ums eating him alive. To explosions and heavy boots stomping down some corridor.

Dawn. Time to die.

Was there a weepy, pink light sifting through the single crack in the ceiling or was he hallucinating again?

Shouts in Spanish were followed by more heavy footsteps. Then the lock on the heavy door clicked. The door banged. Flashlights danced in the dark, blinding him.

"Xavier?" Westin squinted. Terror gripped him like a fist. He felt so weak and vulnerable he muttered a quick prayer.

Cobarde. Xavier's contempt still stung.

In those last fleeting seconds before certain death, Phillip's life flashed in front of him in neon color—his lonely childhood in his mother's Houston mansion with all those rooms that echoed as a solitary little boy walked through them in search of love.

Nobody had ever wanted him...until Patricia, his college sweetheart. For a time she'd seemed so perfect, but in the end, she hadn't wanted him enough to understand his determination to see the world and become a Marine.

Neither had Celeste. Both his loves had left him.

The flashlight zeroed in on his face, blinding him again. What was the use? He held up his hands in surrender. All he said was, "If you're going to kill me, just be done with it."

Cobarde.

"Not tonight, sir," said a familiar respectful voice that slammed Westin back to his days in the Marines, back to the Gulf War. Phillip's eyelids stung when he tried to stand. Once again his legs crumpled beneath his weight. The lights spun and he nearly fainted.

"Friends," came that familiar, husky voice that made Phillip's eyes go even hotter.

"Tyler...."

Westin blinked. Ty Murdoch, his handsome face painted black and green, his night-vision glasses dangling against his broad chest, towered above him like a warrior god.

"Tyler—"

Phillip was trying to stand but was falling again when Tyler's strong arms grabbed him and slung him over his broad back in a fireman's lift.

"You're going home," a woman said.

"Celeste?"

Before the beautiful woman could answer, Phillip fainted.

He was going home. Home to Celeste.

When he opened his eyes, they were beyond the compound, hunkering low in the tangle of bushes on the edge of the lavish lawns. Dimly he was aware of the pretty woman cradling his head in her lap.

"Celeste?"

He was sweating and freezing at the same time.

An eternity later he looked up and saw a chopper coming in hot, kicking up dust and gravel before settling on the ground.

A rock that felt like a piece of hot metal gouged Phillip's cheek.

"Damn."

Then Ty was back lifting him, up...up...into the chopper. They took off in a hurry. They were going home.

Home to Celeste.

He shut his eyes and saw Celeste...blond and pretty, her eyes as blue as a Texas sky. She was crying, her cheeks glistening. The image, even if it was false, was better than a funeral.

Phillip's hand shook as he lifted the razor. He paused, staring at the gaunt face with the slash across the cheek. It had been seven days since the rescue, and he was still as weak as a baby.

When the infirmary door slammed open, he jumped like a scared girl, panicking at the sound of boots because they reminded him of Xavier. The razor fell into the sink with a clatter.

In the mirror, the dark-haired stranger with the hollowed-out silver eyes was pathetic. By comparison the darkly handsome man who strode up behind him was disgustingly robust.

"Mercado?"

Ricky flashed his daredevil grin. "Good to see you up and about."

"Yeah." Westin had to grip the sink with tight fingers so he wouldn't fall. No way was he walking back to the hospital bed. No way would he let Mercado gloat at how wobbly he was.

"After this, you'd better lay low, *amigo.* You stirred up a hornet's nest."

"You think I don't know that."

"El Jefe's big. And not just down here. They're well connected in Texas."

"Why the hell do you think I came down—"

"These guys won't give up. They'll be gunning for you and yours."

"There is no yours. She left me, remember." Phillip shut up. He didn't want to talk about *her.* Still, Mercado was one of the few who knew about Celeste. Most of his buddies believed he'd never gotten over his first love,

Patricia, the classy girl he'd loved in college—the proper girl. It was better that way, better not to cry on their shoulders about a trashy singer he'd picked up in a bar and been stupid enough to fall for.

"Yeah, and Celeste's the reason you've had a death wish for seven damn years."

"Shut up."

"You're forty-one, *amigo.*"

"You make that sound old."

"Too old for this line of work."

"This was personal. You know that. The bastards were moving into Mission Creek. They were using kids to run guns. Kids—"

"Why don't you go back to your ranch? Find a nice, churchgoing girl, get married and hatch some rug rats."

"Sounds like fun. What about you? You straight? Or are you gonna run arms for the family? What the hell were you doing down there?"

Mercado scowled. "Saving your ass."

"You had some help."

"What does it take? A declaration written in blood. Like I told you—I'm straight."

"You'd better be."

His face and eyes dark with pain, Mercado shut up and stared at the floor. Phillip felt instant remorse. "Ty told me you were useful in the Mezcaya rescue," Phillip admitted.

"I'm surprised he said—"

"He did. Thanks. I owe you...for what you did for Ty. And for me."

Suddenly Westin was no longer in the mood to question the character of a man who'd helped save him. The heated exchange had left him so weak, Mercado's dark face began to swirl. His fingers couldn't seem to hold on to the sink. No way could he shave.

"Oh, God," he muttered as the gray tiles rushed up to meet him.

Mercado lunged, barely catching him before he fell.

"Find that nice girl," Mercado muttered. "Lean on my arm, old buddy, and we'll get you back to bed."

"Hell. I don't go for nice girls. I like 'em hot...and shameless."

"Maybe it's time for a change of pace...in your old age."

"Old age?" Stung, Phillip almost howled. The truth was, a ninety-year-old was stronger than he was. Oh, God, why was it such a damn struggle to put one foot in front of the other? When he finally made it to the bed, he was gasping for every breath. He let go of Mercado and fell backward.

His head slammed into the pillow. Even so, they both managed a weak laugh.

"Get the hell out of here, Mercado."

"Forget shameless. Find that churchgoing girl, old man."

Mercado waved jauntily and saluted. Then the door banged behind him and he was gone.

One

Stella Lamour grabbed her guitar and glided out of the storeroom Harry let her use as a dressing room. After all, a star had to have a dressing room. She tried to ignore the fact that the closet was stacked with cases of beer, cocktail napkins and glasses…and that the boxy, airless room gave her claustrophobia when she shut the door.

Some dressing room…. Some star….

As Stella approached the corner to make her entrance, she cocked her glossy head at an angle so that her long yellow hair rippled flirtily down her slim, bare back. At thirty-two, she was still beautiful, and she knew it. Just as she knew how to use it.

"Fake it till you make it, baby," Johnny, her ex-manager, always said.

Fake it? For how much longer? In this business and this city, beauty was everything, at least for a woman.

Every day younger, fresher girls poured into Vegas, girls with big dreams just like hers. Johnny signed them all on, too.

Hips swaying, Stella moved like a feral cat, her lush, curvy, petite body inviting men to watch, not that there were many to do so tonight. There was a broad-shouldered hunk at the bar. He gave her the once-over. Her slanting, thickly-lashed, blue eyes said, "You can look, but keep your distance, big boy—this is my territory."

Johnny Silvers, her no-good ex-manager, who liked fast cars and faster women, had taught Stella how to move, how to walk, how to hold her head, how to look like a star—how to fake it.

Some star. The closest she'd come was to warm the crowd up before the real star came on stage.

Now she'd sunk to Harry's.

Harry's was a dead-end bar in downtown Vegas, a hangout for middle-aged retreads, divorcées, widowers, alcoholics, burned-out gamblers—a dimly lit refuge for the flotsam and jetsam who couldn't quite cut it in real life and were too broke to make their play in the hectic, brightly lit casinos on the strip. They were searching for new lives and new loves. Not that they could do more in Harry's than drown their sorrows and take a brief time-out before they resumed their panicky quests.

In a few more years, I'll be one of them, Stella thought as she grimly shoved a chair aside on her way to the bar.

Her slinky black dress was so tight across the hips, she had to stand at her end of the bar when she finally reached it. She'd put on a pound, maybe two. Not good, not when the new girls kept getting younger and slimmer.

Mo, the bartender, nodded hello and handed her her Saturday night special—water with a juicy lime hanging on the edge of her glass. She squeezed the lime, swirled the water in the glass. Wetting her lips first, she took a long, cool sip.

Aside from Mo and a single, shadowy male figure at the other end of the bar, Harry's was empty tonight. There wasn't a single retread. So, the only paying customer was the wide-shouldered hunk she'd seen come in earlier. She knew men. He was no retread.

There was a big arms-dealer conference in Vegas. For some reason, she imagined he might be connected to the conference. He was hard-edged. Lean and tall and trim. He had thick brown hair. She judged he was around thirty. Something about him made her think of the way Phillip looked in his uniform. Maybe it was the man's air of authority.

Just thinking about Phillip made her remember another bar seven years ago when she'd been a raw kid, singing her heart out, not really caring where she was as long as she could sing. She'd gotten herself in a real jam that night. Lucky for her, or maybe not so lucky as it turned out, Phillip Westin had walked in.

Just the memory of Phillip in that brawl—he'd been wonderful—made her pulse quicken again. It had been four drunks against one Marine, but a Marine whose hands were certified weapons. In the end Phillip had carried her out to his motorcycle, and they'd roared off in the dark. He'd been so tender and understanding that first night, so concerned about her. What had impressed her the most about him was that he hadn't tried to seduce her. They'd talked all night in a motel and had only ended up in bed a couple of days later.

The sex had been so hot, they'd stayed in that motel

bed for a week, making wild, passionate love every day and every night, even eating meals in bed, until finally they were so exhausted, they could only lie side by side laughing because they felt like a pair of limp noodles. When they'd come up for air, she'd said she'd never be able to walk again. And he'd said he'd never get it up again. She'd taken that as a challenge and proved him wrong. Oh, so deliciously wrong. Afterward, he'd asked her to marry him.

She'd said, "I don't even know you."

And he said, "Just say maybe."

"Maybe," she'd purred.

Maybe had been good enough for Phillip, at least for a while. He'd been living on his elderly uncle's ranch alone and supervising the cattle operation because his uncle, who had been ill, was in a nursing home. Everything had been wonderful between Celeste and Phillip until suddenly Phillip had received a call and had gone off on a mission. Alone on the ranch, she'd gotten scared and had felt abandoned and rejected just as she had when her parents had died.

If the days had been long without Phillip, the sleepless nights had seemed even longer. She hadn't known what to do with herself. She wasn't good at waiting or at being alone.

Then a pair of grim-faced Marines had turned up at the door and said Phillip was missing in action. She'd been terrified he was dead—just like her parents. A few weeks later Johnny had driven into town, promising he'd make her a star, saying Larry Martin, *the* Larry Martin wanted to produce her. He'd convinced her to go with him to Vegas. The rest was history.

All of a sudden her throat got scratchier. She knew

better than to think about the past. She swallowed, but the dry lump in her throat wouldn't go down.

How could she sing…tonight? To a man who reminded her of Phillip.

She asked Mo for another glass of water, but the icy drink only made her throat worse.

Did it matter any more how well she sang? This was Harry's. There was only one customer. She picked up her guitar and headed for the stage.

Just when she'd thought she couldn't sink any lower, she'd lost her job two weeks ago and the only guy Johnny could convince to hire her was Harry, a loser buddy of his.

"I can't work at a lowlife place like this," she'd cried when Johnny had brought her here and a cockroach had skittered across her toe.

"You gotta take what you can get, baby. That's life."

"I'm Stella Lamour. I've done TV. You promised I'd be a star."

"You've got to deliver. You're just a one-hit wonder. Wake up and smell the roses, baby."

She'd kicked the roach aside. "All I smell is stale beer."

"My point exactly, baby. You gotta fake it till you make it."

"I'm tired of faking it and not making it. You're fired, Johnny."

"Baby— Stella Lamour, the one-hit wonder." He'd laughed at her. "All right. Fire me. But take the job, baby—if you wanna eat."

She'd taken the job, but every night it was harder to pretend she would ever make it as a singer.

Now, Stella turned on the mike and got a lot of back

feed. When she adjusted it, and it squealed again, the broad-shouldered man at the bar jammed his big hands over his ears but edged closer. Again, the way he moved, reminded her so much of Phillip, her knees went a little weak and her pulse knocked against her rib age. Oh, Phillip....

Don't think about the past or Phillip. Just sing.

Why bother? Nobody's listening.

"I'll start off with a little number I wrote," she purred to Mo and the man. "Back in Texas."

The customer stared at her intently as if he liked what he saw.

"I wrote this seven years ago before I came to Vegas." She fiddled with the mike some more, and then she began to sing, "Nobody but you/Only you/And yet I had to say goodbye..."

She forgot she was in Harry's. She was back on the ranch on Phillip's front porch where the air was hot and dusty, where the long summer nights smelled of warm grass and mesquite, and the nights buzzed with the music of cicadas.

"I thought love cost too much," she purred in the smoky voice she'd counted on to make her famous, to make her somebody like her mother had promised. "But I didn't know."

Then she realized she was in Harry's, and her failures made her voice quiver with regret. "Everywhere I go/There's nobody but you in my heart/Only you."

Somehow she felt so weak all she could do was whisper the last refrain. "And yet I had to say goodbye."

Phillip was the only good man, the only really good thing that had ever happened to her. And she'd walked out on him. Big mistake. Huge.

She'd wanted to make it big to prove to Phillip she

was as good as he was…that she wasn't just some cheap tart he'd picked up in a bar and brought home and bedded…that she was somebody…a real somebody he could be proud of.

She frowned when she heard a car zoom up the back alley. Oh, dear. That sounded like Johnny's Corvette sportscar. The last thing she needed was Johnny on her case. Sure enough, within seconds, the front door banged open and Johnny raced through it on his short legs. His thick, barrel chest was heaving. His eyes bulged out of their deep, pouchy sockets. The poor, little dear looked like a fat, out-of-shape rabbit the hounds were chasing, but his florid face lit up when he saw her.

"Baby!"

Oh, no. He definitely wanted something!

"You and I are through," she mouthed.

Johnny lit a cigarette. Then his short, fat legs went into motion again and carried him across the bar toward her.

He was a heavy smoker, so running wasn't easy. When he reached the stage, he gasped in fits and starts, which made his voice even more hoarse and raspy than usual.

"Take a break, baby…" Pant. Wheeze. "I've got to talk to you." Puff. Puff.

Fanning his smoke out of her face, she turned off the mike and followed him to her end of the bar.

Johnny ordered a drink and belted it down. He ordered a second one and said, "Put some booze in this one, you cheap son of a—"

"Johnny, you can't talk to Mo like—"

Mo slammed the second drink down so hard it sloshed all over Johnny's cigarette. Mo was big. A lot bigger than Johnny. He had a bad temper, too. His face had darkened the way it did when he had an impossible customer and had to play bouncer. Stella was afraid he'd pound Johnny.

"Easy, Mo," she whispered, wondering why she was bothering to defend Johnny, who'd brought her so much bad luck.

Mo whirled and went to tend to his other customer.

Johnny lit another cigarette. "Thanks, babe." Wheeze. Gulp. "I need money fast."

"I don't get paid till Monday." She clamped a hand over her mouth. "It's none of your business when I get paid."

"I got you this great new gig. Your ship's about to come in. You gotta help me, baby."

"That's what you said when you stole my royalties to buy those stolen tires and to pay your—"

"How was I— No-o-o. Baby!" Puff. Wheeze. "I borrowed a little cash to pay a few gambling debts. That's all! Honest! Now a couple of unreasonable guys are making insane demands on a poor guy trying to make his top girl a star—"

"I'm not your girl anymore!"

"Are you going to help me or not?" He was so charged with fear, his eyes stuck out on stems.

When would she ever learn? She hated herself for being such a softie.

"How much?"

"You've gotta big heart. You can't say that about many girls in Vegas."

Just as she slid her fingers into her bra and pulled out what little money she had, the front door banged open and two men in black, who instantly made her think of snakes—and she hated snakes—oozed inside.

"You'd better pay me back this time," she said.

"Sure, baby."

When the snakes yelled Johnny's name, he grabbed the money and ran out the back way, screaming, "She has it."

The two men raced past her after him. There was some sort of scuffle. Bodies thudded against a wall. The men shouted. Johnny squealed in pain. Then his super-charged, fancy black Corvette drove away fast, tires spinning gravel.

She was asking Mo for more water when the two snakes slithered quietly up behind her, grabbed her arms and shoved her against the bar.

"Hey, take your hands off me!"

Both of them had black, beady eyes. When their gazes drifted up and down her body, her heart raced.

"Johnny says you and he…. He says you've got our money." The man who held her had olive skin, a big nose and lots of pimples.

"I don't know what you're talking about." She began to shake. Everybody in Vegas knew guys like this didn't play around.

"Nero has methods to freshen a girl's memory," the taller snake said. "We're in the collection business. We specialize in gambling debts. Our customers lose. They borrow. If they don't want to pay, we motivate them. End of story."

The taller man was potato-pale. Gold-rimmed glasses pinched his nose as he stared at her breasts. "Name's The Pope. You're cute. You could work some of Johnny's debt off…if you get my drift."

"How much money does he owe you?" she whispered. Her heart was really knocking now.

The Pope named a preposterous sum that made her gasp.

"Johnny says you rolled the dice for him," The Pope said. "He says he gave you our money. Pay us, and we're out of here."

"I don't have it."

"Then get it. If you don't, we hurt you. Understand, sexy girl?" Nero said, pinching her arms.

She shivered. Oh, dear. They weren't kidding. Her eyes flew to the front door and to the back. She had to run. But before she took even one step, they read her mind.

"Oh, no you don't—" Nero grabbed her by the hair, intending to haul her out the door with him, when she bit his hand and then screamed for help.

On a howl of pain, he let her go. Since The Pope was blocking the exit, she ran toward the ladies' room. Nero would have chased, but the wide-shouldered customer who reminded her of Phillip had sprung from the bar, stuck out a booted foot and tripped him.

"The lady said to let her go," said a hard voice as the short, dark thug went sprawling into chairs and tables that toppled on top of him.

"Stay out of this. The witch owes us money."

It was an exciting conversation. She would have loved to have stayed and listened, but it didn't seem smart to stick around. There was a window in the ladies' room just big enough for her to squeeze out of.

Once she made it to the ladies' room, the shouts from the bar got louder. Mo must have tackled the other guy.

"You a cop?" The Pope yelled.

"He's got cops' eyes. He moves like a cop, too—"

"We gotta blow this joint."

"What about her?"

"Later—"

As Stella stood on the toilet and opened the window,

she heard gunshots pop in the bar. In a panic, she shoved her guitar through the window. Then she scrambled out of it herself, only to lose her hold on the window frame and fall so hard, she nearly broke her ankle.

She got to her feet, straightened her ripped gown and then fluffed her hair. When she reached down to get her guitar, it wasn't there.

A large hand curved out of the darkness, and she jumped about a mile and then moaned in pain because she'd landed with all her weight on her bad ankle.

"Easy. I won't hurt you."

The big, handsome guy from the other end of the bar, the one who'd tripped Nero, held out her guitar.

She grabbed it and hugged it to her chest.

"Need a ride?" he asked in a hard, precise voice.

"As a matter of fact—" She blurted out her address.

"You can't go home. Can't stay in Vegas, either. Not with those guys after you. They'll kill you…or worse."

She gulped in a breath and then followed him to a sedan that was parked in the shadows. "But—"

"Do you think those guys are going to quit if you can't give them what they want?"

She swallowed.

"Honey, they know where you live."

"You're scaring me."

After he helped her into the front seat of the vehicle, he said, "Didn't your mama ever teach you never to ride with strangers?"

"I didn't have a mama."

He shut her door. "Everybody has a mama."

When he slid behind the wheel, she said, "I was five when she died."

"Too bad." He started the engine and revved it.

"You don't know the half of it. Foster homes. Cinderella. The whole bit. Only without the prince. But when I was little, I used to sing with my mama on stage. She told me I was going to be a star. And…and I believed her. But she died….'' Her voice shook. "On a cheerier note, if you're a bad stranger, I can always beat you up with my guitar.''

He didn't laugh as they sped away. "That'd be a waste of a good guitar.''

"Thanks for saving me.''

"So, where to?''

"The bus station.''

"And then?'' he persisted.

"Texas.'' She was surprised by her answer. *Texas?*

"Is that home?''

"Not exactly. But I have an old boyfriend with a hero complex.'' Phillip—he was the only man she knew tough enough to save her if those guys ever caught up with her. Oh, dear. Phillip—

"The poor sucker your song's about. You left him, didn't you?''

"He'll still help me.'' He would. She knew he would.

"What if he's married?''

"He's not.''

"And you know this how?''

She stared out her window at the bright glitter of Vegas. She wasn't about to admit she'd kept tabs by reading the Mission Creek newspaper online, so she bit her lip and said nothing.

When they got to the bus station, he got out with her and carried her guitar to the ticket window for her. Pulling out his wallet, he said, "You gave your sleazy manager all your money, didn't you—''

"No, but I left my purse in my, er, dressing room.''

He counted out five one-hundred-dollar bills.

"I don't need nearly that much."

"It's a loan." He handed her his card.

"I'll pay it back. All of it. I really will...."

His face was grim as she read his card. "A.T.F. You're A.T.F." Her voice softened when she read his name. "Cole Yardley."

"Good luck," was all he said before he strode away.

"Thank you, Mr. Yardley," she whispered after him. "Thank you." Although he'd refused to open up, something about him made her long for Phillip.

She broke the first hundred and bought a one-way ticket to Mission Creek, Texas, where Phillip now lived. Phillip's uncle had died, and he'd inherited the ranch and made it his home.

Oh, Phillip—

Two

Mission Creek, Texas

It was 10:00 a.m. when the bus driver roared to a stop in front of the café in a swirl of dust under wide, hot, Texas skies. Not that the slim little girl behind him in what looked to be her mama's sophisticated black evening dress noticed. She was curled into a tight ball, her pretty face squashed against the back of her seat cushion.

Stella jumped when the driver shook her gently and said, "Mission Creek."

Not Stella anymore, she reminded herself drowsily. Not in Mission Creek. Here, she was Celeste Cavanaugh, a nobody.

"Didn't mean to scare you," the driver said as she rubbed her eyes and blinked into the white glare.

"Thanks. Give me a minute, okay?"

"Take your time. It's hot out there," he warned.

July. In Texas. Of course it was hot.

"No hotter than Vegas," she replied.

From the frying pan into the fire, she thought as she got up, gathered her guitar and stumbled out of the bus in her low-cut black dress and strappy high heels. For a long moment she just stood there in the dust and the baking heat. Then lifting her torn skirt up so it wouldn't drag in the dirt, she slung her guitar over her bare shoulder. Cocking her head at a saucy angle, she fought to pretend she was a star even though all she was doing was limping across an empty parking lot toward the café that was Mission Creek's answer for a bus station.

The historic square with its southwestern flair hadn't changed much. With a single glance she saw the quaint courthouse, the bank, the post office and the library. She was back in Mission Creek, the town she'd almost chosen to be her home. She was back—not that anybody knew or cared.

Inside the café, she hobbled to the ladies' room before she selected a table. It was a bad feeling to look in the mirror and hate the person she saw. The harsh fluorescent lighting combined with the white glare from the bathroom window revealed the thirty-hour bus ride's damage and way more reality than Celeste could face this early. Shutting her eyes, she splashed cold water on her cheeks and throat.

What would Phillip think when he saw her? Her eyeliner was smudged. What was left of her glossy red lipstick had caked and dried in the middle of her bottom lip. Her long yellow hair was greasy and stringy. She didn't have a comb, but she licked off her lipstick.

When she was done, she had a bad taste in her mouth, so she gargled and rinsed with lukewarm tap water. Oh, how she longed for a shower and a change of underwear and clothes.

Just when she'd thought she couldn't sink lower than Harry's, here she was at the Mission Creek Café in a ripped evening gown with a sprained ankle. Mission Creek Café. Phillip had brought her to lunch here once. The café was noted for its down-home country cooking. Oh, how Phillip had adored the biscuits.

Carbs. Celeste hadn't approved of him eating so many carbs.

She glanced at her reflection again. She was thirty-two. There were faint lines beneath her eyes. Faint.

Seven years later, and she was right back where she started. Still... Someday...

"I'm going to be big! A star! I am!"

A girl could dream, couldn't she?

The smell of biscuits wafted in the air.

Biscuits! In between dreaming, a girl had to eat. She was starving suddenly, and she had nearly four hundred dollars tucked snugly against her heart—more than enough for breakfast. After all, this wasn't the Ritz in Paris. This was Texas where carbs, and lots of them, the greasier the better, came cheap.

Celeste found a table in the back and ordered. When her plump waitress with the mop of curly brown hair returned with platters of eggs and mountains of hash browns and biscuits slathered in butter, Celeste decided to work up her nerve to ask about Phillip.

"More coffee, please," Celeste began.

"Sure, honey."

As the waitress poured, Celeste bit her lip and stared out the window. Not that there was much of a view other than the highway and a mesquite bush and a prickly pear or two.

Celeste could feel the woman's eyes on her. Still, she managed to get out her question in a small, shy voice.

"Does Phillip Westin still hang out at the Lazy W?"

The coffee pouring stopped instantly. "Who's asking?" The friendly, motherly voice had sharpened. The woman's black eyes seared her like lasers.

Celeste cringed a little deeper into her booth. "Can't a girl ask a simple question?"

"Not in this town, honey. Everybody's business is everybody's business."

"And I had such high hopes the town would mature."

"So—who's asking about Phillip?"

"Just an old friend."

"Westin has lots of lady friends."

"He does?" Celeste squeaked, and then covered her mouth.

"He meets them out at those fancy dances at the club."

"The Lone Star Country Club?"

"You been there?"

"A time or two."

"What's your name, honey?"

"Forget it."

"You're mighty secretive all of a sudden."

"Last I heard that wasn't a crime," Celeste said.

The waitress's smile died and she scurried off to the kitchen in a huff. Watching the doors slam, Celeste felt morose with guilt. She was running from killers, deliberately putting Phillip in danger. He'd moved on, made friends with real ladies at that fancy club he'd joined as soon as he'd moved here permanently.

He was wealthy. She was the last thing from a lady, the last thing he needed in his orderly life.

Her appetite gone, she set her fork down with a clatter.

What was the matter with her? Why had she argued with the waitress like that? It was just that she felt so lonely and scared and desperate, and so self-conscious about how cheap she looked. And then the woman had told her Phillip had lots of classy girlfriends.

Oh, why had she come here? Why had she ever thought— If she was smart, she'd catch the next bus to San Antonio. Then she'd lose herself in the big city.

Celeste should have known that wouldn't be the end of her exchange with the waitress. Not in a nosy little town like Mission Creek. Before her eggs had time to congeal, the plump woman was back with a cordless telephone and a great big gottcha smile.

"He's home," the waitress said.

"You didn't call him—"

The waitress winked at her and grinned slyly as she listened to Phillip.

"Oh, no…. You didn't. Hang up."

"She's got long yellow hair. It's sort of dirty. And a low-cut black dress with a rip up the left thigh. Nice legs, though. Sensational figure. And a great big shiny guitar that has a booth seat all to itself." She hesitated. "Yes, a guitar! And…and she's hurt… Her ankle…." Another pause. "What?" Again there was a long silence.

Celeste stared out at the prickly pear and chewed her quivering bottom lip. Then she buried her face in her hands.

"He wants to talk to you."

With a shaky hand, Celeste lifted the phone to her ear. "H-hello…?"

"Celeste?" Phillip's deep Marine Corps-issue voice sliced out her name with a vengeance.

"Phillip?"

"Mabel said you're limping."

"I'm fine. Never better."

"You're in some kind of trouble—"

She bit her lip and coiled a greasy strand of gold around a fingertip with chipped pearly nail polish. What was the use of lying to him? "I—I wish I could deny it."

"And you want me to rescue you...."

She swallowed as she thought of The Pope and Nero. If they followed her and killed Phillip, it would be all her fault.

Her throat burned and her eyes got hot. She squeezed them shut because the waitress was watching.

"How do you intend to play this? Sexy? Repentant? Do you see me riding into town on a white horse and carrying you out of the café in my arms?"

"Don't make this harder."

"What do you want from me then?"

Not to end up in some back alley with my skirt tossed over my head, my panties shredded and my throat slit.

"Just to see you," she said softly.

He laughed, but the brittle sound wasn't that deep chuckle she'd once loved. "You want way more than that and we both know it."

He knew how she hated that military, big man, know-it-all tone. She couldn't bear it any more than she could bear to answer him when he was feeling all self-righteous and judgmental.

"I wasn't born rich...like you.... Maybe if you'd gone through even half of what..." She stopped. That was a low blow. "I—I'm sorry."

For an instant—just for an instant—she saw her mother's white, lifeless face in her coffin and remembered how little and helpless she'd felt.

"Stay at the café. I'll send Juan to get you as soon as he gets back with the truck."

"Juan? I'd... I'd rather you came...."

But he didn't hear her heartfelt plea. He'd already hung up.

Thirty minutes later Phillip's ranch hand arrived in a whirl of dust. When Celeste saw him, she grabbed her guitar.

The waitress stared at the blowing dust and said to no one in particular, "It's awful dry out there. We could do with some rain."

Juan was short and dark, and dressed in a red shirt and baggy jeans coated with a week's supply of dirt. He didn't speak much English, and she didn't speak any Spanish. So she spent the ten-minute drive singing to the radio and watching the scenery go by. If you could call it scenery.

Unlike Vegas, south Texas was flat and covered with thorny brush. When they flew through the gate, Juan braked in front of a tall white house with a wraparound porch. Dust swirled around the truck and the wide front porch as he lit a cigarette.

She coughed. "Where's Mr. Westin?"

"Señor Westin?" Juan clomped up the stairs and pointed inside the house. Then he opened the screen door like a gentleman and beckoned for her to go inside. She nodded. Picking up her long skirt, she hesitantly stepped across the threshold into the living room.

The second she saw the burgundy couch she'd picked out at Sears, her heart began to beat too fast. Nothing much had changed. The same easy chair she'd bought for Phillip still squatted in front of the television set. Maybe the set was a little larger. She wasn't sure.

She knew her way around the house, not that she intended to explore the rooms in the house she'd once called home.

The Lazy W had been a rundown ranch Phillip had visited most summers as a kid. He'd grown up loving it. As an adult, he'd helped his uncle out when he'd been unable to do the work himself. Then a few years back, his elderly uncle had died and left him everything including the ranch.

Phillip had told her several of his friends who'd served under his command in the 14th Unit of the U.S. Marine Corps lived nearby, too. The guys had all belonged to the Lone Star Country Club, so Phillip had joined because they'd told him that's where the prettiest girls in town were. Apparently when the 14th unit was off duty, their favorite sport was chasing women.

Once a Marine, always a Marine, she thought grimly as she set her guitar down by the front door. Oh, dear, now that she was inside, it was all coming back to her. She'd been so crazily in love with Phillip, but at the same time, she'd wanted to be a star for as long as she could remember. Loving Phillip had only made her want it more. She'd wanted to be somebody…somebody special enough for Phillip to love on an equal footing, a somebody like her beautiful mother.

The two obsessions had fought within her. She'd felt deliriously happy when she was in Phillip's arms, and then the minute he'd gone off to war she'd felt scared and trapped. Then he'd gone missing.

How long did a woman wait for a man missing behind enemy lines? Her fear that he'd been dead, like her parents, had driven her mad. She'd felt as if she'd be a nothing forever if she didn't do something besides wait at the ranch. These very walls had seemed to close in on her like a prison. She'd had to run. She'd had to, but Phillip hadn't seen it that way.

When he'd turned up alive and called her, she'd been overjoyed. She'd wanted to see him so badly, to tell him about recording her first song, the song he'd inspired.

Oh, why hadn't he listened? Why hadn't he been able to understand? All he'd understood was that she'd left him.

"But I didn't know you were coming back! I thought you were dead!" she'd cried over and over again.

He hadn't listened. He'd believed the worst of her.

Now she was back in Phillip's living room. How would he treat her? Was he in love with someone else?

"Phillip," she cried, suddenly wanting to stop the bittersweet memories as well as her doubts about the wisdom of coming here.

"Phillip?"

He didn't answer.

Was she really so washed up she no longer had a chance to make it as a country-western star? Should she just give up and settle for some ordinary life filled with babies and chores with some ordinary man? Not that she'd ever thought of Phillip as ordinary.

She wandered into his kitchen. Dishes were piled high in the sink. She didn't have to answer all life's questions today. All she had to do was to convince Phillip to help her until she could find a job and could get back on her feet. He knew people. Maybe he could even get her a job if he wanted to. The Phillip she remembered liked to help people. Surely he'd help her. Even her. Surely—

"Phillip?"

Again, he didn't answer, but when she stepped into the hall, she heard his shower running. At the sound, she almost stopped breathing. Paralyzed, she stood outside his bedroom door until the water was turned off, and she heard the same old pipe that had always moaned groan and rumble. The shuddering sound broke the tension and she laughed.

They'd made love in that shower more times than she could count. She leaned against the wooden wall behind her and fought against the memories.

"Phillip?" she called again just so he wouldn't stomp out into the hall naked.

"Just a minute."

His deep, sexy baritone sent a shiver down her back, and that was before he stepped out of his bedroom into the hall in skintight, faded jeans that weren't zipped all the way up, rubbing his thick, dark hair with a white towel.

Oh, dear, he looked so good, and she was so grimy. She wished her mouth didn't taste so stale.

He tossed the towel back into his bedroom. She'd forgotten that when his dark hair was wet, it had a tendency to curl.

Her eyes fastened on his brown, muscular chest and flat belly, on the whorls of black hair running up and down his lean frame, before roving hungrily back to his rugged face.

Oh, dear. He'd stayed in shape. But, of course, he would. Phillip had the Marine Corps can-do, will-do, damn-it-to-hell-and-back attitude. He was disciplined, focused. He could make a plan and stick to it.

Not like her, who dreamed and wanted and then sometimes got lost in the day-to-day problems that came with living. Things that needed doing didn't always get done, and things she enjoyed doing were savored instead. She tended to drift and get nowhere or go hysterical and do nothing to solve her problem. She could waste days paralyzed by a mood. Which was why she'd landed on his doorstep without a dime of her own and looking even cheaper than the first night they'd met.

Some homecoming.

And Phillip? He was as handsome as ever, dangerously so. His mouth was wide and hard, his lower lip as sensuously kissable as ever. Oh, dear, she felt the old familiar ache to press her lips to his. He'd been so good at kissing, too. Too good.

Seven years on the ranch working outside had hardened his face and etched lines beneath his eyes and around his shapely mouth. He looked older, harsher, and yet…and yet he was still her Phillip.

Her Phillip? Don't be ridiculous!

He hadn't shaved yet, so his square jaw was covered with black bristles that made him look tough and virile and good enough to eat. Used to, he'd let her shave him in the shower before they'd made love.

Quit thinking about "used to."

When her eyes rose to his, he flushed. She felt her own skin heat when she realized he was staring at her breasts.

"I—I didn't have time to buy new clothes."

"How come you left Vegas in such a hurry?"

Her eyes widened in blank shock. The last thing she could tell him was the truth. He'd really despise her. Oh, why hadn't she checked into a motel and freshened up? Why hadn't she given herself a day to get her story together, a day to buy clothes and makeup?

Because unlike him, she wasn't a planner. Besides, she'd been too hysterical.

Instantly his silver eyes went opaque, and he met hers unsmilingly as he waited for her answer that didn't come. Suspicious, his carved face was a mask of mili-

tary, tough-guy expressionlessness. Not by so much as
a flicker of a black eyelash did he reveal that the sight
of her in his hall looking weak and helpless and yet sexy
and wild in a slinky black gown ripped to the thigh
might disturb him.

His hard gaze returned to her breasts. The fact that he
couldn't take his eyes off her body made her feel a little
better. Even though she felt shyly nervous that he still
found her desirable—she still felt better. Which was ridiculous. She wasn't here for sex or love or anything
like that. She didn't want him wanting her. She didn't!

Liar.

"I must look a terrible mess," she said with an air of
innocence that was completely false. Idly she fluffed her
hair.

"You look good," was all he said. But his voice was
bitter.

He stepped into the light and she saw the deep cut on
his cheek.

"You're hurt." She slid across the hall and raised her
hand, intending to touch him.

"It's nothing," he snapped.

Still, she came closer. Before he could move, she had
her hand on the hot, rough skin near the ugly wound,
her fingers tracing its edges tenderly.

"Oh, Phillip...." There were tears in her voice.
"What happened?"

"Don't!"

"Did you go off on some silly mission again?" she
asked.

"As if you give a damn— I could've died for all
you'd care."

She had cared, but better not to go there, she thought.

He grabbed her hand, intending to push her away, but

the minute he touched her, she went strangely breathless. So did he.

Their eyes met, locked. On a raw, tortured note he whispered her name and she whispered his back, her voice as tremulous and lost as his.

Then it was as if they were caught in a spell. Some power outside of them and yet a part of them took over. Before she could stop herself, or he could push her away, she flung herself toward his hard, powerful body. Then she was in his arms, hugging him, clinging with a strength she hadn't known she possessed.

She felt so safe in his arms, so safe and protected after being so afraid. She melted against him like a frightened kitten shaping itself into a warm lap.

His skin was hot, so hot, burning up, and he smelled deliciously of shampoo and soap and yet of real man, too. Again, she remembered those long-ago romps in the shower.

"Hold me," she whispered. "Just hold me. It's been way too long."

He hesitated. Then he groaned and his arms wrapped her in a fierce embrace.

"How did I ever leave you? How?" she whispered. "How? Oh, Phillip, I thought you were—"

"Don't!"

He stiffened. Beneath her ear, his heart slammed in hard, furious strokes. The violent thudding thrilled her. So he wasn't immune to her any more than she was immune to him. He wasn't.

Not that she cared. Not that she could let herself care. She wanted to be a star. Not some rancher's wife in this hellish desert where it almost never rained unless a hurricane roared across the Gulf. Not the wife of some ex-

Marine who might go away to fight and die. Yet she clung to him and kissed his throat.

The kiss proved to be too much for him. The minute her mouth touched his skin, he let out a savage rasp and pushed her away.

"Don't try that again," he said hoarsely in his cruelest Marine Corps voice. "Unless you intend to deliver the goods." His silver eyes stripped her.

"Oh...." She gasped.

He was breathing hard, too.

"Westin, you always wanted me as much as I wanted you, so why does that make me some cheap, sexy tart in your mind?"

"You know the rules. It's not like I made them up."

"What rules? Oh...." Her heart was pounding so fast she could barely breathe, and not from passion now.

"Men can screw around," he said. "Women can't."

"Oh.... I don't... That's a horrible thing to say...in general...and about me. I haven't..."

"You arrive at my doorstep half-naked...in a provocative gown somebody—let's cut the bull, a man probably—tried to tear off you in a bar."

"That's not what—"

"You throw yourself on me, using every cheap trick in the book, and you expect me to believe..."

"I tore my skirt on a window frame."

"Sneaking out of some man's bedroom?"

"Think that if you want to! You're as impossible as ever. As pigheaded...as...as... You don't listen. You think you know everything."

"I know you—Biblically." He laughed. "You're just the same, too."

If that remark made her even madder, his next comment was like a torch thrown onto a pool of gasoline.

"I picked you up in a barroom brawl. I should've known what you were like then. But you came on so soft and sweet and helpless, you fooled me."

"And because of that first night, you think you're better than I am. You always have, and you always will."

"What if I do?"

"I don't know why I came back here."

"Let me guess. You're in some kind of a jam. You probably need money."

"I need a decent job."

"Ha! Dressed like that?"

"Listen to me...please. Just listen."

"You thought I'd be easy pickin's, didn't you? Living out here? Alone? No woman? Well, you were right about one thing, honey. I still want you."

His voice was so hard and filled with hate, she gasped.

"Look at me," he said.

Unwillingly, she met his shrewd gaze and instantly felt stripped to the marrow. Oh, dear. She was afraid she was transparent as glass.

"You feel the same way. So, do you want to stand here and argue, or would you rather just cut this nonsense, and go to bed? But don't flatter yourself. This isn't about love. It's about sex. And money. I'll pay—" He flung her his sexiest, male grin.

Maybe he was a whole lot cuter, but in some ways he was as bad as Nero and The Pope!

But he was her last chance! She clenched her fists and bit her tongue until it bled. Killers, real killers, were after her. She had to focus on why she'd come to see this impossible man she'd once been so foolish to love. Her fury made it hard to remember that besides being an egotistical, macho, oversexed idiot, Westin had a good, dependable, fierce side, too.

Pursuing this particular battle to its conclusion wasn't smart. After all, she had a plan this time. Somehow she had to convince him to help her get a real job. For once, she had to be smart and stick to her plan.

He broke the silence by laughing at her again. "There's no reason to play hard to get, honey. The sooner you go to bed with me, the sooner you get what you really want."

She lifted her chin. His dark gaze made a connection that was way too powerful.

"So I amuse you?" she whispered. "The man I used to know helped people when they came to him in trouble. He didn't insult them and laugh at them and try to take advantage of them…sexually—"

"You conniving— Why are you really here? What do you really want?" he growled.

If only he'd stop looking at her like that. Her heart was still pounding. "Like I said, I need a decent job, a place to live," she persisted.

"Decent?" He wasn't touching her, but his eyes pulled her erotically.

"Is that so hard to believe?" she whispered.

"Simple ambitions for a woman like you. Used to, you wanted fame and fortune."

"Was that really so terrible, Phillip?"

"Do you still want to be a country-western star?"

She wasn't about to admit her dreams to him. In his awful mood, he'd just laugh at her again.

She notched her chin higher. "Would it make you happy to know I've had a few hard knocks and learned a few lessons?"

"Then? What do you want?"

In spite of herself, just being near him made her feel a deep aching need.

"You know people. Maybe you could get me on at the Lone Star Country Club. As a singer. Or even a hostess or a waitress. I need a job."

"You want a job? I'll give you a job."

"I won't go to bed with you for money! And that's final!" Her shaky voice probably gave her away. Was it just chemistry that pulled her to him?

"I need a housekeeper," he stated flatly.

"I don't believe that's what you really—"

"Hear me out. You played Cinderella in all those foster homes. You can live here and do the same for me."

"I don't think it's such a good idea—the two of us living here. Not when you just suggested we go to bed in such a sordid—"

"Don't act like you deserve better. Take it or leave it."

"You didn't used to be this hard," she said softly.

"Maybe I suffered a few hard knocks of my own. I nearly died in the Middle East."

"Oh, Phillip—" Her voice broke.

"Then I came home to marry the woman I loved. Only she'd run off with another man."

His gaze stayed on her face for a long, searching moment.

"I didn't run off with Johnny. It wasn't that way at all and you know it."

"No, I don't know it. How was it, then?"

"You wouldn't listen then."

"You were gone. That's all I know."

"Yes…." She cleared her throat. "And…and I'm sorry if I hurt you."

"You didn't— I don't give a damn about you anymore—understand."

He looked away and she suddenly realized how profoundly she'd hurt him.

"Oh, Phillip—"

He'd cared too much. That's why he hadn't come after her. She'd been so caught up in her own dreams and pain and self-doubt, so sure she'd had to prove herself to him, she hadn't really thought that someone as tough as he was might be as vulnerable and needy as she was. Well, it was too late now. He was hard and cold, and so set against her he was treating her as though she was some trashy stranger.

"What really happened to your face?" she whispered.

"I had an accident. I wasn't wearing a seat belt."

"You should be more careful."

"You gonna stay here and take care of me?"

"Not a good idea. I'm beginning to see we weren't really very good for each other."

"Yet you've come back?"

"Big mistake. I'll go. Forget I ever came...."

He didn't try to stop her when she turned to leave. At the door, she picked up her guitar, which felt as heavy as lead. As soon as she stepped off his front porch into the sun, she realized she was in the middle of nowhere. The sun was so hot, it felt about an inch off her bare shoulders. She felt weak and tired, so tired. So helpless and so hopeless.

With her turned ankle, she'd never be able to walk all the way back to town. Juan was nowhere in sight.

"How the hell do you think you'll get to town?"

She stiffened. No way was she going to beg. "I'll find Juan. He'll give me a ride back to town."

"He's out back."

When she headed out to the barn, she saw the buzzards, which meant there had to be a dead animal out in the pasture. Curious, she let herself through a gate to check on whatever was wrong.

The sun on her face and shoulders grew hotter by the minute, so hot she could almost feel her nose blistering. Holding up her hand to shield her face, she didn't have to walk far before she smelled the stench. Flies hovered above a cow that lay on it side, its belly bloated. Its legs stuck straight out. Black vultures whooshed excitedly around it when she walked up.

Oh, dear. The animal's eyes were gaping sockets. She was about to call for Phillip when a slip of fluttering white caught her attention. Somebody had nailed a note to the dead carcass.

Big block letters read, "You hurt my family, so now I will hurt yours."

She screamed. Then the thick smell of the barnyard and the stench of the dead cow combined with the heat and she felt nauseated. The world seemed to spin, and she grew so unsteady on her feet, she was afraid she'd fall.

Somewhere behind her a screen door slammed. Then The Pope and Nero were grabbing at her long hair.

"Phillip," she whispered groggily. "Save me! Don't let them—"

"Who, my darling— There's nobody here!"

"Thank goodness." Her eyelids felt incredibly heavy as she grabbed a fence railing. The sun burned her face and made her lips feel dry. The sky seemed to blacken. In a halting breath she whispered, "Phillip...."

"I'm here. Right here," he said huskily.

She shook her head back and forth. "Phillip— Phillip— No! Phillip doesn't want me."

Then she felt strong arms around her and her words

were muttered shudderingly against his thick, hard shoulder.

"Don't be too sure about that, honey," his gentle voice soothed.

She felt herself being lifted.

"Celeste...."

For a fleeting moment she realized she really was in Phillip's arms. Only the Phillip who held her now wasn't the harsh Phillip who despised her. No. This Phillip was the gentle, warrior giant she'd fallen in love with.

A weak smile formed at the edges of her lips as she whispered his name and begged him to save her. Then everything went black.

Three

When Celeste regained consciousness, she was in Phillip's bed and he was sitting beside her on the edge of the mattress.

"I'm sorry," he said.

"I'll stay," she whispered.

"Why?"

"Because I need a job. Any job. And I don't have anywhere else to go." Too proud to meet his eyes, she stared guiltily past his dark face until the bright window behind him began to swim. *Because I know you'll help me.*

"Don't cry," he murmured.

She brushed at her damp eyes. "Who's crying?"

He handed her his handkerchief.

She dabbed at her eyes. "I'm not crying!"

He laughed and touched her wet cheek with a blunt fingertip.

"I hate it when this happens." In spite of herself, she smiled at him.

"That's better," he whispered, his deep voice gentle. "For the record, I'm going to call the sheriff and get him to investigate the cow killing. I think I know who's behind this."

"Who—" She shivered guiltily at the thought of Nero or The Pope.

"This isn't about you," Phillip said. "It's about me and some unfinished business in Central America."

"Central America?"

"Never mind. Just be careful. Lock the doors when I'm gone and Juan's not around. I don't want anything to happen to you. I'd never forgive myself if my work endangered you."

"Your work?"

"Shh."

She gulped in a deep breath. He was so concerned for her, she felt ashamed she'd left Vegas with a pair of killers after her. Ashamed that all her dreams and hard work had left her worse off than before she'd started. She was touched that he was so selflessly eager to protect her. There was no way she could confess that she was probably endangering him.

"Thank you, Phillip. I won't stay long—I swear."

"Stay as long as you like," he said.

She yawned and closed her eyes. When she opened them again, he was gone. The shades were drawn and there was a box of clothes on the floor. He must have come in at some point when she'd been asleep. When she got up and knelt to open the box, all the clothes she hadn't taken with her seven years ago were inside.

He'd kept them...packed them away...all these years. Had he been waiting and hoping she'd come back?

"Oh, Phillip—''

Suddenly she almost hated herself. She was using him as a human shield. Maybe The Pope and Nero had followed her. Maybe they'd killed the cow.

Tell him. He deserves the truth. If you don't tell him— he'll be furious.

She pulled a thin white dress out of the box and held it against her body. Memories tugged at her.

They'd driven in to a posh shop in Corpus Christi one afternoon and he'd bought her several outfits shortly before he'd left for the Middle East. He'd liked this particular dress so much, she'd worn it out of the store with the tags still on it. He'd laughed and cut off the tags with his pocketknife. Then they'd driven out to Mustang Island and had gone for a walk on the beach. It had been early spring and the southeasterly breeze had been strong. She'd chased seagulls, her skirts swirling. He'd caught her, and they'd found a secluded spot behind the dunes and made love on their beach towels.

Fingering the tiny buttons, she began to shake as she remembered his fingers fumbling with each pearly stud as he'd undone them one by one. He'd been so clumsy, she'd had to help him.

"Oh, Phillip—'' She buried her face in the soft white cloth, wishing it didn't remind her of how sweet life with Phillip had once been.

"I won't be staying long. I won't. I can't love him. I can't. I'll get myself back on track and he'll never have to know the whole truth. He doesn't still love me. I can't hurt him now.''

She put Phillip out of her mind and took a long hot bath and washed her hair. After towel-drying her hair, she slipped into the white dress with the gleaming pearl buttons. It felt so good to be fresh and clean—to be home.

She turned in front of the mirror and the circular skirt floated around her legs. Then she stopped herself.

"This isn't home. I'm still going to be a star."

Was she really? Or had she just lived on dreams so long, she didn't know how to live any other way? Dreams kept her going. They made it possible for her to face the everyday pain and the hassles of life and find them bearable, made it possible for her to hold her head up even with killers tracking her.

She'd put Phillip in danger. Maybe she'd gotten his cow killed. Would she ever be worthy of a man like Phillip?

He thought he'd seen her at her lowest in the bar brawl. He didn't know. She hadn't told him near everything about what she'd endured in those foster homes. Never once had she told anybody how often she'd had to change homes because her new "father" had started looking at her wrong. And that had meant she'd had to change schools.

So often had she changed schools, she hadn't been able to make friends with the good kids, and, of course, she'd fallen behind in her schoolwork. Once she'd even flunked a grade, which had made the kids, at least the ones she'd admired, believe she was stupid.

The spring of her junior year in high school, she'd painted her lips with bright red lipstick and auditioned for the talent show. Only when she'd stood on that stage had the other kids begun to think she was special. When she'd sung for them, she'd felt reborn, as though she was a whole new person. If she hadn't had that special gift she'd inherited from her mother, she would have stopped believing in herself a long time ago. Every time she remembered standing on that stage behind her mother as a little kid, she knew she couldn't quit.

The days passed. Before she knew it a whole week had flown by. Not once had Phillip hit on her.

She relaxed a little and began to let herself notice him a little more. She tried hard not to smile at him when he said something. Some part of her wanted to get up first thing and make his coffee. But she didn't.

Life as his housekeeper soon became routine. The work itself might be the same everywhere, but Phillip's being around spiced up the most mundane activities. Not that he made any more overt moves.

Still, there were more than a few awkward moments, especially at first, such as when he'd asked her where she wanted to sleep, and she'd eyed his bedroom door, hesitating a second or two before choosing the last bedroom down the hall instead of his, the one they'd once shared.

All he'd said was, "Okay," but his eyes had grown dark and cold, and the military mask had fallen into place when she'd carried her box of clothes from his bedroom down the hall.

Being a Marine, he tried to run his home the way he might run a military base. Maybe that worked when she wasn't around, but she wasn't about to play the grunt to his Lt. Col. Westin. On the first morning after she'd bathed and slipped into her soft white dress, he'd caught her on the back porch when she was towel-drying her hair and had started off with a long list of orders.

"I want you up at 0600 sharp," he'd barked.

"This is a home not some Marine camp," she'd replied.

Laughing at his audacity, she'd saluted him with her

left hand. "I never did get those big old numbers—
0600? Translation, please!" She'd wadded his list of
chores and stuffed it down the scooped neckline of her
soft white dress and into her bra.

"Six a.m. Sharp."

"You can't be serious," she'd said, aware of his silver
eyes lingering on her hand between her breasts. "Only
lunatics or maniacal Marines get up at such an ungodly
hour."

"You didn't even read my list—"

"I know how to keep house! You don't have to tell
me what to do!"

"You could have at least read—"

"Didn't anybody in colonel school ever teach you to
delegate?"

"There's no such thing as colonel school."

"Maybe there should be."

She'd made a habit of sleeping through the alarm he
set for her every night just as she had made a habit of
ignoring the long lists of chores he left on the kitchen
table every morning. Instead, she did what she thought
needed doing, which was more than he ever saw. Naturally, there were some resulting fireworks. He had
started in on her that first night.

No sooner had they sat down to supper than Phillip
had started shooting blunt questions at her, like, "Did
you do…?" Then he'd systematically gone down his
list, which he knew by heart and she hadn't bothered to
read, unerringly selecting the tasks she'd neglected to
do, such as keeping the doors locked all the time, instead
of the chores she'd done.

"Did you iron my shirts?"

"In this heat?"

"Why isn't my bed made?"

"It isn't? Why, I went in—"

She'd stopped. No way could she admit that when she'd lifted his pillow, she'd thought of him lying there and cupped it against her face to breathe in his tangy, male scent. Then the memories of them together in his bed had flooded her and she'd run.

Blushing, she'd toyed with a strand of her hair. Her tongue seemed to stick itself to the roof of her mouth.

He'd turned a little red, too. "Okay. Okay. Forget the bed."

"I can if you can." She'd hardly breathed.

"What about my clothes in the hamper?" he'd growled.

"The…hamper's in your bedroom, too," she'd whispered.

"Oh."

"I—I'll do them tomorrow…if you'll bring the hamper to the laundry room."

"Did you—"

"Phillip, did you memorize your old list—"

"I know what I wrote down—"

This was bad.

Cocking her head saucily, she'd shaken her yellow curls. To gain time she'd fluffed them around her shoulders. "Of course, I didn't do those silly things on your silly list. There were way too many. If you knew anything—you'd know no woman could have done all that in one day—"

"Of course you didn't? What kind of employee are you?"

"The same kind of boss you are. A good boss would praise me for making the kitchen look so wonderful. I rearranged—"

"You hid everything. I couldn't even find a spoon."

"It's called finding a place for things and putting them where they belong. I even dusted behind the canisters and…and I bleached the sink."

He'd glared at her.

"That wasn't on my list."

"The porcelain was all yellow and stained." She'd smiled.

"Don't forget this is my house. You work for me."

"I wouldn't have to if you'd help me get a real job."

He'd jabbed at his eggplant. Then he'd begun to eat in silence. When he helped himself to seconds, she'd beamed. "How's the eggplant Provençale by the way?"

"Eggplant? I don't eat eggplant!"

"Then why is yours all gone?"

He'd eyed his clean plate with amazement. "Because…because I was starving, that's why!"

"Because you liked it," she'd amended gently.

"I wrote steak at the top of my list."

"Have you been listening to me at all? I didn't read your stupid list. I don't do lists."

"I wanted steak."

"Hardening of the arteries," she'd murmured. "Ever hear of that?"

"What?"

"Men in this country eat way too much red meat. You probably eat too much steak. At your age—"

"You work for me."

"Aye. Aye." She'd saluted him with her left hand.

Before he thought, he'd almost saluted her. Then he'd clenched his fingers into a fist and slammed it on the table. "You haven't done one single thing I wrote down today."

"Because you're not a housekeeper or a cook. You

don't think about your health. In short, you don't think like a woman..."

"Thank God!"

"You don't have the least idea what to put on my list. You write down all these silly things that no woman in her right mind would ever do."

"Don't be absurd. You work for me—a man, in case you haven't noticed."

"Oh...." She'd slanted her long-lashed eyes his way. Then she'd batted them and given him a seductive smile. "Oh, I see. This isn't about your list. You're just sulking because I don't want to share your bedroom."

"The hell I am."

"Then fire me."

"And you'd go?"

"All you have to do is get me a real job." She'd flashed him her most brilliant smile. "But if you won't get me a real job, as a tiny concession...because you're so stubborn, we'll have steak tomorrow."

"I'm stubborn?"

She'd giggled. "But no more than five ounces of red meat."

"You're impossible." But he'd grinned back at her.

"Look who's talking."

"You'll really cook steak?"

Over dessert, which was strawberries and fat-free, sugar-free vanilla ice cream, she'd said, "Since you're not going to fire me..."

"It doesn't take much for you to get cocky—"

"Which is a trait I share with you."

She knew she shouldn't tease him. It made her remember how wonderful loving him had been. To break the spell, she'd sat up straighter and said, "Phillip, I need money."

"I knew it."

"Could I have an advance against my paycheck?"

"An advance? Already?"

"It's important...or I wouldn't ask."

"How much?"

She'd named the exact amount she needed to pay Cole Yardley.

Phillip had given her a sharp look, but he hadn't asked what the money was for.

"I owe somebody," she'd blurted, on the defensive because she could tell he was suspicious. "That's all."

"All right. We'll leave it at that."

The next morning, she'd gone to the bank and the post office and sent Mr. Yardley a five-hundred-dollar money order.

In a month, Phillip calmed down. He stopped writing lists. Maybe she'd worn him down. Or maybe he liked the way she did things more than he would admit. She wasn't sure. When there were no more dead cows, she quit worrying that The Pope and Nero had discovered her hiding place.

Growing up in so many homes, she'd learned there were lots of ways to run a household, and if she was going to be the woman of this house, especially when Phillip was a rancher and could pop in at any time, she had to do things her way. No woman in her right mind would let the man have the upper hand in such a situation.

Last night he'd almost said he preferred her menus to his—before he'd caught himself. She cooked lots of vegetables. If she'd left things to him, he would have eaten steak and potatoes every night.

Once things were easier between them, and she'd

taught him she wasn't some grunt he could boss around, new tensions, or maybe the same old tensions, began to build inside her. When they were in the same room, and he followed her with his eyes, she would feel the little hairs on the back of her neck stand up. She would blush and smile at him shyly, and he would look away too quickly.

To avoid such scenes, she kept away from him. When he watched television in the living room, she stayed in the kitchen and read by herself. Not that she could totally ignore him even there. He'd laugh and she'd look up from her woman's magazine and think about him in those ways she didn't want to think about him.

He was so big and broad-chested and tanned. And his mouth. Oh, dear. That warm, gorgeous, delicious-looking mouth of his. Just the thought of his mouth tickling her skin made her knot her hands in her lap and made her body get hot all over. Yes, even in the kitchen all by herself, knowing he was nearby made her edgy and restless and somehow unfulfilled. Before, he'd been affectionate all through the day. Seven years ago he used to come up behind her without warning and she'd feel his fingers at her nape and then his lips.

Now, nights when he didn't come home at his usual hour, she would run to the front door or watch the phone, waiting for it to ring. And all the time an ache in her stomach would worsen as she wondered where he was.

She'd worry herself into a headache. Maybe he'd had an accident and had forgotten to put on his seat belt again. Maybe he'd fallen off the tractor or been gored. Maybe whoever had killed that cow had attacked Phillip. Not that Phillip ever told her his plans. Not that his whereabouts were any of her business. After all, they weren't married. They weren't even lovers. All they were was boss and employee. And as the weeks passed, both were more determined than ever that the other understood that. It was as if they'd drawn lines in the sand and dared one another not to step across. But she worried about him. She couldn't stop herself. And she thought about him constantly. She even sang about him.

When her chores were done, and she had nothing to do, she would go to her bedroom or sit on the front porch with her guitar and write songs. The best ones were always about Phillip. How could that be when he was her boss?

What was she doing here? Was she crazy?

When Phillip was away, she taped the songs and mailed them with a letter to a hot new producer, Greg Furman, in Nashville. Not that Furman ever wrote her back. Even so, she always felt a little guilty, as though she was going behind Phillip's back, as though she should share everything in her heart and soul with him.

But her career was none of his business. What were they to each other, really? She was his maid and that was hardly the career she'd had in mind. Constantly, she had to work to remind herself that this wasn't her home, that Phillip wasn't her husband or even her lover, and that he never would be. But she thought about him when she was in bed, and she dreamed about him when she slept.

She would wake up and tell herself she owed him nothing. Nothing but her friendship! She would tell herself that the next night she would refuse to think about him or dream about him, that she was her own person, and as such, she had to get her career back on track—as soon as possible. And yet…

And yet the very next night, when she was alone in her narrow little bed again and he was such a short distance down the hall in his big double bed they'd shared and made passionate love in, staying in his house even for a few months would seem like a big mistake. A board would creak outside her room and she'd nearly jump out of her skin, thinking it might be Phillip at her door. Hoping it was, her heart would beat faster. She'd imagine his hand on her doorknob, and a bolt of heat would course through her. She'd sit up shivering expectantly. Then she'd realize he wasn't there. She'd wrap her arms around herself and remember how it used to be when they'd lain in bed in each other's arms.

Even when they hadn't been making love, they'd never kept to their own side of the bed. He'd held her close all night. Lying like that in his arms, she'd never felt so safe and so protected, at least, not since her mother had died and left her alone.

"Oh, Phillip, Phillip, you drive me so crazy! What is wrong with me?" The harder she fought not to care about him, the more involved she became.

One day when Celeste was out in the rocking chair, playing her guitar and singing on the porch, Phillip, who was supposed to be out in some far-flung pasture, stalked around the back of the house in a freshly starched white shirt and a pair of pressed jeans. He appeared so suddenly, he caught her singing about him.

"I didn't know I was on the road to nowhere when I left you…"

Rocks spun from under his big boots as he came to a standstill in the gravel beside the back porch. "Celeste…"

Instantly she stopped singing, the last word tumbling out of its phrase as if into a deep pool of clear green water. "You-u-u…."

"You singing about me, girl?"

For no reason at all, she couldn't let go of his silver gaze. She wasn't sure she'd ever noticed before that his pale gray irises were ringed with black.

"Go on," he whispered, looking up at her. "You're great."

She plucked a guitar string, nervous at the thought of him listening. For a tough guy, he sure had pretty eyes.

"Go on—please. You have a beautiful voice."

She leaned back in the rocker and resumed playing. "The lights ahead were so bright, they blinded me…"

He seemed to hold his breath as he looked up at her and listened without comment.

"I couldn't see that fame and fortune weren't enough/ that without you, I'm on the road to nowhere."

"Did you write that?" he whispered.

She nodded.

"You still want to be a star?"

"This star crashed and burned."

"What happened to you in Vegas?" He moved toward the porch.

"I don't want to go there. Please don't ask." Just the thought of Nero and The Pope still scared her to death.

She averted her eyes, so Phillip wouldn't see the guilt she felt for putting him in danger.

"You're a wonderful singer and a wonderful writer," he said softly, placing a booted foot on the first step.

"I was a one-song wonder, remember?" She bit her lip and shut her eyes.

"Celeste—don't be so hard on yourself."

"It's the truth."

"Maybe it doesn't have to be."

"What are you saying?" She couldn't believe he was encouraging her. "Dinner's ready," she said.

"I don't give a damn about dinner."

He sprang up the stairs to the porch two at a time and sank down on his knees beside her rocking chair. She began to shake a little. Did he have to come so close? Did he know what he did to her?

Her palms grew damp and she wiped them on her jeans, but there was no way she could calm the giddy wildness that made her heart flutter.

"If you've got talent the way you do, can you really get it out of your system?" he persisted gently. "Can a dream like that die?"

"I don't want to talk about…"

"What will happen to you if you let it die?"

"I can't believe you're…" She didn't trust herself to go on. His sensitive questions as well as his concern shook her more than anything he could have done or said. "Marines don't talk about dreams."

"Yeah. We're natural-born killing machines."

"Look. You were Alpha Force."

"I know what I was. I'm other things, too."

"I—I didn't mean…"

"Yeah, you did—"

"I'm thirty-two," she said.

"Dreams don't die because you get to a certain age. Thirty-two is young."

"People grow up," she whispered.

"Do they?"

"They're supposed to." Talking about her music made her uncomfortable. "Aren't you still the Marine who wants to serve his country, and you don't care who you have to kill or if you die doing it?"

"I retired. My Marine buddies say I've gone through my nine lives, that I'd better find the right woman, a churchgoing woman and settle down."

His teasing smile gave her a warm buzz. Before she thought, she grinned, too.

"Churchgoing, huh? That's not me, is it?" She blushed. "They're right, you know. You should."

"I don't go to church much—especially since you came home."

Home. This isn't home. Why was that so hard for her to remember?

"What are you saying?" she whispered.

"I'm wondering why you came back to me."

"Back to Texas," she corrected. "Not back to you."

"You knew I was here. Admit it."

Suddenly she started rubbing her arms as if there was a chill in the air.

"Let's quit fooling ourselves," he said, his eyes dark and hot.

"Phillip—"

She stood and set her guitar in the rocker before backing toward the kitchen door.

He crisscrossed his muscular forearms. "Damn it, I've tried not to look at you."

"Me, too," she whispered, her voice thready.

"And I've tried to avoid you."

"Me, too."

He scowled at her. "But you consume me."

"I—I don't want to talk about this, either." Jerkily she grabbed at the screen door.

"Good. I don't want to talk—period." His hand seized hers. "At night I lie awake," he began, his voice rough and strange.

So did she. Not that she could admit it.

"Don't," she whispered even though all her senses were clamoring for him to keep talking.

"I still want you," he rasped, sliding his work-roughened palms up her bare arms and making her gasp.

"Phillip, I…"

"Why the hell do you write songs about me, if it's really over for you?"

"I… That song wasn't really about you."

"Right." He laughed harshly. "You never were much of a liar. That's one of the things I liked about you. You used to tell me everything. About those homes you lived in. About feeling so loved on that stage with your mother. I wanted to make you feel that loved. I tried so damn hard."

"Oh, Phillip. I know you did, and I did feel loved."

He sighed.

She bit her lip. "Until you went away."

He'd made her feel so loved, so adored. Then he'd gotten that phone call in the middle of the night and he'd gone off to the Middle East and gotten himself captured. She stopped herself from reliving the past.

Oh, dear. It was all such a long time ago. Why were her feelings about him still so intense? Why?

Phillip seemed to sense her vulnerability and pressed closer. "Just one kiss," he whispered, clutching her hand again, pulling her into his body. "Is that so much to ask? One kiss? Just to see if you still taste the same. I've got to know."

"Maybe ignorance is bliss."

"Ah—bliss."

His eyes were on her lips, and she was staring at his mouth, too.

When he moved toward her with a predatory male gleam in his eyes, she didn't back away. He let her hand drop and began to stroke her hair and neck soothingly.

She was trembling from his touch, and he was on fire with need.

His skin was so hot, she caught fire, too. He lowered his lips to her temple and rained hot nibbles in her hair that sent little jolts of fire all through her. Without thinking she buried her face in the hollow of his warm throat and weakly kissed his mad pulse beat. He threw back his head, his gray eyes dark and wild with desire.

After a few moments, holding each other made them want more. So much more. Blindly his mouth sought hers.

Blindly, she opened her lips to his. Their mouths clung; their tongues mated. He groaned. His large hands pressed into the small of her back, shaping her against his muscular torso. He was thick and hard against her thigh.

She wanted to unfasten his belt buckle, to rip it out of the denim loops, to unzip him…to…to… And all the time as their lips devoured each other, their hunger grew until she could barely breathe.

There. This. She sighed heedlessly as the tumult from kissing him and holding him possessed her utterly. *This is what I want. What I've wanted every night when I've lain awake. This. You!*

"Oh, Phillip—"

"You're still a perfect fit," he muttered raggedly, his scorching mouth against her hot cheek now.

"So are you."

"Wrap your legs around me."

"Out here?" she murmured.

"Why the hell not? There's nobody to see us."

"Slow down. Maybe because I'm not done kissing you yet," she replied.

"So you want more kisses?"

"Maybe just a few more." She giggled primly, eyeing his lips.

Oh, that mouth of his. That beautiful, beautiful mouth!

His lips claimed hers greedily again, as if he, too, were starved for her loving and would never get his fill. Soon his kisses grew more urgent and she was gasping with such intense pleasure her feelings terrified her.

The dusty cactus and mesquite stretching toward the endless, flat horizon seemed to whirl around her. Soon she felt so dizzy and faint she could barely stand.

"No," she moaned, gripping him by the waist. "We…we can't do this."

"Wrap your legs around me the way you used to," he ordered.

Every sense in her female being went on red alert. But she said, "I'm just your housekeeper now."

"You're way overdue for a promotion. I have a job in mind you're way better qualified for."

"Oh, Phillip— We've got to stop! Really!"

"Really?" he murmured, pressing her closer. He stared at her, his gaze drifting from her lips to her breasts, to her belly and lower…

She had to stop him.

Her hands fell from his neck and pushed against his massive chest. For a minute or two, he resisted.

"If we let this get out of hand, we'd only end up hurting each other."

He didn't say anything, so it was up to her to do the smart thing.

"Find that nice, churchgoing girl," she whispered, lifting her gaze to his. "She's not me, and we both know it."

"Are you really so sure?" he muttered, wrapping an arm around her waist and tugging her toward the door.

She liked being in his arms. She liked it too much. "We tried before. I loved the sound of the guitar and the glitter of bright lights, and you loved the sound of bullets."

"Not anymore. I know what I want now, and it's not war or death. But what do you want, Celeste? You came home. To me. Why?"

"You keep saying that…like it means something. It doesn't."

"Maybe it does."

"This isn't home…. At least, it's not my home."

He let her go. "Maybe it could be. You could stay and keep writing your songs."

"Could I?" She stared at her guitar in the rocker and hugged herself. "Yes, I always write songs wherever I am. I can't seem to stop." She fought to calm herself. It was unbearably exciting to even think she might have him and her music, too. But how? How? He'd said dreams didn't die, and he was right. Hers hadn't. But wasn't that the problem for them?

Besides, because of her early losses and pain, she couldn't trust him or herself or their love. Some part of her thought it would all go away. Still, she couldn't stop her feelings for him any more than she could stop the music in her soul. It was as if he'd claimed a part of her, and she'd never be free again.

If she let this go any further, they'd fall in love all over again. Someday she would have to choose. If they stopped now, maybe they wouldn't have to hurt each other again.

She studied the hollows beneath his cheekbones. She caught the faint scent of laundry detergent from his freshly washed shirt. She wanted him so much, she ached. And she loved the wild loneliness of his ranch.

Maybe he really was tired of war. Well, she was definitely tired of lousy gigs and cheap apartments with rented furniture. It was so nice here with him where she felt safe, where he made her feel beautiful and special. But was he enough for a girl like her? Wouldn't her dream always be there between them? Would the bright lights beckon her again after a few more months?

Confused and lonely as she was, it would be too easy to lead him on, to live here under his protection until she felt safe and had enough money to pursue her real dream, which had always been singing. But she wanted him. Oh, how she wanted him.

She stared at his dark, tanned face, into his wild silver eyes that carved out her soul. In this moment she wanted him even more than she could ever imagine wanting to be a star. But when he leaned down and tried to kiss her again, she shook her head sadly and bit her lip.

Lifting her guitar from the rocker, she began to sing to him, "Without you, I'm on the road to nowhere..."

"So that's how it is!"

"That's how it has to be," she whispered.

"Maybe we're both on the road to nowhere." He lashed out, suddenly angry at her rejection. "When you came back—you put me in hell. Did you know that? You think I'm made of iron? That I'm some kind of cold-blooded killing machine?"

"I didn't mean for it to be like that."

"You're so damned beautiful. So damned sweet. You! It's always about you! Stay away from me—you hear!"

He stomped into the house and slammed the door so hard the whole house shook.

"I've been trying to!" she yelled.

Alone on the porch, she felt as if the big desolate

landscape had swallowed her alive. She sucked in a breath. Panic tore through her.

"I—I didn't want to hurt you. That's the last thing I wanted." She went to the door and then clenched her fingers and sank to the porch floor. "Why do we always end up hurting each other?"

She put down her guitar and fought her tears.

Four

Phillip turned the window unit in the kitchen up full-blast to drown out Celeste's plaintive voice. When he could still hear her singing, he splashed two shots of bourbon onto ice in a short glass and quickly gulped it down, coughing when the stuff burned like acid. Not that he felt it as he began to pace.

A message light blinked on his answering machine. Welcoming any distraction, he strode over to the phone and punched the play button. Justin Wainwright's deep voice came on instantly. Justin was the local sheriff, and with Phillip's help, he was investigating the cow killing that had terrified Celeste.

"Thanks for all your input, Westin. Afraid I still can't pin that dead cow to the Gonzalez character you mentioned even though the FBI is taking your concerns very seriously. The feds are sending an agent to check out our theory about Gonzalez smuggling guns out of Mission Creek—''

Phillip deleted the message, turned the machine off and moved toward the air conditioner so he could watch Celeste through the window. Her golden head was lowered over her guitar, and he realized she was crying as she sang softly to herself.

Despite the bourbon, he could still taste her. A chill shot through him that had nothing to do with the icy air. He'd made her cry again because he was cold and cruel.

Gonzalez and Wainwright were forgotten, as Phillip raked his hand through the thick darkness of his hair. He was a fool to care about her. Furious at both Celeste and himself, he commanded his feelings to shut down. He always shut down before combat. It never took long. In less than five minutes, he'd no longer be human. Tears wouldn't matter. Nothing would matter except accomplishing his objectives.

He moved away from the air conditioner. Maybe it was better this way. He couldn't take another night or another day with her in his house, unless he could have her.

When she came inside, they ate dinner in silence. Oh, she tried to make conversation, and he tried to mumble appropriate answers to her idiotic questions. Why did women always want to talk when you felt like tearing furniture apart with your bare hands or ripping the oak floor up with a claw hammer?

Sweetly she asked if something was wrong with the meal.

How the hell would he know? As if he could taste anything but her. Maybe the steak—she'd actually cooked beef tonight—was delicious. Who the hell cared? He was shutting down, going deep, deep inside himself.

He was good at this game. He'd learned that if he did this before combat, the fear couldn't take over. Instead of going mad or becoming paralyzed with terror, he became inhuman and turned himself into some sort of soulless killing machine. Once, in such a state, he'd run straight at a tank in Iraq.

"We shouldn't have kissed," Celeste said.

"Wouldn't have missed it for the world," he replied.

Her glistening lashes fluttered. Somehow she seemed far away, and he was glad. Her rejection didn't hurt quite so much.

He wasn't good with rejection. The Marines had a policy—they didn't leave anybody behind. That policy was why he'd become a Marine.

He'd been left behind his whole damn life.

Rejection.

His rich socialite mother hadn't wanted him. He'd been an accident and beautiful, glamorous, Kathryn Westin's only child. He'd been a big baby, ten pounds, and she'd never forgiven him for her stretch marks. As soon as he was old enough, she'd packed him off to military school in Harlingen, Texas.

The other boys went home for the summer. He'd been sent to expensive camps near Hunt, Texas, which had an emerald-green river and was some of the most beautiful hill country in central Texas. At Christmas he'd gone to his grandmothers, who were good to him in their way. But he hadn't been close to them, and they weren't his mother. He'd rarely seen his mother. She hadn't even bothered to watch him graduate from high school or college.

Celeste stood and picked up her dinner plate, snapping him back to the present. She walked over to the sink and rinsed her dishes. Even though he knew he was in his own kitchen and she was real, not a phantom, he felt as if he was in a dream. As if she wasn't really there. As if nothing could touch him or hurt him.

"Are you okay?" she whispered, turning around when she was done.

He nodded. "Why?"

"You seem kinda strange."

"I think I'll go for a walk. Don't wait up."

As if she would—

"Oh, Phillip, Sheriff Wainwright called about that cow—"

"I know." He slammed out the door. When the light came on in the living room, he watched her settle herself on his couch to watch his television, which was something she never did, if he was in there.

Rejection. Funny, he couldn't feel a thing now.

Nobody had ever wanted him. Nobody except the Marines.

Boot camp had proved more than even he could bear, so after ten days of abusive military garbage, he'd rejected the Marines and their madmen drill instructors and had gone AWOL. He'd hidden out in the swamp that surrounded the base for a week, with nothing to eat but raw lizards and snakes, with nothing to drink but swamp water. He'd squatted up to his eyeballs in mud and scorpions and mosquitoes while platoons had searched for him. That was when he'd first learned to shut down emotionally.

The MPs had finally found him, of course, and had hauled him to the brig in handcuffs. The meanest sergeant on the base had taken over at that point. He'd made a show of verbally flaying Phillip in front of his platoon. Then he'd collared Phillip and shoved him toward his office for a private torture session. He'd pushed Phillip into a chair and slammed the door.

"A week? You ate lizards? Snakes? What were you thinking about, kid?"

"Wasn't thinking. Shut down."

"Crazy kid. You ate snakes? What the hell were you trying to prove?"

"Shut down."

The sergeant had crossed his arms over his bull-thick chest and eyeballed him. "Either you're going to make one hell of a crazy Marine. Or..."

He let that word hang like a grenade that had been thrown. His eyes narrowed. "Or I'm going to personally take you back to that swamp and feed you to the alligators and snakes myself. Do we have an understanding, kid?"

"Yes, sir."

"Do we have an understanding?" he'd screamed in that awful maniacle tone that had driven Phillip to go AWOL in the first place.

"Yes, sir!"

"Seven days on snakes and swamp water. You're a born Marine. You're crazy enough to be anything you want to be. Don't you ever forget that."

Then the sergeant had given him a fatherly pat. "Now you make me proud, son."

"Yes, sir!"

From that day, the Marines had been Phillip's home and his family. They'd been enough. Until Celeste. Now that she'd come back he wanted more.

He wanted Celeste.

Shut down! Shut down! Dive!

When he got back from his hour-long walk, Celeste was in the middle of watching some chick-flick called

When Harry Met Sally. Curled up at one end of the couch, she was munching fat-free microwave popcorn out of a sack. Her golden hair flowed down her back. Hell, she looked like an angel.

"Want some?" She smiled at him as he shut the front door and then held up her popcorn bag. When he hesitated, she shook it.

He went over to her and scooped out a handful. Their hands brushed, and to his surprise he felt a jolt.

Shut down.

Their eyes met and he felt pulled toward her like an iron filing to a powerful magnet. No matter how hard he tried to ignore her and shut down, he was failing big-time. Just the sight of her on his couch, and her golden female beauty had his blood heating and his heart pounding.

"This is a great movie," she said. "One of the best."

"Never saw it," he mumbled, determined to stumble to bed.

"'Cause you prefer those boring old war movies."

"Movies with no mush."

"Hey, sit down. Watch this! This is my favorite! Meg's in a restaurant—"

Sure enough, Meg Ryan was in a restaurant proving to Billy Crystal that a woman could fake an orgasm. Meg was cute. The scene was hot. Meg got hotter and hotter. Just watching her throw back her head and gasp made Phillip want Celeste in bed, made him want to see Celeste's face when she came.

He went around the sofa and sat beside Celeste. She squirmed a little, relocating as far from him as possible. Meg twisted and writhed and struggled to breathe. Celeste turned beet-red. She didn't look at him, though, and she didn't get up.

They pretended to watch the movie together. Every scene, every piece of dialogue between the mismatched lovers maddened him and made him want Celeste more.

Shut down! But he couldn't.

When it was over, Celeste looked as though she might cry just as she had on the porch.

"What's wrong?" Phillip whispered from his end of the sofa.

"They got together."

"It's called a happy ending. You're supposed to be happy."

She sobbed a little. "I am. I—I am."

He couldn't stand for her to cry, even over a silly movie. Used to, he would have taken her in his arms.

Don't touch her. She doesn't want you. She'll reject you.

Finally, he edged closer and took her hand in his. He fought to ignore that her fingers felt like soft, warm velvet against his rougher palm. "If they could fall in love and make it work, anybody could," he said.

What the hell are you doing, Westin?

She fell for his line—hook, line and sinker.

"Even us?" she whispered, glancing up at him with big, shy, shining eyes.

"Maybe it was too damn easy the first time," he muttered.

"Love at first sight?" she murmured on another little sob, brushing a wild strand of gold behind her ear.

"You were singing in that tight red dress. Every man in that awful bar…"

"Oh, dear, that awful dress—"

"Not awful. Sexy. So sexy."

"You came up and asked me after the fight if I needed

a ride home. You had such beautiful manners...even in that bar.''

"You wiped off my bloody brow with that napkin and said yes, so sweetly, so tenderly.''

"Yes," she whispered. She touched the wound on his cheek.

All of a sudden he couldn't stop looking into her big blue eyes. She had him, right where she wanted him. Or did he have her?

"No seat belt, huh?" she whispered. "What really happened?"

"You don't want to know." He pulled her closer and traced the contours of her face with his hands.

"Some silly war?"

"Can we start over?" He wanted to know. What the hell was he doing? He was supposed to be shutting down. And here he was, coming up for air.

"You mean, sex?"

"Sex would be nice."

"Will you hate me in the morning the way Billy Crystal—"

"I didn't run last time, did I?"

She bit her lip. "I would've come back. You wouldn't let me."

She would've come back. Was that true? He'd been too damned proud to go after her. "If you run off after fame and fortune, why would you want to come back here to me?"

"Maybe they aren't enough. I wouldn't know because I never had them. I thought you'd chase me."

"What are you really doing here? You could have gone anywhere. Why me?"

As always, that particular question made her pale and she refused to answer. And the fact that she refused to answer made him suspicious, made him want to ask that question over and over again even though he knew it made her uncomfortable.

Hell. Why was he so damn sure her coming back here to him meant something? Ego, that's why. Because he wanted to believe she'd come back to him, that was why.

If he was wrong, why had she come? If there was another reason, why wouldn't she tell him?

She leaned into him and kissed him. "You were always in my heart. You've got to believe that."

"That damn song of yours sure got to me."

"So you listened to it?"

"About a million times."

She beamed up at him.

"I've got the CD. I used to lie in bed and drink my bourbon straight from the bottle and listen to it over and over. It was as close as I could get to you."

"I wrote it for you. But I guess you figured that out."

"Yeah." He pulled her close.

"Oh, Phillip—"

To his surprise she circled his neck with her arms.

"Are you sure?" he whispered.

"You mean, about going to bed?"

He ran his hands through her hair. Even that brief contact could twist his gut into a knot. He sucked in a tight breath.

"No. But let's do it anyway," she said.

Without speaking, he carried her to his bedroom and kicked the door shut behind them.

"You can sleep in tomorrow," he murmured gently as he laid her on the bed.

"No more 0600. You're serious."

"You think so?"

"You going to leave me a list on the bedpost?"

"Make your own."

"So I've definitely won another skirmish. And the night is young. I haven't even begun."

"You have some peculiar methods, but you'd make a good combat Marine. You get your way."

"I wage my battles on the domestic front. You'd better look out. When we wake up tomorrow, this base is going to have a new commander."

"You think you're that good?"

"I know *we're* that good."

And they were. Her unsteady hands loosened his shirt buttons and unzipped his fly.

"Oh, Phillip, you smell so good...all musky and male."

When she was done and his jeans were on the floor, he undressed her.

She was as beautiful as he remembered, lush breasts, pink nipples, slim waist, and her skin smelled like flowers. He knelt in front of her and ran his hands all over her. She was like a perfect living sculpture in a museum. No art object was ever more beautiful than she. Every time he looked at her, she blushed and licked her lips. Finally, he took her in his arms and carried her to bed.

As always, this part of love was easy for them. When they touched each other, they burst into flame. Each remembered exactly what to do to give the other the most pleasure. He made love to her as slowly as he could, considering that he felt a raging need and was about to burst.

How else could he show her how much he adored her except with his hands and lips? She arched into him with a fierce passionate response that thrilled him. She clung, kissing his throat, his neck and his chest as he slowly rocked back and forth on top of her.

"Only you. Only you, Phillip," she murmured. "Only you."

"Seven years I wanted this," he said. "Why did you wait so long to come back to me?"

"Why didn't you come after me?"

No way could he tell her about one of the times he'd run away from military school to see his mother. When he'd seen the cars at the house, he'd known she was having one of her parties. She'd been so beautiful in her white sparkly dress that he'd run into her arms. She hadn't even hugged him. She'd stared at the dark stains on her white dress and said, "Your hands are dirty. Why can't you ever remember not to touch Mommy with dirty hands?" Then she'd simply picked up the phone and called the commander of his military school.

"You were the one who left," Phillip said to Celeste.

"But you didn't come…"

"I didn't know you wanted me to."

"Well, I did."

Oh, God— She kept saying that. Was it true? Did she want him? Had she wanted him even then…and…all this time he'd felt rejected?

Thrilled at these musings, he thrust into her deeply. Being inside her tight warmth was everything he'd remembered and more. She completed him as nothing else could.

Oh… This was where he belonged, inside her. He forced himself to move slowly. He wanted this to last, but she was in a hurry.

Clasping his waist, she hugged him hard. "Please… Now! Now! I can't wait!"

When it was over, they talked for hours.

* * *

The next morning Celeste opened her eyes and saw the golden sunlight streaming through the gauzy white curtains she'd hung in Phillip's bedroom. She was alone.

Mourning doves were cooing. Leaves were rustling outside. There were no traffic sounds. She smiled dreamily, hugging herself. The country quiet was so different from the neon glitter of Vegas.

Slowly after she woke up, she got up and raised the window and stuck her head out to breathe in the fresh warm air. Mission Creek wasn't so bad, not even for a girl who wanted to be a star. Not if she had Phillip.

Phillip had been so tender and sweet, so incredibly gentle, and this morning she felt like a woman deeply in love. The angst she'd felt when she'd lived with him before, her heart burning with the desire to be a star, was momentarily gone. Those past seven years had been filled with loneliness and disappointment. For now, last night with Phillip was enough. She felt a peace she'd never known before, a rightness, and a sense of belonging.

Where was he? She wanted him again. She could see her guitar where she'd left it propped outside against the back wall of the porch. It was funny. This morning she could stare at the guitar and feel nothing for it. All she wanted was Phillip to come into the bedroom and smile at her, to take her in his arms again. What did that mean?

The phone rang, jarring her out of her tranquil mood. She didn't answer it because she thought Phillip should answer it since most of the calls were for him. Even when it kept ringing, she let it. She didn't feel like talking to anybody. Then she giggled. Except maybe Phillip. He'd licked her all over. There were so many delicious things she wanted to do with him.

Finally, when the phone wouldn't stop ringing, she picked it up and said hello into the receiver.

"Baby!" Puff. Wheeze.

Alarm bells in her head went off like sirens in a fire station. "Johnny!" Cupping the phone, she lowered her voice. "You and I are through."

"But…baby—"

She turned her back to the door. "Through! *Finito! ¡Terminado!* Do you understand?"

"We have a contract."

"Tear it up! We are through! Do you un-der-stand? Through!"

"O-oh, no," he groaned. She heard a terrible pounding on his end.

"Johnny! That sounds like wood splintering—"

"They're at the door!" Gasp. Puff. Puff. "Call you later."

"Who's— No—don't dare call me here—"

"Catch you later, baby." He hung up.

"Johnny—" When he didn't answer she shook the phone.

Another voice said, "This is Nero. Remember me?"

She began to shake.

"You can't hide," Nero said.

"You'd better not show up here! You'd better not!" She slammed the phone down.

Oh, dear. She had to tell Phillip about this. But how could she tell Phillip? She began to pace. Phillip didn't understand about Johnny. He was jealous and hurt because Johnny had picked her up and driven her to Vegas. Would he believe her if she told him the truth? He was a Marine. Honor mattered to him.

Oh, why hadn't she been smarter? Johnny had been a disaster from start to finish. She'd been an idiot not to dump him long before now. But he'd fed her promises that had kept her dream alive.

Would Johnny tell the loan sharks where she was? Could they trace her by hitting Redial or something? Her heart plummeted. Yes, Johnny would tell. Yes, they could hit Redial. Nero had sounded pretty determined. If Johnny didn't come up with the money, there was no telling what he and The Pope would do.

She had to tell Phillip. He wanted to know why she'd left Vegas. She had to tell him. But he was so stolid and strong. He believed in lists and rules, in living by the book. He wouldn't approve of Johnny and his awful loan sharks. He wouldn't approve of Harry's, either, or of her working there.

In a scared little voice she began to sing, "Johnny, be good." And soon as she did, she felt stronger, strong enough to put Johnny's call and Nero's threat out of her mind.

Phillip's truck roared up in the drive. She had to put on something beautiful. Phillip was home. Phillip—

No sooner had she slipped into a pink cotton dress than the front door banged.

"I'm home," Phillip yelled.

"In here," she cried, tearing the dress off.

He stomped down the hall and opened the door. The pink dress lay over a chair.

"Oh, my. Still in bed?"

She fluffed her hair. "Worn out. You're too good a lover."

"Now that's a complaint a man doesn't mind hearing."

When he sat beside her, she kissed him.

"Hot kiss! Lots of tongue! What's that all about?"

She grinned. "Just checking to see if you're in the mood."

He stripped off his shirt. His boots hit the floor with two loud clunks.

"Looks like you're in the mood—"

"Always with you," he said.

Five

___

Celeste stretched lazily, curling her body against Phillip's. Oh, dear…. She felt limp and happy, completely without a care or a fear. Phillip was as hot as a furnace. Enveloped in his masculine warmth, she felt as if she was sinking into a delicious sensual spell.

"Mmm… I want to stay like this forever."

"Can I shut the windows yet?" Phillip asked, kicking at the sheet with his foot. "It's hotter than the shades of Hades."

"Poor baby," Celeste cooed without the least bit of sympathy as she twisted around playfully and dropped her gaze to the mat of black hair on his wide chest. He had the air conditioner on and she had the window open.

"Or at least turn on a fan?" he grumbled.

It was way after midnight. Awash in moonbeams, the lovers lay awake in a tangle of sheets. Wrapped in each other's arms they were satiated from lovemaking. Or at least Celeste was.

"But the fan makes so much noise we won't be able to hear the cicadas."

"The air in here is as thick and warm as hot jelly."

Phillip was exaggerating. He had the air-conditioning going full blast.

"Jelly. Yummy."

He mopped a hand across his perspiring brow.

"The window being cracked is not why you're so hot, lover buver, and you know it," she teased. "We're like a pair of spent noodles."

"Straight out of the boiling pot."

"I have no complaints." She stroked her hand through the thick matted hair of his chest, down his waist.

He laughed when she circled him down there, and the deep rumble rippled through her and made her nestle against his hot, muscular body.

"Woman, look what you did to my clam digger. It's pretty pitiful."

"What?"

He lay back on the pillow and crossed his arms under his dark head. "It's the punch line in a corny joke about a boy and girl who get shipwrecked on a deserted island. It makes the rounds every time my Marine buddies get together for beers at the Lone Star Country Club or The Saddlebag. On the third or fourth beer Mercado always has to tell it. You wouldn't appreciate it."

"Try me."

"I feel like we've been in bed a week," he said, changing the subject.

"Almost."

He frowned. "The chores are damn sure piling up.

We're running low on feed and I need to break in that new saddle and those chaps.''

"Hey…hey. You talk too much.''

"Hell, I was going to hitch a plow to my bulldozer and clear the mesquite out of the north pasture.''

"That'll wait.''

He groaned. "Maybe if it had rained, I'd agree. I've got a bunch of barely weaned calves that need to eat.''

"Six days,'' she corrected softly, her mind still on their sexual marathon. "Not a whole week.''

"And six nights. Give a guy credit for the nights.''

"You're really something,'' she murmured. "And number six isn't over yet.''

"Yeah, it is. I'm thinking about all those hungry calves and the unrecoverable feed costs plus the extra pasture leases—''

"Quit thinking about them, then.'' She smiled, her heart full of love. "We did this stay-in-bed-a-week, devour-each-other's-bodies routine when we fell in love the first time,'' she mused dreamily. "Is it love at second sight this time all over again?''

He rolled over. "If it isn't, it's a damn good substitute.''

She thought of Vegas, of Johnny and the loan sharks after them both. Terror had driven her back to Phillip. But something else might keep her here. Despite the dead cow and Johnny's call, she felt so safe, so beloved, lying here beside him. It was as if a missing piece of her life had fallen into place.

"But tomorrow, we're getting up…early,'' Phillip said. "We're going to behave ourselves, act like mature adults and go back to work…feed those calves….''

"Oh, dear. End of honeymoon.''

"You're going to clean house and I'm going to pay those bills on the spindle."

"At 0600—sharp?" She saluted. Or rather, she tried. It was an impossible maneuver since she was lying in bed so close to him.

He laughed and pulled her tighter against his chest. "You can sleep as late as you like. Hey, did I tell you that there's a dance tomorrow night at the Lone Star Country Club?"

She remembered what that waitress, Mabel, had said about his girlfriends at the club. "I—I don't fit in there. I—I don't have anything to wear. Anything elegant I mean."

"We'll have to get you something, then."

She'd been dreading something like this. What if she got out and somebody recognized her as Stella Lamour? She remembered Nero's voice on the phone and shuddered. What if word somehow got back to Nero and The Pope? What if they had spies in the neighborhood and figured out where she was and came after her?

"I really wouldn't fit in," she said.

"Of course you fit in, and I'd really like to take you," Phillip persisted.

"I'd rather go for a seventh night in bed."

"We can do that after we get back from the dance. Celeste, I really do want to celebrate our getting back together formally...with my friends."

"Isn't that what we've been doing?" she whispered. "Celebrating?"

"I don't feel too formal when we're both naked."

She laughed.

"You still have doubts, don't you?" he whispered.

"I—I know we're great in bed. That part's like a fairy tale. But what about all the rest of it?" She sighed. "Do you really think such a fairy-tale relationship can last out there in the real world?''

"I want it to. Maybe all we both have to do is decide that's what we want and work at it.''

"But— A girl like me…and a guy like you…" Pain swelled in her chest. "You come from a wealthy family. I have no family.''

"You have me.''

"But—"

"One day at a time. You tell me what's in your heart, what you really want, and I'll try to be there for you.''

Would he? What about her dreams of being a star? Why did taking their relationship to another level scare her so much? What was she so afraid of?

"I've lost everybody I ever loved,'' she blurted.

He traced his lips across her brow. "Me, too. Only I never loved anybody the way I love you.''

"I don't want to hurt you.''

"Celeste, a drill sergeant in the Marines once told me I could be anything I wanted to be. The strange thing was, I believed him, and it's made all the difference in my life.'' He toyed with a tendril of her hair. "So—I'll give you the same advice, believe in yourself. I damn sure do.''

"You're supposed to settle down with a churchgoing girl.''

"I thought that was a dumb idea even before you came home.''

"Home,'' she whispered.

She lifted her head off the pillow and gazed down at him, unconsciously memorizing the way he looked, all sweaty and hot and virile and sexy after their lovemaking.

Home? Was she the one for him? Was he the only

man for her? If so, why was she so afraid? There was so much she hadn't come to terms with—her little-girl dreams, her big-girl dreams, the bad men chasing her and the horrible fact that by staying with Phillip and not telling him about Nero and The Pope she might be deliberately putting him in danger.

She closed her eyes and swallowed the hard lump in her throat. Going out together socially to the Lone Star Country Club would make it seem as though they were a real couple, an ordinary couple. Were they? Was it really that simple? Was she ready for that?

"All the guys will be there," he said, his deep voice hopeful.

"You mean, your Marine buddies?"

"Ricky Mercado and his brother-in-law, Luke...and several of the men who served under my command in the 14th unit."

"I remember Ricky. Talk, dark and handsome—right?"

"Tall, dark..."

"Cute."

"Believe me, he's as anxious as you to renew the acquaintance as you are. Did you two—"

"I was just teasing you. I don't know, Phillip. It seems awful soon to face your friends. We'll have to explain what I'm doing here."

"Well, think about it. I'm proud of you. I want to show you off to the guys and make them jealous as hell." He slid his hand under her nape and stroked the back of her neck with his thumb. "I'm serious, very serious about our relationship."

Her heart swelled. "Oh, Phillip." She felt warmth seep through her being at his stirring words. "But what if somebody recognizes me as Stella..." She shuddered. "That could ruin—"

"They won't," he said gruffly. "And if they do, I'm proud of your CD, proud of the way you worked so hard to make your dream come true."

Her heart missed a beat. *You don't know about Nero and The Pope!*

"You are?" she whispered.

"Damn proud."

You wouldn't be if you knew that the only reason I came here was to use you as a human shield to protect me from two killers.

She remembered the dead cow and the note. Just thinking about why she'd come here made her feel so selfish and so cowardly. He was being so sweet to her.

She bit down on her lower lip. She was using him. She owed him the truth. But the truth might spoil their fragile happiness, and she'd had so little happiness.

"Okay, I'll go, Phillip."

Relief seemed to flow through him as he relaxed and kissed her brow. "Can I turn on the fan now?"

She nodded. He got up and shut the windows and turned on the fan. Then he came back to bed and pulled her close. He was instantly asleep, but she lay in the dark, utterly bewildered, wondering what she should do.

This past week had been pure magic. His every rough and tender kiss had stolen her breath away, stolen her heart, too.

She loved him.

She hadn't wanted to fall in love again, and she didn't want to damage their new relationship by telling him that she was involved in any way with a pair of hoodlums like The Pope and Nero. And if they tracked her here, how would she ever convince him that Johnny had lied about her to the loan sharks, that she'd done nothing wrong?

Nothing except run to Phillip and endanger him and maybe his livestock because she'd been scared out of her wits

Phillip had said he was proud of her. Oh, how wonderful his saying that had made her feel. She wasn't ready to jeopardize Phillip's good opinion of her. Not yet. Their relationship was too new and fragile and precious.

"Do you want to dance?" Phillip whispered in Celeste's ear.

"Oh, yes!" She set her purse on the table. Anything to escape the escalating tension at their table. Her own nerves had started skittering at her first sight of the four-story clubhouse and its rolling lawns.

"Excuse us, gentlemen," Phillip said as he helped Celeste out of her chair.

She smiled at his friends brightly, maybe too brightly—her star-wattage smile. When every man in the room turned to admire her, Phillip swore under his breath.

"Do you have to be so damned sexy?"

She threw her head back and laughed.

"Minx," he said in an awed whisper.

She'd dressed up in a slinky red dress that hugged every curve. She'd put on lots of makeup and fixed her hair because she was so afraid of all the beautiful women Phillip had dated at the club.

She gripped his arm as he led her across the elegant room to the dance floor.

"Relax. You're the most beautiful woman here and the only one for me."

"Really?"

"Really, damn it."

"Is my dress too loud?"

"You look sensational."

She hated being so insecure. She wanted and needed him to say things like that over and over.

Lavish bouquets of long-stemmed roses of all colors decorated the tables of the Lone Star Country Club dining room. Celeste and Phillip had a candlelit table in a corner with Phillip's handsome friends from the 14th unit—Flynt Carson, the local millionaire rancher, Spence Harrison, the former D.A., Tyler Murdoch, a bomb expert, and Luke Callaghan, Ricky's brother-in-law.

Luke was wearing dark glasses because he'd been blinded by scrap metal in a mission and was only just now recovering his vision. Like Phillip, Luke trusted Ricky completely, despite the rest of the gang's doubts.

Unlike her, Phillip seemed so relaxed and at ease in his country club with his successful friends. Celeste knew he wasn't an extremely wealthy man, but he had his Marine retirement and he'd inherited. Compared to her, he was very comfortable financially.

Some of the guys were married and settled now, but this weekend their wives were away in San Antonio shopping. Ricky Mercado, the black sheep of the bunch because his family had Mafia connections, had come in late and was now slouching at the far end of the table. He'd had too many beers and his attitude was that of a sulky jungle cat. Phillip believed Ricky had gone straight, but Mercado was ready to pounce at any remark or glance the other guys made that he didn't like. Not that his attitude slowed his former guys down much.

Even though Phillip and Celeste were sitting between Mercado and the rest of the men, thereby bodily separating them, and Luke, Ricky's brother-in-law, had been hard at work to defuse the situation, the other guys knew what to say and do to irritate Mercado. Thus, Ricky's mood had worsened with each beer.

Not that Phillip seemed upset by Mercado's glowering face. Celeste, however, had wanted everybody to be happy. She'd begun feeling nervous when Mercado had started telling a story about Phillip putting his life in danger by charging three snipers. She hadn't wanted to hear about Phillip's near-death experiences so she was glad Phillip had put his hand on her waist, glad he'd led her to the dance floor.

"Quit twisting that ring 'round and round' your finger. Didn't I tell you, you're stunning?" Phillip whispered when they reached the dance floor. "Didn't all the guys say you were beautiful? Too damn many times? Even Mercado?"

"It was the only nice thing he's said. But why would you take on three snipers?"

"Mercado was exaggerating. Hey, you look good in red. You look like a star. Like Stella—"

"You clean up nice, too," she murmured as he folded her into his arms. Maybe it was best not to think about those stories when she didn't have to. "There are so many beautiful, elegant women here. Have you…dated any of them?"

He frowned. "A few."

"Quite a few?" she asked, feeling even more insecure.

He was silent for a long moment. Then he touched her hair and tilted her chin up so he could meet her troubled gaze.

"Yes." He hesitated. "None of them were you."

She rested her cheek against his chest.

"You're different, Celeste."

"You'd say that to them, too."

"Maybe. But this isn't a line. I'm telling you the truth. I don't care who you are or who you've been or who you've been with before. I don't care where you came from. I need you. Just you. I don't know why. I just do. Honey, you're so damn beautiful and so sweet…not to mention the things you think up to do in bed."

"I've got a good idea for tonight." She whispered a fantasy into his ear.

He chuckled. "Hold that thought."

"Promise you won't think I'm kinky."

"It'll only seem kinky the first time."

The music started and his powerful body moved slowly against her petite frame. As always they were a perfect fit. For a few magic moments she forgot everything but Phillip, but then she grew aware of Mercado's darkening stare. The voices from their table were growing louder.

"Ricky looks so unhappy and the guys, I mean, except for Luke—"

"Hold your head up," Phillip whispered. "Look at me. Forget Ricky and the guys. They'll work out their issues about Mercado. He told me he doesn't work for his family and I believe him. And besides, Luke's holding down the fort while we dance."

She stared so deeply into his silver eyes and forced herself to forget the tension they'd left behind at their table. He was so gorgeous, he mesmerized her. Just looking at him, even in front of all these people, she was sure she lost a piece of her soul to him forever.

"You have nothing to be ashamed of, Celeste. You are as classy as any woman here."

Would he believe that when he found out Vegas loan

sharks were hot on her trail? And what if it turned out they'd killed his cow?

Soon she forgot Nero and The Pope and the guys, and surrendered to the music. Not that Phillip and she really danced. They held each other tightly, their bodies swaying as other beautiful couples swirled around them.

Every woman seemed to cut her eyes at Phillip. Oh, dear. He was so dreamily handsome in his dark suit, dress shirt and dark tie. He didn't have an elegant body as did some of the men at the club. He was too powerfully built and hard-edged. But in his suit he could almost pass for a gentleman.

What woman wouldn't want him? Oh, why had she picked such a flashy dress? The other women were dressed far more conservatively. Next time she'd wear black…long sleeves…

If there was a next time.

"I think this is a waltz," Celeste said a little nervously because the other men weren't crushing their elegant dates and wives to their bodies as sensually as Phillip held her. She didn't want to make a spectacle of herself. "One, two, three. One, two, three…"

"I don't give a damn what kind of dance it is as long as I get to hold you," he murmured, pressing her even closer so that they were thigh to thigh.

"We could have stayed home and done this," she murmured in a shaky tone.

"Things would've gotten a whole lot wilder at home."

His arms tightened around her. She laughed, remembering how he'd caught her on the back porch last night, carried her inside and stripped her in the living room.

They swayed to the music. There was something so sexy about being fully dressed and having to restrain their passion in such a refined setting. Anybody who saw them had to know what they really wanted to do was to strip each other naked.

"The guys love you. They understand why I love you, too."

"I hope I made a good impression. I want you to be proud of me."

"Proud? They're jealous as hell. Especially Mercado."

"Why do the other guys dislike him?"

"Long story. Mercado's okay, though."

"But the other guys..."

"They'll figure out I'm right. You'll see."

The dance ended. When they went back to the table, Ricky, who looked even angrier than before, stood and jerked her chair out. "You call that a waltz, old buddy?" he muttered, attempting a light tone. "You're losing your touch." The other guys frowned at him, but he only scowled back at them.

"Relax, bro," Luke whispered.

Before she could sit, Ricky grabbed Celeste's hand. "My turn," he growled, tugging her away from Phillip. "If it's okay with you, old buddy?"

Of course, after that, all of Phillip's friends had to dance with her. Watching them from the table, Mercado grew more sullen by the minute. Then dinner was served and for a while the tensions at their table eased.

Most of the men had lobster tails with a thick buttery sauce, the kind of sauce Celeste didn't approve of. Mercado refused to eat, saying he'd drink his dinner. Phillip had ordered a slab of steak at least four-inches thick, along with a baked potato he stuffed with sour cream and chives.

When everybody was eating, Ricky said, "I'm glad

you're back, Celeste. Glad you're taming the old war-monger.''

"Warmonger?" she whispered. "He's retired from all that."

"In your dreams," Mercado said.

Ty and the other Marines shot Mercado a warning look, but he ignored them and said, "Now that you're home, sir, maybe I won't receive any sudden calls to go down to Central America."

"Central America?" Terrified, Celeste set her fork down. "What do you mean? Ricky—what on earth are you talking about?"

"Ever heard of a hellhole called Mezcaya?"

"Hell, Mercado," Luke whispered. "See what you've done, she's as pale as a sheet."

"Mezcaya?" she whispered in alarm. "Isn't that the country in Central America that's a breeding ground for terrorists?"

"Ever heard of a particularly nasty little group called El Jefe?" Mercado asked. "They run guns...even from here in Mission Creek."

Phillip interrupted. "Can't we talk about something else? How about the weather?"

"Has he been down to Mezcaya recently?" Celeste whispered, afraid to hear the answer.

"That cut on his cheek. Picked up some shrapnel in Mezcaya right before you showed up on his doorstep, Celeste, didn't you old buddy?"

"It was a rock," Phillip said. "A lousy rock."

"Hell, you nearly bought it," Ricky said.

Spence hissed at Mercado to shut up, but when Phillip shot Spence a warning look, Spence stabbed his potato rather violently.

"All he told me was that he wasn't wearing a seat belt," Celeste murmured tightly.

Ricky laughed. "Why would he be wearing a belt—in The Cave?"

"The Cave?"

"Short for dungeon, sweetheart. He killed a guy, so they locked him up. Ty got him out. When the chopper came—"

"Chopper?" Suddenly her throat squeezed shut and she could barely breathe. "Phillip, you said you'd retired—"

"I am! Damn it, Mercado," Phillip began. "Celeste lost her mother and her father when she was young. She has a thing about close calls and death."

"Don't we all?" Mercado muttered. "So, I guess you didn't tell her about Mendoza or the fact you think his crazy son killed that cow on your ranch to warn you—"

"I'd appreciate it if you didn't upset her—"

"Who's Mendoza?" Celeste asked.

"Nobody. Just this murdering terrorist Westin killed."

"That's enough," Phillip thundered.

Mercado shoved back his chair. "Hey, I know where I'm not welcome."

"Finally," Tyler snapped.

"Easy," Luke said. "Why don't we talk about something else?"

"Because maybe I want to talk about what I want to talk about!" Mercado thundered. "El Jefe is right here in Mission Creek, and all of you know it. Phillip and Wainwright have the FBI looking.... Somebody gave this guy Yardley my name."

"Because of your lousy family," Tyler said.

"Cool it, both of you," Phillip's whisper was even

more deadly than his hard Marine-issue voice. "Don't make a scene. Not here."

"I had nothing to do with any cow or running guns." Ricky threw his napkin down and stood. "Sorry to eat and run."

"Eat and run?" Celeste said, swallowing the lump of fear in her throat.

"Drink and run, you mean," Spence countered.

"Please stay, Ricky," Celeste pleaded.

Luke and Phillip stood as well, and Ricky muttered something under his breath for Phillip and Luke that she could overhear.

"They keep looking at me, making digs about my family and the Mafia...setting the FBI on me.... My former friends...."

"Okay," Phillip said.

"I don't like it. I can't take it."

"Stick it out," Luke advised.

"Maybe I don't feel as comfortable around the old gang anymore as you do—sir. And you do—Luke."

"Look. Nobody said anything to Wainwright or the FBI. You severed your ties with the Mafia," Phillip said.

"Nobody but you and Luke buys that line."

"They will if you hang in there," Phillip said. "Quit drinking. Order dinner."

"Sorry, sir." Ricky leaned down and lightly kissed Celeste's cheek. "Keep up the good work, pretty lady. This *old* rascal is going to take a lot of taming."

Mercado turned on his heel and strode abruptly through the dancing couples, breaking several apart before he made it out the door.

"Good riddance," Spence said.

When Harrison made an obscene gesture, Luke and Phillip gave him warning looks.

"Forget Mercado. All we have to do is get rid of you, old man, and we'll have her all to ourselves," Tyler kidded, attempting to ease the tension.

"*Sir,*" Phillip said.

Ty laughed. "Sir."

"No chance would I leave her with you all," Phillip said, relaxing.

"Any chance of wedding bells?" Spence wanted to know.

Celeste blushed, but she felt relieved now that Mercado had gone and the mood had lightened up.

"How'd the two of you meet?" Luke and Flynt asked in unison.

"She was singing a love song."

They all hooted.

"Well, if she can sing to you, she can damn sure sing to us," Luke said.

One by one, they demanded that she sing to them.

She turned questioningly to Phillip. "I don't think…"

But Ty was on stage with the mike. "We have a star in our midst." Phillip's buddies started clapping and cheering.

"We're outnumbered, honey," Phillip said. "Go on. Let's don't make a scene."

Slowly, she got up and Phillip led her to Ty, who held the mike. Phillip gave the bandleader a big tip, and she told them what to play. Celeste, a natural star, brought the house down when she sang her one big hit. Then she surprised Phillip and sang a song she'd just written called "Lone Star Love Song."

When the last plaintive syllable died, the crowded ballroom was silent. Then everybody started clapping and whistling and screaming for more.

"More… More…" The guys began to stomp.

"Thank you, everybody," she murmured. With a shy blush and a graceful little bow, she demurred, and Phillip led her back to their table.

"You're good. You remind me of somebody I've heard or seen before," Spence said, a frown on his handsome face.

"She's a natural star," Phillip agreed. "Honey, you were the hit of the gathering."

She blushed nervously again with even more glowing pleasure because Phillip was praising her singing, and he was proud of her.

"I know that song," Luke said. "'Nobody but you....' I used to play it all the time. Reminded me of this girl who dumped me. Who sang it? Who wrote it? Stacy? No..."

"I don't know," she lied, squeezing Phillip's hand so he wouldn't give her away.

Spence and Luke said they had to go. Just as their party was beginning to break up, two men entered the ballroom. One was a wide-shouldered hunk whose grim, hard-edged face brought butterflies to Celeste's stomach.

Oh, dear. The man was tall and trim with thick brown hair.

Vegas. Harry's. "Not Cole Yardley," she whispered. "Don't let it be..."

It was.

"What?" Phillip demanded, eyeing her first and then the two newcomers at the door. "Do you know the sheriff?"

"The sheriff?" She began to fidget with her napkin. "I—I've listened to a few of his messages. I—I think I need to go to the ladies' room."

"You just went. Do you know Justin Wainwright or not?"

The sheriff waved and Phillip waved back to him.

Cole Yardley shot her a dark glance.

She lowered her eyes. Oh, dear. This was bad. Cole Yardley was here in Mission Creek with the sheriff, and he remembered her.

If he could find her, anybody could. Oh, dear. What if he said something about that awful night in Harry's to Phillip?

"Can we go home?" she whispered, frantic when Yardley and the sheriff ambled toward their table.

"Not until I find out what Wainwright and the guy who frowned at you wants."

"He did not frown at me."

"Well, he damn sure wasn't looking at me."

If only Cole Yardley would quit glowering at her.

"You know him, don't you?"

"N-no," she said.

The sheriff joined them. "Sorry to interrupt a social gathering, but Yardley here just rolled into town."

Phillip nodded. Everybody introduced himself.

"Glad to meet you, *Celeste*," Yardley said tersely.

"Glad to meet you, Mr. Yardley," she said.

Silently she begged him not to give her away.

"Yardley here is a federal investigator," Justin Wainwright said. Justin handed Cole Yardley's business card to Phillip. "He's here about your dead cow and your suspicions about that arms-dealing ring. Like you, he suspects El Jefe may be operating in our area."

"In Mission Creek?" Celeste blurted.

"Just listen to what he has to say," Wainwright said.

"I admire your work, Westin. I know you've fought for years to bring down El Jefe." Yardley glanced at Celeste when she began to bite her lip.

"Who's El Jefe?" Celeste whispered. "I forget."

"Not who. What! El Jefe is the biggest terrorist ring in Mezcaya."

"Right. Which is in Central America," Celeste said.

"We were just discussing this," Phillip offered.

Yardley cocked his brows, but Phillip didn't embellish.

Mezcaya again. "We were just leaving," Celeste said. The talk about Mezcaya was making her nervous. Phillip had nearly died in Mezcaya right before she'd come. She didn't really want to know about Phillip being involved with terrorists. A second worry was that at any moment Yardley might decide to tell everybody how he and she had met in Vegas.

Phillip had said he was retired. While the men talked, she found herself staring at the red mark on his cheek. She didn't care about the dead cow or El Jefe. She had so many vital questions and they were all personal. Was Phillip capable of settling down even if he loved her? Was she capable of giving up her music for him? Did she even want to? Were they as mismatched as ever? Did people like them settle down? Or did they need a rush other people could live without?

The applause tonight had thrilled her. Still, more than the applause, the gleam of pride in Phillip's eyes when she'd sung had warmed her heart. But was his love enough?

"I believe your friend, Mercado, is still involved in the Mafia," Yardley was saying. "And running guns."

First Mezcaya. Now the Mafia. What was Phillip involved in?

"No way," Phillip countered.

"He just may be the ringleader of this nasty, little weapons-smuggling operation I'm investigating."

"You'll never convince me of that," Phillip said in his flat, Marine-issue voice.

"He was just down in Mezcaya."

"You want to know why? To help Ty Murdoch save my ass. I was slated for execution and he was part of the rescue team."

"Execution!" Celeste gasped. The truth at last!

Phillip had nearly died—again. And he hadn't told her. "Oh, dear. Oh, dear."

"If he wasn't involved with those bastards, how'd he know you were in trouble?" Yardley asked. "Then as soon as you and...and this young lady get back here, somebody kills your cow and leaves you a note."

"You're grilling me but you're looking at my girl. You two know each other or something?"

Yardley and she shook their heads, but neither of them could meet Phillip's gaze.

"Where are you from, anyway, Yardley?" Phillip demanded in a voice charged with both annoyance and jealousy.

Yardley glanced at Celeste.

Phillip skimmed Yardley's business card. "Your card says your office is in Vegas."

"We don't know each other," Celeste whispered, but she blushed hotly.

Phillip stared at Yardley.

"I never saw her before in my life. And believe me, I would remember a face like hers."

"She's a hard woman to forget," Phillip said stiffly. "Well, it's late. I'm tired." He stood.

"If you hear anything, anything at all that's the least bit suspicious, give me a call," Yardley said. "If you lose any more livestock..."

"Sure." Phillip's voice and manner were curt.

When Celeste and Phillip were in his truck, Phillip said, "You never did tell me why you abandoned your career in Las Vegas and came here in such a hurry. Did something happen? Was Yardley your lover?"

"I can't believe..." she whispered. "How could you ask me such a thing?"

"Fasten your seat belt," he muttered. Then he stomped down hard on the accelerator.

She gave a little cry when the truck shot forward into the darkness. Soon the silence inside the cab was so thick between them Celeste hardly dared to breathe.

She stared out the window. He watched the yellow lines in the center of the road fly past.

When they got home, she got out of the truck and ran to the front stairs, only to stumble over something warm and sticky. When she fell forward, black eye sockets stared up at her.

She screamed, and Phillip flew to her when she convulsed in tears and pulled her off the bloated object.

"I—it's a dead...cow," she sobbed. "A-another one. On...on the first step..."

"It's okay."

"There's another note—"

Phillip ripped off the note somebody had nailed to the porch railing.

"'You hurt my family, so now I will hurt yours,'" Phillip read.

"Another cow," she whispered. "Two cows. Why would anybody be killing your cows? I thought Sheriff Wainwright—"

"He's investigating. So am I," Phillip said.

"Is this happening because you killed that bad guy in Mezcaya and didn't tell me about it?"

"I don't know, damn it. With your kind of logic, I

could blame you. Cows didn't start dying till you came here.''

"Oh?'' She felt a rush of guilt and fought to cover it. "Sure! Blame me!'' She turned away, so he couldn't read her face.

"I was making a point.''

"This is about you, not me! What are you doing behind *my* back?''

"What are you doing behind mine, Celeste? You're not telling me where you're coming from, either.''

"Are you about to go off on a mission again and get yourself killed the next time?''

"You're hiding something, too, Celeste. What the hell is going on? Are you going to run off with Yardley or something?''

"What?''

"Did he come here because of you? Is he your next Johnny Silvers?''

"D-don't be ridiculous. He's investigating your gun smugglers!''

"*My* gun smugglers? Hell!'' He stared at her.

"I'm tired,'' she said. "And I'm going to bed. To my old room down the hall. Thank you for a *lovely* evening.''

"My pleasure.'' His tone was hard—pure Marine issue. "I'll call the sheriff and then get rid of the cow.''

She picked up her skirt and walked carefully around him and the mutilated cow. He raced up the stairs and unlocked the door for her. It was hours before the sheriff came and finished his business, hours before Phillip and Juan finished dealing with the dead cow and Phillip finally stomped up the stairs and came inside.

She was still awake, lying in her bed at the end of the hall, staring up at the spidery threads of moonlight on the ceiling. When she heard his heavy tread in the hall, she ached to run into his arms. Instead, she buried her face in her pillow.

His door opened and closed, and he went to bed alone, just as she had.

She hugged herself as she had so many times when she'd lain awake in the dark after her mother had died. Every time she closed her eyes, she saw black eye sockets. She wanted Phillip's arms around her so badly, it was all she could do not to get up and run down the hall to his bed.

Would she always always be that grief-stricken little girl who cried too easily because she was starved for true love?

Six

The honeymoon was over. After a sleepless night worrying about Yardley, and being scared about the second dead cow, and sick that she and Phillip had quarreled, Celeste got up in the dark several hours before 0600. It upset her that Phillip, Mr. Big Macho Marine, could sleep like a baby even when she ran the vacuum down the hall.

She didn't hear a peep from his bedroom until well after ten. When she finally heard him in the shower, she was on the way to the utility room, her arms aching under the weight of a third, huge load of laundry.

There was a lot of dirt on a ranch, at least in dry south Texas. When Phillip came in from a hard day's work in some distant pasture, his carved face would be streaked with mud because he'd perspired so much that the blowing dust had stuck to him. His clothes and hair would be caked with grit. The dirt seeped under doors and through cracks and crannies of the window frames. Dusting had to be done every single day.

That gloomy morning after the dance, Celeste made herself two pots of coffee. Wired from so much caffeine and exhausted from no sleep and the hours of housework, the blissful six days of their marathon lovemaking in Phillip's bed seemed like a long-ago dream. So did her ambition to be a star.

Maybe it was for the best that Mercado, Yardley, rumors about dangerous gunrunners, and the dead cow had turned up to burst her little romantic bubble. Phillip and she were as different as two people could be. Maybe she lusted after him and ached for his sweet smiles and praise. Maybe they really did love each other in their way, but how long could passion alone sustain them? Her failures in the music world had taught her that making it in the real world was an everyday matter. So was love and marriage.

She didn't want to be married to a soldier who left her and went off to war while she stayed home to panic at every phone call because she was so afraid somebody would phone to say he was dead and she'd lose everything again. And did he want a girl who couldn't give up her impractical dreams of being a country-western star?

Mercado had him figured. In between adventures like chasing gunrunners, Phillip needed some nice society, church girl, one of those rich, proper beauties from the country club who dressed like a lady. Someone who was content to be a stay-at-home wife while he was gone.

Celeste was different. She had a voice and a need to be more than she was. Only when she sang did she lose the awful feeling that she was an invisible little nothing. If she dressed flashy and sang her heart out, it was because she craved attention and love. A girl didn't just have talent. Talent had the girl.

When she'd been a kid, all the other kids had had real mothers and daddies to go home to. All she'd had was her music. Singing and writing songs gave her a release from pain and a way to express herself that nothing else did. If she gave all that up for Phillip now, and he kept fooling around with gunrunners and went off again on some dangerous mission and got himself killed, where would she be—too old to make her big dream come true.

If Phillip died, she'd be a nothing. For all the fireworks and tenderness, Phillip might leave her. Her music was the only real anchor she'd ever had.

She was thirty-two. Her shot at the big time was running out. Every spare moment she got, she'd better work on her music. She had greatness in her. She knew she did. This time she'd go to Nashville.

For the rest of that week Celeste kept to her bedroom in the evenings when Phillip came in from work, and Phillip kept to his. She would cook early and leave the food on the stove. They would eat dinner at different times and avoid speaking to each other whenever possible. Even though she was curious about the dead cow, she hadn't asked him what he'd done with it or what he'd said to the sheriff or maybe to Cole Yardley. She knew Phillip was investigating the incident, but she didn't probe for details because the whole thing upset her too much.

At night Phillip went for long walks and watched television. She read and wrote and taped songs in her room. Every chance she got to go into town, she mailed a tape and a letter to Greg Furman, the producer in Nashville, who still hadn't written her back. Phillip seemed too preoccupied to notice that she'd asked for the truck more often.

At night when she was too tired to sing another note, she would crawl into her bed and curl up, lying rigidly in a fetal position, listening to the boards creak and the wind moan in the eaves. After lying in Phillip's arms and enjoying all that soul-stirring sex, it was all the harder to sleep alone without his muscular arms holding her close.

Since Phillip was an ex-Marine, he probably found it easier to stick to his sulk and content himself with investigating his mystery than she did. For him it was second nature to draw lines in the sand and then stay on his side waiting for her to surrender. Well, she wouldn't surrender. She wouldn't.

According to Wainwright and Yardley, Mendoza's men were definitely in the area. Not that Celeste invited Phillip to share his concern on that subject with her. Hell, she was barely civil.

When Phillip stalked into the house late one scorching afternoon intending to bar himself in his bedroom until it was time for dinner, the sound of Celeste's lilting voice in the bathtub brought him to an abrupt halt outside her door. Damn it. She sang those sweet, sad songs every night in her room, probably just to get to him.

The last week had been pure hell. Besides worrying about her safety, it was impossible to live with her, to hear her pour her heart out in those songs, to watch her glide from room to room, without wanting her. Everything she did was sexy, everything she wore—those tight short shorts that revealed her long legs, those skimpy T-shirts that clung to her breasts, the way her yellow hair flowed messily around her shoulders, her dreamy expression when she stared out the window. Did she yearn for bright lights, the stage, fame, and a man who could give her or at least promise her those things?

Every night he'd lain in bed thinking about her, remembering her every smile, smiles that died the minute he entered a room. She'd been driving into town a lot. Why? To flirt with other men? Cole Yardley? To plan her next escape? What did she want, really?

Why couldn't he forget how hot she'd been in his bed before their quarrel, how she'd opened her mouth and given him endless tongue, how she'd stripped and danced for him on the kitchen table? He'd shoved the dishes on the floor, and they'd done it on that table, then in the shower, on the burgundy couch, against the front door, and even in the cab of his pickup before he'd driven into town one morning.

Boots clomping, he stalked noisily down the hall, pausing at her bedroom door, only to gasp when it groaned. Had he touched it by mistake?

Instinctively he grabbed the knob, and the damned door, which had been slightly ajar, opened as if by itself. She was in the tub, splashing water and singing too loudly to notice him. He could see her plain as day.

Beyond her rumpled bed, the path to the bathroom was littered with her clothes and jewelry—those incredible short shorts, her lacy black bra and panties, that little silver chain that disappeared into her T-shirt and hung between her breasts.

Her breasts. His gaze feasted on the lush mounds. She held up a wet rag and squeezed water onto them as she sang some husky melody that he heard all the way to his bones.

It took him a while to catch his breath. She was lying back in her tub sponging her breasts with that damned pink washrag until her nipples peaked like ripe raspberries. His heart knocked violently and he went statue-still. A second glance and he felt as if he'd been slammed in the groin. Instantly he was as hard as a rock.

"I'm just a lonesome girl/lost in the middle of nowhere," she sang. "A lonesome girl in love with a lonesome man…"

But when she squeezed the water out of her rag and folded it neatly on the side of the tub, he knew he should go. She stood up, water dripping off her sleek, dewy body. Oh, God. More than anything he wanted to shove the door open and rush inside to her. But what would she do? She'd barely spoken since she'd stumbled over the dead cow.

His heart thrummed madly in his throat. Soap bubbles clung to her voluptuous, pink body as she reached for a towel. Even from the hall, he could almost smell the rose soap she used, almost taste the warm steamy water that beaded on her skin.

His gaze slid up and down her body, lingering on her breasts and then on that golden triangle of hair lower down. She'd cost him his peace of mind, his very sanity. He didn't know how to win her, but losing her wasn't an option. His objectives weren't clear. He couldn't focus on anything but her.

Oh, man. His physical reaction bothered him. He was a Marine. Where was his iron will, his disciplined Marine Corps brain? Why was it so hard to be tough with her?

Damn it. Xavier Gonzalez and the dead cows didn't bother Phillip nearly as much as his fears of losing Celeste. It took all his control not to rush inside, fall on his knees and beg her forgiveness for being so cold the past week. Fire raced through his veins. Desire had him shaking. Oh, God, she made him weak.

Why had she left Vegas? He'd called Yardley at his motel and asked him the same question. All Yardley had said in that grim voice of his was, "Why don't you ask her?"

The man knew something; that was obvious. Had they gone to bed? Was she in some kind of serious trouble? Damn it, Phillip thought, if Celeste loved him, if she trusted him at all, she would tell him. But she didn't, and he'd been damned before he cut her any slack just because she made him feel so needy.

Somehow even with lust racing through his veins and making him crazy with uncontrollable need, he pivoted and dashed out to the barn to check on his new bulls. And he stayed there until all the lights in the house went out and he knew she was in bed. Then he came inside and called the sheriff. Wainwright and Yardley were still clueless about the dead livestock and the gunrunning activity in the area.

Celeste had the seat of Phillip's big blue pickup jammed as far forward as possible. In spite of her ongoing sulk or feud or whatever you called it with Phillip, she was radiant with excitement this morning as she started the ignition. No more cows had died mysteriously, so her fears regarding the cows had lessened.

"Lonesome Lover" was the best song she'd taped so far. She was proud of it and anxious to get it in the mail. She was sure that this time Mr. Furman would write back.

What did Mr. Greg Furman do with her tapes anyway? Did he listen to them? Or did some secretary simply throw them in the trash? She couldn't bear that last thought.

Phillip and Juan were in the holding pens making sure all their equipment was ready for the big branding next week. Hopefully, she'd make it to town and back before either of them even noticed. But as she backed out of the garage, Phillip stalked up the drive and caught her. His Stetson was off, and he was wiping his mud-caked brow on his soft, blue chambray shirt. When he looked up, his silver eyes drilled her.

His mouth tightened. Then he waved her over. Oh, dear. Her stomach clenched. Not that bossy look. When he frowned, a prickle of alarm skidded up her spine. After barely speaking for days, he suddenly wanted to talk to her! Not good. Quickly she stuffed the incriminating envelope with her new tape in it underneath her seat.

"Hi," she said, rolling down her window as she drove closer to him. "Do you need something from town?"

"Why the hell are you going to town—again?" He leaned on her door, deliberating brushing her hand with his arm.

She jerked her hand inside. "Grocery store."

"But you went this morning."

"Oh… I—I…er, I forgot an ingredient…er, cream."

"Cream?" His gorgeous mouth smiled.

Idiot! Why did you say cream? You never cook with cream!

"My recipe needs cream," she fibbed.

His gaze slid from her scarlet face to the slim silver chain that disappeared between her breasts. "Can I come, too?"

"Aren't you busy getting ready to brand—"

"Juan knows what he's doing."

No! No! No! You can't come! Not today!

"Mind if I drive?" he whispered, opening the door.

The envelope was under the driver's side!

"Sure," she said, her voice casual as she scooted across the seat. "Go ahead. But I'd think you had better things to do."

He climbed inside, and she stared woodenly out the window. As usual the thick silence in the cab soon bristled with her doubts and his edgy hostility. She turned on the radio, the better to ignore him. The first song was about a love-'em-and-leave-'em gal. He opened his window. When he stomped on the accelerator, she leaned over and studied the speedometer. When he slowed down, she stared ahead, her eyes dazed, unfocused.

Were they going to stay mad at each other forever?

"I got an interesting phone call last night when you were at the store." His lazy drawl held an edge of menace that made her nervy with alarm.

"The sheriff? About those old cows?"

"No. Somebody else." He eyed her.

"Oh, really?" she murmured. "Anybody I know?"

"Yeah. Johnny Silver."

"I hope you hung up on him!"

"Well, I didn't."

She swallowed.

He gripped the wheel. She started to say something and then broke off, staring unseeingly ahead. Her chest felt tight.

For a few minutes the only sound in the cab was the plaintive tune about a woman loving the wrong man.

Phillip turned the volume down. "I asked him why you left Vegas in such a hurry."

She gasped and then swallowed. "You had no right—"

"I love you, Celeste." He said it so angrily, the words scared her. "Don't worry. He didn't tell me. The bastard hung up on me."

She sighed in relief.

"So, why won't you tell me why you left? Why you came here?"

"Here we go again. I was in trouble, okay? I did the smart thing and left."

He shot her a contemptuous look. "Can you be more specific?"

"It's all over now."

"All over? So why did the bastard call you?"

"So why does it matter so much to you?"

"Maybe because you matter to me." He paused. "Your friend, or whatever he is, sounded scared. I want to know why. Are you in danger?"

"Why don't you worry about your cows and gunrunners?"

"Are you in danger?"

"No," she lied. "I fired him, okay? And he's the last thing from a friend. I was young and trusting and naive in a word—stupid. He's a snake and a con artist and an out-of-control gambler. He used me. He was no good."

"I'm glad you figured that one out."

"Can we talk about something besides that human rat who can't resist a pair of hot dice?"

"Like what?"

"Like those dead cows and what happened in Mezcaya?"

"Maybe I didn't want to worry you."

"Maybe I don't want to worry you, either," she said softly.

"That's different. I don't need protecting."

"Always, always Mr. Big, Tough Hero? Get real, Phillip. Mercado said you nearly died in Mezcaya. You're human, you know. Bullets don't bounce off you any more than they bounced off those two dead cows of yours." She paused. "I know what it's like to lose someone—"

"And you think I don't—" Phillip snapped. He sucked in a savage breath. "Your friend—I mean, the human rat sounded scared. Real scared."

"Whatever it is, it's his problem."

Phillip rolled up his window and turned off the radio. "Is it?"

She bit her lip and swallowed. "I'm not going to discuss this…until I'm ready."

"When will that be?"

"I don't know, okay?"

He sighed. "Okay."

They drove in silence for a while. Her muscles felt so tense, she ached all over.

It was one of those perfect summer mornings in south Texas. The big sky was blue and so bright she couldn't look at it without blinking, but the heat made everything hazy around the edges, especially at the horizon. A buck and a doe sprang across the road. The southeasterly breezes were playing in the oak and mesquite. Pastures stretched endlessly.

It was such wide-open country that it made their quarrel seem small and insignificant. Gradually, she began to relax.

At exactly the same moment they turned, their eyes locking on each other's faces.

"I—I…"

They both spoke in unison.

"It's beautiful out here," she said.

"Yes."

Before she thought, she smiled at him. To her surprise, his expression softened. When his gaze fell to her lips, her heartbeat came to a shattering halt.

"I've been pretty awful to you this past week," he said, leaning closer.

"Watch the road," she whispered.

"I'm sorry, Celeste."

"An apology?" Another awkward stillness descended upon both of them. "I—I can't believe I'm hearing this."

When his eyes seared her face, she felt an even greater connection.

"Neither the hell can I. Do you have any idea what surrendering costs me?"

She sighed deeply. She knew that tone. A jolt of sheer excitement lit every nerve in her body. Her heart drummed in her ears.

He concentrated on the road again.

"I'm sorry, too," she finally admitted in a rush of elation.

"I've gotta pull over, woman," he growled.

He swerved to a standstill under the deep dark shade of a spreading live oak. He took his time shutting off the engine. As his brown hand fiddled with the ignition, Celeste thought she'd never been so aware of a man.

"You found the only shady place for miles," she said.

"I want to drive home and strip you naked."

A foolish tingle shivered down her spine. The last of her self-control dissolved. "I've got an even sexier idea—"

"If it's better than mine, I can't wait to hear it."

She darted a quick, shy glance at him. When she whispered it in his ear, he laughed. In that instant their quar-

rel was over. Even before the whorls of dust settled on
the cacti and huisache, even before he unfastened her
seat belt and pulled her into his lap, it was as if she had
slipped out of her skin and into his and they were already
one.

His gaze both tender and fierce, he stared at her face
silently until everything inside her went still. She ran a
fingertip down the length of his aquiline nose. Then she
pushed a lock of dark hair from his dirty brow. All she
could hear was his breath coming quick and rasping and
her own heart beating like a savage tattoo.

"You shouldn't work so hard," she whispered.

When she moved, his eyes fell to her nipples that
thrust against her T-shirt.

A little clock on the dash ticked. The sunlight shone
on his carved cheek and black lashes. He was beautiful,
hard, masculine and dangerously virile. And he was hers,
all hers.

No...

"You have sissy eyelashes," she whispered as he
grinned and brushed his calloused fingers through her
hair.

"You're not the first girl to say that, so don't get
yourself all conceited."

"Trying to make me jealous?"

He chuckled. "I'll make it up to you later." Then he
batted his long lashes at her.

A jolt of desire swept through her. Catching her
breath, she wrapped her arms around his neck and
pressed her cheek to his. "Oh, Phillip—"

The week of doing without made it impossible for a
girl with her raging hormones to play hard to get. Even
before he kissed her, even before he drove home and

stripped her, she could already smell and taste the sex that was to come. She couldn't wait.

He tongued her lower lip and every nerve ending in her body caught fire. She melted into him.

He laughed. He knew her that well. He knew her every thought and base desire and reveled in them.

"No goody-goody church girl for me," he whispered eagerly, his eyes darkening.

A slow flush heated her cheeks, and he grinned.

"Oh, dear, you're so gorgeous," she said too breathlessly.

"So are you."

"What do you say we do something about these warm feelings—"

She hugged him. He felt so good, so warm and hard and muscular. And she felt so safe and adored.

A great tenderness welled in her heart as her soul rushed to his. Oh, dear. Not even her music was this essential. It was scary to surrender who she was to anybody, even to Phillip, even in the name of love.

"Do you want to go back to the house or do you want to do it here?" she whispered. "I can't wait much longer."

"A church girl wouldn't say that unless all the lights were out."

She cleared her throat and began to unbutton his shirt.

"I'll start the truck," he rasped thickly when she got to the third button.

"Scared you, didn't I?" she giggled. "You thought I'd really do it out here on the highway, didn't you?"

He laughed. "Wouldn't you?"

It was her turn to laugh. No sooner were they home and inside the front door, than he locked it and started to strip her. When they were both naked, she flung herself into his arms, jumped up, and circled his waist with her legs. He caught her and strutted around the house like a triumphant warrior striding home with his booty.

They never made it to the bedroom. In the hall he sank with her to the floor and kissed her, every part of her, his tongue filling her mouth and then her navel and other moist, intimate places, too, while his hands roamed. She lay still and let him do as he pleased.

When he was done he buried himself to the hilt. Then his huge, muscular body was rising and falling, carrying her with him to heights she'd never glimpsed, never dreamed were possible, and then both of them surrendered to an utter animal wildness that had her sobbing and shaking long after it was over. All the loneliness of their lives dissolved in the blistering explosions that came too quickly and yet seemed to go on and on. In the glorious aftermath she felt bathed in his love and secure; secure, and safe for the first time in her life. She was so happy, she began to cry, but he kissed away her tears and said things to make her laugh.

Afterward, when he helped her up and led her to his bed, he made time for gentle touches and tender words, but she knew that it was the shattering violence in the hall more than her tears or the sweetness in his bed that had wedded her soul to his.

Always, always she would be his no matter how she might dream of other roads to travel, no matter how much she might wish to deny it when her music carried her far away.

Seven

Phillip bathed Celeste's face, which was still hot and flushed from their lovemaking. Squeezing out the sponge, he dribbled it over her breasts and golden hair. She was reclining in the bathtub which was ringed with dozens of low candles she'd lit to give the room a warm, cozy glow. She looked so beautiful, he could have stared at her forever.

"Who are you? Who are you running from?" he murmured, setting the sponge down on the side of the tub.

There was a long silence as she stared into the flickering glow of the candles.

She took a deep breath. "I can't even walk much less run."

He encircled her wrists with his big brown hands. "Will you stay here forever…with me?"

As he gazed into her eyes, the pulse in her throat ticked nervously. "Does my answer matter to you so much? We have this moment. Now. It seems scary to pin everything down Marine-fashion.''

Marine-fashion? What the hell did she mean by that? It required immense control to keep his voice level. He was used to being in charge, to mapping out strategies and seeing them through. Her temperament was more whimsical and artistic. It was the best thing and the worst thing about her.

''What about marriage…children?'' he asked.

''I never had a real home. I can't imagine what all that would be like or if I'd be capable of being a good wife and mother.''

''Frankly, I don't know much about happy homes or happy marriages, either. We'd have to take it a day at a time, make it happen. We could do it, Celeste. I know we could…but we've got to try.''

''You want this perfect housewife.''

''I used to think so.'' He gazed at her. ''You've taught me a lot about what I want.''

''Ready for another lesson in love, Mr. Big, Tough Marine?'' Her voice was soft and a little breathless.

He knew the conversation was making her uncomfortable, so she was seducing him. He should stop her. But it didn't matter what his logical mind knew. A few flicks of her talented fingertips drifting down the flat plain of his stomach and then stroking between his legs was all it took to unleash a floodtide of desire. A few teasing kisses in all the right places had him groaning out loud and begging for more. A few more kisses with a lot of tongue had him grabbing her by the waist and hauling her out of the tub to his bed.

Her skin was steamy warm from the tub, her breath soft and uneven as she lay beneath him, her golden hair fanning out upon the pillows.

"You smell like roses," he growled.

"But I'm all wet. We should get a towel or something."

"Let me look at you."

For a long moment he reveled in her lush, opulent beauty, in her utter femininity. Dark, pointy nipples. Legs that went forever.

"You don't need makeup or flashy dresses. You're a natural beauty."

"You look pretty good yourself—brown, hunky, big."

He grinned. "Big—my favorite compliment."

She'd changed his whole world and in such a short time. Even his room wasn't his anymore. She'd placed flowers and colorful pillows and pictures in every room. There were cumbersome, useless little knickknacks on every flat surface, pictures where once there had been blank spaces on his walls. She'd been here a mere month and already his ranch house felt like home instead of some bachelor's military boot camp.

Damn it. He wanted her. He wanted her here forever. But she had a point. What they had together would do…for now.

Desire burned through him, destroying every well-thought-out plan he had ever made. No perfect, well-bred, society, churchgoing woman, a woman anxious to have a man's ring on her finger and the security of marriage for him. He wanted Celeste—wild, artistic, whimsical, unrealistic Celeste. He wanted whoever or whatever she was. He wanted all of her, every part of her. And every time he had her in bed only made him want her more.

"Honey, you consume me."

"Just love me," she whispered. "I can't get enough of you, either."

For now, he thought grimly. But, at least, he had her for now.

Mabel winked at Phillip as she set his second mug of coffee on the counter. Not that he was in the mood for her chatty attentions today. She was in between husbands, and she liked to gossip and flirt with any man who showed up at the café.

He stirred his coffee and yawned, trying to look bored.

Mabel wasn't fooled. "Missed you," she said, leaning on the counter beside him to show off her ample curves. "You haven't been in to flirt much lately."

"Missed you, too," he replied dryly, but he kept stirring his coffee.

"I nearly called you yesterday," she said.

"Why?"

When he looked up, she smiled slyly and ran a fingertip through her brown curls. "A pair of sleazes came in here asking about that greasy-haired sexpot with the guitar that came here in that ripped, black cocktail dress…. You know…the girl you hired as your maid."

"You don't say." His voice cut like dry ice.

"She still around?"

Mabel knew she was. The whole town knew. She was just fishing for more details, so she could feed the gossip mill.

"What'd you tell 'em?"

"That I never seen nobody like her in my café."

"Thanks."

"Bad-looking pair, if you ask me. Slick and mean. Both of them have snakes' eyes. What'd she do—kill somebody? She's on the run, that's for sure. You'd better be careful."

He thought about his dead, mutilated cattle. Xavier was after him. But who the hell was after her?

"What did they look like?"

"One's dark, and the other is sick and pasty-faced-looking. Oh, and he wears glasses. And they both have cruel, black eyes."

"Their eyes obviously made an impression."

She lifted a brow. "Y'all be careful out there, you here— If I were you, I'd strap on a gun when I left the house—"

"Thanks."

Phillip finished the last of his coffee. Then he gave her a big smile and a tip that made her smile even bigger. Not that Phillip was smiling when he climbed in his truck.

What'd she do—kill somebody?

Phillip remembered Mendoza sailing off that jungle mountain road. Phillip knew what he'd done, but what the hell had she done?

Instead of going to the feed store as he'd planned, he stepped on the gas and rushed home to make sure Celeste was okay. It didn't take a genius to figure out those jerks had to be the reason she'd left Vegas. Phillip remembered Johnny Silver's frightened voice. The guy had panted between every word. He was up to his eyeballs in whatever this was, too. She said she wasn't involved with Silver, but she was.

She'd lied.

Why?

Damn it. She had to tell him what was going on— now. Today. Period.

But he never had the chance to ask her what had gone

down in Vegas because when he roared up to the porch, she ran out of his house in blood-splattered clothes. Tears streamed down her cheeks as she hurled herself into his arms before he could even climb the first stair.

"A-another cow," she gasped brokenly. "Only whoever it was chopped the cow in several pieces in the corral. I—I tripped over...over a leg before I saw... Then I slipped in a pool of blood. Oh, it's all too awful... I—I found this—" She was holding a bloody piece of crumpled paper.

He ripped it out of her trembling hand.

"Oh, Phillip— The...the note's like the others."

He read it out loud. "'You hurt my family, so now I will hurt yours.'"

Celeste shuddered against him. She was so small and petite, so defenseless, really.

Snakes' eyes...? Mabel had said. *What'd she do—kill somebody?*

He pressed her closer. He didn't care what she'd done. If anybody so much as laid a finger on one shiny, golden hair, he'd kill them as coldly and as ruthlessly as he'd run Mendoza off the road.

"Oh, Phillip, I—I thought you were never coming home. I called your cell—"

"It's okay," he whispered, stroking her hair as she shuddered against his chest. "Hey, hey. I was in a no-service area for a while, that's all."

"Does this have something to do with that El Jefe terrorist group?"

"Don't you worry about it. I'll handle it."

He'd better. And fast.

"But...but... I—I'm so afraid.... I don't like the thought of people sneaking around here doing... Why anybody... They could do anything. When I'm here alone...."

Phillip forgot all about the two sleazes in town. His only concern was for her. He had to call Wainwright and Cole Yardley, but that could wait.

"Nobody's going to hurt you," he said gently. "Nobody. Not ever. Because I won't let them. Understand?"

"But what if they come and you aren't here?"

"I'll be here from now on until this blows over. Juan can do most of the errands. I can write lists. He can shop. My credit's good in town."

"Oh, Phillip," she breathed, hugging him closer. "It's you I'm worried about. I called Ricky Mercado and he told me everything that happened in Mezcaya. He told me all about that man you killed and how his son is after you—"

"That bastard."

"Ricky—"

"Oh, so now it's Ricky—"

"He's your friend. He doesn't want you to die anymore than I do, and I don't want El Jefe's men to kill you. I couldn't live if anything happened to you."

"I feel the same way about you. That's what I've been trying to tell you. That's why I asked you to marry me." He waited until her racking sobs subsided and she stood still against him. "It's going to be okay. I swear I'll find out what's going on."

"And you're going to tell the sheriff. You're not going to act like you're so big and tough you won't call the law. You're going to tell him about the cows, about all three cows."

"I'll call him first thing. As soon as you're calm. Shh. Shh..." He stroked her back and her neck and then threaded his fingers into her hair.

When she quieted, he took her hand and led her inside the house. Then he picked up the phone.

"Sheriff…"

She sighed with obvious relief. But her fear didn't go away.

He called Yardley.

Her eyes grew huge when Phillip hung up and strapped on a gun. She followed him around even when he went out to the pastures.

That night he told her to dress up, that they were going out to dinner.

"What's the occasion?"

"No occasion. You'll feel braver somewhere else won't you?"

"Yes. Oh, yes."

Again he took her to dinner and dancing at the Lone Star Country Club. Again she dressed in her flashy red dress. Only tonight they ate in the club's formal dining room, which was decorated in blue and white, and they had a candlelit corner all to themselves. They held hands. They danced again and again, putting on quite a show for the other diners. When their first course arrived, they returned to their table and talked just like an old married couple who were easy and sure of one another, but beneath their conversation, the atmosphere between them sizzled with excitement. Not to mention fear.

After dessert, which was some sort of cream topped with luscious raspberries that melted in his mouth, he blew out their candles. He slid a hand in his suit pocket and laid a small velvet box in front of her. When she gasped, his big brown hand nudged it toward her.

"Open it, darling."

"Darling? I think I can guess what it is." Her voice

was so soft and wistful, he had to lean forward to hear her.

Gingerly she flipped the lid a couple of times before he grabbed it and opened it for her. An enormous solitaire sparkled against black velvet, and she cupped her mouth and cried, ''Oh!''

''What's wrong?''

''It's huge. Too huge.''

''I thought you liked flash. So, do you? Do you like it?'' He took the sparkling gem out of the box and slid it onto her finger.

She flexed her hand. The gem shot fire.

''I—I can't believe this—'' she began, fighting tears. ''Nobody ever gave me...'' Then she strangled on her words and the rest of her sentence was an incoherent jumble.

He looked at her, only at her, his heart pounding painfully against his ribs while he waited, his dread mushrooming when she lowered her eyes and couldn't seem to meet his gaze.

Her lips tightened. Then she began to bite them as if in confusion. Then very slowly she slid his ring off and gently laid it in his palm. Her fingers were shaking convulsively and tears were rolling down her white cheeks.

''Why not?'' he rasped.

''I—I don't know, Phillip. It's too much...too soon. I mean...marriage...forever...you...me...Mission Creek... and children, too... Those cows...''

''We'll solve that mystery.''

''But—''

''Where do you see this relationship going?'' he demanded, changing the subject.

''I...I... Why can't we just be?''

"I'd like to be able to count on...our future. Wouldn't you?"

"You want to plot the rest of our lives all out like a war or something?"

"No. Not like a war. War is hell. What are you running from, Celeste?"

"Nothing. Nobody."

"Is it just me, then? Me that you don't really want?"

"Oh, Phillip, how can you even think such—"

"Or does it have something to do with the two guys that are asking questions about you? What do they have on you?"

"Two guys?" She pushed her chair back and would have raced away in a blind panic if he hadn't grabbed her wrist. "Who? What guys?"

"A couple of men have been asking about you in town. I would have mentioned them earlier, but we had to deal with the dead cow. Who are they?"

Again she struggled to push her chair back, but his grip on her wrist tightened. "Not so fast. There's something else I'm curious about."

"Let me go, Phillip."

With his other hand he pulled an envelope out of the inside of his jacket and read the Nashville address out loud. "There's a tape inside. You're sending stuff to a producer, Greg Furman, aren't you? Why couldn't you tell me?"

"Where did you get that?"

"You still want to be a star, don't you?"

"Oh? I—I left that in the truck, didn't I?" Her hands closed around the envelope, and she stared at him with those big, luminous eyes that undid him. "I love you, Phillip. You have to believe me."

"Then why can't we have a simple conversation? Why can't you confide in me?"

"I didn't think you'd understand."

"You don't give me a chance to."

"You're so big and tough. A Marine."

"A retired Marine, Celeste." He paused. "I'm a human being."

"Your life is precise and… Me, I—I feel…so torn. My life was a mess when I came here. Sending the tapes…"

"So there were more of them?"

"I write him letters, beg him to let me audition. I send him songs, too."

"I see. You can't wait to get out of here."

"No. My musical ability drives me. It's not totally rational. Sending those tapes was something I had to do. I didn't think you'd want me to."

"Life isn't always 'either or' you know."

"It has been for me."

"For me, too, then…because you think it is. When were you going to tell me about the tapes?"

"Oh…oh… I—I don't know. Oh, why does everything have to get so complicated? Why are you asking all these questions?"

"Were you just going to walk out on me again?"

"Phillip, I…"

"Don't say any more." He slid the ring and the little velvet box into his pocket. "You've said way more than enough."

"But—"

"Let's just go home and put this evening behind us."

"But we haven't settled anything—"

"That's up to you—"

He waited. Oh, God, how he hoped she'd say more.

When she didn't, he let go of her wrist, and she stood. He slid his hand to the back of her waist and escorted her out of the elegant blue-and-white room and then through the grand lobby lit with ornate chandeliers. Only when they were outside in the dark beneath a full moon and a starless sky and there was no one to see their livid pain, could they relax a little.

"What are we going to do?" she whispered later when he was driving them home in the truck.

"This is your game. We're playing by your rules. You tell me."

"But I can't. I don't know."

"Then neither the hell do I."

She asked him if he wanted her to leave the next morning and he said no.

Over the next few days Wainwright and Yardley made zero progress on their investigation. The two sleazes from Vegas didn't turn up, either. So, Phillip and Celeste drifted, and drifting was hard for Phillip who was a natural leader who wanted to command not only battles but his life, as well. All he wanted was for her to talk to him and to answer a few simple questions.

But she wasn't used to sharing confidences. Maybe she didn't believe that doing so could bring two people closer. Phillip didn't know, and he didn't ask her. They slept together, but his proposal and his questions had erected an invisible barrier, so sex wasn't as spontaneous or as hot as it had been before.

Now it was sweet and sad and desperate, and yet if it was all he could have of her, he'd settle for the crumbs he could get. He was that pathetic. They were drifting apart, and it was killing him. And there wasn't a damn thing he could do about it but hope that if he waited, somehow, some way, he'd get a break.

And then he did.

Only it wasn't the lucky break, he'd prayed for. It was a disaster that sent their lives spinning out of control in a horrible new direction.

Eight

Later that particular Saturday night after she'd driven off from the Saddlebag in his truck, and left him alone at the bar and he was drowning his sorrows in a bottle, in lots of bottles, all different kinds of bottles, Phillip would relearn one of life's dirtier little tricks. No matter how sudden the catastrophic blow falls, the aftermath is slow and deadly, the better to prolong the victim's agony.

Not that he had the slightest premonition of what was to come as he led Celeste up the steps of the plain-looking, wooden building that was the local bar. He simply felt edgy and unable to face another evening in the house alone watching television while she avoided him, content to read by herself in the kitchen while so many issues in their relationship were unresolved.

Didn't she care about him at all? Maybe she could float through life like a leaf going down a stream, but he needed roots. He needed answers, and he was nearly out of patience.

Feeling close to some dangerous, fatal edge, he shoved the door to the open bar and said in a grim, low tone, "Welcome to The Saddlebag."

As usual she was wearing lots of makeup and that flashy red number that didn't leave a lot to the imagination.

"You come here often?" she whispered, her voice a little shaky even though she was still trying to pretend that everything was all right between them.

"Before you came home I used to hang out here a lot. I shot pool, drank...dated.... And not nice church girls."

Celeste swallowed and wouldn't meet his eyes.

The inside of the bar was dark and cozy. A large bar ran along the far wall and there were about fifteen tables scattered in the middle of the room. In the rear, men were playing pool and shooting darts while their dates watched. A redhead in a tight black mini was yanking at the knob of the lone pinball machine and then pounding the machine and shouting when her balls didn't go where she wanted them to.

The walls were packed with Texas memorabilia. Maybe to avoid his gaze, Celeste was studying the old photographs of early ranchers, cow skulls, antlers, wagon wheels and branding irons with way more interest than they warranted. Somebody had filled a shelf with old beer bottles. She busied herself reading the labels.

Jake Hornung, a local cowboy, set down his pool cue and came over to them, studying her, too. "Long time, no see, Westin."

Westin tipped his Stetson. Nodding, he took Celeste by the elbow and kept walking.

"Nice dress. Real nice…. Hey, I know you." Hornung was practically drooling as he spoke to Celeste. "If you ain't Stella Lamour I ain't Jake Robert Hornung. A buddy said you sang at the Lone Star Country Club the other night, but I didn't believe him. Hey, I bought your album."

"You're the only man in America who did."

"How come you didn't do any more albums? I made copies for all my buddies. Hey," he shouted to his friends at the pool table. "Guys, Karla, this here is Stella Lamour, the country-western star."

A girl in a pink T-shirt that showed too much belly and tight jeans walked up to them and put her arm around Jake. "Stella… You're good, really good."

"I never met a star before," Hornung said. "Will you autograph—"

Celeste took a deep breath. She looked a little uncertain, but her admirers kept smiling at her and fawning over her every remark. Soon she became a little giddy and in the end when she had to sign about ten napkins, she couldn't seem to stop smiling.

A childhood memory came back to Phillip. One night his mother had put him to bed early and told him not to come out of his room because she was having a big party. Famous people were coming. She'd babbled off a few names.

When she'd turned off the light, he'd had a nightmare that he was falling out of an airplane and had awakened right before he'd hit the ground. Screaming for her, he'd run through the house.

She'd been out in the garden laughing with friends near thick banks of azaleas. As thin as a rail, she was exquisite in red, with a low neck that showed off too many glittering jewels. He'd yelled, "Mommy." Her smile had frozen. She'd nodded to his stepfather, who'd clamped a hand on his shoulder and ushered him back to his scary bedroom. His stepfather had been huge, and Phillip had been more terrified of him than of the demons hiding in his dark room.

"If you leave your room again, you know what will happen."

"I want Mommy."

"She's with important people."

"When will she ever want me?"

The next week they'd sent him to military school.

"Let's find a table, Celeste…or should I say Stella," Phillip muttered a little grumpily.

"Sorry about that," she murmured.

He led her away from the excited group, selecting a table as far from the pool tables and her fans as possible. A waitress came and he ordered them drinks and made up his mind to forget about the little incident.

"Sorry about that," Celeste repeated awkwardly.

Phillip was ashamed of his feelings and didn't know what to say. "Let's just get on with our evening."

"I know you don't like thinking about my music or my…career."

"Damn it. Is that what you call it—a career?"

Celeste looked startled. She was about to say something, and then choked back her words when the waitress brought their beers and placed them on tiny white napkins. He shoved a few bills on the table and ordered himself a second beer before he even started the first. "Long day," he said to the waitress.

"Cheers." He lifted his frosty bottle to Celeste and was aware of Hornung and his bunch at the pool tables watching Celeste and talking about her more excitedly than ever. He felt left out, so he drank deeply.

She didn't touch her drink.

"Are you ever going to tell me why you left Vegas?"

"Not now," she whispered.

"When, then?"

"Maybe when you tell me who's killing your live-stock. Okay?"

"Not okay. My livestock has nothing to do with you and me. Your secrets do. Okay?"

They sat at the table, not knowing what to say to each other. Hell, maybe she was listening to the band. Her fingers began to tap the table in time to the beat. Maybe she didn't need him at all. Maybe she just wanted her music. When he finished his second beer, he ordered two more. She frowned when he finished those.

"Don't worry," he muttered, tossing her the truck keys. "You can be the designated driver—*Stella.*"

"Stella? Why…why you're still sulking because I got a little attention."

"The hell I am."

"You hate my music, but it's part of me."

"I don't hate your music, but it led you into a dangerous life. You landed on my doorstep scared and broke, and you won't tell me why."

"Can't we discuss this when we get home?" she asked.

"Ha! You won't talk…except in bed. How long will we last if sex is the only thing holding us together?"

"Sex? You think that's all—" The devastation in her face cut him to the quick, but he wasn't about to let it show.

The band took a break.

"Stella. Stella. We want Stella."

Phillip turned just as Hornung got on the stage and told everybody that his favorite country-western star,

Stella Lamour, was here tonight, and if they were nice and clapped for her, maybe she would sing.

"Hell," Phillip whispered as everybody else began to clap and yell her name.

"Oh, God—" His brown hand curled into a fist.

"Take me home, Phillip."

"Hey, your music's everything to you. Who am I to stop the great star, Stella Lamour? Sing, Celeste, sing your heart out. You know that's what you really want to do."

"I want you, too."

"In bed maybe. But I wonder how much...and for how long? There's something you're keeping—"

She paled. "You keep things from me, too."

"To protect you, damn it."

"I don't want to quarrel like this.... Not with you."

Hornung got down on his knees and said please, pretty, pretty please into the mike.

"Maybe I will sing. It's better than quarreling."

"You're right," he whispered, ashamed suddenly. He didn't hate her music. He hated that she wouldn't level with him. Phillip stood and forced a smile as he helped Celeste out of her chair. "Break a leg—"

She took a deep breath and then, cocking her head to one side, Stella Lamour strutted up to the stage like the star he knew she wanted to be more than anything, more than she wanted him. She took the mike and paced nervously a moment or two.

"I wrote the song I'm about to sing for a very special guy."

Oh, God.

She turned toward Phillip, her gaze locking on his face. Did she have to be so exquisite in that red dress that was almost a carbon copy of the one his mother had worn the night she'd decided to send her little boy to military school?

Celeste shook her blond hair so that it caught the light and sparkled as it tumbled over her slim shoulders. She smiled at Hornung, at the rest of audience, at all the important people in the room. She was a born star. Suddenly Phillip realized that was one of the things that made her so special to him.

Only when she had the attention of every man in the room, did Stella turn back to him and begin to sing. Soon she was belting out her one and only country music hit, which, of course, Phillip knew by heart.

In the middle of her number, a man walked into the bar. Two more let themselves in a minute after he did. Not that anybody noticed them. Stella had everybody spellbound, especially Phillip.

Her blue eyes stared straight into Phillip's and he stared straight back. When she looked at him like that, with her heart in her eyes, he could barely breathe. She held him motionless in his chair until she was done.

"Nobody but you/Only you/And yet I had to say goodbye…"

Why, damn it? Tell me who you are and what you're so afraid of.

Only when she finished singing was he able to look away. Her music truly was a part of her. How strange, he thought that when she'd sung to him, he'd felt as connected to her as he did when they made love.

The other customers must have received a thrill or two themselves because they started clapping and stomping their boots and yelling for more. Hell, one song and she had the place in an uproar. The bar was charged with some new sensual power. Phillip remembered the first night he'd met her. She'd sung more than one song that night, and the place had gotten way too crazy. He'd fallen in love with her voice before he'd even known her.

Stella put the mike down and ran back to Phillip, her slim body carving its way through the excited throng as silently and gracefully as an elegant cat.

"Sorry about that," she whispered.

"No. You were great. Really great," he said.

"You really thought so?" Her big blue eyes seemed to burn his face.

Did his opinion matter so terribly? "Yes. I love to hear you sing. I always feel I'm the only one you're singing to. You were great!"

For an instant he thought he saw the spark of tears in her eyes, and he ached for the lonely little girl who'd grown up in foster homes. Gently he threaded his fingers through hers. Her smile was so radiant, his own heart nearly burst with happiness.

"Yes, you were great," said a hard voice behind them.

"Oh," Celeste gasped, caught off guard. "I didn't see you."

The stranger in the gray flannel suit was one of the newcomers. Phillip didn't know him, so he wasn't a local. The man tossed a business card onto the table. "Mind if I join you?"

Celeste picked up his card and flipped it nervously while she read. "Oh, dear! Greg… Greg Furman?"

The short bald man beamed, his teeth white, when he caught the shock of recognition in her voice. "The one and only."

"But you never once answered my letters— How'd you find me—"

"You put your address on every single envelope. I'm

closing a deal in Texas. So, I went out to your ranch, and this guy on a tractor said you were here. The last song you sent me was pretty good. Oh, it needs some work—''

"Pretty good? Oh, dear.'' She flicked a rapid glance up at him. "Pretty good? You really think so—''

"Good enough for an audition in Nashville, Miss Lamour.''

"I—I can't believe…'' She turned to Philip. "Oh, Phillip, this is wonderful. Just when I was about to give up forever…and settle….''

Settle? The word jarred Phillip's soul.

She looked past Phillip, but her dazzling smile faded when she focused on something or somebody behind him.

"Oh, dear….'' Her dying words were low-pitched and nearly inaudible. Phillip felt an icy prickle of danger. Something cold and deadly suddenly charged the air. Celeste went paper-white.

Furman was too full of himself to notice. "Sorry, this has to be a short meeting, doll. So, look me up if you're ever in Nashville.''

When Furman got to his feet, he had to dodge a dark man and his paler companion, who were rapidly approaching their table.

The men sidestepped out of Furman's way and stared at Celeste with cold, flat eyes. Her lips quivered and she seemed to forget Furman and his exciting offer.

The two men were obviously some sort of threat. Her eyes grew huge when the dark man and his pale companion yanked chairs out and sat beside her without an invitation.

Phillip placed his hand over hers and pulled her closer.

He didn't need a formal introduction to know these were the two sleazes Mabel had warned him about.

"Please don't hate me forever," she pleaded under her breath to Phillip. The sadness in her eyes brought a bleak feeling of inevitability over him, too.

"Don't be ridiculous—" He broke off. "I couldn't ever—"

The band was still on break. The bar grew ominously quiet. Phillip's heart slammed against his chest.

"Whatever it is, it's time we face it…together," he said, tightening his hand over hers as the men stared at Celeste.

She licked her tongue over her dry lips and kept her wet lashes lowered.

"You two want something?" Phillip asked sharply. "I don't remember asking you to sit down."

"Yeah, we do…something from your lady friend…if you could call her a lady. You been hidin' out, using him to protect you?"

Celeste winced.

Using him? "Go to the ladies' room, Celeste," Phillip ordered in his Marine-issue drawl.

"They're my problem, not yours." Her guilt-stricken tone was jerky. Her hand was shaking in his.

"No arguments, Celeste."

She pushed back her chair.

"Hey, now, you ain't gonna run off from The Pope here, without giving him a little kiss for old times' sake?" jeered the pale reptile with the pimples and glasses.

"Go, Celeste!" Phillip's lips barely moved. "Now!"

"Hey, wait a minute, buster. We got business with Stella here." No sooner had the man with the pitted olive skin and big nose spoken than he lunged for Celeste.

Faster than lightning Phillip sprang between them.

"Whatever it is you're after, you're dealing with me from now on. Understand?"

Celeste swallowed a sharp, convulsive sob as Phillip pushed her away. "Go," he repeated.

"Phillip, please, please, please…let me stay and explain…." Her breathing was labored, and her beautiful blue eyes were luminous. "I didn't know how or where to begin before, but—"

He shook his head. "You're a little late."

She stared at him, as if to memorize his frozen features. "Oh, Phillip—"

The two men beside him began to fidget. They were getting restless. Celeste's eyes grew huge as she waited for them to tell Phillip about her.

Was it really so terrible? Why couldn't she have opened up to him before? If only she had trusted him enough to tell him whatever it was, dealing with these lowlifes would have been child's play.

But she hadn't. Just as she hadn't told him about her secret correspondence with Furman. His home had been a hiding place, a rest stop, a brief interval in a journey she'd intended to take alone to stardom.

Celeste's yellow hair gleamed. Why did she have to look like an angel even in her flashy red dress? She was very pale, scared to death and yet gorgeous. So gorgeous. A natural-born star.

Suddenly she seemed so far away…unreachable, like a star, heaven bound while he would always be an earthling. As he looked at her, he could feel his heart hardening, his body shutting down as it always did before a battle.

She seemed to sense the change in him, sense the total coldness. After a long time her breathing came under control and she raced toward the back of the bar.

Because of Celeste Phillip was about to cross a line he'd never crossed before. He was going to pay off these thugs or do whatever it took to get them off Celeste's back forever. He didn't care what she'd done, even if it was murder.

"How much?" he said angrily to the two men.

Nine

A hand with long black fingernails curled over the top of the metal door to Celeste's toilet stall. "Celeste, you in there?"

Celeste had put paper on the toilet seat and was sitting down with her shoulders hunched forward. Elbows in her red silk lap, her head was in her hands. When she didn't answer, the door jiggled.

"Go away," Celeste pleaded.

"Your big guy's right outside. He wants to talk to you somethin' awful. Says your friends from Vegas are gone and won't be back to bother you ever again."

"Not right now—"

A door banged open. "Man in the ladies' room!" Phillip shouted.

"Oh, my," the woman on the other side of Celeste's stall said. "Do you want me to call security?"

"No," Phillip said. "I want you to get the hell out of here."

"You're rude. That's my purse you're throwing…." The woman screamed and ran out the door after her purse.

A door lock clicked. Then a large brown hand jimmied her stall door.

"Celeste, damn it, do you think that flimsy door is really going to keep me out—"

She opened it. "I can explain—"

"Nero and your friend The Pope saved you the trouble."

"What…"

"Let's just say, I agreed to pay them a great deal of money. You're free to follow your big dream."

"But what if I don't want—"

"You came here to hide from those goons. True or false?"

"It's complicated."

"True or false?"

"True."

"You used me."

"No… I just wanted to hide. I needed a job."

"You seduced me so I'd protect you from them and pay them off so you'd be free to go on your merry little way."

"No…"

"Well, now you're free. Everything, the pretty smiles, the sex…. It's all been an act. Lies. You never wanted me. You wanted to be Stella Lamour, and you used me to make that happen."

"I love you."

"You knew they'd come."

"I didn't owe them anything. You shouldn't have paid…"

"They said they'd kill you if I didn't. They threatened me, too."

She blinked nervously. "They were after Johnny. He set them on me. I didn't tell you…because I couldn't bear for you to think badly of me. I didn't do any of those things they probably said I did. I'm not some—"

"I know exactly what you are—a woman I paid a great deal to sleep with. You let me use your body, but you gave me nothing else."

The room seemed to spin. His dark face was at the center of whirling white tiles and mirrors and fluorescent lights. Somebody was pounding on the door outside.

"Security!" a man shouted.

"Don't worry," Phillip said. "You were worth every penny. You've got Furman's card. And this, too." He pulled out a wad of cash and stuffed it into her red purse. "That's way more than you'll need to get to Nashville. Give your friend Johnny a call—"

"He's not my manager. He used their money to gamble and told them he gave it to me. Why won't you listen—"

"Maybe because you never trusted me enough to talk. Get the hell out of my life. A girl with your talents should go far."

"You said you loved me."

"Love." He laughed shortly. "There's no such thing. Not between us. You taught me that lesson—twice. We had sex. We used each other. You were scared and needed a soft landing. I was bored and needed a diversion in between wars. It was fun while it lasted, honey. But now it's goodbye. If we're smart, we won't pretend it was more than it was."

"You asked me to marry you."

"That's before I knew who and what you were. Why would I marry a shameless woman I've bought and paid for?"

"Shameless… How dare… Oh… You big, stupid lunk! You were a fool to pay them money I didn't even owe. You… I hate you. You're heartless…. You won't listen."

"Oh, so this is all my fault. I saved your life, and it's my fault?"

"You asked me why I wouldn't talk to you. Well, it was because I knew you wouldn't listen. You didn't before. You're arrogant and pigheaded. I knew you'd think the worst of me just like everybody else did when I was a kid. And you do. I just wanted a few more days with you…and a few more nights. I was that starved for love, that pitiful."

"Shut the hell up!"

"No wonder you're all alone in the middle of no-where—"

She flung open the door and raced past a short, fat man in a brown uniform.

"Miss—"

Phillip leaped after her, forgetting that she had the keys to his truck.

She was inside his truck and backing out before he caught up with her. Lunging at her door, he pounded on her window. She floored it, and roared out of the parking lot, her tires shooting gravel at him just like the chopper had in Mezcaya. All he could do was step back and cough in the dust. Another truck roared to life and raced out of the lot after her.

Hell. She was in no condition to drive. He stumbled

after the trucks. His booted toe hit a thick root in the drive, and he nearly fell.

Hell. He wasn't any more fit to drive than she.

"Celeste! Come back!"

His stomach went hollow when her red taillights disappeared into the gloom. Then the thick humid night wrapped him. Anything could happen to her out there.

"Damn it!"

He couldn't allow himself to feel protective or to worry about her. She didn't want him—period. Now that she was gone, now that he knew why she'd come and stayed, he felt gut-sick, rejected. He was alone. And there wasn't a damn thing he could do about it…except drink.

Tears clogged Celeste's throat and blurred her vision. She was driving so fast the truck was weaving from side to side, but she was too upset and irrational to think about slowing down.

So, Phillip thought she was low and cheap, did he? The weeks they'd lived together, all the lovemaking, everything they'd said to each other and shared, meant nothing to him. He believed every sordid word The Pope and Nero had told him.

She'd been right not to talk to him. Dead right. Well, at least she had her memories. She sniffed. They would have to hold her for a lifetime.

The straight black road was like an inky river under the stars through the wild, wide-open brush country. Why was she crying over a pigheaded hunk? She had what she wanted. She'd saved her paychecks, Phillip had paid off those devils and even given her more money. Furman wanted to cut an album.

Stardom had never seemed so close. So why were tears streaming down her cheeks?

High beams flared in her rearview mirror, blinding her. She'd noticed another truck had left the lot at the same time she had, but she hadn't really thought much about it. The driver flashed his brights and caught up to her. She slowed down and moved onto the shoulder so he could pass her.

Instead, he rear-ended her bumper so hard she could barely keep the truck on the road. Oh, dear! He hit her again. Whoever it was, was trying to flip her or hijack her.

She gasped. Nero and The Pope! They must've gone outside to wait for her. She should have known the money hadn't been enough. Then she remembered the dead cows and the threatening notes. Could these thugs be from Mezcaya? Whoever they were, they wanted to hurt her.

When she stomped down hard on the gas pedal, the goons behind her did the same.

Where could she go? Not back to the ranch. Not without Phillip there. No, somehow she had to find a wide place and turn around. She had to get back to The Saddlebag and Phillip.

Oh, Phillip. She loved him so much. Now she realized she'd been so afraid of losing his admiration she'd kept the bad things in her life to herself. But love had to be about sharing, even the bad things. This time she would explain, and she would make him tell her everything about Mezcaya. She wasn't going anywhere until she made him listen. She wasn't leaving him until she was sure he knew how much she loved him.

The truck rammed her again. Even as she struggled to hold on to the wheel, her truck veered off the road, bumping over rocks and cacti, thrashing through tall grasses.

Her heart was hammering when she fought to turn the wheel and get back on the road. No matter what happened, she had to make it back onto the highway, turn around and get back to Phillip. When she was on asphalt again, she risked a glance at the speedometer. She was doing more than ninety-five.

So were the devils behind her, flashing their lights.

Phillip... Just when she saw yellow signs that indicated a rest area up ahead where she might turn around, the truck hit her again so hard she skidded out of control.

The truck was flying straight at a tangled clump of oak trees.

"Oh, dear..."

She slammed her foot on the brake and screamed for Phillip, but the truck was like a roller-coaster car out of control.

The dense black trees with their spreading branches loomed like a wall in front of her. She screamed again right before she hit them. After that everything seemed all right.

She was back home in bed with Phillip. They were laughing and kissing, and he was caressing her hair and telling her he loved her.

He understood. He loved her.

Everything was all right.

She wasn't dying. She couldn't be.

She was going to cut an album in Nashville, and Phillip was beaming proudly, begging her to marry him. She had Phillip and her music. He was right. Life and love and woman's dreams weren't an "either or" proposition. She could have it all.

A young thug with a permanent tan and a cigarette danging from his pretty mouth leaned close to her.

"Help me," she whispered. "Phillip…"

He laughed and began to scribble something on a piece of paper. His handsome face blurred. Then she heard voices in a foreign language.

The next time she opened her eyes, the pretty thug and his friends were gone.

Everything was all right.

Time ticked by slowly. Then a light shone in her face, blinding her. She tried to move and a hot pain stabbed her in the right thigh.

"Phillip—" Her voice cracked in agony.

"Don't try to move," Sheriff Wainwright warned gently. "We're gonna have to get the Jaws of Life and cut you out of there."

"Phillip… I want Phillip… I love Phillip." Her voice broke. Nothing mattered nearly so much as Phillip.

Ten

The beer bottles he'd lined up like soldiers on his table blurred. Phillip blinked but, in the dimly lit corner of The Saddlebag where he sat sprawled, that only made bottles bob like swimmers. He whirled around, grinning drunkenly as he held up two fingers, signaling to the bartender that he wanted a couple more.

The door opened and a tall, dark man stalked inside and looked around. Not that Phillip noticed Ricky Mercado at first. All his attention was focused on the bartender, who was scrubbing dirty glasses and seemed to be deliberately ignoring him. Even when Phillip heard his friend's heavy tread behind him, he paid no attention. Instead he picked up a bottle and began to beat his table like a drum. The maddening bartender looked up and scowled at him.

"It's about time," Phillip rumbled, swallowing a string of curse words.

"Enough, old buddy," came Ricky's deep voice behind him.

"Leave me the hell alone, Mercado."

With a charming smile Mercado pulled up a chair and sat.

"You deaf?"

"There's an old raccoon that hisses and spits at me every time I walk out my back door. He radiates more charm than you, old buddy."

"Did you come here to insult me—"

"I came here to warn you and Celeste. Wainwright and Yardley grilled me about Mezcaya all afternoon. They think I'm to blame for your dead cows. I did some checking, and I'm pretty sure that crazy thug, Xavier Gonzalez, is in the neighborhood gunning for you."

Oh, God. "How the hell would you know that unless—" Phillip began in a hard, ugly tone as he nastily swung around on Mercado. *Unless you had secret dealings with the arms dealers?* Even in his inebriated state, he wasn't ready to accuse Mercado.

Still, Mercado's voice got icy, too. "My source is very reliable. He knew all about the cows and the threatening notes— If the feds didn't know something, that A.T.F. agent, Cole Yardley, wouldn't be here trying to sniff out Gonzalez's little gun-smuggling ring. Yardley keeps showing up at my place, suggesting I'm involved with running guns to Mezcaya. No matter what I say, he won't believe I quit the family."

"Go away and leave me alone. I've got worse things to deal with than Xavier Gonzalez or your personal problems."

"Do you? If Xavier's hell-bent on murder?"

"Get out!"

"So where's Celeste?"

"Where's my damn beer?" Westin spun his chair around. "Bartender—"

"So she's gone. For good this time?"

"Get the hell out of my face," Phillip muttered between his gritted teeth. Then he slouched back against the wall.

When Mercado leaned forward to say something else, Phillip whipped out of his seat so fast, the chair fell over. The cozily lit room swirled. Phillip's gut wrenched queasily and he felt himself swaying. Mercado shot to his feet and grabbed his arm to steady him.

"I don't need your help. I don't need anybody's help." He bent and swiped at the beer bottles, laughing when they fell like bowling pins and rolled off the table.

The phone rang, and the bartender rushed up to them and said something fast to Mercado.

Pushing his friend, who suddenly looked dazed out of his way, Phillip stumbled toward the door, blearily amazed at how heavy his feet were and how damned hard it was to walk in a straight line.

Mercado caught up with him and lunged at the massive door beneath the exit sign, barring his way. He was holding a cordless phone against his broad chest with one hand.

"You're in no condition to drive." Mercado's expression was strange, scarily strange. His dark eyes held pity and compassion and something else—was it fear?

Mercado said something—maybe Phillip's name, but the words ran together in a jumble.

"Celeste," Mercado said in a low, shaken voice. Then he held out the cordless phone. "It's Wainwright, the sheriff…. They've made headway on their investigation. But there's been an accident. Celeste… They think Xavier or his thugs—"

"Celeste?" *Oh, God.*

Phillip took a sharp, painful breath and then he grabbed the phone. But he was so clumsy, he knocked it out of Mercado's hand onto the floor. Then he toppled to his knees, scrambling for it like a madman. By the time he picked it up, it was dead.

"She's in the Mission Creek Memorial Hospital," Mercado said.

"She's alive?"

"Somebody ran her off the road."

"Deliberately?"

Mercado nodded. "The bastards left another note. Celeste gave them a description of Xavier Gonzalez."

"Xavier?" *Oh, God.* He'd find Gonzalez and make him pay.

He shouldn't have been so rough on her. She'd been too upset to drive. If she died, it would be his fault—

"An ambulance took her to the hospital. That's all I know."

"She could be dead already."

Just the thought caused a blackness to close around his soul. He was a rejected little boy again with no place to call home.

What a bleak, dead place the world would be if anything happened to Celeste. He imagined her face still and white in a coffin. He had to get a grip, to shut down. Only he couldn't.

Terror that she was gone and it was too late for them wrenched him out of his self-indulgent abyss of idiotic self-torment into a totally different kind of hell, a hell that didn't allow him to shut down, a scary hell he had to face.

"I have to see her. I have to make sure they're taking

good care of her. You can't trust hospitals. Terrible things happen in hospitals. People die.''

"I'll drive you," Mercado said. "But first, I'm getting a cup of coffee down you—"

"Just get me to the damn hospital."

On the way over, all Phillip could think about was Celeste. Who'd hurt her? Xavier's men?

She'd been driving his truck. Xavier's men could have gone after her just because she'd been in his truck. He'd get to the bottom of this mystery, but first he had to make sure Celeste was okay.

If she wasn't all right, he'd die, too. Maybe not physically, but without her, his life would be flat and empty like before. Only worse.

He remembered the seven years after she'd left him. Seven years of fighting other men's wars. He hadn't cared whether he'd lived or died. When he'd been home rumbling around the empty ranch house without her, he'd seen her in every room. He'd tried dating other women, but nobody had ever come close to filling the void.

When he'd gotten home from the Middle East and found her gone, he'd been so hurt and furious that when she'd invited him to Vegas or offered to come back for a visit, all he'd said was, "Follow your dream. You don't want me."

What if she had? Maybe it was his fault she'd gotten into so much trouble. Maybe she could have found a way to be a singer and a wife. Maybe he should have supported her instead of demanding her on his terms. He thought of how she'd smiled when her fans had praised her tonight. Her music and the thrill of singing to an audience was part of her. Her voice thrilled him, too. It was why he'd fallen in love with her. She was a natural star. He'd been a selfish bastard to even try to take all that away from her the first time. He just hadn't realized back then how much her music mattered to her. And to him. To hold her, he had to give her her freedom.

As for Xavier... Phillip shouldn't have left Mezcaya with him alive.

He buried his face in his hands. The fear that gripped him was worse than anything he'd ever experienced in combat. He was helpless and scared, and his macho, tough guy act wasn't going to work this time. He couldn't shut down. The pain and the fear were inescapable. Never in his whole life had he felt so vulnerable and exposed.

"Celeste. Please, God, or whoever's listening up there... Please don't let her die."

"Phillip. I want Phillip...."

Celeste was in the hospital. Her broken leg was in a cast. Tubes were attached to her arms.

The door to her hospital room opened.

"Phillip..."

But it wasn't Phillip. It was a redheaded nurse with a syringe in her hand.

"I don't want a shot. I want..."

"You need your rest."

Even as she shook her head, Celeste felt the faintest prick in her arm and sweet fire tingling in her vein.

"Do you remember crashing your truck?"

She swallowed. "There's a weird taste in my mouth."

"Here, sip some water."

When she tried, she could barely lift her head or swallow. Within minutes her eyes felt heavy and her mind was drifting. "Phillip..." But Phillip wasn't coming. He didn't want her. He'd made that clear. She wasn't worthy.

Sick at heart, she shut her eyes.

Hours later she woke up and Phillip was there. Only this time she didn't believe he really was. It was a dream, like the one she'd had after the accident. Oh, the heartache when she realized her mind was playing another cruel trick.

"Go away," she whispered. "You don't really love me. You don't..." She shut her eyes, willing him to vanish.

"Celeste," he drawled in that velvet tone he used when they made love. "I'm sorry. I don't care what you did. I love you. You're the most wonderful thing that has ever happened to me. I love you."

"Hello," she said softly, opening her eyes.

He smiled.

"Hold my hand," she murmured. "Touch me so I'll know you're real."

He smoothed her hair out of her eyes. "I'm real."

"I'm okay," she said. "I have a broken leg. A minor fracture..."

"The doctor told me."

His hand stroked her cheek lovingly.

"Your truck's totaled, though. I—I was driving too fast when that other truck..."

"I don't care about my truck or even about who did this, just as long as you're..." His voice broke. He crumpled a piece of paper viciously in his hand.

"What's that you're holding?" she whispered.

"Just a note somebody left... Nothing."

"Did somebody kill another cow and leave you a note?"

"It's not important."

For a second or two her tough Marine stared past her out the window. He was too choked up to talk.

"Another warning?"

He pressed his lips together and nodded. "You're all that matters," he whispered. "You have to believe me."

She squeezed his hand. "So are you. I won't go to Nashville. I'll give it all up for you. I wanted to be somebody because I thought I was nothing. But you make me feel…special. Our life together, our future, is everything. I want children. Your children. Oh, Phillip, I was such a fool."

"You don't have to give anything up for me. You have a big dream and you tried to make it come true. You wouldn't be you without your dreams. I want to help you make them come true."

"You're my big dream. I just didn't know it. I was on a path. I had tunnel vision. You're everything."

"We'll work it out. Your music is a part of you. If fame and fortune ever threatens to overpower us, we'll deal with that, too. Together. If you want to sing, I want you to. We'll hire a housekeeper."

"Oh, Phillip I don't know. We'll have to see. Right now just knowing you love me is enough. But you'll let me sing if I feel I have to? You love me that much?"

He rained gentle kisses along her brow. "Now that I'm sure of you, I'm not intimidated by your music."

"Maybe I have a broken leg, but I feel so wonderful, so cherished. I—I didn't want to discuss my past life…because I was ashamed of it, or my dreams because I thought they threatened you."

"You don't have to explain anything. I was a jerk…. Pigheaded…I believe you said."

"No. You took me in when first came here with nothing even though I'd hurt you terribly."

"We hurt each other. You're a wonderful woman."

"I—I was so ashamed…when I got here. So ashamed of being such a miserable failure. I was afraid those guys might show up, and you'd think the worst."

"Which I did—"

"I—I wanted you to think well of me—"

"I do, in spite of how I acted tonight. Forgive me for that momentary lapse of sanity. I was jealous. It drove me crazy that you refused my ring and that you didn't trust me enough…"

"I do trust you. I was crazy not to before. Nobody's ever been so good to me before."

"That's all that matters." He cupped her face with his hands. "You made a mistake. You didn't do anything really wrong."

"Johnny gambled and didn't pay the money back he lost. When I gave him some money because he was desperate and I felt sorry for him, the goons after him came after me."

"No good deed goes unpunished." Grimly, Phillip thought of Xavier and what he'd nearly done to Celeste.

Phillip forced a hollow laugh. Then her eyes welled with unshed tears.

"Let's forget them…and concentrate on each other," Phillip said, leaning forward to kiss her as he stuffed Xavier's note into his pocket.

"What about the dead cows?"

"I'm almost certain a creep named Xavier Gonzalez from Mezcaya killed them and did this to you. He will pay. Apparently, he's got a nasty little operation running guns from Texas to Mezcaya, and he sees me as a personal threat to his business. Nobody knows where Gonzalez is right now, but I swear we'll catch him. So, your focus is to get well. Mine is to keep you safe."

She ran her hands through his hair and sighed.

"The mystery is all but solved. The bad guys will be brought to justice," he promised as he traced her cheek with a rough fingertip. "You have nothing to be afraid of. Nothing—"

"Nothing…to be afraid of…because I have you to protect me." She smiled at him with joy and love in her eyes. "I was right to come home to you." She felt completely happy, maybe for the first time in her life.

"Oh, Phillip, Phillip, my darling…. When I drove off from The Saddlebag I thought I wouldn't ever see you again, that you wouldn't want me. I was in hell."

"Me, too. I love you."

Tenderness at his velvet, reverent tone burst inside her like a new flower even before he put his arms around her and buried his face in her hair. Gently, without speaking, they held on to each other. Then he kissed her, a deep, long kiss that Celeste wished would go on forever.

Their souls and hearts were in that kiss.

"Forever," she whispered. "No more goodbyes. Only you."

"Forever."

He patted his pocket. "It's a good thing I held on to this big chunk of ice." He pulled out a familiar black velvet box and opened it.

"Oh, Phillip—" When she looked at it and then at him, her blue eyes flashed with more fire than his diamond.

"I've been carrying it around, waiting for the right moment."

"Looks like you found it."

He slipped it onto her finger. Bringing her hand to his

mouth, he kissed each fingertip. Not saying anything, he gazed into her eyes.

"Oh, Phillip—"

"Home. You've come home," he whispered. "To me, where you belong."

Epilogue

The long white limousine raced through gray storm clouds and thick driving rain toward the Lazy W. Dozens of cans tied to the back bumper rattled noisily behind them.

"Not very good planning…getting married during a hurricane," Celeste whispered as Phillip kissed her.

"Tropical depression," he corrected gently.

In the rear seat of the vehicle, the bride and groom soon forgot the cans and the rain or the damp satin streamers glued to the trunk of the car. They were kissing and holding each other so tightly, their bodies seemed glued together.

After another long kiss that left her breathless, Celeste held up her hand and gazed at her rings. All day, all during the reception, she hadn't been able to stop looking at them.

"Mrs. Phillip Westin," she murmured, glancing up at him. "Oh, darling, I can't believe you did it."

"We did it."

"I'm a respectable married woman."

"Don't let it go to your head. I mean, I don't want you to start acting...too respectable."

"You mean in bed?"

"Exactly."

She laughed. "I can't believe the whole town came to our wedding. Why, the reception at the Lone Star Country Club filled the club to its maximum capacity."

"And maybe then some." He grinned. "Free food and booze. It's going to cost us."

"I don't care. Everybody was so nice to me."

She still couldn't believe that the town accepted her because Phillip had chosen her to be his wife. They didn't care who she'd been before or if her wedding gown was low-cut and clung to every curve.

Now she was somebody, really somebody. Finally she had a family and a home...even a town to call home. She was loved and accepted. She was safe.

When the chauffeur pulled up to the big white house and got out and opened their door, Phillip wasted no time in getting her out of the rain. As soon as Celeste managed to get out of the car, he gathered her into his arms and carried her up the stairs and through the front door.

Inside, he let her go even though his eyes continued to hold her. Her knees felt weak because at last they were alone again. She knew what he wanted, what he'd wanted ever since the preacher had made them one.

Without speaking she reached up and began to undo the studs of his shirt. He slipped out of his tuxedo jacket as eagerly as if this was their first time. Soon she had the studs undone, and she'd managed to get him out of his shirt, too. He flung it on the floor impatiently, and she wrapped her hands around his lean waist.

His brown skin was hot. His eyes burned her.

"Oh, Phillip…"

"I can't wait," he said. "But then, I never can."

"Who says you have to? We're married."

"All those guests… I thought they'd dance forever."

"They're still dancing," she said. "We're the only ones who snuck out early."

"It's our honeymoon. We're entitled," he murmured, kissing her earlobe.

With awkward hands, he began to unfasten the tiny satin buttons at the back of her dress.

Then they were on the floor, and he covered her with his body. She closed her eyes and ran her hands over his thighs.

She felt something touch her abdomen, and she began to tingle all over. She giggled and grabbed at his hand blindly. "What…"

"Don't open your eyes," he whispered, "or I'll have to blindfold you."

Satin ribbons curled over her nipples, her eyelashes, and her throat. And then he touched her with something ice-cold.

"What's that?"

"Just be quiet. Enjoy."

"But it's kinky."

"Only the first time."

She knew Phillip deserved a proper, virginal bride. Not her. And yet he had told her over and over he wanted no one else.

She kept her eyes shut and surrendered to the sense of touch. For a long time different sensations played over her until she was quivery and nervy, and still he wouldn't take her. Then he licked her in sensitive places, and still with her eyes closed, she licked and touched him back.

He leaned over her. "Wrap me with your legs."

Instantly her legs came around him. When he drove inside her, thunder clashed outside and rain began to beat at the windows with gale force. The storm wasn't nearly as wild as she felt.

He said her name above the roar of the storm and she whispered his.

Never had she felt so hot or so desired. She was married. She belonged to him—utterly.

"I love you," he said. "I love you, Mrs. Phillip Westin."

Then he came, and she exploded, too.

"Being married just makes it better," she whispered a long time later.

"Every day, I'll love you more," he said.

"Oh, me, too. Me, too. You're my dream, my everything."

"Sing to me," he murmured.

"Nobody but you," she began. "Only you…" Her throat was suddenly too tight to sing.

"Don't ever say goodbye," he commanded.

"Everywhere I go, there's nobody in my heart…only you." She paused. "Enough singing."

"But not nearly enough loving—" He picked her up and carried her to bed.

"It's about time, cowboy," she purred when her golden head hit the pillow and he covered her with his much larger body.

She circled him with her arms.

He was all man, all hers, at last, forever.

* * * * * *

What the Rancher Wants...

LUCY MONROE

Lucy Monroe started reading at age four. After gone through the children's books at home, her mother caught her reading adult novels pilfered from the higher shelves on the bookcase... Alas, it was nine years before she got her hands on a Mills & Boon® romance her older sister had brought home. She loves to create the strong alpha males and independent women that people Mills & Boon® books. When she's not immersed in a romance novel (whether reading or writing it) she enjoys travel with her family, having tea with the neighbours, gardening and visits from her numerous nieces and nephews.

For my children... Your support means the world, and no mom could be prouder of what amazing women and young man you have become

CHAPTER ONE

CARLENE DANIELS parked her car in the circular drive in front of the most imposing ranch house she'd ever seen.

Being from oil-rich Texas, she'd seen a few too…not to mention the beautiful homes built locally by millionaire celebs looking for *anonymous* vacation homes.

Anonymous. Right.

Built in the California Mission style, this home's three-story stucco walls gleamed pristinely in the bright sunshine, the red-tiled roof and wrought-iron accents looking elegant rather than historic. She wondered who lived here. Typical for the area, the ad had given no particulars about the family she would be working for. *If* she would be working for them.

Sunshine Springs was not a hotbed for career opportunities, especially for an ex-schoolteacher turned cocktail waitress. But it was time to stop hiding behind spandex miniskirts and her job at the bar. Her experiences with Grant Strickland had made her realize that.

She'd left Texas in pain and determined to leave her old life behind completely. When the only opening available when she arrived in town had been working in a bar, she'd taken it because in no way would it remind her of the job and the kids she'd loved so much back home. But memories didn't go away with a change in setting and she wanted her life back.

Carlene opened her car windows a crack and put a sunshade on the dash to protect the car from turning into a portable oven before sliding out of the driver's seat and slamming the door. Swinging the wrought-iron gate open to the entryway, she slipped inside and rang the doorbell. After a couple of minutes and no answer, she rang it again.

They were advertising for a housekeeper after all. If the bell hadn't been answered by now, it probably hadn't been heard.

The door swept open. "What's the rush?"

The husky, masculine demand caught her completely off guard. Oh, wow...this man was...totally yummy. Black hair, cobalt-blue eyes and a tall, drool-worthy muscular body.

"I...uh..."

The piercing blue gaze traveled from her hair to her toes and back up again. Then it made a return journey, leaving chills in its wake. Wow...again.

She knew what she wanted him to see: a woman

from another time in her life, before she'd taken the job as bartender at the Dry Gulch. A time when her clothes and manners matched the woman she was on the inside.

Instead of the revealing outfits she wore to work nowadays, she had donned a long straight denim skirt, a loose white scooped-neck top, and white sandals. Flats. After months of wearing nothing but spiked heels that added inches to her diminutive height, these shoes almost felt as if she were wearing bedroom slippers.

The only concession she'd made to the glitz she'd grown accustomed to was the silver and turquoise belt around her hips. Even her normally riotous brown curls had been tamed in a loose French braid and she'd left off everything but the barest of makeup. She looked exactly like what she wanted to convey: a nice girl. Non-threatening in the feminine stakes and perfect for the role of housekeeper.

She stifled a cynical snort at the thought. Even her oversized top could not disguise her generous curves. Curves that had been causing her trouble since the sixth grade. And she was pretty sure it was those curves that had caused the second once over and small tilt at the corner of the man's otherwise rather grim lips.

However, she was darned if she was going to have breast reduction surgery, as her mother had suggested in order to make herself appear more respectable. She liked her figure. She just didn't like the things it made people assume about her character. An old familiar ache tried to work its way to the surface and she forced it back down.

That part of her life was over. She wasn't going to let it dictate her present any longer and she sure as shootin' wasn't going to let it dictate her future.

"You Carlene Daniels?"

She nodded, experiencing an odd inability to speak.

"I'm Win Garrison. Expected someone older."

"So did I." The words were out before she even realized she was going to say them.

She'd set this interview up with the former housekeeper. The woman had spoken little English, adding no further details about the family she was leaving behind than the ad had given. All Carlene knew was that Rosa's last day had been yesterday and that she, Carlene, had an interview for the position of housekeeper with Rosa's former employers today.

However, Carlene had heard of Win's ranch, the Bar G. Who hadn't? Only it had never occurred to her that the owner of a ranch that bred free-range mustangs, not to mention having the most prestigious thoroughbred horse breeding and training program this side of the Rockies, would be younger than fifty. Win Garrison was maybe thirty, but certainly not much older.

Making no effort to respond to her comment, he turned around and started walking down the hall, clearly expecting her to follow him. "I'll interview you out in the courtyard."

She walked behind him, cataloging his attributes like an inventory control clerk and powerless to focus her attention elsewhere. Despite his obvious wealth, Win's clothes were that of a working cowboy. His long legs were encased in a pair of jeans washed to a comfortable, faded softness that clung to his backside with almost indecent snugness. His ebony hair brushed the collar of the dark T-shirt that rippled with his muscles as he walked.

The man was too hot for Carlene's peace of mind. Maybe this job was not such a good idea…but hand-tooled boots clicked on the tile floor ahead of her drawing her inescapably toward a future as uncertain as the past she'd left behind.

Where was his wife? Why would *he* conduct the interview for a housekeeper and cook?

Win led her through the entrance hall to another interior hallway that surrounded the courtyard. An intelligent concession to central Oregon's cold winters, she thought. They went outside through one set of four sliding glass doors placed in the walls of windows that faced the courtyard from the house. She followed him to a large brick patio and couldn't help but admire the beautifully kept foliage along the way. Small shrubs and patches of grass, broken by stone pathways leading to the house, surrounded a two-tiered cement fountain. "It's lovely."

"Thank you."

He moved forward and pulled out a chair from the wrought-iron patio set. She sat down.

"Want anything to drink?"

She shook her head. "I'm fine, thanks."

He nodded and sat across from her.

When he didn't immediately begin asking questions, she decided to ask a few of her own. "Mr Garrison, I'm afraid I have almost no information regarding you and your family. When I called on the ad in the paper and spoke to your housekeeper, she told me little more than that she planned to be gone as of yesterday. Do you have children? Will Mrs Garrison wish to interview me as well?"

It made her nervous to have to go through a two-interview process for the job of housekeeper, but she would survive. It just meant that much longer before she knew whether or not she had the position. What she really wanted to ask was if there had been a lot of other applicants.

He leaned back in his chair, his boots scraping on the stone tile. "No."

No? No, what? She smiled faintly. "Would you care to expand on that a little?"

"No kids. No wife. No other interview."

She wasn't sure if she was relieved or worried by

that bit of news. "Then perhaps you would like to commence with this one?"

His eyes narrowed. "You sure you wouldn't like to do it? You seem to be doing fine so far."

Crud. It was the teacher's instincts coming out again. She would have thought, after all this time out of the classroom, she'd have no problem treating adults differently than the children she used to work with. But then a lot of times patrons at the bar needed the same kind of handling.

She tried another smile. "Um…okay. We can get the rest of my questions out of the way first. Is this a live-in position?"

"No."

She managed to bite back a sigh of relief. The job of live-in housekeeper to a man as good-looking as the one before her was rife with the potential for gossip. The last thing she wanted was any more gossip. "What are the hours, then?"

"Rosa worked from seven-thirty to four."

Carlene nodded. "What exactly do the duties entail?"

He frowned and shrugged.

She stared at him in shock. "You don't know?"

"Why do you think I need a housekeeper? It's the house stuff. I don't want to have to worry about it. A cleaning service comes in a few times a week. Rosa took care of setting that up."

Great. His Spanish-speaking housekeeper had set

up the cleaning service…which meant that the maids probably spoke Spanish as well. She could hope they were bilingual because her college French wasn't going to do her a lot of good here.

"What else did Rosa do?"

Win's frown deepened. "I told you…I'm not sure. I run my ranch and the stables. She ran the house."

"And that's what you want me to do…run the house?"

He nodded, almost smiling. "Yes."

"Did Rosa cook all your meals?"

"Yes. Both for me and the hands."

"Okay." Now they were getting somewhere.

"Did she make your bed?" Oh, nuts…why had she asked that? Not that she didn't need to know, but she really didn't need to be thinking about bed and this man in the same sentence.

But Win looked as if he was thinking. "The service only comes in maybe three times a week… my bed is made every night when I climb into it, the towels and such are gone from the bathroom too. Yes…guess she made my bed."

"And did the laundry." Not to mention a pile of domestic stuff that Carlene was quickly coming to realize Win never even *thought* about.

Must be nice to be rich enough to leave all those details to someone else.

"Well, yeah."

"It sounds like you want to hire a wife," she quipped.

He didn't smile at her small joke. Instead, his brows drew together in his fiercest frown yet. "The last thing I want is a wife, hired or otherwise. If you've got any ideas in that direction, we might as well part company right now."

She experienced an odd combination of amusement and anger at his words. Amusement that anyone could be this blunt and anger that he would assume she was angling for such a thing.

Okay, so she *had* come to the conclusion that she wanted the husband, the white picket fence and the two point five children playing in the yard after the last decent guy she dated ended up married to someone else. And she wanted that yard well manicured, not full of rusty automobile parts. The guys she met at the Gulch had not been candidates for the "two point five kids and white picket fence" scenario. They were generally interested in one thing and, with her figure, they expected to get it.

But there was no way that Win Garrison could know about her secret dreams and she certainly hadn't implied she was auditioning him for the role of husband in them.

"I'm here to apply for the position of housekeeper, not wife. Furthermore, I'm certainly not interested in marriage to a man who thinks monosyllabic replies pass for communication and rudeness is socially acceptable behavior. Don't worry. If I were to take the job of your housekeeper, your unmarried status would remain perfectly safe."

"Good." He looked satisfied, her insults seeming to go right over his head. "Then we can finish the interview."

She stood up. "I don't think that's a good idea, Mr Garrison." That she was using his rudeness as an excuse to get away from a man she was far too attracted to was not a thought she wanted to contemplate at the moment. "Thank you for your time, but I think it's best if I leave."

There had to be another job she could get that would get her out of the Dry Gulch and maybe make her application to teach in the Sunshine Springs school district a little more appealing. Just because this was the first good prospect she'd seen in the two weeks since she started looking, didn't mean it was the only possibility.

"Sit down, Carlene, and call me Win."

"No, really. I need to go." She turned to leave.

But his voice stopped her. "I said sit down." His tone made the quietly spoken command more intense than shouting could have.

She turned back to face him.

He smiled and her stomach dipped and that was so not good. "If you can't follow one simple direction, we're going to have a pretty rough working relationship."

Frowning, she remained standing. "I don't think we can have a working relationship at all, Mr Garrison."

"Why? Because I sometimes talk in monosyllable?"

"No. Because you *are* rude and I don't work well with rude people." It was the truth. She'd gotten chewed out more than once at the Dry Gulch for taking a bad-mannered customer to task for their behavior.

"If I apologize, will you finish the interview?"

She didn't think he was the kind of man that apologized often. "It depends."

"On what?"

"On why you were discourteous to begin with."

"What exactly did you consider the discourtesy, if you don't mind me asking? My one-word replies or my warning?"

She felt herself blush because she'd been rude too. Insulting even and it hadn't gone over his head. He'd simply opted not to make an issue of it.

She sighed. "The warning. Most women would not find your assumption that they are looking at you as a potential mate on such short acquaintance flattering."

Even as she said the words, she felt silly. She was taking them far too personally. Really.

His cynical laugh didn't make her feel any better. "Honey, I'm a rich man with a lifestyle a lot of people covet. A fair number of women would consider marriage a nice way to ensure they share it. I learned a long time ago to make my lack of interest in marriage clear from the beginning, no matter what relationship between me and the woman." He certainly wasn't talking in single syllables right now.

"You mean you warn all your dates and hands the same way?"

"Yes. I don't have any women working the Bar G right now, but the female vet got her warning the first time she came out to check the horses."

"It's like a religion with you," she said, a little awed by his vehemence.

He sat up, planting his booted feet securely under him. "You could see it that way. You sure talk fancy for a housekeeper."

But not for a high school English teacher with a degree in French literature, she thought. "Is that a strike against me?"

"I don't know. Why don't you sit down and we'll discuss it?"

She acquiesced.

He smiled again and she decided that she preferred it when he frowned. His smile was entirely too sexy and the last thing she needed was to think of her employer, particularly this one, as sexy in any way. He wasn't interested in marriage and she wasn't interested in an affair.

That left *sexy* out of their equation.

"What kind of experience do you have?" he asked.

"Not a lot," she admitted. "Not any paid, but I can cook and I've been keeping house for myself since I went away to college."

Of course, keeping up with her dorm room and then small apartments was nothing on the scale of his three-story mansion, but she would cope.

"If you can cook as well as you talk, the hands are going to love you." He gave her another once-over, this time, instead of chills, his gaze making her go hot in places an employer should not affect. "Then again, once they get a look at you, they'll think they've gone to heaven even if your food tastes like cow pies."

This she was used to. This she could handle. At least that was what she tried to convince herself. Men had been making comments about her figure for years. She had learned long ago that the best way to deal with the comments was to ignore them. "Ever eaten any?"

"Any what?"

"Cow pies?"

"No," he said, with a hint of smile in his voice.

"Then I guess you won't know if my cooking falls under that category, now, will you?"

The smile became a full-blown chuckle. "Guess not. You start tomorrow morning, Tex."

"My name is Carlene."

"But you talk like a Texan."

"I'll have to work harder on that. I'll never live there again." Too much pain she never wanted to revisit.

Relaxing against the brown leather couch in his living room, Win swirled the whiskey in his glass before taking a swallow. It had been several hours since Carlene Daniels had left. His new housekeeper. He grinned.

She had a body that would make most men uncomfortable in their jeans and talked like a prissy little schoolmarm. Remembering the curves her loose top had been unable to hide, he amended his thoughts. The lady wasn't exactly little, at least not in some places. She wasn't too big either. She was a perfect pocket Venus, with womanly curves that led to a naturally small waist. She was the stuff of most adolescent male dreams, maybe most adult ones as well.

She'd certainly been the subject of too many of his waking thoughts today. He still couldn't figure out what gremlin had gotten into him and prompted him to offer her the job. She had no experience. He sure as hell hoped she could cook. His hands might like looking at a sexy woman like her, but that would grow old pretty darn quick if she didn't feed them right. He sighed.

Maybe he should assign Shorty to help her until she got used to the routine. The diminutive man made lousy biscuits, but he knew the quantities and types of food horsemen ate.

She'd probably talk Shorty's ears off. The woman had a mouth on her and it was plain as the day was long that she was used to being in charge. So long as she limited that bossy streak to the house, they wouldn't have any problems. He didn't want to have to worry about anything but running the Bar G and Garrison Stables. With mares ready to foal he didn't have time to concern himself with stuff like meals and cleaning house.

He wondered where she'd gotten such a bossy streak. If she didn't have any experience as a house-keeper and cook, what types of jobs had she held before? He couldn't believe he hadn't asked her. He hadn't even asked her to fill out an employment ap-plication. He had hired her based on sheer instinct and that wasn't like him. He was a careful man.

He hated admitting it, but his hormones had played their part too. It was disconcerting to realize that he'd reached the age of thirty and he could still be swayed so strongly by the sight of a beautiful woman. He'd just gone too long without. He hadn't had a date in months and hadn't slept with a woman in even longer. He'd gotten tired of the games. Tired of empty sex. Both things seemed to come along with the territory for a man uninterested in marriage.

There were times the big house felt empty too, times he felt empty. His certainty that marriage was for idiots didn't waver. He'd learned the lesson too well at his mother's knee. Hadn't she married five men and divorced four? The only reason she hadn't divorced her last husband was because she'd died before she could get bored again with marital bliss.

There had been a time when Win had been willing to believe that there were women out there that weren't like his mother. He'd been young and foolish. Barely out of high school and overwhelmed with the responsibility of caring for his thirteen-year-old sister, he'd met a shy, sweet little gal who wanted to get married—Rachel. He had believed that Rachel could help with his sister, could make their household, devastated by the death of his mom and stepdad, a home again.

It hadn't worked that way. Rachel had wanted him to sell the Bar G and move to the big city. She had dreams and no one was going to stand in her way, least of all her young husband and his needy little sister. He hadn't wanted to risk marriage since then. He'd learned his lesson the hard way, but he *had* learned it.

Carlene sure had been offended when he laid it out flat for her. She'd bristled with feminine pride and it had been all he could do not to laugh. She was naïve if she thought most of the women who entered his life didn't see him as a potential meal ticket complete with caviar and silver spoons.

She didn't know it, but it hadn't been rude for him to set things straight from the beginning. It had been fair and he was a fair man. She had a right to know where he was coming from. He wanted her and he meant to have her, but he wasn't interested in marriage.

He'd wanted her from the moment he opened his door, irritated by the second ringing of chimes set off by the impatient person waiting on the other side. The woman standing on the other side had been so far from what he'd expected that he'd felt sucker punched. And horny.

No doubt about it. He had been too long without the company of a woman, but he'd had the good sense to hire Carlene and soon that would be rectified.

CHAPTER TWO

CARLENE liked Shorty, the ranch hand Win had assigned to help her in the kitchen, the minute she met him. He had a grin that more than made up for his lack in stature. Soft gray eyes twinkled under a crown of silvered hair. "Well, missy, Win says you don't got a hill of beans in experience, but I'm to help you learn the ropes. You know anything about cooking?"

She laughed. "I'd have to be pretty dumb to take a job as housekeeper and cook if I didn't, now, wouldn't I? Do I look dumb to you?"

Shorty sized her up as if he was seriously contemplating his answer to that question and Carlene's respect for him went up a notch. The man kept his eyes focused mainly on her face.

"No, missy, you don't look dumb at all. That must mean you can cook." He sighed with relief. "It's a good thing. Win and the hands ain't real fond of my vittles."

Then why had Win assigned the man to help her in the kitchen? Shorty answered that question for her with his next statement. "None of the hands, including our boss, can do any better. At least I know how to cook food without burning it, even if it isn't real appetizin'."

Carlene walked over to the sink and washed her hands. "I'll let you in on a little secret, Shorty. I can cook without burning the food and I've been told that my food is better than passable by more than one person."

"Well, glory be, that's a relief."

Carlene hoped that the rest of the ranch hands would share Shorty's enthusiasm when they filed into the large kitchen for lunch. She'd made French dip sandwiches, Caesar salad and cookies for dessert.

Win took a seat at one end of the table. Shorty sat to his left and a man they called Joe, who looked about the same age as Win, sat to Win's right. He was introduced as the ranch foreman in charge of the horse and mustang training. Four other hands, ranging in age from just out of high school to another man who looked as wizened and gray as Shorty, sat down. Apparently, most of the hands worked for Joe, while Shorty and one of the youngest men, a brunette with cold gray eyes they introduced as Lonny, worked in the thoroughbred stables with Win.

Carlene placed filled plates in front of each man, beginning with Win. She didn't realize that she'd been waiting for his approval until he looked up and nodded. "Looks good."

She quietly said, "Thank you," and continued passing out plates, feeling ridiculously pleased. After serving everyone, she turned back to the counter where she had lined up the ingredients for the pies she planned to make.

"Aren't you going to eat with us, ma'am?" Joe asked.

She turned around, waiting to see if Win would second the hand's invitation to join them. When he didn't, she replied, "I'll eat later. I've got work to do."

"Aw shucks, ma'am, we'd be pleased for your company," a redhead said.

Lonny gave Carlene a knowing look and patted the bench next to him. "You can sit right here, Carlene."

Normally, she would have just laughed off an invitation like that from such a young man, but there was an intensity about Lonny that made Carlene nervous. The cold ruthlessness in his eyes reminded her of the student that had torn her life in Texas to shreds. She suppressed a shiver, reminding herself that there was no disgruntled principal here to help Lonny hurt her. There was just Win and she could not see him stooping to the lengths her ex-boss had even if she rejected him.

She managed to swallow a rude comeback to

Lonny's comment, not wanting to offend Win's other employees her first day on the job. "No, thank you. As I said, I've got work to do."

She shifted her gaze to Win, wondering what he thought of the exchange.

The look he was giving the younger man was cold and deadly. He turned slightly so that he was looking directly at her, his gaze warming several degrees. "Do what's comfortable for your schedule, but don't skip your lunch."

She smiled at the order. "Yes, boss."

He nodded. "If you're hungry now, the men'll move so you can sit by Shorty."

It didn't escape her notice, or that of his men, if Lonny's narrowed eyes were an indication, that Win's dictate would place her next to him as well. Carlene didn't mind. Compared to Lonny, Win was a much safer bet. She had no doubt that sitting between him and Shorty she wouldn't have to fend off any roaming hands under the table.

She considered Win's offer. It shouldn't be such a big deal, but it would set a precedent for the future. If she ate with them now, human nature dictated that the hands would recognize that whenever she shared their table, her place would be between Win and Shorty.

Her stomach chose that moment to make a rumbling sound and the men laughed while she smiled, embarrassed. "I guess I'll eat now."

* * *

Several hours later after preparing a dinner that only required Shorty to heat things through before serving them, Carlene got ready to leave. Her feet didn't hurt as much as after a night tending bar, but her back ached from a different kind of labor. She'd spent the day cooking, cleaning and trying to decipher the written instructions Rosa had left behind in a confusing mixture of Spanish and English.

She wondered what had caused the other woman to abandon her job so abruptly.

"You sure know your way around a ranch kitchen," Shorty commented from behind as she pulled off her apron and hung it on the hook by the refrigerator.

She turned and smiled at him. "Thanks. I grew up in west Texas cow country."

"Congratulations, Shorty. You got more information out of her in five minutes than I was able to do during her interview."

Carlene's head snapped up at the sound of Win's amused voice from the doorway to the dining room. He leaned against the doorjamb, a lazy smile on his face and looking handsome as sin. He was dressed much as he'd been for her interview, except today his T-shirt was black instead of dark blue and a cowboy hat hung loosely from his fingers next to his thigh.

She wished he'd stop smiling at her like that. It made her forget what she was going to do next.

Forcing herself to focus on his words and not his mouth, she said, "You didn't ask."

He came into the kitchen sniffing at the casserole in the oven with an appreciative air. "Smells good."

"Thank you."

He lifted the linen towel covering the two marionberry pies she'd made for dinner. She'd used the native Oregon fruit, figuring the men would appreciate the plump, tangy blackberry-style filling. "You're wrong, you know," he said as he put the cover back over the pies.

"Wrong about what?" she asked, feeling breathless for no apparent reason.

"I did ask." He turned to face her. "I distinctly remember asking if you had any experience."

"You asked about experience as a housekeeper and cook. I don't have any formal experience, but I do know how to cook and clean house. I told you that."

She didn't understand his enigmatic expression. He asked, "Why'd you leave Texas? Were you looking for adventure?"

She couldn't hold back the laughter that bubbled forth. "If I'd been looking for adventure, I wouldn't have ended up in Sunshine Springs." Though the small town was a lot more than what she'd thought it was when she'd first arrived.

She'd had no idea at the time that it was a winter playground for the rich and famous.

He relaxed his tense posture and returned her smile. "No. You wouldn't have."

"So, why did you leave?" Shorty asked, reminding Carlene of his presence.

"It was time to move on," she replied noncommittally.

"Leave behind a disgruntled lover?" asked the irrepressible Shorty.

Carlene frowned. It was too near the truth. "I left behind a life that didn't fit me any longer."

Win's expression turned distinctly chilled. "Did that life include a husband? Children?"

"No." She was inexplicably hurt that he would have such a low opinion of her as to believe she would leave her own children behind, and her voice came out tight. "I've never been married."

His expression didn't lighten. "Do you do that often?"

"What? Move on?" Was he worried that she would move and leave him in the lurch looking for a housekeeper as Rosa had? "Don't worry, I'll give you plenty of notice when I'm ready to leave."

His expression turned even more forbidding. "I see."

She hated it when people used that catch all phrase. It made for lousy communication. For instance, what exactly did Win believe he saw and why had it put him in such a dour mood?

"There's nothing to see. I'm a responsible employee, Win. I won't leave you in the lurch."

"You said *when,* not *if.* You're already planning to leave."

He didn't need to make it sound as if she were betraying him. She was just an employee. A housekeeper…a job easy to fill again, as she was testament to. But perhaps she should tell him about her plans to get a teaching position in the fall. She discarded the idea as quickly as it came. This wasn't exactly a position with a contract and long-range career plans. She would do the job she'd been hired to do as long as she worked for Win Garrison, and she'd do it well.

And she'd give him sufficient notice to find someone else. He couldn't ask for more than that.

She did say, "I'd have to be a different person to be content with the position of cook and housekeeper for the rest of my life."

Win nodded, his face blank. "Yes. You would."

A couple of days later, Carlene was washing up the dishes left over from breakfast when Lonny came in. Once they learned she knew her way around the kitchen, Shorty no longer came up to the house to help. So, she was alone with the stable hand. She pushed the discomfort that thought caused aside. She could handle a young man like Lonny, even if he did have eyes colder than a meat locker.

Determined to take control of the encounter right from the start, she forced a smile to her lips. "If you're looking for Shorty, he's down at the stables."

"I didn't come to talk to Shorty. I came to talk to you." Lonny leaned negligently against the counter about a foot from where she stood at the sink.

She put the last plate into the bottom rack of the dishwasher and then closed it. Standing straight, she dried her hands on the kitchen towel she kept by the sink. "What can I do for you?"

Lonny's smile didn't travel from his lips to his eyes. Carlene suppressed a shiver.

"I don't want anything special," he said.

She knew he was lying. There was purpose along with unmistakable confidence in the younger man's eyes. Well, that confidence would turn to surprise if he tried anything. He would learn just as her former boss had that Carlene was not, nor would she ever be, easy prey. She was grateful that Lonny had no way of exacting the terrible price that her former principal had for her rejection. At least this time, she could say no without losing her job and her reputation in the process.

She stepped around him to pull down the platter she intended to use for lunch, using it as an excuse to move away from Lonny. She needn't have bothered. He moved with her.

"Aren't you supposed to be working right now?" she asked with no little exasperation. Really, Win could keep better track of his hands.

"You know the old saying. All work and no play makes Lonny a very dull boy and I'm anything but dull, babe."

Carlene set the platter down with more force than necessary. "My name is Carlene, not babe." She took a deep breath to recenter. "And the truth? I *am* a bit dull. I believe in working when I'm paid to work. I've got lunch to prepare and a house to clean, so if you'll excuse me."

Lonny moved forward, crowding her against the wall. He put one hand on the wall and the other on her hip, effectively caging her in. "Don't worry. I'll teach you how to have a little fun." He squeezed her hip and she pushed against his chest, but he didn't move.

Letting his gaze travel down her body, he paused at her breasts hidden behind the big white apron, before moving on. His leer sent her insides churning. She really didn't want to have to deal with this. "Although, with the way you're built, I bet you know plenty about fun, don't you, *babe?*"

His head came down as if he planned to kiss her.

Enough was enough. Some guys just didn't comprehend when a woman wasn't interested. Lonny might be young, but he was old enough to learn this lesson. She'd worn a pair of her more conservative heels today, her body too used to spending hours on heels to be comfortable in her flat sandals.

She was glad she'd done so now. Using the short, but very spiked heel of her shoe, she came down with all her weight on the top of his boot. He grunted and stumbled back a step. Before he could steady himself, she'd curled her fingers into a fist and punched him right below his ribcage just as her self-defense instructor back in Texas had taught her.

Letting out a high-pitched curse that ended on a big oof, he doubled over.

She drew herself to her full five-feet-four-inch height. "I am not anyone's babe, least of all yours. Do I make myself clear?"

He lifted his head, his arms still curved protectively around his midsection. "Yeah."

She nodded. Good. "Though I may not be old enough to be your mother, I'm certainly too old to be your anything else. I can't even be your friend because I don't offer that kind of trust to idiots who don't know any better than to make a pass at a co-worker on their boss's time."

He glared at her, but he didn't argue.

"I work for the same man you do and I expect the same respect that you give any of the other hands. Is that understood?"

He finally stood up straight, but his breathing was still a little shallow. "Understood, but you don't know what you're missing."

She let that slide. A man needed some pride, after all.

She had only one final thing to say to him. "As far as how I'm built having anything to do with my ability to have fun, I'm here to tell you that I've got all the same parts that other women do. Fun, especially the kind you appear to want, is a state of mind, not body. How I look has nothing to do with it, unless we're talking how my brain works and then maybe you'd have a clue."

Lonny nodded and sidled out of the kitchen without further comment.

Win came in the door as Lonny was leaving. "You forget what I told you to do this morning?"

Lonny shook his head. "Just needed to talk to Carlene about something."

Win looked at Carlene and then back at Lonny. "Anything I need to know about?"

Lonny's cheeks, which had taken on a slight pallor, turned red. "No, boss. Nothing important."

Win looked at Carlene. "That true?"

Carlene nodded. "It definitely wasn't anything important."

It appeared as if Win wanted to ask more questions, but Lonny was already headed toward the stables. Win stepped completely into the kitchen.

"I'm going into town to pick up some things. Do you want to come along and get groceries?"

She took longer to consider his question than she was sure he expected. She did need groceries. Rosa, the previous housekeeper, had left some things well stocked and some nearly empty. The problem was going to town with Win. She avoided him and the intensity she experienced whenever he was around as much as possible. And after her little dust-up with

Lonny, she did not want any more challenges from the male of the species.

He raised a mocking brow. "I didn't realize it would be such a difficult question."

She frowned. Why did she get the feeling that he knew exactly why she hesitated? Inexplicably, the thought stung her pride. "That would be fine, Win. Just let me get my purse."

He shrugged. "You don't need it. I'll buy the groceries."

"Don't you know that a woman feels naked without her purse?" she asked.

His eyes took on a distinctly disturbing quality and she tensed in preparation for some ribald comment, but none came. He merely said, "My sister's mentioned that a time or two."

He led her out to the car and she said, "I didn't realize that you had a sister. Does she live around here?"

Maybe Carlene had met her.

"No. She and her husband live in Portland."

Carlene settled into the passenger seat of Win's midnight-blue Ram pickup and buckled her seat belt. "Oh. What's her name?"

If he thought she was nosy, he didn't say so. He started the truck and headed toward the highway. "Leah Branson. Her husband runs Branson Consulting out of Portland. Maybe you've heard of it. They get their names in the paper from time to time."

Carlene searched her memory, but couldn't

remember ever reading about the consulting firm. "No. Sorry."

"I guess you aren't real interested in the financial section of the paper?"

She bristled at his condescending tone. "As a matter of fact, no. I like to read human interest stories, not dry articles on the state of the economy."

She also liked to read popular fiction. She'd been teased at college because of her taste in reading material, but she refused to conform to someone else's idea of what a French Literature major should want to read.

She realized she was taking easy offense again and sighed. "Sorry. I didn't mean to get defensive."

"I didn't mean to offend you, honey."

Now why didn't Win calling her honey bother her a bit when Lonny calling her babe was like nails scoring a chalkboard?

"You didn't. Not really. But just because I'm not interested in the financial section of the paper doesn't mean I'm a bimbo."

He took his gaze off the road for a few seconds to meet hers. "Does that happen often?"

"What?"

"People think you're a bimbo."

"Because I don't read the stock reports?"

"Because of how you look."

The man saw too much.

"People assume a lot of things about me based on

the way I look." She joked, "I guess it's a good thing I'm not blonde. I'd have a whole slew of assumptions made about my intelligence based on the color of my hair."

Win frowned. "Is that why you left Texas? Were too many people judging you based on your looks?"

His insight startled her and she didn't answer immediately. How much did she want to say? "You could say that," she hedged.

"I'd rather hear what you have to say about it."

"I don't like revisiting my past."

"Okay."

His easy agreement should have set her mind at rest, but she had the distinct impression that he was just biding his time. She was almost certain the subject wasn't closed as far as Win Garrison was concerned.

Looking for something besides herself to discuss, she said, "Tell me more about your sister."

His expression softened. "She's five years younger than me. She and Mark have got a couple of real cute kids."

"Where are your parents?"

His fingers gripped the steering wheel a little tighter. "I don't know where our dads are. Mom moved after each divorce and we lost touch. Neither of them were big on visitation rights."

"And your mom?" she asked.

"She died in a plane crash twelve years ago."

"Who raised your sister?"

"I did." He spoke with no inflection in his voice.

"That must have been really hard, taking on the responsibility to raise a teenage sister and losing your mom at the same time."

"Raising Leah was nothing new. Mom was too busy getting married and divorced to pay much attention to either of us. Leah was my responsibility from the day Mom brought her home from the hospital." He smiled ruefully. "I still get tied up in knots every time she cries."

His admission touched something deep inside Carlene. It was so far from something she would have expected him to say. "Divorce is incredibly traumatic for children. I can't imagine what it must have been like for you to go through two of them."

"Four."

She stared at his profile. "Your mom was married four times?"

"Five. She was divorced four times. I guess modern pop psychologists would say she had a problem with commitment."

"What happened to her fifth husband?" Carlene knew she was being unforgivably inquisitive, but she couldn't seem to help herself.

"Hank Garrison died in the plane crash with my mom."

"You use your stepfather's name. Did he adopt you?"

Win gave a harsh, bitter laugh. "Nothing so

formal. Every time Mom remarried, she insisted Leah and I take her husband's name. I had more last names growing up than pets."

"But you stuck with Garrison."

"Yeah." His terse answer didn't invite further comment.

She laid her hand on his arm. "I'm sorry."

He spared her a brief, cold glance as he pulled into a parking spot in front of the grocery store. "Save your pity. I survived."

She yanked her hand back, feeling chastised. She'd reserve her sympathy for someone who needed it, someone who had a little softness left in him. She just wished her heart didn't constrict every time she thought of Win's childhood. At least she understood the aversion to marriage he'd expressed at their first meeting. The man had a reason for distrusting the institution.

Win watched Carlene walk across the grocery store parking lot and couldn't help admiring the sway of her hips in her snug-fitting denim jeans. She looked back when she reached the front door, and waved him on impatiently. He sighed and obeyed her imperious little wave.

Pulling onto the main road, he mulled over the conversation they'd had in the car.

He didn't like talking about his mother, but he'd hoped that if he opened up to Carlene a little about his past, she'd be willing to do the same with hers. His was an open book anyway. Anything she wanted to know she could find out from one of Sunshine Spring's long time residents.

He took her curiosity as a good sign. Women wanted to know about the men they were interested in. Carlene was definitely interested in him, but she'd given a lot of mixed signals. Something was holding her back.

He had a feeling that something had happened to Carlene in Texas that left her skittish as an untried filly. He figured it was his job to help her get over her past and move on. Because he wanted her warm and willing.

CHAPTER THREE

THE next morning, Win came into the kitchen to ask Carlene a question and stopped dead in his tracks. She was bent over pulling something out of one of the low cupboards. She had the sweetest little behind he'd seen in a very long time. Hell, maybe ever. And it was positioned up in the air in a position guaranteed to turn him hard as a rock.

He took a minute just to appreciate the view.

Her jeans weren't exactly tight but they couldn't hide the sweet curve of her cheeks. He'd noticed she liked to wear her clothes loose and wondered why. Not that he minded. He didn't want the hands getting any randy ideas and he had a suspicion that Lonny already had. So far, though, the boy had done nothing overt. He just watched Carlene with hungry, hot eyes and Win didn't like it.

Along with his own randy thoughts toward the sexy little lady, Win had developed a whole passel full of possessive feelings. The only other woman he

felt this protective toward was his sister, Leah, but he
damn sure didn't want to see her naked. Now,
Carlene was another story. He figured once he got her
into his bed, he wasn't going to let her out for a good
long while.

Thinking about what he planned to spend that
time doing sent his temperature spiking. If he
wasn't careful, he was going to fantasize himself
right into a state of unrequited lust and, as much as
he wanted Carlene, he had a horse ranch and
training stables to run.

"You find what you're looking for yet?" he asked
by way of saying hello.

A muffled scream came from inside the cupboard
and she jumped. Her head must have hit something
because he heard a loud thump followed by a groan.
Shimmying backward, she got herself out of the
cupboard and turned to face him.

Her glare was as hot as his loins. "You startled
me." She made it sound as if she'd just accused him
of horse stealing.

"You didn't hear me come in?" he asked, knowing
good and well she hadn't.

She never would have remained in such a tantalizing position otherwise. When it came to desire,
Carlene acted like an untried filly. He'd seen her
looking at him with something hot in her pretty
brown eyes and that gave him hope, but she didn't
flirt or encourage him in any other way. She was like

a mare going into heat, not sure she wanted to be covered by the stallion and playing hard to get.

He'd let her dance around the corral some, but eventually he was going to corner her.

She rubbed her head, the action pressing her generous breasts against the big white apron she wore from the moment she arrived until she went home in the afternoon. "No. I didn't hear you. Why didn't you say something?"

"I did." Just not right away.

She ignored that. "Those cabinets aren't very convenient. It's almost impossible to reach the back without climbing right in."

He shrugged. "I can reach them just fine."

She went all squinty-eyed. "Well, I can't and I'm the housekeeper. Unless you want to do the cooking, you'd better find some way to make the pots and pans stored down there more accessible."

He thought about it. "Maybe I could have a pull-out shelf installed by one of the ranch hands. Would that work?"

She looked nonplussed by his easy acquiescence. "Yes. That would be fine. Terrific, in fact." Then her eyes took on a wary cast. "Not Lonny."

He narrowed his own eyes, trying to read the expression on her face. "Has he said something to you? Made you uncomfortable?"

She turned and picked up the big stew pot she'd

been after. "I'd just rather not have him underfoot. I like Shorty. Can he build the shelf?"

She set the stew pot in the sink and turned on the water.

Win didn't like dropping the subject of Lonny, but he had the impression that Carlene had said all she wanted to. Maybe she'd noticed the way Lonny looked at her too and was embarrassed by it.

With her looks, you might think she was used to that sort of male attention, but Win got the impression that she didn't like it. "Shorty's handy, but I need him in the stables right now. Call a carpenter to install the pull-out."

Turning off the water, she looked at him over her shoulder, a smile of gratitude playing on her lips. "Are you sure?"

"Honey, you can't be wondering if I can afford it." Hell, most women were only too happy to spend his money.

She laughed. "No, more wondering if you thought it was worth it. I'm glad you do. I'll call the carpenter tomorrow. Thank you."

"You're welcome."

She went to lift the cast-iron pot and water sloshed over the side. "I forgot how heavy these things are."

He sidled up behind her and put his arms around her. Taking a firm grip on the handle, he lifted it. "You want it on the stove?"

She stood still, like a rabbit caught in a snare. "Yes, please."

Her voice came out all breathy and soft. He wanted to lean down and kiss the creamy skin of her neck and see what that did to her voice, but he controlled himself. A mare couldn't be broken to bit if the handler startled her early on with demands she wasn't prepared to meet.

He stepped back, using one hand to carry the pot. He set it on the stove for her.

She turned to face him, the skin of her cheeks a rosy hue. He liked this additional evidence that his nearness had an effect on her. Standing so close to her had a pretty strong impact on him too. He'd be walking like a saddle-sore greenhorn, if he weren't careful. His usually comfortable jeans felt tight enough to do damage right now.

"Thank you."

"Anytime, honey."

She busied herself putting the stew together and he just watched. He liked the way she moved, her actions fluid and graceful. When she opened the fridge to pull out the meat, she squatted rather than bending over to get it. Amusement at the action tugged at him. If she thought the view of her thighs pressed against blue denim was any less exciting than her backside, she had a lot to learn about men.

She straightened and put the meat on the cutting block. *"What?"*

"Something the matter, honey?"

She took in a deep breath and blew it out with her eyes shut, then she opened them. "What are you doing in here? I don't think you want cooking lessons, so why are you hanging around watching me prepare dinner when you've got a stable to return to?"

Her surly tone made him grin. "You're bossy, aren't you?"

He could just about hear her teeth grinding together. "You're the one that told me you want to work uninterrupted—not have to deal with anything domestic. You must have come up to the house for a reason."

"Yeah."

"What is it?" She looked as if she'd like to wrap her fingers around his neck, but not with the intention of doing anything nice.

Why had he come up to the house? Oh, yeah. "I was wondering if you could put together a couple of casseroles for the weekend. Rosa used to do it and it helped me out a heap."

She nodded. "That won't be any problem."

"Good." He turned to leave and then stopped. "Maybe I'll put that shelf in for you myself, tomorrow."

"No, really…your idea of calling a carpenter is a good one."

"If you insist."

He left the kitchen with the look of consternation on her face fixed clearly in his mind. She noticed him all right. She hadn't look horrified, just thrown for a loop and he figured that was a good sign.

He'd break that filly to bridle, but first he had to get her used to having him around. Then he'd work on the touching.

Just like a nervous mare and he had a real special touch with nervous fillies, just ask anyone.

Carlene was ready to quit her job as Win's housekeeper two weeks later. Between Lonny's glares and Win's bedroom eyes, she was at her wit's end.

Win never implied that her job was even slightly reliant on her sleeping with him, but then again he made no bones about the fact that he wanted her in his bed. He hadn't actually come out and said so, but he watched her with a hot gaze that made her insides melt. It didn't help that he found more excuses than a student with spring fever did to skip class, to get close to her.

Just yesterday he had insisted on helping her get a large ceramic bowl down from the top shelf in the pantry. That would have been fine except that he didn't allow her to move out of the way before his strong, masculine body was stretching up and leaning over her to reach the bowl. Again, no problem.

Except that the effect Win's closeness had on her senses couldn't be denied. She'd forgotten for one full minute what she'd been planning to do and just stood there, breathing in his scent. He'd noticed.

Darn him. And he'd laughed. No doubt he thought she was like a plump peach, ripe and ready to be picked off the tree.

She sighed and cut some more shortening into the flour for the biscuits she was preparing to go with dinner.

She didn't want to quit.

She liked her new job. Shorty might not know much about cooking, but he was a sweetheart. She liked the rest of the ranch hands as well…except Lonny. She enjoyed cooking for them and Win was a tidy person. Keeping his house clean was a cinch, especially with the help of maid service that came in three times a week. Mondays and Wednesdays and once on the weekend.

She liked everything about working at the Bar G except the way its owner made her feel.

Dealing with an interested male shouldn't be so difficult. Men had been interested in her since she started wearing a bra, but Win was different. She had an almost overwhelming desire to give in to the invitation she saw in his eyes and that scared her spitless. He'd made it very clear that he wasn't interested in marriage and she hadn't changed her mind about an affair. First, because she believed that she deserved more than that and second, because no school board for a small town like Sunshine Springs was going to hire a teacher with a reputation for loose morals. Gossip always got around.

Awareness skittered down her spine and she spun around, dropping the pastry cutter into the ceramic bowl with a clang.

Win leaned against the wall watching her. He did a lot of that, leaning against a wall or something and just watching her. It made her nervous and hot and jittery besides, something she definitely didn't want to deal with.

She forced a smile to her lips. "Hi."

He pushed away from the wall and walked toward her. She started getting nervous again as the distance between them closed to less than a few inches.

She backed up, but ran into the counter behind her. "Win?"

He reached out and brushed her cheek. "I thought the flour was for the biscuits."

"It is." She couldn't think of anything else to say. She couldn't seem to move away either.

"It's not real attractive makeup, but on you it's kinda cute."

"No." Then understanding dawned. She whipped her hands up and scrubbed at her cheeks, getting rid of any remaining flour Win hadn't brushed away with his hand. "I didn't realize I was wearing dinner."

"I wouldn't mind," he said.

"What?" Was it just that his proximity had scrambled her brains, or was he really not making any sense?

His voice dropped to a husky drawl. "I wouldn't mind you wearing my dinner."

As the words registered Carlene felt her blood spike with both anger and desire. She forced the anger to the forefront. Placing her hands on Win's chest, she shoved. Hard. He fell back a couple of paces.

She untied the big white apron she wore to protect her clothes with jerky movements. She yanked it off and tossed it on the table. "That's it. I quit."

When Win didn't say anything, particularly, "I'm sorry and won't you please stay?" she reached her hand out and poked him in the chest with her forefinger. "Listen here, Mr Bedroom Eyes. I've had my fill of you watching me like I'm a mare in heat and you're the stallion sent to cover me. Do you understand me?"

His smile infuriated her. "I think so."

She crossed her arms over her chest and glared at him. "Just what do you understand?"

"You don't want me to look at you like I want you."

"Well?" she asked.

"Well, what?"

She blew out an exasperated breath. "Are you going to stop?"

He reached out and brushed his fingers down her arm. Desire pooled in her lower belly and she bit back a groan. "I don't know if I can. I do want you, Carlene. I'm not real sure why that bothers you so much. I haven't pushed you to do anything about it, have I?"

She had to give him that. "No. You haven't, but that's not the point."

"What is the point? You don't like feeling like you want me too? I can fix that for you, honey."

The promise in his voice made her shiver with feelings she did not want to acknowledge or give in to. "Forget it. I'm not interested in a one-night stand and that's all you're offering, isn't it, Win? You don't want marriage or commitment."

His fingers curled around her upper arm. "I made my feelings on marriage plain the day I interviewed you, but there's a whole lot of ground between a one-night stand and marriage. I never said I wasn't interested in any kind of commitment. I can guarantee you that while you share my bed, no one else will."

"An affair?" Outrage burned through her and she twisted from his grasp. "You think a no-strings, open ended affair is an appreciable improvement over a one-night stand?"

His eyes narrowed. "You aren't going to convince me that you've married every man you've slept with."

The warmth of desire she had been feeling shifted to a frozen sort of pain. Win was like all the others, making assumptions based on how she looked and not who she was. Wouldn't he just die laughing if he found out that she was a twenty-six-year-old virgin? She might look like a pinup in a girlie calendar, but she'd fought against the image her entire life.

She dated very little, in high school because she had been more interested in her studies than in boys and in college because once the men she dated figured out that she didn't put out, they went looking for greener pastures. She had planned to change her innocent status a while ago with Grant Strickland, a truly nice man.

She had decided the time had come. Unfortunately, or fortunately, depending on how you looked at it, her timing had been off. Grant had been in love with another woman and hadn't been interested. She still felt the heat of embarrassment when she considered how she'd thrown herself at the man. She had truly lousy instincts when it came to men she was attracted to.

And Win was no exception. Their situation made her want to cry. He affected her as no other man ever had, including Grant, but she wasn't willing to risk her reputation and her goals for something as transitory as an affair, especially an affair with a man who made it clear that long-term commitment would never be an option.

She moved to the door.

She couldn't stay here. She wanted Win too much. The risk was too great. Grabbing her purse from the broom cupboard, she said, "You can send my check in the mail."

She had to get out of there before her resolve to keep a lid on her emotions faltered.

Her hand was on the knob to open the door when his fingers clamped around her wrist in a vicelike grip.

* * *

Win knew he couldn't let Carlene walk out that door. He didn't get what she was so upset about, but he was going to find out. They were attracted to each other. That was not a bad thing. At least, not to his way of thinking.

He kept his fingers locked firmly around her wrist as he pulled her around to face him. "What the hell do you think you are doing?"

She looked at him as if he'd lost a few marbles. "I'm leaving. Now, let go of my arm."

"No. I'm not letting go of you and you aren't leaving." He leaned forward until his face was close enough to hers that their breath mingled. "Do I make myself clear?"

She glared at him and said, "Yes," between clenched teeth.

He leaned back a little, but didn't let go of her wrist. "We're going to talk this out."

The stubborn woman shook her head at him. Didn't she know that women were supposed to want to talk things out?

"We have nothing to discuss. You want a convenient sex object for your housekeeper. Only you neglected to mention that as part of my job description. I'm wondering why though...you were quick enough to tell me your no marriage policy. I am not interested in being *anyone's* temporary squeeze, so I'm leaving."

Sex object? Temporary squeeze? Putting a tight

lid on his temper, he hooked one hand under her knees and the other behind her back. She screeched something about overbearing, insufferable cowboys, when he picked her up. He ignored her. The powder keg that was his temper was liable to go off if he paid attention.

She kept up a litany of complaints all the way out of the kitchen, through the courtyard, and into his living room. She was shoving at his chest with her fists by the time he dropped her gently onto the couch.

She shot right back up again and stood toe to toe with him, her eyes shooting sparks. "You cannot treat your employees this way and expect them to stay. What did you do, manhandle Rosa until she left?"

The thought of anyone manhandling the two-hundred-and-fifty-pound Mexican grandmother of twelve surprised a smile out of him. "No. Rosa left because her daughter went into early labor with baby number four."

When Carlene just scowled at him, he sighed and shoveled his fingers through his hair. "Damn it. I didn't mean to manhandle you either, honey."

"Don't call me honey. Employees take just as dim a view of being referred to in a too familiar fashion as they do to being manhandled."

"Will you be reasonable? I didn't manhandle you."

Her eyebrows shot up. "What would you call carrying me through the house against my will?"

"Trying to get you someplace where we weren't

going to be interrupted by Shorty or one of the other hands," he was goaded into shouting.

She settled her hands on her shapely hips. "What's wrong with Shorty overhearing me quit? It's not like a state secret or something."

He'd about had all the sass he was going to take off of her, but he tried once more to discuss the situation rationally. "You aren't going to quit. I didn't want Shorty, or anyone else, listening to us discuss our *relationship*."

Her toe started tapping and he actually moved his booted foot back a couple of inches, to get it out of range, before he realized what he was doing.

"We don't have a relationship except that of an employer and employee. As far as I'm concerned, that one is over."

"Fine. Quit your job as my housekeeper, but don't expect that to end it."

Her eyes narrowed. "Are you threatening me? What do you plan to do? Stalk me?"

That did it. He'd reached his limit. She seemed to realize it as soon as he had because she tensed, ready to run. He didn't give her the chance. Grabbing her arms, he yanked her up against him and slammed his mouth down on hers.

The only problem was that the moment his lips touched hers, all his anger evaporated and was replaced by raging desire.

* * *

Carlene could have remained an unwilling partici-
pant in Win's passionate assault if he'd stayed angry.
He didn't. The grip he had on her arms, which hadn't
been that fierce to begin with, loosened. He reached
up and unclipped the barrette she'd been using to
hold her hair back and tunneled his fingers into the
unruly curls.

Suddenly their argument…her fury…everything
but the feel of Win's lips on hers ceased to exist. She
allowed her hands, which had been fisted against his
shirtfront, to relax against him. His muscles felt solid
under the soft fabric of his shirt.

His lips moved over hers, softly, coaxingly. He
licked her bottom lip and she shivered.

"Open for me, honey. I'm desperate to taste you."

She couldn't deny the agonized need she heard in
his voice. Allowing her lips to part, she silently invited
Win in. He didn't need any urging. His tongue swept
inside and took complete dominion of her mouth.

Feelings that she'd never experienced roared to
life inside Carlene and she clung to Win, afraid that
if she didn't she would fall down.

He groaned and pulled her close against his body,
cupping her backside with one strong hand and
locking his other hand behind her head, tangling it
in her hair.

She allowed her hands to trail up his neck and
twined her fingers together once her hands were firmly
anchored behind his head. His tongue demanded a

response in her mouth and she eagerly gave it. She met him thrust for thrust and reveled in the sound of hungry need he emitted.

Using the hand on her bottom, he rocked her pelvis against his and an electric current shot through her feminine core. Heat and dampness grew between her legs. She whimpered and he broke his mouth away from hers to trail kisses down her neck and up again toward her ear. Her breath came rushing out on a high-pitched wail. It just felt so good, better than anything she'd ever known.

"Oh, yes, baby, just like that."

His husky voice grated against her ear and his hot breath made her shiver uncontrollably. Suddenly the world tilted and she found herself lying under Win on the leather sofa.

Her world had shrunk down to the soft cushions at her back and the hard man lying on top of her.

"We're going to be so good together, honey. I promise."

His words broke through the passionate daze she had slipped into and she started to struggle. "Let me up, Win."

He didn't seem to hear her as he unbuttoned the top three buttons on her blouse in quick succession. He slipped his hand inside and the feel of his fingers on her aching flesh almost sent her spinning back toward the passion filled no man's land she'd been caught up in since Win's lips had first touched hers.

His next words acted like a cold shower on her senses, however. "Don't worry, honey, I've got a condom."

She started to struggle in earnest. "Let me up. I mean it, Win. Let me go."

He stopped kissing her and lifted his head to stare into her eyes. "What?"

"Please, let me go." Foolish tears gathered in the corner of her eyes.

Win slowly moved off of her body, his expression wary, and then pulled her into a sitting position next to him. "I was going too fast, wasn't I?"

She nodded, unable to speak past the frustrated tears clogging her throat. He no doubt now believed he had all the evidence he needed that she was exactly what he thought, a woman willing to share a no-strings affair. Her fingers trembled as she tried to rebutton her blouse. She muttered an expletive when they slipped for the third time off the button.

Win brushed her fingers out of the way. "Let me do that."

He had her buttoned up in less than ten seconds. The man was fast, about a lot of things. He tipped her chin up so that she had to meet his gaze. His blue eyes had grown dark and in them she could see the remnants of the wanting he'd been forced to control.

"Okay now?" he asked.

She'd never be okay again. "Yes," she nevertheless said.

He nodded. He turned and brushed around the floor with his fingers. "Got it."

He held up her barrette as if it were first prize on the show circuit.

She took it from him and managed to clip her hair into some semblance of order. "Thank you."

"Any time, honey."

She took a deep breath and let it out slowly, praying for strength as she did so. "We need to talk, Win."

He nodded, his expression serious. "I know."

The problem was, she didn't know what to say.

He saved her from having to come up with the right words by speaking first. "I owe you an apology." He pushed his fingers through his hair. "Hell, honey, I'm not used to the feelings you bring out in me. My only excuse is that when you threatened to leave, I knew I had to do something to stop you. Picking you up and bringing you in here seemed like the most straightforward approach to keeping you around."

She smiled at his explanation. "What were you planning to do tomorrow when I didn't show up for work? Kidnap me?"

She meant it as a joke, but he took her seriously. His face took on a pained expression. "I didn't get that far in my thinking. I guess this he-man stuff only takes a guy so far, huh?"

A guy who understood the word no. Earlier

evidence to the contrary, she had a strong feeling that Win was one of those men. "Yes."

He nodded. "What are you going to do?"

CHAPTER FOUR

THE question surprised Carlene. She would have assumed that after the way she responded to his kiss, Win would think he had her full cooperation in his plans for an affair. Surprisingly, it was his doubt that precipitated her own. If he'd gone on demanding that she stay, she would have been able to walk out.

"I don't know," she answered.

"Would you stay if I promised to take things at your pace?"

The offer threw her. She didn't want to set the pace to an affair and yet she couldn't bring herself to throw the offer back in Win's face. She didn't doubt it had taken a toll on his pride to make it. He was not a man used to women saying no...or letting anyone else be in control. She decided honesty was the only alternative.

"I'm attracted to you."

He smiled. "I could tell."

She swallowed. "Yes. Well. Although I find you

more attractive than any man I've ever met, I'm not interested in an affair. I'm too old to play those games."

Instead of the angry frown she expected, he smiled. "What are you? Twenty-four, twenty-five? You're not exactly at the age when most women's biological clocks start ticking."

"I'm twenty-six and it isn't my biological clock I'm worried about. At the risk of sounding hopelessly old-fashioned, it's my reputation." And her heart, but she didn't think she needed to admit that right now.

He stared at her for several taut moments, as if testing the strength of her will. Finally, he nodded. "I can't say that the idea of sneaking around thrills me, but I can understand your desire to be discreet."

In for a penny, in for a pound, her mother had always said. "Discreet isn't what I was thinking about exactly. I meant it when I said I didn't want to have an affair."

His hands flexed, then fisted against his thighs. "Are you saying that the kiss we just shared didn't change your mind?"

She nodded, feeling miserable. "That's exactly what I'm saying. I'm not going to pretend that I don't want you, Win."

He gave a harsh laugh. "Thanks for that much at least."

"But, I'm not in the market for a no-strings affair."

"Are you really going to quit?"

She sighed. She didn't want to, now more than

ever. "No. I'm a big girl and I can handle a little sexual attraction."

She hoped and prayed with all her heart that was true. She needed this job and the thought of never seeing Win again went through her soul like an arctic wind. It might not be the safest course of action, but it was the only one she could live with.

He gave her a slow sexy wink, his relief evident. "I can too, honey, but I'm telling you right now that I want you and that isn't going to change either."

She nodded, accepting his statement for what it was—a challenge. She just hoped she wasn't being irreparably stupid in believing she could meet it.

"So is it true you carried Carlene through the house like a sack of potatoes yesterday?"

Shorty's questions caught Win by surprise and he damn near yanked on the bridle of the horse he was leading. His head shot up and he met the older man's gaze. "Where'd you hear a fool story like that?"

He'd never carried a sack of potatoes cradled in his arms in his life.

"Joe said he came into the kitchen looking for a leftover piece of pie just as you were carrying our new cook to parts unknown." Shorty stopped and adjusted his hat back on his head. "Said Carlene was yelling her head off."

Win would have to teach Joe a lesson about gossip. He didn't much like the thought of his hands

discussing him and Carlene, but he was smart
enough to realize he probably couldn't stop it. "He
said that, did he?"

Shorty hooked his thumb in his belt. "Yeah. We
was all pretty sure the little lady was gonna quit. No
one was looking forward to going back to my vittles,
I can tell ya."

"She didn't quit." Win was still a little surprised
and very pleased by that fact.

"Uh, huh. I noticed. She's in there making lasagna
for dinner tonight." Shorty rubbed his stomach in appreciation. "Makes a man relish working up an appetite
for the kind of cookin' *that* little lady provides."

Win figured there was a point to this conversation,
so he remained silent, waiting for Shorty to get to it.

"A gal like that needs a hand gentle on the leads,
boss."

Win wasn't surprised by the warning. Carlene had
won the hearts of his hands within a couple of days
of her arrival. It wasn't just her cooking either. She had
a ready smile and kind word for just about everyone.

Everyone except Lonny.

Win still didn't know what had happened that day
he'd come upon Lonny leaving the kitchen with the
expression of a newly branded calf on his face. He
could guess though and it irritated the hell out of Win
that another man felt he had a right to make a pass
at Carlene. The way she'd acted about having Lonny
make the shelf in the kitchen had made him even

more suspicious, but until he knew for sure he couldn't feed the other man his teeth.

Win wanted his hands and the rest of the world to know that Carlene was his woman. Only she wasn't his woman, not yet anyway. And when she finally gave in, he had an ugly feeling the woman was going to want to be "discreet".

He didn't know what women thought they were gaining by hiding a relationship, but he figured she wasn't going to back down real easy on that point. Hell, nothing said she'd back down about getting involved either. Nothing, but the way she responded to his touch.

A man could find a lot of hope in having a woman respond to him the way Carlene responded to Win.

Shorty cleared his throat, reminding Win that he wasn't alone with his thoughts.

"You know what I mean, boss?"

What had the man said? Oh, yeah, something about a gentle hand on the leads. "Carlene's not a horse, Shorty," he said, ignoring the fact that he'd used similar comparisons himself in his own mind.

Shorty shrugged. "Women and horses got a lot in common. They don't take kindly to rough treatment and you've gotta coax 'em into trusting you."

"Where'd you learn that? The cowboy school for seduction?"

"I was married a heap o' years, boy, and a man learns something about women living with one day in and day out."

Win wouldn't argue that. Living with his mom for eighteen years and his wife for less than two had taught him plenty about the opposite sex, the most important lesson being that they didn't stick around. From what Carlene had said about moving on the first day she'd come to work for him, he figured she'd follow the same pattern. But he'd damn well have her in his bed before that happened.

"Will it make you feel better to know that I apologized?"

Shorty's eyes widened and then his wrinkled face split in a grin. "She's got you apologizing already, boss? Now that's a good sign, a mighty good sign."

"I'd appreciate it if you and the rest of the hands would leave off speculating on my relationship with Carlene."

Chuckling, Shorty pulled his hat back down over his brow. "Didn't realize you two was already at the *relationship* stage. Lonny ain't going to like hearing that."

Win frowned. "If Lonny's smart, he'll keep his opinions on the matter to himself."

"Oh, he ain't stupid, boss. Don't figure he'll say anything, but don't know that he's gonna give up on Carlene either. I've seen the way he watches her. He's got ideas, that's for sure."

Win watched Carlene with wanting in his eyes too, but what he wanted from Carlene and what that young punk that worked for him wanted were very different things. Weren't they? *Hell, yes,* he told himself. He wanted more than a quick toss in the sheets. He wanted Carlene for as long as it took to work out whatever it was they had going between them.

He figured Lonny was just looking for some experience with a beautiful woman. Well, he wasn't going to get it with Carlene. Win toyed with the thought of firing the young stable hand, but decided that in all fairness he couldn't fire the boy for having feelings. At least not today.

A warning might be in order though. Win scowled at Shorty. "If he wants to keep his job, he'll keep his hormones under control when he's around Carlene."

Satisfaction settled over Shorty's features. "It's like that, is it? Glad to see that you ain't so blind after all. Women like Carlene don't come along in a man's life every day, you know? 'Bout time you settled down and had yourself a family. Carlene'll make a mighty fine mother, if you ask me."

Win's scowl deepened. "You can forget any pipe-dreams about marriage, old man. The only kids I need around are my sister's. I see them when she visits and then she takes them home, just the way I like."

An empty feeling in his gut belied Win's words, but he refused to withdraw them.

Shorty snorted in disgust. "Thought you was finally smartening up, boss. Guess you ain't." His gaze slid toward the house where Carlene stood beating rugs in the spring sun. "Then again, maybe there's hope for you yet."

"Don't count on it," Win replied.

Shorty turned and walked away, muttering about mule-headed horses' asses that passed for men.

Win watched Shorty's retreating figure, his thoughts in turmoil, and it was all Carlene's fault. She had him so twisted in knots he didn't know if he was coming or going. One thing he did know—he wasn't going to give up a lifetime of hard-learned lessons for any woman, even one as appealing as his housekeeper.

She acted like a woman who was looking for marriage, but Win didn't buy it. She'd already made it clear that she was moving on. She wasn't really interested in permanence either. So why was she so bothered with the idea of an affair? She was bringing up marriage as some sort of barrier between them.

He didn't know why she felt as if she needed one, but he'd find out. Once he did, he'd overcome it and any others she planned to erect. After all, he was a man that knew how to get what he wanted and he wanted Carlene Daniels.

A week later, he wasn't one step closer to breaching Carlene's defenses. In fact, he felt as if she built a better corral to keep in her emotions than the one he used to exercise his horses. The woman was as stubborn and frustrating as they came.

He sighed and leaned back in his chair, putting his booted feet up on the table. Satisfaction that no one was there to scold settled over him. Now if he were a married man, he'd have to listen to some woman reprimand him for putting his boots on the furniture, even the outside furniture.

When his ex-wife wasn't complaining about the lack of social life and opportunities in Sunshine Springs, she had nagged Win about his manners, or lack thereof. She found his cowboy ways too earthy for her delicate tastes. Too bad she hadn't figured that out *before* marrying him. Too bad he hadn't figured it out either. There had been some clues, but his judgment had been clouded by fear, grief and unsatisfied lust.

Rachel had insisted on waiting to go to bed together until they got married.

As far as he could see, she'd used sex and anything else that came handy to try to manipulate him, first into marriage and then into selling the Bar G and Garrison Stables so they could move to the city. He'd learned a lot in his short association with Rachel, that was for sure. Lessons he wasn't about to ignore.

Thoughts of his ex-wife always put him in a bad mood, so he welcomed the interruption of a ringing doorbell. He stood up and headed toward the front of the house, thinking of Carlene when the chimes rang out a second time before he had a chance to open the door.

When he finally opened it, however, it wasn't Carlene standing on the other side. It was his baby sister. He felt guilty almost immediately for the sense of disappointment he had to squelch.

Leah threw herself in his arms. "Win, you've got to help me. I don't know what to do anymore. It's just too much," she said between broken sobs against his shirtfront.

He patted her back and looked past her to the small compact parked near the front of his house. In the fading light, he could make out the outline of two tiny heads, but no other adult. She'd brought Win's four-year-old niece and two-year-old nephew, but her husband, Mark, hadn't accompanied her.

He hugged his sister and then set her away from him. "Hush, Leah. Let's get the kids inside and then you can tell me all about what's bothering you."

She nodded, swallowing a sob. Shoot. He hated it when she cried. His insides twisted like the strands of a lariat.

It wasn't any surprise that an hour later he found himself agreeing to keep the kids for a few days while Leah tried to get her head on straight. She needed a break and it sounded as if her marriage was on the skids.

He sure hoped Carlene liked children because her job description was about to change. He needed a nanny as well as a housekeeper. Hell, he'd give her a raise—that should help get her to agree.

Especially when he told her the other change he needed her to make.

* * *

"Move in here? Are you nuts?" Carlene stared at him, her eyes clearly showing every bit of what she was thinking for the first time that week. The little woman was furious. "I took this job expecting to clean house and cook. Now you want a live-in nanny? No way, Win. I'm not doing it. You'll have to find someone else."

He had to convince her and soon. He had a full day of work ahead of him and he was already a couple of hours behind, having had to wait to leave the house until Carlene showed up.

"I told you when I interviewed you, it's your job to deal with the domestic stuff." He smiled in what he hoped was a coaxing manner. "I know taking care of the kids is above and beyond what I hired you to do, but it's not permanent and I'll give you a big bonus."

She erupted all over him like Mt. St. Helens, bristling with outrage as she drew herself up. "You think you can *bribe* me to put my reputation on the line, not to mention exhaust myself caring for two toddlers?"

He didn't know what her fixation with her reputation was, but she must know something about children if she knew taking care of a couple of toddlers was so tiring. He had to agree. Shelly had woken in the night calling for her mom. It had been all Win could do to get the little girl to go back to sleep. He didn't look forward to more nights of the same. Children needed a woman's touch. Carlene talked as if she'd had personal experience along those lines.

"You taken care of a lot of kids?"

She eyed him warily, but nodded. "I babysat all through high school. I started watching one set of twins the year they were born and helped their mom potty-train them before I went off to college. I have no doubt your sister needs a break, especially if her husband travels so much, but you agreeing to give her that break does not make it my responsibility."

He opened his mouth to answer and she forestalled him. "You're going to have to find someone else."

He frowned, starting to get a little annoyed. He didn't think a woman as kind as Carlene would be so difficult to convince to help him. Didn't she fall all over herself mixing herbal teas for Shorty's arthritis? Hadn't she refused to let him fire Lonny when Win had finally cornered her about the scene in the kitchen?

He'd think that kindness and understanding would extend to her boss as well. "Well, your job description just got changed. Now it includes watching my sister's children while I'm busy at the stables."

"Hire a teenager to help you," she shot back.

"Don't know any well enough to trust my sister's children into their care."

That seemed to stymie her. Her mouth, which had been open, ready to level another sally at him, closed with a snap.

Before she could marshal her thoughts, he went in for the kill. "Come on, honey. It's only for a few days. Don't tell me that you can turn your back on two defenseless little kids that need you."

A frown wiped the expression of thoughtful concern she had been wearing right off her face. "I'm not turning my back on 'two defenseless little children'. I'm refusing to do what their overbearing, arrogant, thickheaded uncle is demanding I do. There's a big difference in my mind."

"That 'overbearing, arrogant, thickheaded' man is also your boss and like I reminded you...it's your job to take care of the domestic stuff. You want help with the kids? Call a service to send someone to help you with the cooking and other household stuff, but I'm not leaving my niece and nephew under the responsibility of a stranger. I want *you* with them. Just for this little bit," he reiterated.

"Win! *You're* the one that told your sister you would take care of her kids."

The pocket spitfire was stubborn, he'd give her that, but he wasn't giving in on this. He couldn't. He had too much going on both with the free range horses and the stables to take time off right now. "Rosa would have done it, no problem. She would have insisted."

Carlene looked like a tea kettle ready to whistle. "And that matters to me why?"

"Because she was a good housekeeper and you are too."

Laughter burst from the woman in front of him.

"You think I aspire to golden-star status as a house-keeper?"

"You are the kind of person who takes pride in doing her job to the best of her ability, no matter what that job is."

"I've been a great housekeeper for you."

"And now I'm asking you for something extra. No different than asking Shorty to stay with a foaling mare or myself to get up two hours early for a month to take an extra training project on." He took a breath, thought of saying something else and then sighed. "Please, Carlene. I need your help."

The starch went right out of her as he said the final words and he wondered why he hadn't thought to use that approach before. Mostly his pride. He hated saying please or admitting he needed anything from anybody, but especially a woman. He'd been let down too many times.

"Okay. I'll work something out, but not the nights. You're going to have to handle those on your own."

"As far as caring for the children, that's not a problem, but I've got mares ready to foal. If I'm needed in the stable at night, I can't leave Shelly and Jared in the house alone. Besides, they're going to miss their mama something fierce. They'll need comforting. A woman's touch."

"I don't see how a perfect stranger could comfort them any better than their uncle."

That made his lips twitch. Was she really that

ignorant of the effect she had on people? "Honey, you could comfort a wounded lion cub. Shelly and Jared are going to love you."

Her cheeks turned an interesting shade of pink. "Thank you, but don't think that flattery is going to win this argument."

He didn't. He figured Carlene's soft heart could do that for him. He heard a noise come through the door he'd left open to the courtyard. His spirits lifted. The kids were awake. He knew Carlene wouldn't stay stubborn on the issue of staying the nights once she'd met Jared and Shelly. They were great kids.

"Can you at least stay tonight?"

"Yes." She fixed him with a steely stare. "But just this one night. Got it?"

He smiled. He had it all right and he had her. After the first night of holding Shelly when she woke up calling for her mommy, Carlene would be hooked. She'd see the kids needed her. If having her stay the nights made her that much more accessible to him, well, a smart man knew when to take advantage of his good fortune.

Another noise came, this one a tad louder.

Carlene's head shot up. "One of them is awake."

"Sounds like Jared. He's probably hungry for some breakfast. Why don't you rustle up something? I'll go get him."

He left Carlene staring after him with a pretty darn adorable look of confusion on her face.

He had been right. Jared was awake and standing in the playpen that Leah had brought with her. His baby-fine blond hair stuck to the side of his head. He stopped crying and smiled when Win entered the room. Chubby little arms reached up from the playpen. "Up, Unca Win, up."

Win obliged willingly, letting his gaze shift to the sofa where his niece still slept. He'd put the kids in the study because all the bedrooms were on the upper levels, he'd move them to the bedroom when they were asleep. He carried Jared to the floor and saw about changing the little guy's clothes. By the time he was finished, Shelly had woken up.

She knelt in the middle of the sofa that looked a whole lot bigger under her than when he sat on it and rubbed sleep from her eyes. "Uncle Win, where's Mommy?"

Win scooped Jared off the dresser and used his free arm to pick up Shelly. He carried them out the door and through the courtyard toward the kitchen. "Your mommy let me have you two for company for a few days. You know how lonely Uncle Win gets when you aren't around."

Shelly contemplated Win, her gaze serious as only a four-year-old's could be. "Mommy said she needed a break. She was crying. Is she done crying, Uncle Win?"

Pain lanced through Win at the question. Shelly had seen too much of Leah's unhappiness.

He carried her and Jared through the kitchen door. "Yeah, sweetpea, I think she's done crying, except for maybe a little because she misses you."

"Uncle Win."

He set the kids down at the table and knelt down to Shelly's eye level. "Yeah, sweetpea?"

Shelly's lower lip trembled and her baby-soft brown eyes filled with moisture. "I want my mommy."

Hell.

Carlene stepped forward. Her smile was bright enough to light a stadium. "Good morning. You must be Shelly. I'm Carlene. You know, sometimes I want my mom too."

Win watched his niece's eyes widen. "You do?"

Carlene nodded, her expression sincere. "You bet. She lives in Texas. That's a long way from here. When I miss her, I try to do things I like to do with her so I won't miss her so much. Do you think that would work for you?"

Shelly pursed her lips in thought, but she'd stopped crying. "I don't know."

"What do you like to do with your mom?"

"I like it when she rocks me and reads me a story. Mostly she holds both me and Jared," Shelly said.

Carlene nodded with enthusiasm as if Shelly had just revealed the secret to eternal youth. "You know, I like to rock little children and read to them too.

Maybe you'd let me rock you and Jared—what do you think?"

A little of Shelly's unhappiness faded from her eyes. "I guess."

Carlene smiled that thousand-watt smile again. "Okay. What do you say we have some breakfast first?"

"I's hungry," announced Jared. "I's wants beck-fast."

Carlene and Shelly both giggled and Win relaxed. Everything was going to be just fine. He met Carlene's eyes over the top of Shelly's head and mouthed a "thank you". She shrugged and returned to cooking pancakes.

He walked over to her and kissed her softly on the temple in gratitude. "Thank you. You're one in a million, honey."

She turned startled eyes to him, her lips soft and inviting. The only thing that stopped him from accepting that invitation was the presence of the two little people at the table. They stared at Win and Carlene with identical looks of interest on their faces. He sighed. Another time.

CHAPTER FIVE

CARLENE tossed her cotton nightgown in the overnight bag along with clothes for the next day.

Taking advantage of the fact that she had managed to get both Jared and Shelly to take an afternoon nap, she had left Shorty in charge and rushed to her apartment to pack for her overnight at Win's. She didn't want the children to wake up while she was gone, although she couldn't have said why. They undoubtedly knew Shorty much better than they knew her, but she felt the need to be there in case they woke wanting their mom.

She made quick work of her packing and was back in her car in a matter of minutes. She flipped on the air-conditioning. Summer in Oregon's desert wasn't as scorching as west Texas, but it was hot enough. She breathed an air of relief as the refrigerated air from the vents cooled her skin.

If only she could cool her reaction to Win as easily. She'd fought him over watching his niece and nephew not because she truly had a problem with taking care of the children, but because she didn't want another link between herself and Win. She felt the strings tying her to her sexy boss tightening each day. His desire beat at her whenever they were in the same room together and that wouldn't be so bad if there weren't a corresponding cadence inside of her.

There hadn't been another incident like the one when he'd kissed her until she'd forgotten common sense. Win had been a perfect gentleman, but that didn't alleviate the pressure she felt. She got the sense that Win was just biding his time until she surrendered to the feelings between them. He seemed to think that them making love was a foregone conclusion.

The thing that terrified her was that she was beginning to wonder if he was right.

She went to sleep every night with his image fixed firmly in her mind and woke up each morning anticipating seeing him again. His prominence in her thoughts both scared and exhilarated her. She'd never felt this drawn to another man, not even Grant. She wanted Win, but she wanted more than a short-term affair.

She wanted it all and Win acted as if marriage was one step away from maximum-security prison. She sighed. Was it any wonder that she was scared? Well, one thing was for certain. She wasn't going to stay the nights at Win's after tonight. He'd have to find someone else.

Despite its celebrity part-time residents, Sunshine Springs was a small town with small-town attitudes. She wasn't about to risk her prospects of getting hired as a teacher again by living with Win. It didn't matter if she slept with him or not, plenty of people would take it as a foregone conclusion. Look at the way the principal at the grade school Zoe taught at had reacted to her living with Grant. Grant had been Zoe's best friend for pretty much all of her life too. Tyler had told Carlene all about it and she knew better than to push her own luck.

High-school teachers got just as much, if not more, scrutiny. Especially one with her track record.

She pulled her car to a stop near Win's house. It would make the perfect house for a family.

A sudden image of a little boy with Win's startling blue eyes and black hair playing in the courtyard fountain took her breath away. More staggering than the vision of the little boy playing in the pond was the absolute certainty that the child belonged to both *her* and Win. It seemed so real that she was surprised to realize that she hadn't yet gotten out.

She shook her head ruefully and stepped out of her car. The heat was doing things to her brain, that or the knowledge that she was tempted to chuck all her requirements out the window and give herself to Win, no commitments.

Making a baby with Win would be fairly easy.

Making a family with the man would be another matter entirely.

The cry woke Carlene from a fitful sleep. She sat straight up in bed and tried desperately to make sense of the shadowy images she could barely make out in the darkness. This wasn't her bed. This wasn't her room in her cozy little apartment either.

Another cry rent the air. *"Mommy!"*

Everything crystallized in Carlene's brain. She was sleeping in the guest room next to Shelly and Jared's. When the cry was followed by audible sobs, she jumped out of bed. Taking no time to put on a bathrobe, she rushed from the room. *Where was Win?* Couldn't he hear Shelly's heart-rending cries? Carlene stepped on a toy and let out a squeak as she stumbled into the children's room.

The night-light that Win had put in at Shelly's request illuminated the distraught little girl sitting in the center of the double bed. Carlene didn't hesitate. She put her arms out and Shelly flew into them.

Locking her arms around Carlene's neck, Shelly choked out words between her tears. "I'm s-scared. I want my mommy."

Carlene hugged the little girl fiercely. "Shh, sugar-bear. It's going to be okay."

Continuing to speak softly to Shelly, Carlene crossed to the rocking-chair in the corner of the room. It was a roomy, old-fashioned wooden rocker; the kind Carlene's mom had used to rock her when she woke scared in the night. She sat down and cradled Shelly on her lap. Rubbing the little girl's back, Carlene continued to speak comforting words and rocked the chair in a soothing motion until Shelly's crying subsided.

She didn't stop rocking until Shelly's limp posture and deep breathing indicated she had once again fallen asleep. Even then, Carlene stayed in the chair, holding the child. The feel of the small body tucked against hers filled Carlene with longing. Win said she was too young to be worried about her biological clock, but what about her heart's desires?

Stifling a sigh, she stood up. Carlene put Shelly back into the bed, tucking the covers around her small form. She turned and checked on Jared, surprised he had slept through his sister's upset. His blanket had slipped down and Carlene pulled it up to cover him before turning to leave the room.

She stepped into the hall and stifled a scream as a shadow unattached itself from the wall and came toward her. *"Win."*

"Is she okay?"

Carlene nodded, her heart beating too frantically for her to form a proper response.

He had obviously come straight from bed. His hair was disheveled as if he'd recently run his fingers through it. He hadn't bothered to put on a shirt or shoes and the top button on his Levis was undone. Her fingers itched to reach out and touch the muscled planes of his chest. All in all, he looked much too tempting for her peace of mind.

He wrapped his fingers around her upper arm and tugged her through the doorway into the open-air corridor that looked out over the courtyard. "Thank you."

She turned so that she could see his profile in the moonlight. "You're welcome. Why didn't you come in?"

"I told you. Children need a woman's touch."

"Win, that's silly. Are you saying you don't think a father has a responsibility to comfort his children?" She whispered, not wanting to risk waking Shelly again.

Win's teeth flashed in the darkness as he smiled. "Don't get on your high horse, honey. I'm not saying that at all. It's just that right now, Shelly wants her mom. It makes sense that she'd accept more comfort from a woman."

"What about her dad?" Carlene asked, "Don't you think she misses him as well?"

Win snorted. "It wasn't her dad she was calling for."

Carlene had to acknowledge the truth in that statement. She shivered. The night chill reminded her that she'd forgotten to put on a robe, so did the expression in Win's eyes.

She tried valiantly to stay on topic. "That doesn't mean the children don't miss their dad."

He rubbed his hands up and down her arms, sending frissons of excitement through her as well as welcome warmth. "Mark travels a lot. They're used to him being gone for a few days at a time. This is the first time that Leah has left them with anyone for even overnight."

"Your sister must really be feeling pressed against a wall to have left them here."

"Yes." He pulled Carlene against him and wrapped his arms around her back. His heat enveloped her. "It's too cold out here for you wearing nothing but that thin gown."

She smiled at the censure in his voice and pulled back slightly so she could see his face. He looked dangerous in the reflected light of the moon.

"I was in too much of a hurry to find my robe. Besides, you're the one that pulled me out here instead of letting me return to my room and my warm bed. Why did you?"

"I wanted to talk to you."

"About Leah?"

His head lowered until his lips were centimeters from hers. "No."

Thoughts of Leah's emotional crisis faded as the flames of Win's desire reached out to lick her. She shivered again, but this time not from the cold. "Oh."

He smiled and lowered his mouth the remaining distance for their lips to touch.

* * *

Win waited a heartbeat, his lips pressed against Carlene's. Would she reject him? Desperation seized him as gaping hunger gnawed at his insides. He needed her softness so much, but he couldn't afford to push her tonight. He wanted her to agree to stay while Shelly and Jared were with him.

She gave a small, feminine moan and her lips softened under his. Exultation filled him as he deepened the kiss. He had been aching to taste and touch her since that one steamy encounter on his couch. Letting his hands slide down her back, he pressed her body more firmly against his. It felt so good.

Too good.

If he didn't sit down, he might well fall down. The acknowledgement of his weakness made him want to laugh. None of his men would believe that this tiny mite of a woman could bring him to his knees like this. Sweeping her into his arms, he carried her along to a wrought-iron lounger situated at the corner of the outdoor corridor. He liked to lie in it and watch the rain come down during a storm.

Without allowing their lips to break contact, he laid her on the cushion covering the lounger and came down on top of her.

She gasped as his body settled against hers.

Suddenly her fingers were all over him, touching his chest, his back, and finally burrowing into his hair as she pulled his face closer. She parted her lips and he eagerly accepted the invitation she offered. He swept her mouth with his tongue, reveling in the sounds of need emanating from her.

He wasn't sure, but he thought that her tiny little moans alone might be enough to make him spill his seed.

Still kissing her, he slipped to lie on the narrow width of cushion next to her. He kept one thigh locked over hers and pressed his erection against her hip, enjoying the sweet torture the position elicited. He wanted to touch her. He *needed* to touch her.

He undid the buttons on her prim cotton night-gown, pleased when she made no move to stop him. It was a far cry from the black lace he had been fantasizing her wearing, but the sight of her to-die-for body outlined by the thin cotton in the hall outside the kids' room had sent his temperature through the roof. It had also had an instant hardening effect on his sex.

Once her buttons were undone, he pulled back slightly and parted the soft white fabric to expose the perfection of her breasts. Strawberry-pink, velvet-soft nipples pointed proudly from the center of the creamy white mounds and it was all he could do not to bury his face between them.

He sucked in his breath. "You are incredible, honey. You know that? Looking at you is like being up close and personal to a piece of art."

The skin of her breasts flushed and he didn't think it was from arousal. "Win?"

"Hmm?" he asked as he slipped his hand inside and cupped one of her full breasts.

Damn. It felt as if he'd died and gone to heaven. Her nipple tightened under his palm and he couldn't resist brushing his hand back and forth, back and forth until she was pressing her generous flesh against the callused skin of his palms.

"I want to taste you."

Her head moved restlessly on the cushion. "Yes. Please. Win. *Yes*."

Pushing the fabric of her gown further to the side he lowered his head and closed his mouth over the puckered flesh.

She groaned and arched against his mouth. "Win, that feels… It's so… Please, don't stop."

He was happy to oblige. Hell, he was ecstatic. He suckled her sweet little nubbin while using his hand to gently squeeze and caress her other breast. He took her other nipple between his thumb and forefinger and pinched lightly. She cried out and arched against him, pressing his face into her breasts. Man, she was hot.

He could not wait to feel the slick warmth of her most private place. He wanted to touch it, to taste it, but most of all to bury himself in her until all that sweetness surrounded him and was branded with his touch.

He gripped her nightgown and started edging the fabric up until he could feel the bare skin on her leg. So soft. She was so incredibly soft. He inched his fingers up her thigh, seeking the tender flesh between her legs.

"Win? What are you doing?"

Did she really need him to explain it to her? He encountered the soft cotton of her panties. He rubbed her through the cotton, satisfied when it grew damp under his touch.

She gripped his shoulder, her fingernails digging into his skin. She would leave her mark on him and he didn't mind. Not at all.

"Win, please… This is too…"

He slipped one finger under the elastic of her panties and yes, right there. Yes. Wet. Hot. Slick feminine flesh.

"You can't touch me there," she shrieked.

He mentally disagreed even as he wondered at the panic in her voice. She acted like a nervous virgin.

Lifting his head, he tried to reassure her. "It's okay, honey. I like touching you there. I'll like it even more when we get your panties off. So will you."

Her eyes, which had been cloudy with passion, widened with something that looked like fear. "I don't want to take them off."

He begged to differ. "I think you want to, but you're scared. Tell me what's scaring you. I'll go slow. I swear."

"It's not that. It's just that I'm not sure I'm ready to make love with you, Win."

He felt irritation rising in him. "Why the hell not? You want me. You can't deny it."

He rubbed his finger over the feminine flesh hidden by her panties to prove his point. It worked too. She arched against his hand even as she shook her head.

"Don't shake your head at me, damn it. I won't let you lie to me. Not now. Not ever." He leaned over her, letting her see that he meant what he said.

She stared back at him, her eyes filled with some emotion he didn't understand. Finally, she nodded. "You're right. I *do* want you. Very much, but I *am* scared. Win, I don't want to be somebody's convenient bed partner for a short affair. Not even yours."

"I told you. I'm not looking for a sleazy affair," he ground out.

"Then what exactly are you looking for, Win? We both know it isn't a wife."

Helpless rage welled up in him. He wouldn't let another woman manipulate him into promising marriage in exchange for sex. He was a lot smarter at thirty than he had been at nineteen.

He jumped off the lounger and stood up, glaring down at her. "You're right. I don't want a wife, but I told you once before that there's a lot of ground between a one-night stand and marriage."

She stood and adjusted her nightgown so that her beautiful breasts and legs were back under cover. "Maybe there is for you, but I'm having a hard time accepting that."

Sexual frustration and anger made him lash out. "We both know that with a body like yours, you've had plenty of opportunity to figure it out. So, would you stop talking like a Victorian spinster, fearful of losing her virginity?"

She blanched as if he'd struck her. He felt about an inch tall and shrinking by the second as her eyes widened with pain and filled with tears.

Hell.

Before he had a chance to try to undo the damage he'd done with his mouth, she drew herself up and blinked away the moisture in her eyes.

"I'm getting awfully tired of explaining to the men around here that my bra size has no direct correlation to my desire to bed every male within a fifty-mile radius. I can understand Lonny's ridiculously immature view, but I expected more from you, Win. I really did."

She impatiently brushed an errant tear from her cheek. "Furthermore, I may not be Victorian, but I am a virgin and I can damn well talk like one if I want to."

With that she whirled and ran back down the corridor.

Win stood in stunned silence for a full thirty seconds, long enough for her to disappear inside her room. Then he swore a blue streak. Who would have guessed that a woman as good-looking as Carlene would be a virgin at twenty-six?

It wasn't natural.

He wanted to slam his fist into something.

* * *

The next morning, Win had already headed down to the stables by the time Carlene entered the kitchen.

She was a little late. She normally arrived for work at seven-thirty, but this morning she had dawdled getting dressed. She'd told herself that she had been busy listening for Shelly and Jared to wake, but the truth was that she was doing her level best to avoid Win.

She couldn't believe she'd done what she had with Win the night before…and enjoyed it so much. But he made her feel such intense things. Not only sexually, but different about herself—like her body was something truly beautiful. Something to be admired, not just lusted over. Which was pretty funny when lust and sex came together, but no way could she describe what happened last night as pure lust.

Win wanted her in a way that touched her so much more deeply than any man's interest had before because it felt deeper. He made her feel proud of her femininity…her figure.

But she still went hot with embarrassment every time she thought of the way she'd blurted out her virginity to him.

He must have had a good laugh at her expense after she fled like a frightened rabbit. Once he'd calmed his raging hormones, that was. The fear that he would accuse her of being a tease was another reason she was avoiding him. There was no denying that she'd encouraged him. And she'd been accused of being a tease by other men for a whole lot less.

Men like her ex-boss.

Shorty came into the kitchen. "Mornin', Carlene. Win says you'll need my help while the little 'uns are staying."

Carlene digested that. Win had made no such offer the day before and she knew he needed Shorty down in the stables, but she wasn't about to turn down the help, not when she had to cook for seven hungry men and keep two active toddlers occupied so they wouldn't miss their mom too much. "I could use a hand later getting lunch ready and started on dinner. It shouldn't take more than a couple of hours from your day."

"Good enough. Kitchen duty is a piece of cake compared to working with the boss today. He's ornery as a wounded mountain cat. I don't suppose you know anything about it, do you?"

She affected a nonchalance she didn't feel. "He's probably just a little stressed from worrying about his sister."

She opened the fridge and pulled out the meat she'd defrosted for tonight's dinner.

Shorty peered at her, his eyes intense. "I don't think so. He's used to dealing with Leah's troubles. Nope. It's something else and it's got him snapping at anyone fool enough to look cross-eyed. Thought for sure he was gonna take Lonny's head right off over something Win would have normally let go."

That got her attention. "He was mad at Lonny? Why?"

Shrugging, Shorty pulled out the big cast-iron stew pot and put it on the stove for her. "Can't rightly say. No real reason as far as I could see."

"Oh."

He turned and gave her another probing glance.

She forced a smile to her lips. "Why don't you go back to work? I won't need any help for a couple of hours."

Shorty shook his head. "Can't. Win said for me to watch the kiddies while you go to your apartment."

She stopped dicing the steak she planned to stew for shepherd's pie. "I wasn't planning to go to my apartment this morning."

"Win says you're going to need more things."

Win said this, Win said that. And just who said that Win was king and she one of his subjects?

When she didn't respond, Shorty added, "So you can stay the nights."

Carlene frowned at that. Win couldn't possibly know that she had changed her mind about staying. She hadn't said a thing. If anything, after last night, he should expect her to be even more entrenched in her certainty it was the wrong thing to do. She was a little surprised at herself that she wasn't. However, after holding Shelly while she cried the night before, Carlene knew she couldn't turn her back on Leah's children.

They did need her.

"I didn't tell Win I planned to stay the nights. In fact, I told him to find someone else."

"Kiddies need a woman's touch when they miss their mama."

Win and Shorty had hopelessly outdated views on the roles of gender in comfort. When she told Shorty she thought so, he shook his head, more serious than she'd ever seen him.

"Win spent a heap o' years being both parents to his little sister, long before his mama died in that plane crash. He's pretty determined to give Leah's kids what he couldn't give her, a woman to comfort them."

Sounds from the hall indicated the children had woken up. She moved to the sink to wash her hands. "I've got to feed the children right now. You might as well go back to work, Shorty."

She didn't admit that she planned to go to her apartment later. Win had no right to assume she meant to stay. The very least he could do was confirm it with her rather than sending Shorty to her with the news like a royal edict. She had valid reasons for not wanting to stay on Win's ranch and even if those reasons didn't weigh heavily against the feel of Shelly's little arms clinging around her neck, he didn't know she'd changed her mind. He was too arrogant for belief.

Shorty frowned, but didn't argue. It wouldn't have mattered if he had, she was already on her way to get the children up and dressed.

She decided that they could both use a bath after breakfast since she and Win hadn't bathed them the night before.

Two hours later, she was cutting fruit for a salad while Shelly and Jared played on the kitchen floor with the brightly colored plastic dishes Carlene used to store leftovers when Win entered the kitchen.

Both children shot up off the floor and wrapped themselves around Win's legs.

"Unca Win, I's a cook. See?" Jared stood proudly, covered from chest to toes in one of Carlene's white aprons that had been folded in half.

Win smiled down at his nephew and ruffled Jared's blond curls. "You making our dinner tonight, sport?"

Jared nodded. "In the *big* bowl. See?"

Win pretended to see an amazing array of dishes in the big bowl and commented on all of them. He gave Shelly a smacking kiss and told her to take Jared to see Shorty who would take them to visit the horses.

Shelly and Jared headed for Shorty, who was waiting by the outside kitchen door, with squeals of delight.

Win turned to Carlene, who had finished her salad and was sliding it onto an empty shelf in the refrigerator.

"Shorty and I'll keep an eye on the kids while you go to your apartment and pick up more spare clothes."

Not a word about last night. For which she should be grateful, but perversely wasn't.

She frowned at him. "I thought we agreed that you would find someone else to help you at night."

"Are you saying you're leaving?" Challenge radiated in his voice and stance, but she thought she saw fear in his eyes.

The fear decided her, but she wasn't going to make it easy for him. He could darn well have asked.

"We're not talking about me quitting my job. We're talking about me moving in here."

"Shelly and Jared need you. You saw that last night."

Sudden understanding dawned. "You waited, didn't you? You heard Shelly. Probably before I did, but you waited because you wanted me to go to her and to comfort her."

He had the grace to look guilty. "It was the hardest five minutes of my life. I hated hearing her cry," he admitted.

"And if I tell you it didn't work. That I still refuse to move in here until Leah comes back for her children?"

"Is that what you are saying?" he asked harshly.

He had told her last night never to lie to him. She didn't think she ever could.

She sighed. "No. That's not what I'm saying."

He nodded, the relief evident in his eyes, though she could see that he tried to hide it. He didn't sound relieved when he spoke however. He sounded irritated. "So, why the big scene about it?"

"You could have asked. Don't you realize how

arrogant you are to just assume I'll agree to stay, especially after last night?"

"So this is about last night? You want me to apologize? Fine. I'm sorry."

Unaccountable moisture burned the backs of her eyes. "I didn't ask for an apology."

He grabbed her arms and pulled her until their faces were inches apart. "Then what do you want?"

She closed her eyes against the anger in his and told him the truth. "I don't know anymore."

He let her go and she opened her eyes. He looked wary. "Are you ready to go to your apartment?"

She took a deep breath and nodded. "Yes. I'll be back after lunch. Everything is ready and in the refrigerator. Shorty will have to serve it, though."

"Fine." He turned to go back outside.

"Win."

He stopped at the door. "Yeah?"

"Do you have any idea how long Leah will be gone?"

He looked back over his shoulder, his expression closed. "No. Why?"

"It would be nice to know how much to pack and how long I'll be staying, but I guess that's out, huh?"

"I don't know. I wish I did."

The words were stark and suddenly it hit her that it bothered Win a whole lot more than it bothered her that he didn't know when his sister was coming back.

She tried to smile reassuringly at him. "It's going to be okay."

He nodded, but she could tell that he wasn't convinced.

"By the way, do you think she'd mind if I potty-trained Jared?"

His eyes widened. "I doubt it."

"Good."

"You sure you want to do it? I've heard potty-training can be pretty tough, especially for boys. I think that's why Leah's been putting it off."

She shrugged. "Trust me, a day and a half of changing a two-year-old's diapers is enough incentive for *me*."

She just wished she could find similar incentive to keep her hands and her thoughts off of her boss.

CHAPTER SIX

"YOU told me that Lonny asked you out and you turned him down."

Carlene looked up from the book she'd been trying to read.

His face set in an expression of disapproval, Win stood just inside her open bedroom door. She'd left it that way when she had put Shelly and Jared to bed. She wanted to be able to hear them if they needed her. Unfortunately, she had not heard Win's approach.

He had been busy down at the stables with a pregnant mare since after dinner and she hadn't expected to see him again until the following morning. She'd come to the conclusion late that afternoon that he was doing just as good a job of avoiding her as she had been doing to avoid him.

The knowledge had irritated her.

Especially after her trip to her apartment. She'd found herself packing lacy underwear and a couple of items of clothing that showed off her figure. She'd stopped in mid-packing, staring at a very pretty bra she hadn't worn since leaving Texas. It had been a symbol of her acceptance of herself then...something she'd lost when she left.

But she'd brought it with her to Win's house.

She shifted to sit up more squarely against the headboard and laid her book aside. "That's essentially what happened."

He ran his fingers through wet hair. He must have showered before hunting her down in her room. "I don't think so."

The dangerous emotion she sensed in him made her want to tread very carefully. "What do you mean?"

"Last night you said that he thought you wanted to go to bed with him."

She'd said several things she shouldn't have last night. "He offered. I turned him down. That's all there is to it."

"Lady, there's a hell of a difference between a man asking you to go out and offering to take you to bed." He pushed away from the doorway and stepped further into the room.

She felt as if the mountain cat Shorty had mentioned that morning had come in. She was tired of the feelings that overwhelmed her when Win was around. His interrogation over Lonny set off a recklessness she didn't understand, but she wasn't going to squelch either.

"Don't you think I know that? Don't you think

I've had enough experience with the latter my whole life to know that?"

He stopped prowling the room and fixed his blue-eyed gaze on her. "What do you mean?"

She slid her legs off the opposite side of the bed from where Win was standing and went to stand at the window. It looked out over the desert surrounding the ranch house. Moonlight reflected off the sagebrush and sparse Douglas Fir trees.

She started talking with her gaze still fixed on the night outside her window. "I started wearing a bra in the sixth grade and not some little-girl training bra either. Ever since then boys and then men assumed I was interested in sex."

"You telling me that some little ten-year-old tried to get you to drop your drawers behind the school building?"

She whipped around and glared at him. She was opening her heart to him; he could darn well take her seriously. "No. But, more than one not so little ten year old tried to get a feel of what was under my shirt."

She turned back to face the window, her face growing red with remembered shame. "It was humiliating. I was still playing with Barbies and boys thought I wanted to be their plaything. It just got worse as I got older. It wasn't just my breasts that developed. My whole body changed."

He spoke from right behind her, laying his hand on her shoulder. "Honey, you have a very nice body."

She almost laughed. "That was the whole problem. People assumed that I was a brainless twit because of the way I looked. By the time I hit high school, I lived in oversized clothes, kept my hair in an unstylish pony-tail and my nose buried in my books."

He turned her around to face him. "You're smart and you set out to prove that to everyone."

She nodded, surprised at his understanding. "Yes. I did it too. I graduated valedictorian with a full scholarship to a private university."

He tipped her chin up until their eyes met. "That's not the end of the story."

"How do you know?" she whispered the question.

"Because if it was you wouldn't still be so sensitive about a man's appreciation for your body."

That made her angry. "You think I should just laugh it off when men like Lonny try to cop a feel when no one else is around?"

Win's fingers on her shoulders went rigid. "He tried to cop a feel? You said he propositioned you."

"He did. He's obviously a believer in using multiple media to make a point."

"Hell."

His angry concern warmed her. "Look, Win. I handled it. Lonny won't be making any more passes."

He didn't look as if he believed her. "Like you handled it with me last night?"

"What do you mean? You think I let him kiss me and then called a halt to the whole thing? You think

I'm a tease?" She didn't care about Lonny any longer. She just wanted to know if Win's avoiding her meant that he thought she had led him on the night before and was disgusted with her for it.

"No. That's not what I meant and you can stop putting words into my mouth. I think you are a beautiful woman afraid of her own body, not a tease. You were just as desperate to touch me as I was to touch you, until you got scared. What I want to know is if you thought you handled Lonny by telling him you are a virgin. Because if you think that did it, I've got bad news for you."

"What do you mean?" she asked, curious.

"He's more likely to see you as a challenge than just let it go. He'll think that taking your virginity will prove he's more of a man."

"Is that how you see me now, Win? A challenge? Someone you need to bed to prove that you can do what no other man has been able to accomplish?" She had to know.

"We aren't talking about me. We're talking about Lonny. Now tell me if you told him what you told me," he demanded.

"No." she smiled wryly. "If you must know I used multimedia as well."

"Explain," he demanded with typical Win-style arrogance.

"I stomped on his foot to get him to back up and when he did, I punched him."

His smile was slow and sexy. "You're some little Amazon when you're riled, aren't you, honey?"

She shrugged, secretly pleased at the approval she saw in his eyes. "When you grow up in west Texas, you learn how to take care of yourself. Now, answer my question. Am I just a challenge to you?"

His smile faded and his eyes became very intense. "Carlene, I need you like I haven't needed a woman in a long time, maybe ever. It hasn't got a damn thing to do with your lack of experience. In fact, I spent most of last night trying to convince myself to leave you the hell alone."

She looked around her room and then back at Win. "But you didn't succeed."

"No."

"I still don't want an affair."

"I'm still not interested in marriage." He released her and swung away. He walked over to her bed and picked up the book she had been reading.

It was a romantic suspense by her favorite author. She should have known she was in trouble when she'd been unable to concentrate on it.

He laid the book back down and turned around to face her again. The expression on his face chilled her. "My ex-wife used sex to manipulate me into marriage, Carlene. I won't let that happen again."

The knowledge that he'd been married before hurt her. "Where does that leave us, Win?"

"I don't know. Are you going to use my attraction to you to try to force marriage?"

A painful lump formed in her throat. "No, but I'm not going to have a casual affair with you either."

His hands clenched at his sides. "I guess there's nothing left to say, then, is there?"

He turned and headed toward the door. With each step he took, she wanted to stop him, to call him back. But for what?

She didn't have an answer to the impasse they found themselves in either.

Three days later, Carlene was exhausted and cranky as she shucked the corn on the cob she planned to serve Win and the hands for dinner that night. Grateful that she had a smaller number to feed than usual, she yanked the husk off the outside of the corn and tossed it in the bag at her feet. A couple of the ranch hands were delivering a stud Win had sold to another Mustang breeder in Wyoming. They weren't expected back until tomorrow.

She kept an eye on Shelly and Jared out of the corner of her eye. They were playing in a small plastic pool that Win had purchased for them. She'd wanted to set it up in the courtyard, but they wanted to watch the horses and she'd compromised, setting the pool up outside the back entrance to the kitchen, telling the kids they'd have to watch the horses from that distance. Jared splashed Shelly and the little girl gave a gleeful shout.

Carlene smiled despite her irritable mood. Win had been right when he said they were "a couple of real cute kids". Watching them had confirmed her own desire to be a mother. Something she wasn't likely to become anytime soon.

"Miss Carlene, Miss Carlene. Jared has to go potty. Can I take him?" asked Shelly while Jared hopped on one foot, looking desperate.

Shelly loved escorting her brother to the bathroom and setting up the potty chair for him. It made her feel like a big girl, so Carlene agreed.

She'd just finish shucking the corn and then go make sure Jared got his big-boy underwear pulled up right.

She brushed the back of her hand against the slight perspiration on her forehead. She needed a nap. Between Shelly waking up in the middle of the night and thoughts of Win that disturbed Carlene's rest, she had been getting precious little sleep the past few days.

Shelly hadn't woken the night before last. She seemed to be settling into the routine of the ranch, but then Leah had called last night and spoken to the children. It had been almost impossible to get Shelly and Jared to sleep and then, predictably, Shelly had woken around midnight calling for her mother.

Carlene had rocked the little girl for over an hour before Shelly had fallen back asleep.

Win told Carlene that Leah had said she just

needed a few more days and then she'd be back. He hadn't volunteered anything else and Carlene hadn't asked. Truthfully, she didn't care when Leah got back except how it affected Shelly and Jared.

Carlene's main concern was the fear that she was falling in love with her boss, a man who would probably never let himself love her. He'd been very careful to avoid any physical contact with her for the last three days and it was driving her crazy. When their hands accidentally collided while bathing the children, he would yank his away as if she burned him.

His constant rejection made her want to cry, but not half so much as the haunted expression she saw on his face whenever he really looked at her.

Win still wanted her, of that she was certain. But how long would he want her? He wasn't looking for a lifetime commitment and Carlene wasn't foolish enough to believe that a temporary physical attraction would lead to anything more than heartache for her. She hated the fact that Win equated her desire for a strong commitment to manipulation. It wasn't that she wanted to force him to marry her.

What she needed was the security that they were both going into the relationship wanting to make it last, looking at the possibility of a future together. She couldn't have a future with a man who refused to marry, could she?

The knowledge that he'd been married once

before gnawed at her. He had loved one woman enough to risk the commitment despite his experience growing up with a mother who changed husbands as often as some women changed hairstyles. What had ended his first marriage? Did he still love his ex-wife?

That question tormented Carlene more than any other. The thought of Win loving another woman made her want to throw up.

She finished shucking the corn and stood up. Time to check on the kids. She was surprised that they hadn't come back outside to continue playing in the pool. When she tried to open the kitchen door, though, she found it locked. Panic pulsed through her until she heard giggles from the inside.

The children weren't hurt.

She rushed around to the kitchen window and, standing on her tip-toes, tried to peer inside. She wasn't tall enough. She looked around her for something to stand on; her gaze fell on a wooden crate one of the hands had left near the house. She dragged it over to the window and stepped up, this time getting a clear view of the kitchen.

The sight that met her eyes made her sigh with relief and groan in exasperation. Jared stood in the center of the floor wearing one of Carlene's large white aprons and holding a wooden spoon. Shelly stood on a chair with a box of cereal. She poured the cereal onto the floor into a large puddle of milk as

Carlene watched helplessly through the window. Jared stirred it with the spoon.

"Something wrong, Carlene?"

Win's voice startled her and she lost her balance. Her arms windmilled and the bag of corn she had been holding went flying just before she did. Win caught her, but several small thuds indicated the corn hadn't been so lucky.

Landing against Win's chest, she expelled air in a big whoosh. For a brief moment in time, she forgot the children making cereal on the floor she'd mopped just that morning. She forgot her fears for the future. She forgot that Win had been avoiding her. All she could think about was the feel of Win's strong arms locked around her and his rock-hard body pressed against her own.

It didn't matter that he only held her because she'd literally flown through the air to land in his arms. He was holding her and it felt good, too good. Her eyes wide, she licked her lips, trying to find something to say.

He swore and then lowered his mouth to hers.

The kiss was brief, but explosive. Although he pulled back almost immediately, she had felt the desperate hunger in him and it called to a matching emotion in her.

He set her away from him. "I didn't mean to do that."

"I know."

She did too. He'd made it abundantly clear that he didn't want to start anything under her terms. She forced herself to look away from him and noticed the corn strewn on the ground. She wanted to scream out her frustration, but swallowed the urge. She bent down and started to gather the corn.

"Just rinse it and it'll be fine," Win said as he picked up the corn near him and tossed it into her bag.

She raised her head and glared at him. "Easy for you to say. You're not responsible for feeding the hands. I am."

Win's eyes narrowed. "Take it easy, honey. No one's going to notice that the corn took a detour on the way to the table."

"Maybe not, but they're bound to notice when they have to eat it raw because Shelly and Jared locked the cook out of the kitchen."

Win's smile infuriated her. It wasn't funny, darn it. "Don't you dare laugh. This is not in the least amusing."

He tried to hide his smile. "No. I can see that."

"Just what do you think Leah would say if she drove up right now? She wouldn't be very impressed that the woman you hired to watch her children had managed to get herself locked out of the house while they had a merry old time making cereal on the floor."

"Is that what they're doing? Making cereal?" he asked.

"Yes, with an entire box of toasted oats and about a gallon of milk from the looks of things." Just the thought of all that milk spilled on her newly mopped floor made her wince.

Win turned toward the house. "Come on."

She followed him to the kitchen door. Win pounded on the door. "Shelly, open up. Miss Carlene and I want to come inside."

Carlene heard movement from within and then the door scraped open. Shelly stood on the other side, her face split in a happy grin. "Hi. Me and Jared got hungry. We made cereal."

Carlene's gaze settled on the little boy sitting in the middle of floor, eating the soggy cereal with his fingers. He looked up and smiled proudly. "I's a cook. See?"

Part of her wanted to laugh and the other part wanted to make sure the children knew that locking her out of the kitchen and making cereal on the floor was not appropriate behavior.

She settled on turning to glare at Win, who had swung Shelly up into his arms. "Do you still think this is humorous?"

Win indicated his nephew with a flick of his eyes. "Yep. You can't tell me that's not funny, Carlene."

She sighed. So much for help from that quarter. She walked over to Jared and lifted him from the puddle of cereal. "Come on, sweetie, let's get you cleaned up."

Jared protested, "But I's a cook. Don't wanna get cleaned."

"You're a good cook too, Jared. As a matter of fact, I'm going to let you and Shelly help me make dinner, but first we've got to wash you up. Cooks have to be very clean when they're making food for other people."

"Oh."

She took that for agreement and headed toward the bathroom.

She looked at Win over her shoulder. "You can bring Shelly. I'll need your help getting them both bathed before I clean up the mess in the kitchen."

Win's eyes narrowed. "I've got stuff to do in the stable. I don't have time to give the kids a bath right now."

Carlene gave him her sweetest, most insincere, smile. "Just think of it as an *amusing* blip in your schedule."

Win growled something that made Shelly laugh.

By the time she and Win had Jared and Shelly bathed and changed, both children were showing signs that they needed a nap. Carlene got them to lie down with the promise that she would wait to finish preparing dinner until they woke up.

Win followed her back into the kitchen. "Need help cleaning up this mess?" he asked, indicating the cereal drying to the floor.

"I thought you had things to do."

"They'll keep."

She shook her head. "That's okay. Cleaning it up is my penance for letting this happen in the first place."

"How did you?"

She wasn't about to admit that she'd gotten side-tracked thinking about him.

She shrugged. "I guess I'm a little tired. I let Shelly take Jared to the bathroom and I didn't keep very close track of the time that had passed. The next thing I knew, they had locked me out and were pouring milk on my newly mopped floor."

Win's eyes filled with concern. "You aren't getting enough sleep."

"It was just sitting out in the sunshine being lazy. It made me tired. I'm fine now." A yawn surprised her before she could stifle it, giving lie to her words.

He reached out and brushed her cheek. "You've got shadows under your eyes. I should have noticed. You're working too hard."

"I'm fine, really." She didn't think her heart could handle his concern. She'd rather he went back to ignoring her.

He shook his head. "You need a nap as much as the kids do. Go lie down and I'll take care of cleaning up this mess."

A nap sounded so tempting, but cleaning was her job after all. "Don't be silly. You didn't hire me so you'd have to clean up when I'm feeling a little sleepy."

"Forget the mess," he growled. "You're taking a nap."

She would have argued, but another yawn slipped out and she knew Win would never believe that she didn't need the rest. She nodded. "Fine, but don't complain to me about getting behind on your own work."

He nudged her toward the door. "You're welcome."

She didn't need to be such a fishwife. Turning around, she gave him a conciliatory smile. "I'm sorry, Win. Thank you. Though I'm sure Lonny and Shorty won't be thanking me for keeping you from the stables."

She turned to go, but his words stopped her. "Lonny isn't with Shorty."

Her tired brain had a difficult time making sense of his statement, but she sensed there was something important there that she needed to understand.

She turned around to face him again. "Where is he, then?"

Win's shoulder's lifted in a negligent gesture that said he didn't know. "I fired him."

"You fired him? Why?" She couldn't believe it.

Win looked at her as if her brain wasn't functioning very well, which it wasn't. However, her question was a reasonable one.

"He made a pass at you," Win said.

"But, I took care of it. You didn't have to fire him."

A frown creased Win's features. "He signed his own pink slip the moment he touched you."

She couldn't take it in. "That's ridiculous, Win. This is your busiest time of year. You can't have fired one of your hands just because he made a play for your housekeeper."

Suddenly he was right in front of her, his hands holding her in place. "You aren't just my house-keeper, damn it."

"Yes, I am. You're interested in sleeping with me like Lonny was, but I'm no more than your employee."

His expression turned fierce. "I'm not like Lonny and you know it."

Weary of fighting over the same ground, she conceded. "You're right. You are old enough to go out with me for one thing, but you want the same thing he did."

Win released her and let his arms drop to his side. "Lonny's a horny kid on the prowl for a good lay. I want *you,* honey. There's a difference and one of these days you're going to figure it out. Then you'll put us both out of our misery."

She opened her mouth to deny what he had said, but he pressed one of his fingers against her lips. "Shh. Go take your nap. We'll talk about this later."

She swallowed her denial and, pulling away from him, she turned to go.

Win finished cleaning the kitchen, careful to get every last bit of milk mopped up. Carlene wouldn't appreciate the smell of sour milk in her kitchen. He liked the possessiveness with which she referred to the kitchen. Other housekeeper-cooks had said similar things, but hearing it had never affected Win the same way. It made him feel a sense of permanence with Carlene; like maybe she wouldn't quit and move on the way she'd told him she planned to do eventually.

He rinsed the mop with bleach water and put it away in the broom closet. Then, although he knew he needed to get to the stable, he found himself climbing the stairs to the second level and walking down the corridor toward Carlene's room. He took a minute to check on Jared and Shelly. Both kids were sleeping soundly, which didn't surprise Win at all. They expended enough energy to fuel a small town. He didn't know how Carlene handled it. Even with Shorty's help in the afternoons, she must be running herself ragged, but she hadn't contacted a service to send someone out to help her.

When he had asked her why, she shrugged and said she didn't think the kids needed another stranger in their life right now.

She was an amazing woman.

He pushed open her bedroom door and his gaze settled on the woman sleeping in the bed. She'd undressed and her bare shoulder peaked above the light blanket she slept under. His fingers itched to touch the silky smooth skin. How long was she going to keep him waiting? When would she accept that they could be good together?

Good, nothing. They would be spectacular.

She sighed in her sleep and turned her head on the pillow, giving him an unencumbered view of her gentle features. Bruises from lack of sleep marked the skin under her eyes. He felt guilt settle on him. Hell. He should have noticed how tired she was getting, but he'd been so busy trying to avoid her. He'd spent the last three days trying to give her space.

He realized now that the strategy hadn't worked worth a hill of beans.

She was still focused on his desire to remain single. She couldn't seem to grasp the fact that he wanted more than some tawdry affair or a one-night stand. He almost laughed. One night with Carlene would only leave him hungry for more. As he'd told her, there was a whole range of possibilities between marriage and a quick roll in the hay.

Wasn't there?

Of course there was, he admonished himself.

She didn't think so.

Hell. She'd even compared him to that idiot, Lonny. It was not a flattering comparison. Lonny would bed any willing woman. Win should have realized the potential for trouble when he hired Carlene. He hadn't. The knowledge rankled.

She should never have found herself in the position of having to defend her virtue from a lecher like Lonny.

Well, Win would be much more careful when he hired a replacement hand. He wouldn't hire another jerk looking for an easy lay, even if it meant working the busy spring season short one stable hand. He would protect Carlene, even if she didn't think she needed it.

CHAPTER SEVEN

"ANYBODY up for some ice cream?" Win asked after dinner.

His question was immediately greeted with delighted shouts by his niece and nephew.

"I wants some. I do," shouted Jared.

"Me too. I want bubble gum flavor. Can I have bubble gum, Uncle Win?" Shelly asked, hopping excitedly from one foot to the other in the middle of the kitchen.

Win turned to Carlene and she felt the force of his gaze as it locked with hers over the children's heads. "How about you, Carlene? Would you like something sweet and cool?"

She wanted *something,* but ice cream didn't come into it. Ever since she'd woken from her nap, she'd been feeling a curious tension. It felt as if something had shifted in her relationship with Win that afternoon, but she didn't yet understand what.

Perhaps it had something to do with his remark

about putting them both out of their misery. About wanting her, not just any woman. She had the distinct impression that a showdown over their relationship was coming, one in which she might not be victorious. She wasn't even sure she wanted to be any longer. Ice cream, however, was safe.

So she nodded. "Sure, just let me do something to my hair and I'll be ready to go."

Gazing at her reflection in the vanity mirror in the bathroom attached to her room a few minutes later, she critically surveyed the dark curls framing her makeup-free face. She hadn't had time to apply any sort of cosmetics since the first morning after she started watching Win's niece and nephew. Children were time-consuming. No wonder so many mothers went for the natural look.

Grimacing at the unkempt woman in the mirror, she made a decision. Twenty minutes later, she had changed her clothes, swept her hair up in a riot of curls on top of her head and applied subtle makeup. She moved into the bedroom and took inventory of her improved appearance. She looked much more feminine in the form-fitting, coral knit top, emerald-green designer jeans and gold sandals than she had in her oversized white T-shirt, blue jeans and tennis shoes she'd been wearing earlier.

Win called impatiently from the courtyard. She could hear the children playing in the fountain through the opening she had left cracked in her door.

"Carlene, by the time you're ready it's going to be winter already and ice cream isn't going to sound so good."

She smiled at the jibe, anticipating Win's reaction to the change from frumpy housekeeper to attractive female. Taking the time to apply coral lip-gloss over the too-subtle lipstick she had originally picked out, Carlene finished getting ready. She seized her purse off the dresser and headed to the courtyard to meet Win and the children.

The minute she stepped onto the stone pathway, she knew her time primping had been well spent.

Win's eyes locked on her with the precision of a homing missile. A slow, wicked grin split his face. "Honey, it's a good thing for you that we've got these two around or you'd never make it to town for ice cream."

His hand swept out, indicating the children, who were sailing two small plastic vessels in the pool below the fountain.

She returned his smile with one of her own and winked. "Maybe I wouldn't want to."

The intensity in his look shot up another ten degrees. He took a deep breath. "You're playing with fire, honey. Watch it or you're going to end up singed."

"Uncle Win, Mama says never to play with fire. It's dangerous." Shelly's sweet face was set in serious lines.

Win laughed and the sound of masculine amusement shivered along Carlene's nerve endings with as much force as a touch.

He swept Shelly up in his arms and tickled her. "You're right, sweetpea. Fire is dangerous."

Turning his head, he met Carlene's gaze and she knew the words were meant for her as much as for his niece.

Feeling too good to be cautious, Carlene just smiled and turned to collect Jared.

That nap had done wonders.

Several other families shared Win's brilliant plans for after-dinner ice cream. The place was packed.

Families. The word didn't really describe himself, Carlene and the children. Technically, he, Shelly and Jared could be considered family, but it wasn't the same. He didn't plan on getting married again and that meant he wasn't going to be a father. It also meant he didn't have to worry about disappointing his children as his parents had disappointed him. It meant he wouldn't bring another child into the world that would have to face the devastation of divorce and his *family* getting ripped apart.

It also meant that Win would never have a wife or children to share the simple pleasures in life, like going out for ice cream on a warm summer evening.

Thoughts that used to underline his hard-won independence were now just a little depressing. He gave himself a mental shake and focused on the pleasure of the moment. He was with his two favorite kids and a warm, sexy woman. What more could a man ask for?

Answers that he didn't want to deal with whispered at the back of his mind, but he ignored them in favor of glaring at a couple of teenage boys that were ogling Carlene. One of the boys caught his gaze and quickly turned away, nudging his friend as he did so. The friend wasn't so quick to look away, but when Win indicated the outside with a tilt to his head and a raised eyebrow, the boy swallowed and found a renewed interest in the menu board.

He'd never felt this possessive about anyone, not even his ex-wife. Rachel had been pretty. Men had looked and all Win had experienced had been male satisfaction in having a pretty wife. Carlene would probably call him sexist. Hell, maybe he was...a little. Anyway, things were different with Carlene and they weren't even involved yet.

"What are you going to have?" Her question pulled Win from his reverie.

He shrugged. "Double scoop of Rocky Road. It's what I always have."

She stared at him as if he'd just said that he ate his ice cream while riding buck naked through town.

"What?" he demanded. "You don't like Rocky Road?"

"I love Rocky Road, but I can't imagine getting

the same flavor of ice cream every single time. They've got thirty-two flavors, Win. How can you not want to try something new? I can't even get two scoops of the same thing," she admitted.

"I'm not much on change I guess."

"Life without change is boring. It's too…it's too…*predictable*."

Yeah. Like waking up next to the same husband for the rest of your life. His mom hadn't liked that sort of predictability either. "That's me, boring."

Making a grab for Jared's shirt before he could get out the door someone had just opened, Carlene laughed. She led Jared over to the case that displayed ice-cream cones decorated like clowns and animals. "Here, sugarbear. Why don't you pick one of these to have for your treat?"

Shelly decided she wanted a decorated cone as well and joined Jared at the case as they discussed the merits of the ones displayed there.

Carlene turned back to Win, lingering laughter in her eyes. "One thing you could never be, Win, is boring. Irritating. Arrogant and sometimes even pre-dictable, but never boring."

"Tell me that six months from now." That was about how long his mom's euphoria over a new marriage would last. Then the fighting would start. The tantrums came next and then, finally, divorce.

Carlene's smile slipped. "I get the feeling we're talking about more than preferences in ice cream here."

He shrugged. A crowded restaurant was not the place to get into such a discussion. In fact, he didn't think he wanted to have this particular discussion at all. "What two different flavors are you going to have this time?"

She eyed him speculatively, as if she was testing his determination to change the subject, and then she too shrugged. "I was thinking about the flavor of the month and mocha almond fudge. I'll have it as a sundae with hot fudge, whip cream, nuts and a cherry, of course."

It was his turn to eye her askance. "What is the point of ordering two different flavors if you're going to drown them with toppings?"

The sparkle came back to her eyes. Laying her hand against his chest, she said, "You've definitely got to learn to live a little, Win. Your ice-cream-eating education has been severely limited. I suggest you let me order for you tonight."

He couldn't resist the teasing glint in her eyes. She'd been like this ever since she came into the courtyard looking like a million bucks. He liked it when she teased him, he realized. Taking the plunge, he said, "Okay."

Her smile went up about one hundred watts. "Great."

For a minute he thought she was going to seal her approval with a kiss. She had slipped her hand up from his chest to the back of his neck and her gaze had gone soft, her lips parting. He started to lean down to make it easy for her and she blinked. Then she looked around, seeming to remember their surroundings.

Lightning quick, she removed her hand from his neck and moved back a step. "Uh, I'll find out which cones Shelly and Jared have decided on."

Stifling his disappointment, he nodded. "You do that."

His voice came out harsher than he intended. He knew she wanted to be discreet, but he didn't have to like it.

She didn't waste any time moving further away from him toward the kids.

"I want the puppy," Shelly said in response to Carlene's question.

Jared wanted a lime-green clown.

Win took the kids to a table to sit down while Carlene made the order. He wondered what kind of ice cream he was going to end up having. He doubted it would matter. Ten to one, she was going to have it all doctored up like hers.

A few minutes later when she appeared at their table with two fully loaded sundaes and the kids' cones, his guess was confirmed. Carlene laid a huge stack of napkins in the middle of the table along with a cup of water. She handed each of the kids their cones before placing what looked like a mound of whip cream in front of Win. He speculated on what the innocent-looking white fluff hid before scooping into it with his spoon.

His trepidation must have shown on his face because she giggled. "Don't worry, it isn't going to bite back."

"That's what they said before the giant banana split destroyed that small Midwestern town."

Shelly's eyes rounded. "What giant 'nana split? Did you see it?"

He reached out and ruffled his niece's hair. "No, sweetpea. I was just kidding."

"Oh. Does that mean the giant 'nana split isn't true, Uncle Win?"

He nodded. "Yes, sweetpea, that's what it means."

"Mama says you aren't supposed to lie, Uncle Win."

He groaned and looked to Carlene for help. Her gaze was fixed on someone behind him and he got the feeling she'd missed most of the frustrating exchange he was having with Shelly.

He wanted to turn and see who she was looking at with that expression of chagrin, but he had to answer Shelly's question first. He didn't want her telling Leah that he lied.

"A joke isn't a lie, sweetpea, because nobody is supposed to believe it. They're supposed to think it's funny."

"When somethin's funny I laugh," Shelly informed him.

"It was a joke for Carlene," he said, feeling just a little irritated at both the constant questions and Carlene's fixation with whoever had just walked in.

"Miss Carlene didn't laugh." Shelly's observation didn't improve Win's mood any.

He fixed Carlene with an irritated frown. "No, she didn't."

Shelly turned her attention to Carlene as well. "Miss Carlene, why didn't you laugh?"

Carlene turned to Shelly, making an obvious effort to collect her thoughts. "What was I supposed to laugh at?"

Shelly gave an exaggerated sigh. "Uncle Win's joke, silly. He said it was funny, but you didn't laugh."

Carlene shifted her gaze to Win. He stared back, letting her see his irritation. She let out her own little sigh. "I'm sorry, Win. I missed it. Do you want to repeat it?"

He wanted to know what had her so rattled. "No. Humor lacks something when the spontaneity is missing."

She winced. "Sorry. Uh, what do you think of your sundae?"

He looked down at the melting whip cream covering a mound of ice cream and toppings he had barely touched. "What is it?"

"French vanilla with hot fudge." She reached over and dipped one of the napkins in the cup of water. Then, using the wetted napkin, she wiped the dripping ice cream from Jared's fingers before handing him back his cone.

Then she turned her attention to Win. She

reached across the table and picked up his spoon. After scooping a bite of the concoction in his bowl onto it, she offered it to him. "Here, scaredy-cat. Take a bite."

He would have told her he wasn't afraid to try it, but when he opened his mouth she slid the spoon inside, managing to make it feel like a caress in his mouth. He licked the ice cream off the pink plastic spoon and she slowly withdrew it from his mouth. Then, spying a smidgen of fudge left on the plastic, she put it in her own mouth and licked it off.

"It's one of my favorites. Do you like it?"

The sundae was delicious, but the sight of Carlene licking the spoon was sweet enough to give him a sugar rush. He took another bite of ice cream and swirled it around in his mouth pretending to think about it.

Carlene waited with anxious anticipation on her face for his verdict. He took another bite, making this one last longer than the last one. She seemed mesmerized by the way he ate his ice cream.

"It's fine."

Her eyes narrowed, but she couldn't hide her small, shallow breaths. "Fine? I order you the classic of all classics in ice cream confectionery and you say it's just fine?"

He kept his expression neutral. "It's not quite the same experience as a double-scoop cone of Rocky Road."

She sized him up with her gaze. "I see. I guess

next time I'll let you order your own ice cream. Some people just don't adjust well to change."

He laughed. "Honey, it's ambrosia and you know it." Did she know how much he'd enjoyed her feeding him as well?

She must have because every once in a while she'd offer him a bite of her ice cream, or dip her spoon in his and feed it to him. The kids wanted to get in on the act, so Carlene shared hers with them, too. How she managed to be sweet and motherly with his niece and nephew and in almost the same breath turn around and send his hormones raging, he didn't know. But, man, he liked. He liked it a lot.

They were finishing their ice cream when he heard his name.

"Win Garrison. That you?"

He turned and looked up. Grant Strickland was striding toward them. Win stood and shook hands with the other man. "Strickland. How's married life treating you?"

Grant's new wife, Zoe, had been one of Leah's friends when they were younger. Win hadn't gone to the wedding because he actually didn't know Grant and Zoe all that well. Leah was the one that had actually done part of her growing up and schooling here in Sunshine Springs. He and his sister had moved into Hank Garrison's ranch home with their mother when Win was seventeen. Grant had been in his class in high school, but Win had been too busy learning the ropes of ranch life from Hank after school to make many friends.

Besides, Win made it a policy to avoid weddings whenever possible.

Grant's smile was so blissful it was almost painful. "I'm a happy man."

Win believed him. Maybe marrying your best friend was the one way a man could figure she wasn't going to grow bored and leave. If she wanted to marry you after knowing you most of her life, she wasn't likely to change her mind six months down the road.

Grant focused his gaze over Win's shoulder. "Hey, Carlene."

"Hi, Grant." Her voice was quiet.

"You two know each other?" Win asked.

"I met him at the Dry Gulch."

Win nodded. "She's working for me now, as my housekeeper."

Grant's eyes widened in surprise, but his attention didn't linger on Carlene. Leaning down, he ruffled Jared's hair. "Hi, little guy. Leah's your momma, isn't she?"

Jared just ducked his head, but Win nodded. "Yep, these are Leah's little ones."

"I didn't realize that Leah was in town. Zoe'll want to see her."

Carlene's smile slipped and Win wondered if she was worried about him telling Grant that she was living at Win's ranch temporarily while Leah's kids were staying.

Win shrugged. "Actually, she's not in town. Leah left the kids with me for a few days."

Grant didn't ask any questions as a woman would have. He just nodded. "I don't know if you've heard, but I've decided to shift the focus of my ranch from cattle to horses."

"I heard."

Leah had told him that Zoe, a vegetarian, got too upset when the cattle went to the stock sale. Grant was changing his ranch and the way he made his livelihood to make his wife happy. Win wondered if he'd be willing to do the same thing for Carlene. The thought was so alien it made him frown. He had no plans to marry, not Carlene. Not anyone. She affected him as no other woman had, but he was still in control of his future and that future did not include a wedding.

"I was hoping you'd let me pick your brain on the running of a horse ranch. I'm not going to try to run a stable as well like you have, but I'm real interested in the Mustang herd. You've got one of the best reputations in the business."

Win nodded, not at all flustered by the praise. It was true and he'd worked damn hard to make it that way. No sense denying it. "Come out anytime. I'll show you around the operation although the ranch is pretty much Joe's baby now. I'm damn busy with the stables."

Grant laughed. "That's what happens when you're the best at what you do."

"Or at least in the top ten," Win said with a smile.

Grant nodded. "Well, Zoe's at the pizza place. I saw your truck outside and decided to come in. I'd better not keep her waiting."

Grant turned to go, waiving a quick farewell over his shoulder to Carlene and Leah's children.

When Win turned around, Carlene was busy washing Shelly's face and hands. Jared looked as if he could use a little help too. Win dipped another napkin in the water and went to work on his nephew.

When he was finished, he asked Carlene, "You ready to go?"

"Sure. We'd better get these two in bed soon." She didn't quite meet his eyes and he wondered what she was thinking.

Was she regretting her earlier teasing? Did she think he would make her follow through on the offer she'd made in the courtyard before they left? The kids would be in bed soon, but he didn't know what that was going to buy him.

Sometimes the female mind was too complicated for a mere man to comprehend.

Carlene tucked the blankets around Shelly and prayed that the little girl would sleep through the night.

Leaning down to kiss the soft skin of Shelly's cheek, Carlene said, "Goodnight, sweet girl."

Shelly smiled sleepily. "Goodnight, Miss Carlene."

Her eyes were closed before Carlene had turned to take Jared from Win's arms. Win had changed the boy into pajamas and night-time underwear in case of accidents. Win shook his head at Carlene. "I'll tuck him in."

She nodded and left the room. She hadn't expected Win to give her such an easy escape after her earlier teasing, but she certainly wasn't going to make things more difficult for herself by sticking around.

The rumble of Win's voice as he spoke to Jared trickled down the hall as Carlene made her way to her bedroom. She turned on the light and shut the door, relief flowing over her that she was saved from the confrontation over their relationship—at least for tonight.

What had possessed her to tease Win as she had in the courtyard, and then later at the ice cream shop? She had been playing with fire and Win was right. If she didn't watch it, she was going to end up good and burned. Kicking off her sandals, she headed to the bathroom to wash off her makeup and brush her teeth.

Seeing Grant tonight had been a shock. She should have expected it. After all, he and Zoe lived on a ranch on the other side of Sunshine Springs. Carlene was bound to run into them once in a while. It wasn't as if there were hard feelings between them either. She'd been invited to their wedding…and she'd gone. But seeing Grant while she was with Win had been disconcerting.

It made her realize how much of a mistake she'd made with him.

Unclipping her hair, she let it fall to her shoulders in a springy mass of dark curls. She finger-combed it, knowing the tight natural curls would just frizz out if she attempted to brush her hair out now that it was dry.

She had tried straightening it once. Her mother had thought that doing so might give her a more staid appearance, a more *acceptable* appearance. Carlene had found the procedure and the results less than pleasant. As she finished detangling her hair with her fingers she realized that her mother might never accept her as she was. She looked in the mirror and conceded that after her parent's refusal to stand by her during the problems she had faced back home, that was no longer as important as it once had been.

However, that didn't mean she couldn't accept herself. Life was too complicated as it was without trying to be someone else.

So, who was she?

Was she the woman who had dressed in spandex miniskirts and tended bar at the Dry Gulch or was she the woman who wore her clothes loose and comfortable while tending house and cooking for Win Garrison?

She moved back into her bedroom and took a fleeting glance at the woman in the mirror. Perhaps she wasn't either of those women. Perhaps she was the woman standing before her, looking back from the mirror. A woman comfortable enough with her own body that she could wear clothes that enhanced her figure without needing to flamboyantly display every curve.

One thing was certain, she wasn't the woman who had donned her work gear and tried to seduce Grant Strickland. Her face heated at the memory. Grant had asked her out first. The date had ended in disaster when Zoe's pet hamster had come running into the kitchen.

Carlene had an unreasonable fear of rodents.

The second date, if you could call it that, had been entirely her idea. Grant had stopped by the Dry Gulch with a dozen red roses and Carlene had assumed that meant he was interested in pursuing a relationship.

Looking back, she couldn't understand what had prompted her to act like a siren. The only explanation that she could think of was that for a month or two before Grant asked her out, she had become increasingly depressed and lonely, not to mention restless with her innocent and single status.

Grant was the first man that she had any real interest in for so long that she went for it. She acted out the part she assumed he had been expecting when he asked her out, that of the seductress. She didn't seduce him. She succeeded in humiliating herself and causing a rift between Grant and Zoe. In her own defense, she had not realized that the two had become a couple. They'd been friends so long, no one, including Carlene, thought they ever would.

She didn't think that mid-life crises occurred at twenty-six, but she didn't have a better explanation for her behavior. It certainly bore no resemblance to her refusal to sleep with Win. It wasn't as if she had asked Grant if he were interested in marriage either. So, why make such a big deal out of it with Win? Why refuse herself and Win the sensual relief they both craved because of their lack of a future? It wasn't as if she'd been sure she could have a future with Grant Strickland.

In a moment of stunning clarity she realized that although she had been attracted to Grant, she had been in no danger of falling in love with him. Their lack of a future hadn't bothered her because she hadn't necessarily wanted one with him, but she did with Win. She knew instinctively that if she gave herself to Win, she would be opening herself up to heartache beyond anything she had ever experienced—even the rejection of her parents.

She plopped down onto the side of the bed, unable to accept what her heart was trying to tell her. She could not allow herself to love a man who believed the solution to life's problems lay in a no strings attached, short term affair. She couldn't.

The only problem was that she had a horrible feeling that she already had.

She was so overwhelmed by her thoughts that she

only vaguely registered the knock on her door. It wasn't until the door swung open and Win walked into the room that she forced her scattering thoughts back into a pattern she could identify.

That pattern filled her with irritation.

"Win! What do you think you are doing just walking into my room? I could have been getting dressed, or something."

His brow lifted in sardonic amusement. "Since we know the only 'or something' you are going to be engaging in will be with me and you are still decently covered, you might as well relax, honey."

She shot to her feet, channeling all her tumultuous thoughts into the safer venue of anger. "That's not the point and you know it. I am your employee, not your wife, and I deserve some privacy."

His frown at the word wife only underscored the differences between them. "Listen, honey, right now you're a woman that has me tied up in knots. I'm definitely not thinking of you as my employee."

She crossed her arms under her chest. "Well, maybe you should and save us both a lot of trouble."

He shook his head. "Uh uh. It isn't going to work. You aren't built anything like my other employees."

"Just what is that supposed to mean?"

He made a placating gesture with his hand. "Calm down, Carlene. I didn't come in here to start the next range war."

She harrumphed. "Then why did you come in here?"

His sigh would have parted her hair if he were two feet closer. "I came to invite you to join me for a nightcap."

CHAPTER EIGHT

CARLENE'S eyes filled with shock. "A nightcap? You want me to come have a drink with you?"

Her voice came out a high squeak and Win wondered why she sounded so disbelieving. She didn't think he was going to let her get away with avoiding him for ever, did she? They had things to work out and that wasn't going to happen with her hiding in her bedroom every time the kids were asleep.

"I opened a bottle of wine and it's waiting in the living room." That should please her. Women thought wine was romantic. Given his choice, he would have preferred a nice glass of Macallan scotch on the rocks.

"I don't think that's a good idea. We both have to get up early and Shelly will probably wake up again in the middle of the night, needing to be rocked back to sleep. I don't want to miss hearing her because I've anesthetized my brain with alcohol. We've just had ice cream. It isn't a good idea to mix alcohol with a big sugar rush, I'm sure." She talked so fast, she sounded like the auctioneer for the Cattleman's Association annual fundraiser.

Maybe she thought if she said it fast enough, he wouldn't find her excuses downright bizarre. He laughed out loud. "Honey, you're being ridiculous. One glass of wine isn't going to dull your senses to the point that you won't hear Shelly if she wakes up. As for mixing sugar and alcohol—"

She didn't let him finish. "Never mind that. We both still have to get up early. I need my sleep. You said so this afternoon."

She stood next to her bed, her hair a wild mass around her shoulders, looking triumphant. She thought she'd made an iron-clad argument. He reached for her and hooked her wrist. If he didn't get her out of the vicinity of her bed very soon, he'd be making his arguments with his body, not his mouth.

"You can take a nap while the kids are sleeping again tomorrow, if you want. It's not that late and I want some company," he said as he pulled her from the room.

"So, what you want is all that matters?" She lowered her voice as he pulled her past the kids' door.

He sighed with irritation as he pulled her down the stairs to the courtyard. She gave a low exclamation.

He turned around. "What's the matter?"

She glared at him, her face illuminated by moonlight. "I stepped on something."

He looked down at her feet and realized for the first time that she'd already taken off her shoes. If he'd waited a few more minutes to come to her room, there was a strong possibility he would have found her already undressed. The thought was too damned tempting to contemplate for very long. He swung her up into his arms. This time instead of fighting him, she put her arms around his neck and held on.

He liked this way a whole lot better.

He carried her through the courtyard into the living room and reluctantly let her go. Turning to the tray he had brought in before going to get Carlene, he asked, "Wine okay?"

"I suppose I should be grateful you didn't throw me over you shoulder and carry me in here like a sack of potatoes again," she said, her feisty nature asserting itself.

He remained silent, waiting for an answer to his earlier question.

She sighed. "Wine is fine."

He poured the golden liquid into a wineglass and handed it to her. "Let's get something straight. I didn't carry you like a sack of potatoes last time and I sure as certain didn't put you over my shoulder. Got that?"

She looked taken aback by his vehemence. Too bad. He was tired of everybody and his mother telling him he'd manhandled her. She'd been a whole lot more squirmy on the first trip through the courtyard in his arms, but she had in no way resembled a sack of potatoes.

"Got it," she said.

"Good. Now, drink your wine."

She sat down in an overstuffed chair that matched the leather sofa. Her choice amused him. Did she think if she sat on the couch, he'd seduce her? Even funnier, did she believe that sitting in a chair was going to stop him? He poured himself a glass of wine and sat on the sofa where it rested kitty corner to her chair. He stretched his legs out in front of him. She shifted hers a few inches to the left so they wouldn't touch.

Taking a sip of her wine, she looked at him over the rim of her glass. "Did anyone ever tell you that charm is not your strong suit?"

He felt a slow smile grow on his face. The woman sure could put her tongue to good use. "Now that you mention it, Leah has said something a time or two about my lack of tact."

She looked thoughtful for a moment. "I suppose that doesn't bother you?"

The question surprised him. "What?"

"Having others think less of you."

"My sister doesn't think less of me because I don't attend to every social nicety."

Carlene's gaze traveled around the room before coming back to settle on him. "No, I don't suppose she does."

They were both silent for a minute.

"It bothers me, you know," she said.

"What bothers you?" he asked. Her pensive mood confused him after her earlier nervousness, but he wasn't going to discourage it. Maybe he'd finally get the answers about her past that he'd been wanting.

"Having others think less of me. Having them believe the worst of me, particularly those I care about and respect."

"Who thought the worst of you, honey?"

Her eyes focused on something that he could not see. Perhaps the past. "When I graduated from high school, I knew just what I wanted, to be a teacher. So, I took an accelerated masters program. I was twenty-three when I finished my practicum and got my first real job teaching. I was offered a position at the high school near my hometown." She let out a long breath. "Maybe I was too young to teach high school, too close to the kids in age. I don't know."

The image of Carlene teaching fit his view of her a whole lot better than her working at the Dry Gulch. Despite the fact she was working as his housekeeper, he wasn't really surprised by her true profession. He wanted to know why she wasn't teaching now, though.

When she didn't go on, he asked an innocuous question he hoped would open her up further. "What did you teach?"

For a moment, her concentration returned to him. "English Lit."

He took a sip of his wine. It wasn't that bad. "Not my favorite subject."

She smiled, her expression indulgent. "I understand. It isn't everybody's, but I loved it. I still do."

"What happened?" Something pretty serious for her to end up his housekeeper, cook and nanny.

An expression of pain flitted across her face as her eyes lost focus again. "The first year was great. I established a strong rapport with my students and the rest of the faculty seemed to like me."

"The second year things changed?" he guessed.

"Yes. Our principal retired. The new one the district hired was really different. His methods and attitudes didn't mesh with my own. We had a few dust-ups, but nothing I couldn't handle until he decided that I would make a good after-school buddy."

Fury washed through Win before he had a chance to fully digest her words. "He made a pass at you?"

"You could say that. He was much too smart to do anything for which I could accuse him of sexual harassment. He made several innuendos, brushed up against me when we passed in the halls, things like that."

"The bastard."

She took a long drink of her wine and then wiped the back of her mouth with her hand. "My sentiments exactly. The worst part was that he was married to one of the sweetest women I'd ever met. It made everything ten times worse. Finally, one day he made a comment that I couldn't ignore and I let him know in no uncertain terms that I wasn't interested."

"Like you did with Lonny?" He could just see the resulting scandal if the English Lit teacher got caught punching the principal of the local high school.

She smiled ruefully. "Not that drastic, but he got the picture. Things got worse after that. He questioned my decisions, dropped in unannounced on my classes. He said he was checking up on me, making sure there were no discipline problems. All of a sudden he had a problem with a single woman my age teaching high school. I still thought I could handle it. I was such a fool."

The defeat and self-condemnation in her voice touched a chord deep inside him. He knew what it meant to play the part of the fool. "What happened?"

"I had the star quarterback in my third-period class. He was a smart boy, but he skimmed on his work. I made the mistake of grading him according to the work he turned in to my class and not on his football-playing ability."

Win had heard stories of teachers being forced to alter grades for star athletes. "You tried to flunk him?"

"He failed one assignment. With his other low grades, that put his playing for the school team at risk." She crossed one green-denim-clad leg over the other. "The principal tried to get me to give him a passing grade."

He thought he knew what was coming. "You wouldn't back down."

"No." The single word said it all. Carlene wouldn't lie for anyone. Her personal code of honor was too high.

"So, they removed him from your class?"

She gave a short bitter laugh. "If only it had been that easy. The student filed a harassment charge against me. He said I'd made a play for him and flunked him when he refused to have anything to do with me."

Cold anger surged through Win. If that lying little weasel had been within spitting distance, Win would have made sure he wasn't up to playing quarterback for a very long time, if ever.

Unaware of the rage pulsing through him, Carlene went on. "It was ridiculous and I didn't take it very seriously at first. I assumed no one would believe him. I was wrong."

He couldn't stand it any longer. Needing to comfort the pain he heard in her voice, Win pulled her gently from her chair into his arms.

She was stiff at first, but suddenly she just snuggled against him and spoke into his chest. "It was horrible. Everyone gossiped about me and somehow my looks and my body were considered the measure of my morality rather than my personality or past. I got calls in the middle of the night making threats and accusing me of things I hadn't even heard of. My principal asked me to resign."

He rubbed her back with continuous downward strokes. "What did you do?"

"I refused to resign. I fought back. I still had my grading records and the last assignment that clearly deserved a failing grade. I hired a lawyer who took depositions on my behalf. He was able to prove the spuriousness of the student's claim. We'd never been in the same room alone."

Win sensed that wasn't the end of the story. If it had been, she would still be in west Texas teaching high school.

"If the principal had stood behind you, things would have been a lot better," he said, trying to get a feel for the rest of the story.

"Yes. It would have. However, he was the one that insisted on opening a full-scale investigation— even after the boy admitted he'd made it up to get on the team."

The yellow-bellied snake. "You were acquitted."

She pulled back so that she could see his face. What he saw on hers made him tighten his hold on her. Her eyes mirrored a wound that was not completely healed.

"In the eyes of the law, absolutely, but not that town. The day I won the case, I went to my parents' house. They were about the only two people in town I was certain were still speaking to me."

"Did they celebrate your victory with you?" He had to ask, although the truth was there in her eyes.

She surprised him when she said, "Sort of."

Maybe it wasn't that bad, but his gut told him it was.

Her lip trembled and she took a calming breath before going on. "They congratulated me on winning the case, but my dad suggested I look for

a job somewhere else. He said he wanted me to
have a new start. To get away from the gossip, but
I realized that a good deal of his motivation was that
he and mom had been humiliated by my problems
and they wanted peace in their lives again. Mom
told me later that some of Dad's golfing buddies
had refused to play with him any longer. She said
their friends had been pressuring them to get me to
leave town."

Win couldn't believe the lack of loyalty and
weakness her parents had shown. How had they
managed to raise a woman as strong and dependable
as Carlene? But then, his mom had raised him, hadn't
she? "Did your mom want you to leave town?"

"Yes, but she was a little more subtle. She suggested I take a vacation before going back to work."

"A vacation?" he asked.

"She thought I should go to Southern California."

"Why there?"

"Lots of plastic surgeons, or so she had been told."

"So?" He was confused.

"She suggested I get a breast reduction.
Apparently women with a figure like mine invite the
sort of trouble I had at my school."

Win could not believe her mother had been so incredibly stupid. "It wasn't your fault!"

Her eyes glistened. "Thanks."

"You don't have to thank me for the truth." He'd
like some time to talk about the truth with her

parents. They certainly didn't deserve a daughter as wonderful as Carlene.

She settled back against his chest. "I decided that Mom and Dad deserved some peace, so I resigned from my position at the high school, packed my car and left."

"You didn't go to California," he said with satisfaction.

He felt her smile against his shirtfront. "No. I won't say I didn't think about it, but I came to the conclusion that I like myself. It wasn't my fault my boss was a lecher or that I had a student with the morals of a bull moose."

He smiled at the return of her feistiness. "You came here instead."

"Sunshine Springs was just a little dot on the map. I liked the name of the town and so I came. Once I got here, I found a job right away, so I decided to stay."

"Not as a teacher."

She grimaced. "No, definitely not as a teacher. But I'm tired of hiding from what might happen. I want to teach again."

"You still want to teach high school?" he asked, awed by her courage.

"You probably think I'm nuts, but yes. I was a good high-school teacher. I want my dreams back. I want my life back. I've let other people, not very nice people, have too much of it as it is."

* * *

The next night, Carlene went looking for Win after she finished tucking the children into bed. She found him down by the stables. He was giving Shorty instructions about one of the pregnant mares.

"Win."

Both he and Shorty turned toward her at the sound of her voice.

Win smiled. "Hi, honey. What do you need?"

"I need to talk to you. Do you have a minute?"

He nodded. "Sure."

Turning to Shorty, Win asked, "You got everything covered here?"

"Yeah, boss."

Win turned and headed toward Carlene and the house.

She watched Shorty go into the building behind Win. "Is Shorty staying the night with the horses?"

Win nodded. "Yeah. One of my mares is ready to foal anytime. He'll call my beeper if she goes into labor."

They went through the house and into the courtyard as if by one accord. Win sat on a chair near the fountain. It was next to the table with the ice tea Carlene had set out in anticipation of their talk. She took the chair on the other side of the small table.

Win picked up one of the glasses and took a long swallow. "What did you want to talk about?" he asked.

"Leah."

His eyes widened. "What about her?"

"When is she coming back, Win?"

He shrugged, as if the answer were of no importance at all. "Soon, I imagine."

She wasn't going to let him sidestep this issue. "When is soon? Tomorrow, the next day, next week?"

His eyes narrowed. "Why are you so interested all of a sudden? You tired of taking care of the kids?"

She didn't like the accusation in his tone. "You know that's not true, but they miss her. It was very difficult to get them both to sleep tonight, but particularly Shelly. She wants her mom."

He looked placated by her answer. "Leah needs some space."

Frustration filled Carlene. "Well, her children need *her*."

"Shelly and Jared will be fine." Win smiled at her. "You're doing great with them."

"I'm not their mom, Win, and that's who they need right now. Leah is going to have to work her problems out with her children around."

Win's expression closed. "Leah knows what is best for her kids. She's a good mother, a better one than she ever had."

Why wouldn't he listen to what Carlene was saying? "I did not mean to imply that I thought anything different. I'm simply pointing out that it's time for Leah to come back."

Win slammed his ice tea down on the table. Brown liquid sloshed over the sides. "You're my housekeeper and the kids' temporary nanny. It's not up to you to tell me what my sister should or should not do."

The attack was so unexpected that it left Carlene speechless.

Win's fury was gone almost as fast as it had come. He reached out and brushed his hand down her arm. "I'm sorry, honey. I didn't mean to snap at you."

She jerked away from his touch. "No problem. I was clearly stepping outside the bounds of our employee-employer relationship by expressing my concern for the two children in my care."

He put his hands on his thighs and blew out a long breath. "I said I was sorry. I know you're worried about the kids, but you've got to trust their mom to know what's best for them."

"Why? Did your mom always know what was best for you? Being a parent doesn't make you infallible."

She'd learned that lesson very well as a teacher.

Win's expression turned dangerous. "Leah is nothing like our mother. She cares more for Jared and Shelly than Mom ever cared for us."

He wasn't shouting, but the cold fury in his voice was just as intimidating.

Carlene refused to back down. "For the second time, I'm not implying that Leah is a poor mother. I am saying that she needs to get back here and comfort her children."

"That's enough." His hands fisted against his thighs. "Leah will get here when she gets here and until then we will take care of Shelly and Jared. Understood?"

"Can't we at least contact their father? Maybe Leah's husband is back from his business trip and would come get the children."

Win's glare knifed through her with the precision of a surgeon's scalpel. "Why don't you just come right out and say it? You're bored watching the kids and you want a change."

The injustice of the accusation caught her on the raw. She exploded from her chair and stormed over to Win. She was so angry she was shaking. Leaning over him, she found it difficult to control her trembling limbs. No one had ever made her mad as Win could.

"Listen closely, you stubborn cowboy, because I've taken about all the insults I'm going to off of you. I am concerned about Leah's children. I believe they need their mother. If she won't make herself available, then we try to find their father. I don't care if they are used to him being gone for weeks at a time. He's still their father and having him around will give them more security than they've got right now."

She punctuated the last sentence with jabs to Win's sternum. The cold fury in Win's eyes made her nervous and she stepped back, but he didn't move. He just caught her gaze and held it captive with an intensity that could have been physical.

"We will not call Mark. If my sister says he's out of town, then that is where he is."

Carlene couldn't help trying again. "Maybe he got back early."

"Forget it."

"But, Win—"

He cut her off. "I said forget it and I meant it, Carlene. You are my employee. You have nothing to say in the matter and I damn well don't want to hear anything else on the subject. Leah will be back in a couple of days and then you'll be free from the burden of watching her children. If you don't think you can handle it, I'll find someone else. What's it to be?"

An iron fist squeezed Carlene's heart, making it difficult to breathe past the pain. "I'll watch the children and be your employee, but *nothing more*."

She turned and stumbled toward her bedroom, tears clouding her vision. Blinking furiously, she willed herself not to cry until she had reached the relative safety of her room.

She hadn't reached the inner hallway before strong fingers clamped onto her shoulders from behind, halting her in mid-step. She struggled against his hold. "Let me go!"

"No. I can't."

The raw fear in his voice had barely registered when he spun her around and pulled her into a tight embrace against his chest. "I was wrong, honey. You're more than an employee and we both know it."

She struggled against the strength of his arms and argued against his shirtfront. "No, we don't know it. You don't want my interference and I don't want you. Let me go, Win."

He had to release her before she lost it. The pain in her chest was so tight, she could barely breathe. She'd been falling in love with this man and he wanted sex. Nothing more. Not her concern for the children. Not her interference in his life. Nothing, but her body. And she didn't know how to give only that. If she ever let Win make love to her, she'd give him everything and she knew it.

Frantic to get him to let her go, she swung her foot forward and kicked his shin. "Let me loose."

He grunted, but his hold didn't so much as loosen a fraction of an inch. Her toes felt as if they had a run-in with a cement wall.

"Please, Carlene, you've got to listen to me."

She threw her head back so she could glare up into his face. "Like you listened to me?"

"I made a mistake. I'm sorry. Give me a chance to make it right."

"Why? So you can come to my bed? You don't really care that you've hurt me. You don't care what I think about your sister, or her children, or how much they're hurting. You're just trying to placate me so I'll let you seduce me, but it's not going to happen. I've been an idiot, but I won't be one any longer."

Blue eyes shot fire at her. "No. Damn it. That's not the way it is."

"Oh, really?" she asked with as much sarcasm as she could put into the two words. "Then how is it? Are you going to deny that you want me?"

His grip on her tightened. "Hell, no. I want you so much that I spend most of the time when I'm with you damned uncomfortable in my pants, but that isn't why I apologized."

"Then why?"

"Because I was wrong. Because I can't stand hurting you. Because your opinion matters to me and I'm sorry I went ballistic on you. Truly, deeply sorry. Please, honey, don't walk away from me."

"Let me go." She said it quietly, but he listened this time.

He released her with obvious reluctance. "Come back and sit down. Please," he said again. "We'll talk this out."

CHAPTER NINE

CARLENE shook her head. "Talk what out? You've already informed me that I have nothing to say in this matter. I can't imagine what we've got to discuss."

Win surprised her by smiling, though it looked ragged around the edges. "Honey, the day you have nothing to say about something is the day I'll be rushing you to the emergency room worried about the condition of your vocal cords. Besides, I *also* said your opinion matters to me."

"If I say something you don't like, are you going to yell at me again?" she demanded quietly.

"No," he put up his hand. "Scouts' honor."

Some of the tension drained from her. If he was willing to talk rationally, then she could too. She returned to her seat near the fountain. Win joined her. She waited in silence, sipping at her ice tea. If he thought she was going to reopen the subject after the way he'd shot her down, he didn't know her very well.

Win took a deep breath and let it out slowly. Then

he turned to her. "I've been protecting my baby sister since my mom brought her home from the hospital when I was five years old. I'm a little sensitive when I think someone else is criticizing her, I guess."

Carlene raised her brows. "You don't say?"

Win frowned. "Look, I'm trying to explain and I've already said I was sorry. Cut me a little slack."

He'd done more than apologize. He'd begged. She could do as he asked.

"You don't explain yourself very often, do you?" she asked.

"No. I don't." He ran his fingers through his black hair. "What I'm trying to say is that I understand your concerns. I know the kids miss her. It scares the hell out of me that she left them here. I don't know what's going on with her and Mark."

"You're afraid that she's like your mother and that's why you overreacted when I expressed my concern."

Once she'd said the words, Carlene waited, barely breathing, to see how Win would react to them.

He rubbed a hand across his eyes. "Yes."

The word was a bare whisper of sound.

"Listen to me, Win. Leah is not your mother. Whatever is going on in her head right now must be pretty devastating, or she wouldn't have left her children."

His eyes pleaded with her. "How do you know? You've never even met her."

"Shelly and Jared are too well adjusted and loving

for her to be anything but a terrific mother. Win, you do know her and you know she isn't like your mom."

"You're right, but then what is the point of the things you said earlier?"

She knew her smile was tinged with exasperation. He really didn't get it. "The point of what I was trying to say is that I think you should tell your sister to come back or call her husband. Shelly and Jared need their parents."

"I don't want to call Mark."

"Why?" she asked.

"I don't think he knows that Leah left the kids with me. If I call him, it could cause problems in their marriage," Win said.

"It sounds like there are already problems, or Leah wouldn't be having the crisis she's having right now."

Win nodded. "I know, but if she has some time alone, maybe she'll get over wanting to leave him. She doesn't need me calling him and making things worse."

"You really are afraid that she's like your mom, aren't you? Win, you've got to accept that if Leah is thinking about leaving Mark, she's got solid reasons. She's too committed a parent to divorce him on a whim and I think deep down you know that."

Win's expression relaxed a little. "Yes. I do know that. Hell, I don't even know if she's thinking about divorce. She just told me she needed some time to think. When I talked to her on the phone the other day, I could tell that she misses the kids as much as they miss her. I don't know what's going on."

Carlene understood Win's quandary. He didn't want to cause more ripples in a marriage that might already be on the brink and he was confused by his sister's behavior. From everything he'd said and the impression Carlene got from others, it was entirely out of character.

"Do you have a phone number for her for emergencies?" she asked Win.

"Yes. She really is a good mother, Carlene."

"I believe you. She isn't going to mind you calling her and telling her that her children need her. Maybe that's something *she* needs to hear right now."

He stood up. "You're right. Guess I'll go call her before it gets too late."

Carlene watched him go, her heart aching for the pain both he and Leah were suffering right now. Carlene had no doubt that Leah was just as terrified as Win that she was like their mother.

Carlene carried the ice tea glasses into the kitchen and wondered if Win would come looking for her after he had spoken to Leah. Would he understand that Carlene was anxious to know the outcome of the telephone conversation?

More importantly, would he want to share it with her as a man shared important things with a woman who was more than just an employee?

* * *

Win sat down in his chair and stared at the number he'd written on a slip of paper by the phone. Carlene was right. He knew it. He had to call Leah. If for nothing else, but to make sure that she was okay. He inhaled deeply, trying to gather his thoughts. He wanted to express his concern for the kids without making Leah feel worse than she already did. It wasn't going to be easy.

He wished that he'd shown the same forethought before running off at the mouth at Carlene. He'd hurt her. When she went running from the courtyard, he'd been filled with fear. Part of him had known that if he let her go without making things right, he would lose his chance with her. She was already fighting a relationship with him for all she was worth.

His idiotic comment that she was no more than an employee would give her ammunition in the war she waged against becoming his lover. He couldn't risk losing her. So he had done something he rarely did— apologized. Then he'd tried to explain. That hadn't been easy. He didn't like analyzing his emotions and he hated talking about the past, but she needed to understand why he'd been so defensive.

He didn't know if she forgave him completely, but she had listened. She hadn't pouted and she'd comforted him.

She had been right. He was afraid that Leah was turning out like their mother. Carlene's assertion that if his sister was considering ending her marriage, she'd have a darn good reason, rang true. Leah loved Mark. She loved her kids and she wasn't just bored. Something was going on. Something serious. Win just wished he knew what it was.

He picked up the phone and dialed.

Carlene checked the clock on the bedside table for the third time in fifteen minutes. She had left her door cracked open so that Win wouldn't assume she was asleep, but an hour had passed and he still hadn't come. Could his conversation with Leah have lasted this long? Doubt gnawed at her. Maybe he didn't see Carlene as someone with whom he could or should share his family's problems.

She'd pinned her hopes on the fact that he apologized for his outburst. She had believed he was truly sorry for hurting her, for implying she had no place in his life outside that of employee and perhaps casual bed partner.

The soft knock sent hope surging through her. Jumping up off the bed, she called, "Come in."

Win pushed the door open wider and stepped inside. His face wore a more relaxed expression than she'd seen all evening. He smiled. "Hi. Mind if I come in and talk for a while?"

Win in an asking mood pushed her a little off center.

She indicated the chair and ottoman in the corner. "Uh, take a seat."

He pulled the ottoman away from the chair and straddled it, putting his hands on his knees.

She edged around him and sat on the chair. "So how did the call to your sister go?" she asked, impatient to hear the details.

"You were right. She needed to hear that the kids missed her. She'd gotten some crazy ideas in her head."

"Like what?" Carlene asked.

"Like her husband and children didn't really need her. That she was just a glorified housekeeper and nanny. Crazy stuff like that."

"She must really be hurting."

Win's expression turned to one of concern. "Yeah. I think she is. She and Mark need to talk. I told her that."

"You did?" Carlene couldn't hide the surprise in her voice. Win was not what one would consider a modern male with sensitivity training.

"Yeah, I did. You don't have to be a pop psychologist to know that a married couple needs to talk out their problems," he said, indicating he had guessed her thoughts.

She smiled. "No. You don't. When is she coming back?"

"It could be as early as tomorrow. I told her not to rush, but that the kids would be real happy when she got here."

He had said it just right. "You're a nice man, Win."

"If you believe that, why won't you go to bed with me?"

After she recovered from the shock of his blunt query, Carlene frowned. "Don't tell me that tactless questions like that have gotten you past first base before."

Win grinned. "I haven't dated all that many women, but the ones I did didn't seem to be bothered by my 'lack of tact'."

Irritation at the mention of women in Win's past made Carlene reckless. "What about your ex-wife? Did she have a problem with your lack of tact?"

She regretted the words the moment they left her mouth. She wished with all her heart she could call them back when Win's expression of amused tolerance turned cold and stony. Darn it.

When would she learn to control her tongue? "I'm sorry I asked that."

"Why? Don't you want an answer?" His voice held no inflection, as if the discussion had no importance for him. His eyes told another story.

"I don't want you to feel obligated to tell me anything you don't want to." Of course she wanted to know about his ex-wife. What woman in Carlene's position wouldn't want to know about the one female that Win had been willing to take the risk of marriage on?

He contemplated her answer for several long seconds. She began to fidget, shifting nervously in her chair. Resting his elbows on his thighs, he leaned forward and examined her eyes.

Like a jackrabbit who sensed the presence of a predator, her entire body went still. What was he thinking? He kept his gaze fixed on her so long that the sound of his voice surprised her when he spoke.

"By the time she left me, Rachel let me know that she pretty much hated everything about me, my lack of tact included."

Impossible. No woman could hate everything about this man. He had too much loyalty, too much honor; too much of what made a man a good man.

She instinctively shook her head. "She must have been crazy."

He didn't smile. He didn't even blink. "Not crazy. Determined. She wanted out of this little hole-in-the-wall town and she thought I was her ticket out of here."

Carlene's chest tightened. "I don't understand."

"It's simple. Rachel married me, believing she could convince me to sell the ranch and stake her life in the big city. When she discovered that I had no desire to uproot Leah's new life, or my own, Rachel made it clear that she found me lacking in just about everything. I wore my boots too scuffed and my hair too long. According to her, I was rude and uncouth. Toward the end, she couldn't even stand me touching her at night. Not that I wanted to all that much. The town was just starting to attract a certain clientele for winter sports. She hitched her star to one of their hangers-on and left Sunshine Springs behind just like she wanted."

Pain for Win's loss ripped through Carlene. His marriage sounded more like a civil war.

"How long were you married?" She almost asked how long he'd had to endure Rachel.

"Less than two years."

"All of that happened in less than two years?" She couldn't keep the disbelief from her voice.

His grim features relaxed into a smile. "Yeah. One thing you can say for me, when I screw up, I do it fast and well."

Carlene could not digest his attitude. "You didn't screw up. You married her believing she wanted the same things from life that you did. It's hardly your fault she lied to you. You must have loved her very much."

"I married her because I wanted a woman's touch raising Leah and because I was tired of walking around with a perpetual hard-on. I told you, she made me wait for sex until we got married. I thought she was just an old-fashioned girl. Hell, she wasn't even a virgin."

The self-disgust in Win's voice tore at Carlene's defenses. "Win, there's nothing wrong with your wanting a woman to help Leah through the difficult years of adolescence. It's unfortunate that Rachel wasn't interested in making you a proper wife or your sister a suitable mentor."

He stared at her as if she had just spoken in Portuguese. "Well, at least now you understand why I'm not going to jump into the trap of marriage again."

The certainty in his voice crushed the hope that

had been blossoming since Win knocked on her bedroom door. How could she prove to him that marriage didn't have to be a trap if he wouldn't take a chance on it, on her? She needed more time than a short-term affair provided to prove that she wasn't like his mother. Carlene wouldn't get bored with him after six months.

If he wouldn't risk a committed relationship with her, how could Carlene show him that she wasn't like Rachel either? She didn't want him to give up his life and his roots in the community to make her happy and she knew that she would never grow immune to his touch. She couldn't. She loved him.

There was no point in denying the truth any longer. She was crazy in love with the stubborn, sexy rancher and her life was never going to be the same.

"I understand that you got burned and that you are leery of committing yourself to another woman."

He leaned further forward until his blue eyes burned into her own. "Listen to me, Carlene. Listen close. I'm not just leery. I am not interested in marriage."

He spoke each word with precision, leaving her in no doubt that he meant exactly what he said. She would have to be a fool to believe that she might be able to change his mind. The earlier recklessness she had experienced returned. So what? Men and women had been doing foolish things in the name of love throughout history and it didn't always end in heartache. Sometimes love conquered.

She had to believe that this would be one of those times. She couldn't accept the alternative—a future without Win.

She reached out and wrapped her fingers around one of his fists. "But, you are interested in me."

He closed his eyes, his expression that of a man in pain. "Yes, honey. I want you so much it's killing me."

She believed him.

Reaching out with her other hand, she traced the line of his jaw. "Where will we end up in that whole range of possibilities between a one-night stand and marriage that you told me about?"

His eyes flew open and she felt his muscles go battle-ready under her fingertips. "Are you saying that you're willing to give us a try?"

How odd that he would put it in those terms. To her way of thinking, it had been Win who refused to give them a chance. He didn't see things that way. The knowledge gave her hope.

"Maybe. I can't promise anything, Win. You have to tell me where we'll fit on that spectrum of possibilities first."

He turned his face and kissed the palm of her hand that rested against his cheek. "I guess just taking it one day at a time won't work for you?"

She shook her head. "I need some assurance that I'm not simply a convenient body."

He laughed, relieving some of the pent-up tension

between them. "Honey, you are a ways from being convenient. That's for damn sure."

She didn't return his smile. She couldn't. She had to know the answer. "Then what am I?"

She was giving up her dreams to go back to teaching school for a chance with Win. A small town like Sunshine Springs was never going to hire an ex-bartender who was living with her lover to teach their children. She could practice discretion, she supposed, but doubted that would last very long. Besides, she didn't want to hide her love for Win from the rest of the world. She had the feeling that he needed her public commitment as much as she needed to know where she stood with him.

"You're my woman."

She digested that. "For how long?"

His eyes widened in shock. "You want me to put a time limit on our relationship?"

"No."

"Then what do you want?" Frustration radiated off him in waves.

What did she want? Some sort of commitment. A promise, but not marriage. She didn't know. "You're the one that said there's all sorts of ground between a one-night stand and marriage. I just want to know what ground we're talking about. Is that so much to ask?"

"There *is* a lot of ground between the two. I've just

never had to define it before," he said with exasperation.

Dread snaked through her. She pulled her hands from him and scooted back in the large chair. "Have you had a lot of situations where you might have had to, but they didn't ask?"

If she sounded confused, that was only fair. After all, she *felt* confused.

"No! I told you. There haven't been *that* many women."

"Believe it or not, your attitude is not helping to set my mind at ease," she replied, her own frustration lacing her words.

He smiled ruefully. "Look, honey, I don't have a string of lovers in my past. It's been so long since my last date that Shorty was starting to get worried."

Somewhat mollified, she nodded. "Okay, then. I can see that defining what our relationship is might be a little difficult for you. You obviously need some time to think about it."

He swore. "You aren't going to let me make love to you tonight, are you?"

She stood and indicated the door with her hand. "You need time and I'm willing to give it to you. Goodnight, Win. Go get some sleep."

He didn't go. He stood too and towered over her, his entire body emanating male desire. He fixed her with a piercing blue gaze and settled his hands on her shoulders, the heat of his fingers burning through the cloth of her shirt.

"What I need right now, honey, is you. The question is, are you ready to put me out of my misery?"

CHAPTER TEN

CARLENE shivered at the suppressed desire in Win's voice.

Was she willing to put him out of his misery? Was she willing to risk letting him make love to her without defining their relationship?

His face took on a serious, almost feral, expression. "I don't know the *words* for what we have, but I can show you, if you'll let me."

She couldn't speak. She wanted him so much and suddenly the idea of talking didn't hold all that much appeal. He didn't want marriage, but he did want her. Not a nameless, faceless woman to warm his body, but *her.* And she loved him.

In all her dreams of love and a family, they never included this desperate edgy feeling. This despair and pain mixed with joy and desire. They might not be married, but she knew with every pulse of her heart that she belonged to him. Completely. Her heart. Her body. Her desire. They were all his. If she refused to let him make love to her, that would not change. If he made love to her tonight and then walked away tomorrow, that still wouldn't change the truth of her love.

She loved him.

She needed him.

She *wanted* him.

His thumbs brushed the sensitive skin of her neck up to the underside of her chin. "Please. Let me make you mine tonight."

For the second time that night, her proud, arrogant cowboy was reduced to pleading with her.

She reached up and curled her fingers over his wrists, awed by the strength that held her so gently. "Yes, Win."

His eyes turned stormy blue and his nostrils contracted. He didn't waste time asking if she were sure or saying anything else at all. He closed the distance between their mouths and locked his over hers in a possessive kiss that shook her to her toes. Flicking his tongue over the seam of her lips, he silently demanded entry into her mouth.

She gave it without so much as a thought.

She expected him to sweep her mouth with branding passion, but, from the moment he entered her mouth, his kiss gentled. He explored her with lazy thoroughness letting her adjust to his possession while she relearned his taste.

Wanting more, but not knowing how to get it, she

released his wrists and tunneled her fingers into the black silk of his hair. She tugged against his head while trying to press her body against his. The hold on her shoulders prevented her. She moaned in protest.

Now that she'd decided to make love to Win, she wanted it all. Immediately.

He refused to be rushed and kept going with that slow, tantalizing kiss. Heavens, the man knew how to use his mouth to advantage. Her nipples grew tight and aching, though he hadn't so much as touched them. The confines of her bra and shirt seemed too much all of a sudden. She wanted them off.

Now.

She tried to let Win know without breaking that incredible kiss. She squirmed. She made needy little sounds low in her throat, but she couldn't make herself break contact with his lips. Maybe if she touched him, he'd get the idea.

Reluctantly, she slid her fingers from his hair; mourning the loss of one erotic touch even as she lowered her hands to grasp his shirt near the waist-band of his jeans. She tugged until she could get her hands under the hem. She brushed his stomach and the muscles under her fingers tightened convulsively.

Win growled and let go of her shoulders to yank her closer, trapping her hands between their bodies. The relief of having her breasts crushed against the work-hardened muscles of his chest was short-lived. It just wasn't enough.

She wanted skin on skin, but couldn't even move her hands against the bare skin of belly, he held her so tight.

She forced herself to tear her mouth from his. "Please, Win. I need… I want…" She couldn't make herself say it.

She'd never made love with a man. Her experiences with Win were the closest she'd ever come and she didn't know how to tell him she wanted him to touch her body.

He rocked against her, sending jolts of pleasure rocketing through her feminine core. "What do you want, baby? Tell me."

"I can't," she wailed.

He let his hands slide down to cup her bottom and squeezed.

Oh, my goodness, that felt good.

"Sure you can, honey. Tell me what you want."

She shook her head, but he ignored the refusal and just kept tormenting her with almost touches. He'd press his erection against the juncture of her thighs and then pull back. One erotic squeeze of her bottom and then his hands would move back up to knead her back. All the while he kept her hands trapped against heated, tantalizing flesh.

"I want you to touch me like you did in the courtyard," she finally blurted out when she could take no more of his teasing. Once she got started, she couldn't stop. "I want you to take off my top and my bra and touch my breasts. With your hands and your mouth.

I want you touch me between my legs. Only this time, I won't make you stop. I want to touch you too."

She brushed her thumbs up and down, moving them as much as the tight position they were in would allow. His arms tightened around her and he groaned.

"That's good because I want to do all those things and more."

More? What more? She almost asked him, but decided she probably wasn't prepared for the answer. She'd let him show her. *"Then do it,"* she all but shouted.

He chuckled. "You'd better keep it down, honey."

She stifled a scream of mounting frustration.

And then she forgot her frustration as Win pulled away and started undressing her. He tugged off her top, pulling it over her head and letting it fall to the floor.

When he'd looked at her before, there had only been the illumination of moonlight. Now they were in her room with both the overhead light and the lamp on. Embarrassment heated her skin. She wanted his touch, but she didn't want him looking at her. She crossed her arms over her chest and gazed fixedly at the black T-shirt covering his torso.

"Look at me, baby." The words were spoken soft and low, but held such an unmistakable air of authority that she raised her head.

His eyes were midnight blue pools of wanting. "I want to see you. Will you let me?"

She nodded her head, but still didn't move her arms.

He waited.

She chewed on her lip. "Could we turn off the lights?"

He shook his head, but said, "I'll compromise."

And he walked over to flip down the switch for the overhead light, leaving the room bathed in the soft yellow glow from the reading lamp by the bed.

Then he waited. Right where he was. On the other side of the room and somehow the distance between them gave her the courage to lower her arms.

His focus did not at first waver from her face and she was grateful. "Are you okay?"

She nodded, mute.

"Good." Then he let his gaze slide down and she felt as if he were touching her breasts with his fingertips.

Her nipples, already tight, puckered further against the lace of her bra.

"Take it off," he demanded in a guttural voice.

Taking a deep breath, she reached behind and unhooked the clasp of her bra. Then, shrugging her shoulders, she let it fall to the carpet with her shirt.

His breathing turned shallow and raspy. "I'm really glad you didn't listen to your mom."

For a minute his words confused her and then she remembered telling him about her mom suggesting a breast reduction. "They're not *that* big." And they weren't. Certainly not large enough to justify surgery, even if she'd agreed with her mom.

"They're perfect."

She felt her mouth tip in a smile and for the first time she was glad her body was built like a centerfold instead of a schoolmarm. "Thank you."

His hands fisted and then relaxed at his side as if he wanted to reach out and touch her, but had stopped himself.

"Your turn. Take off your T-shirt." She waited to see if he would comply.

He did. With a sexy smile that made her toes curl into the carpet. He did it slowly, revealing an inch of his rock-hard chest at a time until he finally pulled the black knit over his head and tossed it aside. The partial striptease had a direct effect on the spot between her legs and she could *feel* herself growing wetter.

"Now your pants," he said.

She thought about refusing, unsure if she could strip for him, but then realized that he would remove his too and the anticipation of watching such a spectacle made up her mind for her. She unsnapped her jeans and following his lead, unzipped her fly one little centimeter at a time. By the time she had the zipper down and had started pushing the waistband over her hips, Win had a fine sheen of sweat on his body.

He swallowed convulsively as she pushed the colored denim completely down her legs and kicked it away. She stood naked except for the silky panties covering her most feminine place. Could he see how wet they were?

"Now you."

He didn't make her say it again, or explain what she meant. He had to take off his boots first. Then his socks. The only sound in the room was their breathing as he unbuttoned his placket one brass button at a time until he could pull the worn blue denim completely off. He wore knit boxers that fit like a second skin, outlining the awesome length and breadth of his erection.

She knew she didn't have a lot of experience with men, had never actually seen a man's engorged penis up close, but he looked big. Really big. Being inquisitive by nature, she'd seen pictures and none of them had prepared her for Win in the flesh.

She swallowed and then licked her lips, unable to break her gaze away from his manhood.

Laughter rumbled in his chest. "You look like you're staring down a bobcat, hoping it won't attack, baby."

The sound of his voice broke her reverie and she looked up to meet amused blue eyes. "I sort of feel like it, if you want the truth."

All amusement melted from his expression. "I'm not going to hurt you, baby." Then he grimaced. "At least no more than absolutely necessary. I've heard it isn't a picnic the first time for a woman."

"You've never made love to a virgin before?" Only the Lord knew why, but that knowledge comforted her.

"No, but I'll take care of you. I promise."

"I believe you, Win. I trust you."

He nodded. "Good." Then he smiled. "Enough to take off those sexy little panties?"

Her hands shook as she gave him her answer with action. Hooking her thumbs in the side elastic, she shimmied the silk down her hips until it slipped off and landed in a puddle at her feet. She stepped out of it.

He didn't wait for her to remind him it was his turn before following suit. Once his boxers were off, his erection jutted out from his body in imposing, bold glory. Bending down, he drew a foil packet from the pocket of his jeans and she wanted to tell him not to bother, but the dream for marriage and a family was hers. He didn't share it and for just a moment pain cut through her excitement.

Then he ripped open the packet and slid the protection over his hardness, bringing her attention back to his manhood. Somehow *that* was supposed to fit inside of her. She didn't see how it could be possible, but she'd read romance novels. She wasn't a complete innocent. Women stretched to accommodate their lovers, or so she'd read. She sure hoped that part of the romance wasn't fantasy.

He put his hand out. "Come here, baby."

She knew what he was asking. He wanted her to trust him. To come to him and show him that she knew she belonged to him. The message was in his eyes as his hand reached toward her. Without conscious volition, her feet started to move toward him, taking the rest of her body with them.

When she reached him, he bent down and kissed her lips with surprising force.

"You belong to me."

"Yes." She couldn't deny it and even if she had, he would know the truth.

He swung her up into his arms, high against his chest, and carried her to the bed. "Hold my neck."

She did and he released her back in order to pull back the bedspread, blanket and sheet.

Then he laid her with infinite care onto the cool sheet of the bed. She didn't release his neck and he came down on top of her, allowing her to feel the entire length of his body against her own for a full minute before rolling to the side. She protested the lack of contact with a soft murmur that turned into a moan as his hand cupped her breast.

Then he touched her, just as he had in the courtyard, only this time she felt as if each whisper of his fingertips were a branding iron making her more completely his. His hands would not leave behind any marks, except on her heart, but she would be his all the same.

And she would make him hers. She would brand him with her touch so that he would never be able to find fulfillment with another woman.

She reached out and circled one turgid, small, male nipple. The hand on her breast tightened. Pleased with that response, she leaned forward and made the same circling motion, only this time with her tongue. He groaned and she did it again. Then, because she couldn't help herself, she took that small, hard nub into her mouth and sucked.

He shouted her name and pushed her away. "No more of that. I'm hanging on by a thread here, baby, and I can't handle any more assaults from that talented little mouth of yours."

She didn't argue, but she had every intention of assaulting him all over his body. Later. Right after she caught her breath from the feelings coursing through her as his mouth closed over her nipple. He suckled her softly at first, his hand on her other nipple, gently rolling it between thumb and forefinger. She squirmed against him and he increased the pressure of both his fingers and his mouth.

The sensation was so exquisite, so overwhelming, she didn't know if she could stand it. Her pelvis rocked off the bed, seeking, needing, wanting. *"Win."*

He sucked harder and she bit back a scream. Then his hand was no longer on her breast, but had slid down her body to claim her feminine flesh. He continued the suckling of her nipple while slipping one hard finger between the folds of her tender flesh. She pushed against that invading finger, until it slid into her wet heat.

Oh, my goodness. Oh, wow. "Win. That's too... It's way more... I can't..." She couldn't finish a sentence to save her life.

It just felt so good. He slid in and out of her tight

channel, stretching the previously untouched flesh, and she almost cried from the wonder of it. Then his thumb pressed between her lips at their apex and made a slow circle around the aroused bud there. She arched off the bed, the sensation so strong that she shook with it.

And a delicious feeling began to throb within her. She felt as if nerve endings attached to her feminine core were radiating outward with a pleasure she'd never known. "Oh, please, oh, please, oh, please. Don't stop. Win. Just don't stop."

And then she was convulsing and crying and shuddering and he wasn't stopping, even when she begged him. Even when it was so intense she thought she'd die from it and then he moved down her body until his mouth was where his thumb had been and he slipped two fingers inside of her. And it felt too tight, but she couldn't make herself say so because his tongue and teeth were touching her intimately and it had begun all over again. This time her body went rigid and then it shook, and shook, and shook. Tears spilled over from her eyes, their damp warmth making tracks down her temples into her hair.

Then she went limp. Unbelievably, bonelessly limp.

He swarmed up her body, laying on top of her, dominating her flesh, though he hadn't yet entered her. His mouth rocked over hers in a claiming kiss, his tongue thrusting inside. She tasted herself and she should have found that distasteful, but she didn't.

She reveled in the carnality of his kiss, in the heated eroticism of his tongue in her mouth.

Then she felt him at the opening of her femininity. The broad head of his penis pushing against her, inexorably. He would take her now and she would welcome him and as he marked her with his body's possession, she would mark him with hers.

It hurt.

It stretched.

"Do you want me to stop?" His voice shook with strain.

"No. Please, Win. Make me yours."

And he did, with one hard, painful thrust. She was so slick from her two orgasms that her body let him in, but she felt stretched to the limit and she lay under him in a state of semi-shock.

He stilled and kissed her again. Soft, comforting kisses. She could feel his entire body tremble from the strain of not moving and yet his kisses held only patient reassurance.

She loved him so much in that moment, the emotion nearly exploded from her chest. She shifted up, just a little bit, to show him that he could move.

He did. Gently stroking in and out. She moaned in a combination of pain and pleasure. His control broke and he thrust in and out of her with hard, decisive thrusts. She cried out, startled by the pain. He stopped and would have drawn out, but she locked her legs around his hips and held him tight.

"No. Don't stop."

The new position opened her more fully to him and relieved some of the pressure between her legs. He must have felt the way her feminine flesh softened around him because he started thrusting again and this time although there was still some discomfort, it felt good too.

He clamped his mouth back over hers and when he came, she absorbed his masculine shout of pleasure. He held her tightly for several minutes after he found his release and then rolled off of her and stood.

He looked down at her thighs. "You bled."

She could see the evidence on him. "A little."

"I'll take care of you." Then he disappeared into the bathroom.

She heard water running and he reappeared a few minutes later, a damp washcloth in his hand. He used it to wash between her thighs and the warmth soothed her flesh. He took it back into the bathroom and then returned to slide into the bed next to her.

She went into his arms without protest, needing the assurance of his touch after the overwhelming events of the night.

Win held Carlene's soft, warm body against his and wondered how in the hell she expected him to define what they'd just done. She'd let him make love to her, had in fact given herself with a sweet generosity that still had him reeling, but he knew she expected him to tell her where their relationship fit between a one-night stand and an affair.

He didn't have the words. Not now. Not when he felt as if his entire world had just been thrust into a new dimension. One that included the knowledge that no other man must ever see Carlene as Win had seen her tonight. All passion and promise.

Tensed for a confrontation, it took him a moment to realize that Carlene was already dozing. Her body lay curled against his in trusting relaxation. She'd tucked her knee between his legs and her hand rested on his chest while she used his shoulder for a pillow, cuddling him as if she'd done it all her life...or would willingly do it for the remainder of his.

Now that he knew about her plans to get back into teaching, his assumption that she was the type of woman to move on didn't hold water. The way she talked, Carlene planned to hang around Sunshine Springs indefinitely. Her commitment to the community was definite.

Was she as committed to him? More importantly, could her commitment to him last for a lifetime?

The questions spinning through his head were interrupted when his beeper went off. The mare must have gone into labor. He gently eased out from Carlene's clinging embrace, taking care not to wake her. He dressed quietly and turned off the lamp before tiptoeing from the room, waiting to put on his boots until he reached outside.

CHAPTER ELEVEN

THE next afternoon, Carlene had just gotten Shelly and Jared down for a nap when the doorbell rang.

She hadn't seen Win all day, but he'd called…just to see how she was. To tell her thank you for last night in a low, gravelly voice that made her wish he were with her in person—and naked. He couldn't leave the stable and things sounded too tense down there for her to offer to bring the kids down to see the horses as she wanted to. With Lonny gone, Win and Shorty had their hands full.

One of the ranch hands had taken food down to the stables at lunchtime and Carlene would have offered to do it, but she didn't want the first time she saw Win after last night to be in front of an audience.

She rushed through the courtyard now to answer the door, wondering who it could be. She didn't think that Leah would bother to ring. Besides, Win wasn't expecting her for another day. Grant had said something about stopping by, but wouldn't he have gone straight down to the stable?

She quit her useless speculation and hurried to the door, wanting to open it before the visitor rang the bell again and perhaps woke one of the children. Carlene swung the door open and stared in open-mouthed amazement at the person standing on the other side.

Zoe Strickland smiled. "Hi. Grant's down at the stable picking Win's brain. I thought I'd come up and say hello to Shelly and Jared."

Carlene forced her mouth to close and then form a somewhat strained smile of greeting. She stepped away from the door. "Come in. Um...the children just went down for their nap. I'm sorry, but I'd prefer not to wake them if you don't mind."

Zoe smiled again. "Of course. Maybe if you're not too busy, we could have some coffee, or something."

Zoe impressed her. A lot. If she was in Zoe's place and someone had tried to seduce Win, she'd want to scratch the woman's eyes out, not invite her to the wedding or drink coffee with her. "Sure. How about iced coffee in the courtyard?"

"That sounds great." Zoe followed Carlene down the hall and out into the courtyard.

"Why don't you wait here while I get the drinks?" Carlene asked. She needed a few moments alone to collect herself.

When she returned, Carlene found Zoe playing

idly with the children's boats in the fountain. Zoe turned when Carlene set the tray down on the wrought iron table. "Shelly and Jared are really special."

"Yes. They are," Carlene agreed.

Zoe sat down. "Leah must be feeling pretty stressed to have left them with Win. I guess you're helping him out?"

Carlene didn't want to gossip, but she didn't see any harm in telling Zoe the circumstances surrounding her watching Leah's children. "Win hired me as his cook and housekeeper a couple of weeks before Leah dropped by with Shelly and Jared. He asked me to add nanny duties to my job description, so here I am."

Zoe smiled. "I don't know Win nearly as well as I know Leah, but I'd say he doesn't ask for much. I'll bet it came out more a command."

Carlene smiled. "You could say that."

"I didn't realize that you wanted to quit your job as a bartender," Zoe said neutrally.

"It didn't fit anymore." Carlene thought of her plans, plans that would go up in smoke if she began an affair with Win, and sighed. She wasn't sure those plans were as important as they once were. When she put them on the scales with a possible future with Win, they didn't weigh as heavily as she thought they would.

Zoe looked at her curiously. "Do you regret it? I imagine you don't make near the money as a house-keeper that you did tending bar."

Carlene smiled wryly. "You're right, but it pays the bills and, no, I don't regret quitting. You're going to find this hard to believe, but working at the Dry Gulch really didn't fit my temperament."

Zoe nodded, but didn't say anything. She relaxed against her chair and took another sip of her drink. "This feels nice. Things have been hectic with Grant making the changes at the ranch and my class's preparations for the spring program at school."

Carlene felt a stab of envy at Zoe's mention of the school program. "Zoe…" She let her words trail off.

Zoe turned her head slightly. "Yes?"

"I just wanted to say that I'm sorry about Grant. I really didn't mean to cause any problems for you two."

Zoe's look was filled with understanding. "I believe you. I think that Grant really deserves the most credit for the snafu, if you want my opinion."

"He gave me roses, I assumed he—"

Zoe nodded. "Exactly. A man shouldn't give flowers to one woman when he wants another."

The words were so like some that Carlene had said to Grant on the fateful second date that she felt an affinity with Zoe. "Precisely."

Seconds ticked by as the two women sat in companionable silence.

Carlene took a deep breath and spoke again. "But I still want you to know that if I had realized you and Grant were a couple, I would never have shown up at his house like that."

Zoe met Carlene's gaze, her expression intent. "I know that, Carlene. I'll admit that I didn't at first, but later I realized that you weren't trying to hurt me, or Grant."

"Thank you. You can't know what a relief that is for me."

Zoe smiled. "I'm glad."

Carlene returned the smile, feeling warm. Amazing as it might seem, she believed she was making a new friend.

Win came out of the stable, dog tired, hungry and smelling like a horse. He'd spent the good part of last night and today with not one, but two foaling mares. Then Grant Strickland had come by and he'd had to have Joe give the other rancher the grand tour. But that wasn't what had him in a dreadful mood and had his insides clenching. It was something Grant had said.

They'd been standing in the stable outside the mare's stall and Grant had asked, "How is Carlene working out as your housekeeper?"

"Damn fine."

Grant nodded. "I can see that. To tell the truth, once I got to know her some, I had a hard time seeing her working as a cocktail waitress at the Dry Gulch."

Win couldn't see it himself, so he grunted in agreement.

Grant smiled, kind of with a wince. "Wish she'd gotten her job here a few months earlier though."

"Why's that?"

"I almost caked it up with Zoe over Carlene and I think I hurt her feelings too."

"What are you talking about?"

"I asked Carlene out, thinking I could use her to keep my distance from Zoe."

"She didn't tell me you two had dated."

"Don't know why she would. It wasn't exactly a big romance. One failed date and one failed seduction attempt." A look of guilt washed over Grant's features, as if the man regretted saying what he had.

Win felt his entire body tense. "You tried to seduce Carlene?"

Grant seemed to realize all at once that Win was more interested than an employer should be. "Uh...not exactly. Look, nothing came of it."

But Win saw something in the other man's eyes and he asked, "She tried to seduce you?" not believing it, but letting the words come out anyway.

"Forget what I said, Win. Carlene's a nice woman."

"Yes, she is. She's also mine." So much for being discreet, but he felt a very primitive, undeniable need to stake his claim.

Grant smiled, this time the look one of commiseration. "I get that. I'd build a fence around Zoe if she'd let me."

Win felt the same way and laughed, but something inside felt wrong. He couldn't get the thought out of his head that his innocent Carlene had tried to seduce the man in front of him. Another part of his brain denied the possibility vehemently. She would never have gone after Grant like that.

She wasn't the type and she'd guarded her innocence too damn strictly.

Carlene would have to be in love to give herself to a man and she'd given herself to Win. He had no doubts about her feelings for him.

Any more than he could doubt his feelings for her. Not any longer.

The sound of a vehicle on the drive brought his attention back to the present and he veered away from the back entrance to his house. Walking around the front, he saw Leah's car come into view.

She pulled up next to Carlene's stylish compact. Win couldn't help comparing his sister's family sedan to Carlene's bright red sporty coupé. There were a lot of other differences between the two women as well, but not where it counted. They both had integrity and they were both willing to sacrifice for the people they loved. He'd seen Leah do it time and again in her marriage and hadn't Carlene left her hometown to make life easier on her folks? They had something else in common too.

He loved them.

He'd reached that conclusion about three o'clock this morning as he soothed a hurting mare. He had not meant to love the feisty little brunette keeping house for him, but he didn't have a choice. After making love to her last night, he couldn't lie to himself about it either. They hadn't shared sex; they'd shared themselves. He wanted Carlene, but more importantly, he needed her. She brought sunshine into his life, as well as a passion he wanted to grow old with.

She wasn't anything like his mother. No more than Leah was. Carlene wouldn't grow bored with him and just move on. And unlike Rachel, Carlene wanted the same life that he did. A settled life, right here in Sunshine Springs.

Leah got out of her car. She looked exactly as Win had felt walking out of the stable a few minutes ago. Pain lanced through him at the knowledge that she'd gotten to that point because of her emotional turmoil, not something as simple as a birthing mare.

"How you holding up, baby-girl?" he asked, using the childhood nickname.

Her eyes filled with tears and she rushed into his arms. He closed them around her, wishing he could protect her with his love and strength, but knowing that this time all he could do was be there for her.

She didn't say anything. She just held on and cried for about five minutes. Finally, the storm of weeping passed. She pulled back from his arms. "I suppose you want an explanation?"

He shook his head. "No. I just want you to be happy."

She gave a small, watery smile. "Thank you. I don't think I'm ready to talk about it to anyone just yet."

He understood. Sometimes things needed to settle

before you could talk them out. "You ready to see the kids now?"

Her eyes lit up. "I'm dying to see them. I don't know what I was thinking, leaving them behind while I tried to figure out my future. They are my future and any decisions I make have to include their well-being."

Win's heart warmed at her words. He put his hand out and she placed hers in it. "Come on. I know two little kids that are gonna be real happy to see you. I want you to meet my new housekeeper, too. She's been helping me take care of the kids."

Leah stayed close as he led her into the house, her excitement at the prospect of seeing Shelly and Jared a palpable presence in the air around them. "What's her name? Maybe I know her."

"Carlene Daniels, but that may change soon."

He couldn't believe he was thinking about getting married again. After spending the night mulling over his newfound love and Carlene's request for him to define their relationship, he'd realized the only definition he'd been comfortable with had been one that included commitment. Permanent commitment.

He wondered how she'd react to the news. Probably totally differently than he expected. The woman was not exactly predictable.

Leah stopped dead still. "Who?"

"Carlene Daniels."

"The woman who used to be a bartender at the Dry Gulch?"

"Yes, but she's mine now."

Leah's eyes widened. "Yours?"

"My housekeeper." Other claims could wait until Carlene understood what they were.

"Oh, wow. And she's watching the kids?"

"Yeah. She did real good with them too."

"I…um…I wouldn't have expected that."

"You know Carlene?"

"Not personally, no. I just…I've heard of her. From Zoe."

"What did you hear?"

"Nothing important."

Leah tried to walk away, but Win wasn't letting her. He hugged her to him, refusing to go anywhere. "What do you know about Carlene?"

"Just she and Grant had a thing."

"One date and a failed seduction hardly makes a 'thing'," he said, borrowing Grant's words from earlier.

"So, you do know about it?" She laughed. "I guess Carlene is a lot less racy than I was led to believe if you've got her watching my children. I know how protective you are."

"Carlene is as far from racy as it's possible to get." The woman had been a virgin until last night.

"Her attempt at seduction must have been a one-time deal. She must have really been taken with Grant, I mean…" Leah's words trailed off as she realized she said too much. "I mean obviously it wasn't a big romance or anything."

But Win wasn't listening.

He was picturing Carlene with Grant and it was making him sick. "Let's go see the kids," he managed to force out.

Damn...after everything, was Carlene like his mom and Rachel after all?

He led Leah into the kitchen, then stopped and stared. Carlene sat in the middle of the floor, surrounded by dry pasta of every shape and size. Shelly and Jared perched beside her. It was Shelly wearing the apron this time.

She looked up and grinned. "Hi, Uncle Win. Me and Jared wanted to make sgetti."

"I's making noodles," chimed in Jared.

Carlene looked up at Win, her rueful smile and innocent eyes belying his sister's accusations. He saw knowledge of what they'd shared last night there too and it made him want to grab her and kiss her, ignoring his worries about what Grant had been to her. "I walked in here after putting a load of laundry in the washer and found Jared and Shelly practically buried beneath the pile of pasta. Defeated by their superior wit and speed, I decided to join them."

He felt himself smile in response to her teasing.

Leah laughed out loud. "Oh, you little hooligans!"

Before he could formally introduce Carlene and Leah, exuberant whoops sounded and the kids launched themselves off the floor and at their mother.

Leah dropped to her knees and gathered her children to her. She hugged them fiercely, whispering silly words of love and how much she had missed them.

Shelly pulled back from her mother's arms. "Mama."

Leah smiled. "Yes, dolly-girl?"

"I missed you."

"I missed you, too." Tears streaked down Leah's face, but she was all smiles as the kids dragged her to the courtyard to show her their toy sailboats in the fountain.

Carlene pulled out the broom and started sweeping up the pasta mess on the floor. "Your sister seems happy to be back with her children."

"She is, almost as happy as I'm going to be getting you all to myself again."

Carlene blushed. "Me too."

He pulled her to him for a quick, but hard kiss.

She smiled, looking a little dazed as she went back to sweeping. "I could get used to that."

"Me kissing you?"

"In the kitchen...just like a normal couple."

"We are a couple, honey."

"Is that right?"

"Yes."

"So, that's how you decided to define our relationship, the one that falls somewhere between a one-night stand and marriage."

Win grimaced, but Carlene didn't see it. Her attention was focused on the dry noodles she was trying to sweep together into a manageable pile. But he wasn't ready to discuss the life-altering decisions he'd made in the stable.

So, even though he knew it was not the right time to be talking about this, he asked baldly, "Did you try to seduce Grant Strickland?"

He didn't need Carlene to answer him. Her look said it all. She turned pale as milk and her lips trembled. She looked guilty as hell.

Indescribable pain lanced through Win. "Tell me you didn't."

"I can't."

He spun away and stormed out of the kitchen. He had to get away from her before he said or did something he'd regret until his dying day.

She'd loved another man enough to try to seduce him, but she'd made Win beg. The fact that she had given in and let him make love to her last night only seemed to make it worse, not better. He'd thought it was something better than he'd ever known, but if the evidence before him was any indication, she was more a master game player than Rachel had ever been.

Carlene had made him beg.

Carlene moved around her bedroom, packing her things. Leah was here now. There was no reason for the housekeeper to continue staying at Win's ranch. If he'd wanted her to stay, he would have said something. Apparently what they had between them—being a couple—didn't extend to the commitment of living together, or trust. As she folded the top she'd worn the night Win took her and the children out for ice cream she considered Win's reaction to her admission regarding Grant.

He'd just walked away. There had been no opportunity to explain, no chance to tell him she was sorry. Though why she should apologize to him for something that happened before they even met stymied her. It wasn't as if she expected him to apologize for marrying Rachel.

Win had taken Leah and her children into town for an early dinner and been avoiding Carlene ever since. That said it all, didn't it?

How had he known about Grant? Had the other man told Win? Or had Leah said something? After all, she and Zoe were friends. If that were the case, Carlene wondered who else Zoe had told. Was the tale of her botched attempt at seduction all over town? Carlene wished that Zoe had warned her, but she realized that was a foolish expectation.

Zoe was a really nice woman. If she'd told Leah, she wouldn't have expected the story to spread. Probably more than most people, Carlene understood how gossip worked. Even people who cared about you, like her parents, could do their share in spreading rumor and innuendo. Silence wasn't always golden and the truth could be taken out of context.

She pulled a pair of jeans from the closet and folded them before placing them neatly into the rapidly filling suitcase. She wasn't going to cry. There was still a chance for her with Win. It wasn't as if she'd demanded marriage from him. Surely, he wouldn't balk at being her lover because of the thing with Grant.

He just needed to cool down a little. She'd seen his possessiveness. He had a streak of it about a mile wide. He'd fired a stable hand he needed very badly simply because Lonny'd made a pass at her. He would get over his anger about Grant though. He had to. She didn't think her heart would survive if Win rejected her completely.

When she was finished packing, she carried her suitcase out to her car. Win was waiting, framed by the open front door, when she turned around to go back inside.

"Leaving?"

The covered entryway threw his face into shadow and she couldn't read his expression.

"Now that Leah's here, there's no reason for me to stay the night."

He didn't say anything and she couldn't stand the distance between them. Not the emotional or the mental one. She stepped forward until she could see his face, until she was close enough to reach out and touch him. His eyes were expressionless.

She put her hand out, touching his arm—feeling

the heat of his skin like a brand on her palm. "Win, we need to talk."

"Later, not now."

A lead weight settled where her heart had once been. "When?"

"I don't know. This just isn't working." He sounded so tired, as lost as she felt.

"What isn't working? Our affair? You're saying that you don't want me anymore because of what *didn't* happen with Grant Strickland?"

Win's eyes mirrored the pain she felt, but then his gaze turned hard. "I still want you." He raked her body with his eyes. "But that'll pass once you leave."

The words stung. Did he realize he could have slapped her and it wouldn't have hurt any more? He was making it sound as if she were just a body to him and she knew she was more. She had to be more. "Do you really think you can forget me so easily?"

For a brief moment the stoicism vanished and she saw her answer. Fear and pain mirrored in his eyes, but there was also anger. "I believe I have to try. Rachel did a number on me, but she had nothing on you."

"You don't mean that."

His stoicism cracked and he glared as if he hated her. "You tried to seduce another man, but you made me beg."

"It wasn't like that.

"I was lonely…depressed…I missed my real life. Grant came along and I don't know…I guess I thought we could have something. Something more than nights spent fending off advances from drunks and carding teenagers trying to buy beer on a dare."

"You couldn't expect him to marry you."

"No, we never even talked about it."

Win said a really ugly word.

"I didn't want to talk about marriage to Grant, Win. I didn't love him!"

"Are you saying you love me?" he asked, trying to sound like his old hard self, but she heard the emotion bleeding through. The need that matched her own.

Oh, please let it match her own.

"Yes, I love you, Win, and making love with you was a hugely scary step because of it. I knew I would lose myself."

"Did you?"

"Yes."

"You're leaving."

"I thought that was what you wanted."

"No."

"No?"

"Never."

"Never?" she asked, feeling light-headed.

"I don't ever want you to leave."

"That sounds an awful lot like marriage," she choked out.

"Doesn't it?"

"Win?"

"Come back inside, honey."

She nodded, her throat too clogged with tears to speak.

Carlene expected Win to come to her bed that night, but he didn't. She'd come back inside to find Leah waiting. The other woman had seemed keen to get to know Carlene. No doubt because she'd spent so much time with the other woman's children. Leah had thanked her profusely for potty-training Jared and then invited her to come to Portland to visit anytime she liked, the next day before she left town.

Win hadn't been cold to Carlene, but he hadn't acted like a man who wanted her to stay forever either and that oblique reference to marriage had her insides tied up in knots. He disappeared into town for a couple of hours after his sister left and then returned after the hands had eaten lunch.

He found her in the kitchen. He walked up behind her and kissed her neck.

She melted into him, the relief at his touch intense. "Hey big man. Did you get what you needed in town?"

"Yes."

She turned around to face him. "I want to talk. Is that all right?"

He nodded and then kissed her lips, softly, gently.

They went into the living room and he pulled her onto the sofa beside him.

She bit her lip and then made herself speak. "I didn't mean to make you beg."

"I thought you loved him more than me, but—"

"Oh, no," she said, talking over what he would have said next. "I didn't love him at all, but you...I think I've loved you since the beginning. And it scared me."

"You said you gave me your whole self when we made love."

"I did."

"That's going to make my next question a little redundant, but definitely necessary."

He pulled a small velvet box from his jeans pocket and laid it on her thigh. "Will you marry me, honey?"

She stared at the ring box and blinked back tears. When she made no move to touch it, Win flipped the lid up. Inside nestled the most beautiful diamond ring she'd ever seen. Its oval brilliance shone.

"Why is the question redundant?" she asked with a hitch in her voice she couldn't hide.

"You said you gave yourself to me, that means you're already mine. But I want the rest of the world to know it too."

"Do you love me?"

"More than anything in life. More than my fears. More than my certainty marriage is a trap for the unwary."

"I love you too."

"So the answer is?"

"Do you really have any doubt?"

"No." But his eyes said something else. "I wouldn't mind hearing an answer though."

She dropped to her knees in front of him and said. "Yes, Win. I want to marry you. Please, be my husband and my love for a lifetime. Please."

"You begging me, honey?"

"Love is worth pleading for."

"Yes, it is."

"What do you mean we aren't sleeping together again until after we're married?" Carlene demanded when Win kissed her outside her bedroom door and made to leave her there.

Alone.

Win watched her warily, but smiled. "I want to prove that I love you, that you're more than your body to me."

"You don't have to prove anything to me. We're past that."

"Yes, I do. You deserve it," he vowed. "You've spent your whole life being seen as a body and I need you to know you have always been and will always be more than just a sex partner for me."

"I know that, Win. You told me you love me...that you want to marry me, for goodness' sake."

She twined her arms around his neck and pressed against him. "Who appointed you the decision maker in this matter? I want to make love right now."

He grabbed her shoulders and held her away from

him in a cast-iron grip. "Honey, you are going to appreciate my restraint later. Trust me."

She laughed. "You are so darn arrogant."

He nodded, his expression pained. "I know."

What was she supposed to say to that? "Well, stop it!"

"I can't. Not this time. I need to prove to you that I love you enough to wait."

Of all the idiotic ideas…but also incredibly sweet and…she was not going to start crying. How had she ever gotten so lucky as to have this man return her love? "Win, that is ridiculous! I'm the one you're proving it to and I already believe you love me."

He smiled. "Good."

Finally. "So, we can make love now."

He shook his head, slow and easy. "No. This is important to me. Are you willing to wait for my sake?"

Darn him. He couldn't turn the tables like this. "Are you asking me to prove my love for you?"

"No. I know you love me, honey. You're willing to marry me knowing my worst flaws. I'm asking you to trust me. I'm asking you to let me do this right."

"Okay." What else could she say?

He let his hands fall away from her shoulders. "So, when are we getting married?"

She studied him for several seconds. "If we left now, we'd be in Reno by tomorrow morning."

He jerked as if shocked by a jolt of electricity. "What about the white dress and all the trimmings?"

"I've got a white dress. I don't care about the trimmings," she assured him.

"Your parents? Don't you care if they are there?"

She thought about that. "Nope. I'll send them an announcement. They'll be thrilled, of course. Married women are so much more respectable."

"I kind of thought we'd get married here in Sunshine Springs," Win replied.

She gripped the bottom of her top with both hands and peeled it off in one smooth movement.

Win gasped and his eyes turned dark blue. "What the hell are you doing?"

"Negotiating."

She put her hands behind her back, which pressed her breasts against the silk cups of her bra. She grasped the clasp on the back of her bra.

Beads of sweat formed on Win's forehead.

"Now, either you agree to Reno today or I unclasp this bra. I'm warning you. The next thing to go is my jeans. You're going to love my silk panties."

Win glared at her, but the unmistakable bulge in the front of his pants negated the intimidating effect of his stare. That and the fact that she knew he loved her.

"That's not negotiation, that's blackmail," he ground out.

She shrugged and Win's gaze zeroed in on her cleavage like an arrow to a target. "Call it whatever you like, but I'm one second away from taking this off."

Win swallowed and then he grinned. "How soon can you be packed?"

"Give me fifteen minutes." Then she bit her lip. "What about the stable?"

"The mares have foaled. One of the ranch hands can help Shorty and I can take a few days off, no problem."

Her smile was brighter than the noonday sun. "I'm so glad."

"Me, too, honey…me too."

CHAPTER TWELVE

Twelve hours later, Carlene unclasped the bra.

They'd flown to Reno and gotten married in the nicest wedding chapel Win could find and now he was getting his reward.

Carlene had her husband's full attention as she let the piece of white silk fall to the thick midnight-blue carpet of their honeymoon suite. Win's gaze was riveted to her beautiful breasts and the small scrap of silk that covered her feminine secrets.

"I told you that you'd love my panties," Carlene purred as she walked over to join him on the bed.

He'd already undressed and he waited for her on top of the white satin covering the huge round bed that dominated the room.

"They're every bit as sexy as the little white dress you wore to our wedding," he assured her.

As wedding dresses went, he had to admit that it had been unique. The white lace mini-dress that so obviously had been former work gear from the Dry Gulch lay in a pool at Carlene's feet. In fact, she had bought it to wear to work, but never got up the nerve to do so. He was glad. It had outlined her curves in a way that would have set more than one man's hormones roaring out of control. Win had been hard pressed to make it through the wedding vows. Literally.

Carlene covered the last couple of feet to the bed in a little rush. She landed against Win's chest, bearing him back on the bed. "This time, I'm going to lick you all over."

He grinned. "Sure you're up to it?"

She didn't answer. She was too busy licking a slow path down his throat to his collar-bone. She sucked lightly on the base of his neck and he groaned.

"Baby, that feels so good." He caressed her, brushing the sides of her breasts with his hands. "So do these."

She didn't answer, but kept moving down until she was making those sexy little circles around his nipples as she had the other night. Oh, man, he didn't know if he could take this. "If you aren't careful, honey, I'm going to lose it before I get anywhere near being inside you."

She laughed, the sound low and throaty. "I'm not worried, Win. I have tremendous confidence in your powers of rejuvenation."

Then she took his nipple into her mouth and sucked and he felt an electric jolt all the way to his penis. He bucked up off the bed and shouted something feral. He figured turnabout was fair play. He might not be able to reach her with his mouth, but he'd always had long arms. He started off by kneading the sides of her breasts until she was squirming against him, rubbing her hard little buds against his torso. He pushed against her until she lifted just enough for him to get his hands under her and play with the pretty pink raspberries.

She didn't stop torturing him with her mouth, though, and pretty soon she'd scooted down far enough that he was forced to reluctantly release the soft, velvety flesh of her breasts. She pressed wet, heated kisses down his stomach making him tense in anticipation of her going lower.

"Baby, maybe this isn't such a good idea. Let me love you."

She shook her head and her curly hair tickled against his lower abdomen. "You are loving me, darling, but it's my turn to pleasure you."

Who was he to disagree with the little woman when she got stubborn? Besides, it felt so damn good.

And then her hot little mouth was there, right on his engorged shaft and she was kissing the head with her tongue and lips. She made one long, slow pass from the tip of his shaft to the base with her tongue and then back up again before taking him back into her mouth and sucking. He wanted to explode, but not without taking her with him.

He grabbed her head and gently, but firmly, lifted her away from his erection. She murmured a protest, but he was past listening. He tossed her on her back and set about bringing her to the same brink he was trying so desperately not to go over yet. At the first touch of his mouth to her breasts, she cried out. By the time he'd suckled them both, she was writhing under him, her legs spread wide to make room for him.

He pressed his penis against the now slick opening of her body. "I'm not wearing a condom."

She stilled and met his gaze. "I don't want you to."

"Are you sure?"

"Yes. I want babies."

"Me too, honey. Me too." And then he was inside her and they were straining together toward ultimate fulfillment.

She cried out and convulsed around him, sending him over the edge, and he pumped his seed into her. "I love you," he shouted.

"I love you," she whispered in return.

Several hours and more than one bout of lovemaking later, she lay cradled in his arms. "Honey?"

She yawned. "Yes?"

"About your job."

She snuggled closer. "I like being your housekeeper, Win. It's fun cooking for the hands—though I'm not sure it's technically kosher for a wife to accept payment from her husband for that kind of thing."

He caressed her backside and wondered how soon

he could sustain another round of lovemaking. "I wasn't thinking about you being my housekeeper."

"You weren't?" She moved so that she lay on top of his chest, her chin resting on her hands.

"No. I don't think I mentioned it, but the principal of the high school is a friend of mine."

"She is?" Carlene sounded sleepy.

"Uh-huh. I gave her a call, she said that there's a position teaching English Lit for you, if you want it."

Carlene sat straight up, her nude body glowing in neon lights reflected through the window. "She said what? What about an interview? What about my résumé?"

Win chuckled. "Calm down, honey. The interview is set up for next week, but you're a shoe in."

"How can you be so sure? Did you tell her about what happened in Texas? I don't want to take a job and then have them hear about that debacle later. She'll think I lied to her, or didn't tell her the whole truth."

"I told her already, honey. She knew about it anyway. I guess you submitted your resume to the school district awhile back. She'd already run the checks. There weren't any openings then, so she didn't call."

Carlene nodded. "I never heard anything. There's an opening now?"

He reached out and touched the sweet bud on her breast. She shivered.

"Yes. It's only part-time, but I figured that would be okay with you."

"Any job teaching would be okay with me."

He reached for her and pulled her across his chest. "That's what I thought."

He kissed her, long and thoroughly. She was making sexy noises and moving against his body by the time he started trailing kisses down the side of her throat.

"Win?"

"Yeah, honey?"

"Thank you."

He stopped kissing her and took her head in his hands, forcing her to meet his gaze. "You could have done it yourself, but I like helping you."

She grinned, her eyes misty. "You're amazing."

Win's future stretched out before him, a golden road he would travel with Carlene, his wife. The wife he'd been sure he'd never have.

He flipped her over onto her back and set about making the other part of the dream he'd never even acknowledged come true. The dream of a family and a wife who loved him—who would love him for a lifetime.

0810/25/MB300

Ambition. Passion. Scandal.

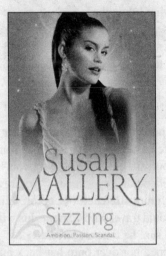

Cold, powerful matriarch Gloria controls the Buchanan dynasty. But, after falling ill, she's forced to rely on home help Lori Johnson.

Lori has struggled out of poverty and has no time for spoiled playboy Reid Buchanan. Especially when he's embroiled in a tabloid sex scandal.

Lori must show the Buchanans what's really important – before secrets and lies destroy them all.

Susan Mallery's Buchanan Dynasty –
secrets are about to be revealed…

Available 6th August 2010

www.millsandboon.co.uk

THE

LEGACY

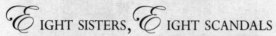

IGHT SISTERS, IGHT SCANDALS

VOLUME 1 – JUNE 2010
Mia's Scandal
by Michelle Reid

VOLUME 2 – JULY 2010
Kat's Pride
by Sharon Kendrick

VOLUME 3 – AUGUST 2010
Emily's Innocence
by India Grey

VOLUME 4 – SEPTEMBER 2010
Sophie's Seduction
by Kim Lawrence

8 VOLUMES IN ALL TO COLLECT!

0610_24_MB290

Fill your summer with four volumes
of red-hot Australians!

Convenient Possession
by Helen Bianchin

Available 4th June 2010

Billionaires' Marriages
by Emma Darcy

Available 2nd July 2010

Ruthless Seduction
by Miranda Lee

Available 6th August 2010

Outback Engagements
by Margaret Way

Available 3rd September 2010

www.millsandboon.co.uk

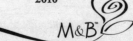

0810_10_MB292

Three volumes of gorgeous, hot-blooded Italian heroes

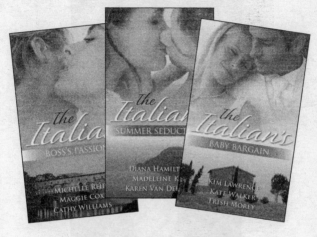

The Italian Boss's Passion
Available 16th July 2010

The Italian's Summer Seduction
Available 20th August 2010

The Italian's Baby Bargain
Available 17th September 2010

COLLECT ALL THREE!

www.millsandboon.co.uk

0810/009/MB298

DESERT HEAT...

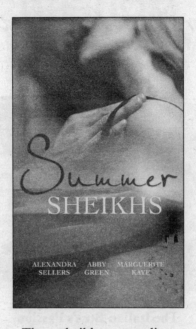

Three sheikhs are sending
temperatures soaring in:

Sheikh's Betrayal by Alexandra Sellers

Breaking the Sheikh's Rules by Abby Green

Innocent in the Sheikh's Harem
by Marguerite Kaye

Available 16th July 2010

www.millsandboon.co.uk

M&B

GENERIC_01_10

MILLS & BOON®
MODERN™

...International affairs, seduction and passion guaranteed

8 brand-new titles each month

4 available on the first Friday of every month and
4 available on the third Friday of every month from
WHSmith, ASDA, Tesco, Eason
and all good bookshops
Also available as eBooks
www.millsandboon.co.uk

GENERIC_06

MILLS & BOON®

MODERN
Heat

Sizzling, stylish, sensual –
the ultimate temptation

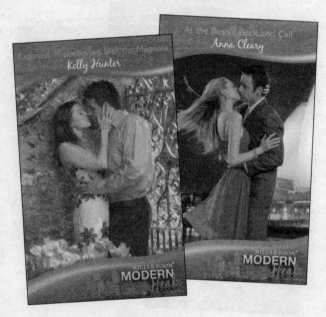

2 brand-new titles each month

1 available on the first Friday of every month and
1 available on the third Friday of every month from
WHSmith, ASDA, Tesco, Eason
and all good bookshops
Also available as eBooks
www.millsandboon.co.uk

GENERIC_51

MILLS & BOON®
Desire™ 2-in-1

2 passionate, dramatic love stories in each book

3 brand-new titles to choose from each month

Available on the third Friday of every month
from WHSmith, ASDA, Tesco, Eason
and all good bookshops
Also available as eBooks
www.millsandboon.co.uk

WEB/M&B/RTL2

Discover Pure Reading Pleasure with

**Visit the Mills & Boon website for all
the latest in romance**

- ◎ **Buy** all the latest releases, backlist and eBooks

- ◎ **Find out** more about our authors and their books

- ◎ **Join** our community and chat to authors and other readers

- ◎ **Free** online reads from your favourite authors

- ◎ **Win** with our fantastic online competitions

- ◎ **Sign** up for our free monthly eNewsletter

- ◎ **Tell us** what you think by signing up to our reader panel

- ◎ **Rate** and review books with our star system

www.millsandboon.co.uk

 Follow us at twitter.com/millsandboonuk

 Become a fan at facebook.com/romancehq